"A veritable casserole mixing history, musicology, travel, biography, and multiple murder. . . . [A] skillful, accessible inclusion of Mozartiana and music history . . . evocative portraits of storied cities like Salzburg, Venice, and Prague." —*The Raleigh News & Observer*

"Fusing the magic of Mozart with the literary suspense genre, first novelist Slater, a concert pianist and author of *In Mozart's Footsteps*, delves deeply into Mozartiana to deliver a picaresque tale. . . . In a spectacular . . . scene, Slater mirrors the satisfying climax of a great evening of opera. Any reader who can hum a few bars of Mozart will relish this oratorio of crime and commerce." —*Library Journal*

"Mozart lovers are in for a treat." —*Publishers Weekly*

"This is a gripping, deeply satisfying read, difficult to put down, impossible to forget—a novel to fascinate lovers of Mozart and of whodunits. Letters and diaries of Mozart and his circle, both genuine and forged, appear and disappear. There is murder as well as mystery, a strong narrative line as well as a wealth of detail." —Peter Branscombe, University of St. Andrews

"[A] liberal use of aristocratic venues and titillating vignettes . . . a picaresque fantasy." —*Kirkus Reviews*

"The Mozart material is fascinating and provides a compelling background for a thriller." —*Booklist*

# Night Music

## Harrison Gradwell Slater

NAL BOOKS

NEW AMERICAN LIBRARY

New American Library
Published by New American Library, a division of
Penguin Group (USA) Inc., 375 Hudson Street,
New York, New York 10014, U.S.A.
Penguin Books Ltd, 80 Strand,
London WC2R 0RL, England
Penguin Books Australia Ltd, 250 Camberwell Road,
Camberwell, Victoria 3124, Australia
Penguin Books Canada Ltd, 10 Alcorn Avenue,
Toronto, Ontario, Canada M4V 3B2
Penguin Books (N.Z.) Ltd, Cnr Rosedale and Airborne Roads,
Albany, Auckland 1310, New Zealand

Penguin Books Ltd, Registered Offices:
80 Strand, London WC2R 0RL, England

Published by New American Library, a division of Penguin Group (USA) Inc. This is an authorized
reprint of a hardcover edition published by Harcourt, Inc. For information address Harcourt, Inc.,
6277 Sea Harbor Drive, Orlando, Florida 32887-6777.

First New American Library Printing, October 2003
10  9  8  7  6  5  4  3  2  1

 REGISTERED TRADEMARK—MARCA REGISTRADA

LIBRARY OF CONGRESS CATALOGING IN PUBLICATION DATA

Slater, Harrison Gradwell.
Night Music / Harrison Gradwell Slater.
p. cm.
ISBN 0-451-20972-9
1. Mozart, Wolfgang Amadeus, 1756–1791—Diaries—Fiction. 2. Manuscripts—Collectors and
collecting—Fiction. 3. Americans—Europe—Fiction. 4. Musicologists—Fiction. 5. Composers—
Fiction. 6. Europe—Fiction. I. Title.
PS3619.L37N44 2003
813'.54—dc21          2003044939

Set in Adobe Caslon
Printed in the United States of America

# PART ONE

# Milan, Boston, Nancy

# PRELUDE

*Footfalls echo in the memory . . .*
—T. S. ELIOT

"Sir, can you hear me?" A nurse in white, her forehead glistening with tiny beads of perspiration, was involved in frenetic activity. Under the glare of harsh, burning lights, I could make out dangling bags of clear plastic that rattled violently with each turn of the wheeled stretcher through the endless corridors. Unable to move or even bend my neck, I looked down at my body with great effort. Trying to focus, to get my bearings, I made a grisly discovery—surrounded by a mound of bloody gauze was a five-inch knife handle protruding from my chest.

Stretched out on a long board and wearing a stiff neck collar, I could see a complicated labyrinth of canvas cords holding me down tightly: straps across my chin, my waist, and all the way down my legs.

"Sir, can you hear me?" she repeated with a thick accent, startling me. When I raised my index finger to indicate yes, she continued, "We're here to help you. Do you know where you are?"

After a few seconds, I waved my finger, No.

"Do you know what happened to you?"

Again I indicated no.

Turning to her colleague, she spoke in a language that I recognized as Czech. In haste, they were hanging intravenous bags with tubing, and as they worked she explained to me, "You've lost a lot of blood and we need to replace it. Do you know what your blood type is?"

Weakly, I responded, "Can't remember."

"That's all right," she said.

"Am I dying?" I blurted out.

As she debated what to say, her silence indicated the worst. Then, quietly, she replied, "We're doing everything possible to prevent that."

The level of feverish activity in the room continued unabated, when a young doctor appeared abruptly and began pinching my earlobe. "What are you doing?" I asked weakly.

"Testing your level of consciousness," he said, his eyes darting around the room as technicians and nurses ripped hurriedly through their procedures. "While waiting for the X-ray machine to be brought into the operating room. We're about to do a cross-table lateral C-spine."

"Where am I?" I asked.

"In Prague, at the Zaradník Clinic," he replied. With the end of a small hammer, he began stroking the soles of my feet brusquely and said, "I'm testing your reflexes."

For a split second, his expression alarmed me. "What is it?" I asked.

"You have a positive Babinski," he replied soberly. "Instead of curling down, your toes spread up and out. It means you have a spinal injury."

Stunned by his bluntness, I started to ask, "What . . ." but my question lodged in my throat, choking me. Suddenly I was aware that I couldn't feel anything below my waist. A desperate urge to move, to sit up, swept through me.

"Stay still," he ordered. "First we have to worry about the knife in your chest. When we remove it, we might have to replace the blood vessel."

Half speaking the words, I asked, weakly, "Who did this to . . ."

His words began to fade out slowly: ". . . wouldbebettr-fyoutriednottalk."

As the massive X-ray machine was rolled into the room, I closed my eyes and felt myself drifting, finally releasing my hold on the tangible world. Slowly I began to enter a universe of mist and uncertainty, a stream of consciousness that led me tentatively, reluctantly into my past. *How did this happen?* I continued to ask myself. Vaguely I remembered being home in Boston during the summer. It was night and I was walking over large cut stones of gray-green and dark turquoise slate, which transformed the pavement of Copley Square into a luxuriant Oriental carpet. In the distance, I could hear the ominous rumbling of skateboards, their riders displaying their skills on the spacious steps of the Boston Public Library to a soft accompaniment—the murmur of a dozen jets of water splashing tirelessly. Lights were flickering and the reflection of streetlamps in the shimmering pool of the fountain created a counterpoint to the somber shadows of two stylized Egyptian obelisks. Tall spires of blue larkspur and salvia filled the summer air with a damp, seductive perfume and—

Suddenly, the glimmer of an image interrupted my thoughts: an express letter arriving from France. And something about a diary, some old pages I had found. Something grotesque—unfathomably violent—had happened. I slowly sensed my memory returning with the relentless inevitability of a dripping faucet, and with the same tortured rhythm. Dimly I could picture gold embossed letters on heavy ivory laid paper, a world of immense wealth, articulate and brilliant, concealing a simmering, brooding sexuality threatening to explode.

The pieces from my past began falling into place.

# CHAPTER I

*The life of every man is a diary . . .*
—J. M. BARRIE

At the ticket window in the central station, there was a huge line of anxious, impatient travelers, mostly Italian. When I finally reached the counter, the agent informed me, "Trains heading south are running several hours late." Standing behind me in line, a traveler accustomed to the caprices of the Italian railways added that he had heard a group of disgruntled workers had blockaded the tracks at Salerno with their own bodies.

"Nothing serious," the agent at the window concluded. "Just the usual Christmas strike." But to me it suggested serious delays, and I envisioned spending hours in an immobile train packed to capacity with restless holiday travelers.

"The best thing to do?" I asked.

"Wait a day and see what happens," the ticket agent replied, and the veteran traveler concurred.

After checking into a small hotel, I crossed the street to Via Mecenate, where the windows of a large auction house caught my eye. A preview was taking place and although I suspected I would be gone by the time the items were auctioned, the quality and number of antiques were imposing enough to capture my imagination, and so I entered. Spread out over many rooms was an infinite number of impressive pieces: inlaid period furniture, marble busts, and eighteenth-century engravings, all competing for the eye. In a room dedicated entirely to leather-bound volumes and illuminated manuscripts, I noticed a dusty archival folder marked *"di scarsa importanza"* (of little importance). Untying it, I found a thick stack of tawny ochre pages covered with columns of script and numbers penned meticulously in Italian. The random words *olio, vino,* and *legno*—oil, wine, and firewood—caught my eye, indicating that the pages were a balance sheet for household expenditures. As I proceeded through the stack, the color of the pages shifted gradually to ashen gray and I began to detect a musky stench, the smell of damp paper.

In peeling the layers apart, my hands were continuing to search long after my mind had decided that I had better things to do on my vacation. But my fingers persisted in their silent hunt, since I realized that the folder, after making it through so many centuries, could easily end up in a Dumpster if no one bought it.

The ink, a rich sepia, glistened with a syrupy viscosity, and the enigmatic quality of the leaves and layers intrigued me. Dampness had weakened the folios, but the paper was from virile stock—much like the rich, sturdy pages used today for artistic writing paper and fine private editions from exclusive bookmakers—and seemed to have stood up to the ravages of time. After prying apart a new layer, I was surprised to find myself staring at a set of pages completely different from the anonymous ledgerlike household accounts that preceded them; these were not in Italian, but in German.

As I peeled back another page, a name caught my eye: Nannerl. The name was so special—the nickname of Mozart's sister. In fact, I realized I had never heard of anyone else using the name Nannerl. But my thoughts were interrupted when I spied numerous tiny burrows and tunnels traversing the pages, apparently made by worms eating their way through the layers. An involuntary shudder swept through my body as I searched for a date, aware that I might at any moment unpeel a page and find one or a dozen of the voracious creatures squirming and wriggling before my eyes.

The mere glimpse of the name Nannerl triggered a flood of impressions. In some ways her life had been unfortunate; she had been a child prodigy on the harpsichord, but the extraordinary abilities of her younger brother gradually eclipsed her own talent and usefulness. Although she had appeared before the sovereigns of the greatest courts in Europe, she was eventually relegated to staying home in Salzburg with her mother while her father, Leopold, traveled with Mozart to Italy in search of fame. Attractive, well mannered, and educated, she was prevented by her father from marrying the man she loved in favor of a nobleman who was almost twenty years older. And she died alone, almost blind and in poverty. The birth of a genius in her family had proven both a blessing and a curse.

Despite the damage, the pages were almost pristine: no smudged edges, no signs of reading and rereading. In fact, I had the distinct impression they had never been touched. When I found the scrawled date, "January 24, 1770," my mind shut down momentarily and my heart began to pound. Looking around surreptitiously, I tried to see if anyone had noticed my reaction, but customers were too busy discussing how items would look in their apartments, and the sales and security personnel were too interested in guarding small silver objects on display.

To avoid attracting attention, I resisted the temptation of reading through the folios and debated canceling the rest of my trip, which had been undertaken at great financial risk. Not having received any word about several job prospects, I had decided to toss caution to the wind and buy an airline ticket on my last credit card. And I was now paying my travel expenses with the remaining trickle of available credit. All because I had come to realize that Europe—that rich, elusive sanctuary of Western art and culture— was necessary to my existence. For years, my precarious financial situation kept me from traveling outside America. But I had begun to wonder what the purpose of all my hard work was. Unwisely, and regardless of the consequences, I had put up my last dollar to travel, and now I was considering giving it up in midstream.

Somehow the innocuous little stack of papers made sense of it all. The prospect of a serendipitous discovery sent a wave of optimism racing through me: for once, fate was smiling on this impoverished, unemployed scholar. Briefly, I even imagined a few lines in the Associated Press, an event that could give me an edge over hundreds of other candidates for a permanent teaching position.

Maybe it was all just by instinct but I decided to cancel the rest of my trip. After all, even established, well-paid university professors would do the same thing. And if the diary were authentic, nearly any one of them would kill for what I had in my hands.

On the evening of my fourth day in Milan, I arrived early at the imposing, frescoed auction room, where seventy or eighty buyers were seated. A huge lot of inlaid Italian furniture from the time of Louis XVI immediately drew intense activity, followed by keen interest in a splendid oil painting of the Madonna by Murillo. The language in the room was unknown to me: a pen or an index finger raised aloft almost imperceptibly, a brief raising of the chin or a subtle nod. After an hour and a half, the grimy folder that had caught my attention came up for bid, and I waited in the uncomfortable silence while the auctioneer opened the bidding at *dieci* . . . ten euros. About ten dollars.

The moment he was ready to move on, I said, "*Dieci*," using my best poker voice.

After a painfully silent pause, no one was interested in making a higher bid. "Once, twice . . ." the auctioneer announced.

"*Venti*." Glancing over my shoulder, I saw an extraordinarily well-dressed man with a thick black mustache who raised an eyebrow when my eye caught his. Was he a professional, hired to push up the bidding? Or was his curiosity suddenly stimulated by a foreigner bidding on a worthless stack of papers?

My heart suddenly pounding, I hesitated to respond too quickly. "*Trenta*," I finally said. It was only about thirty dollars, but I realized I could soon find myself outside my possibilities for bidding.

After a pause, I heard, "*Cinquanta*." Raising his bid to fifty dollars, the only other bidder seemed to be playing a game with me. Although I tried to be inconspicuous as I examined the contents of my wallet, I sensed every eye in the room was riveted on me.

"*Cinquantacinque*," I responded. About fifty-five dollars.

"*No, Signore*," the auctioneer replied in Italian, with a reprimanding tone. "*Dieci* is the minimum bid."

"*Scusi,*" I replied, apologizing, furious that I hadn't thought of bringing more cash. "*Sessanta.*" Sixty dollars.

The next half minute was excruciating. With my temples pounding, the silence was interminable. The ear-splitting rap of his gavel on the desk struck me with the force of a thunderbolt. "*Aggiudicato!*"

*That's me!* I suddenly realized, *I have it.* Looking over my shoulder, I caught the eye of the impeccably dressed Italian, who shrugged his shoulders casually, with an ironic expression.

My precious, unexplored trophy held tightly under my arm, I exited quickly, with a slight degree of paranoia, as if an invisible gauntlet of pickpockets was poised and waiting. Walking back toward my hotel, I was both ecstatic and skeptical. Had I just been scammed by a professional bidder into paying my entire week's budget for a stack of worthless papers?

The massive paving stones of the Piazza Duomo, just washed, glistened with a tired dignity, and it surprised me to see hundreds of people out at night, crowded into cafés, huddling in small groups, smoking or enjoying a leisurely stroll after dinner, just as incalculable generations before them had done. Bright lights illuminated the facade of the immense Gothic cathedral, giving the impression of daylight. Detail, so much detail, overwhelmed the exterior, a masterpiece of mannered, cluttered elegance. Sculptures of transcendental lightness, thousands, competed for attention, and tons of stone hewn into lace soared above me, more like fragile paper cutouts than marble. And from the highest pillar, a tiny gold Madonna looked down upon the mad frenzy beneath her with helpless incomprehension.

Near the cathedral was the entrance to the Galleria Vittorio Emanuele, a massive structure of glass and wrought-iron filigree reminiscent of some great nineteenth-century horticultural exhibition. At a small indoor café, I ordered the house aperitif and then stopped short. Checking my remaining cash, I quickly changed my order to *una piccola birra alla spina,* a small draft beer, realizing I couldn't even afford to leave the waiter a tip.

Slowly, I began to evaluate my newly acquired treasure. Again I unearthed the folio dated January 24, 1770, and tried to remember where Mozart was living at that period of his life—an easy task thanks to Leopold Mozart, who had planned to write a biography of his famous son and had chronicled and documented his life more than that of any composer in modern history. Mozart was born in 1756, so I calculated he would have been about fourteen years old in 1770, and in Italy for the first time with his father, where they hoped to secure a commission for Mozart to write a serious opera for the theater that preceded La Scala opera house.

Although the weight and quality of the paper suggested that it could have come from the eighteenth century, I returned to the folio that had caught my eye with a more critical, even skeptical, approach and started to make a careful transcription of the text.

*January 24, 1770*

*This journal will, of necessity, be brief. It will be my silent companion and faithful confidant. It will be the only possession that is mine alone, the one part of my life that is truly my own.*

*Papa is in the next room discussing practical matters with two gentlemen. He knows my usual pace in composing so it would not be wise to spend too much time on this diary. For this reason, my journal will have to be comprised of short passages.*

*Perhaps a diary is the only way to understand the many feelings I am experiencing. After all, we are alone in Italy for the first time, without Mama and Nannerl, and the sense of freedom is exhilarating. My impressions of this new world are too powerful to suppress, they burst from my pen like themes flowing from my fingers at the keyboard.*

*Papa would certainly disapprove of my "ill use" of the gifts God has given me in my writing a diary instead of a new composition. But he himself keeps a precious book of notes, and his weekly letters to Mama are just like a journal, carefully preserved each week in our heavy*

*wooden chest in Salzburg. Why should the same privilege
be denied me?*

*Each day a ferocious thought returns to torment me: I
have been denied a great deal. Over and over again, I
hear, "The most fortunate, the most blessed of children. A
miracle, a gift of God." All this and more. Yet something
has been missing for a long time: my childhood
evaporated like snowflakes on the windowpane. Like an
inquisitive bird peering from the nest, I desire to spread
my wings. And I fear the inevitable, that the days of my
adolescence will be denied me as well.*

*Papa insists that the tailor, the wigmaker, and even
the artist who just painted my portrait emphasize my
youth, and he has even told people that I am younger
than my true age. Yet, regardless of his determination to
portray me as a child, since our arrival in Italy, I have
become a man, and nothing Papa can do will ever
change that.*

As I leafed through the folios, a mounting rush of excitement surged through me: discovering a Mozart diary could be my first big break, my chance of establishing a foothold in the tight, closed world of academia. Somehow, all the struggles to make ends meet now seemed worth it—the nights researching and writing until 2 A.M., knowing that I still had to prepare music classes for the next day. Perhaps the meager times were coming to an end. The diary began to represent that elusive, seductive light at the end of the tunnel.

The text of the document was certainly credible since, at that time in his life, Mozart consistently referred to his father, Leopold, as Papa. And what a father Leopold was: a renowned educator who supervised every aspect of his children's development and a keen businessman who controlled every detail of the many journeys made with Mozart. Perhaps, as the diary suggested, he controlled too much and too successfully. But the material was convincing—either it was the work of an expert forger who knew Mozart's life well, or I had stumbled onto something authentic.

It was my last night in Milan, so I was reluctant to surrender myself to the barren, unadorned walls of my hotel room. Instead, in the Galleria Vittorio Emanuele, I was immersed in a world of frescoes, mosaic floors, and sculpted ornaments, lit theatrically to evoke space and perspective—a stage set of scrolls, shells, and sculptures and of tiny wrought-iron balconies where no one could walk. And the Galleria was overflowing with a vibrant celebration of life.

It was time for me to make an important decision: whether to try my luck with the diary in the lucrative commercial world of international auctions or in the academic world. Unfortunately, my life in the world of academia had brought nothing but disappointment. I thought that my total devotion to Mozart, music, and my students would mean something. But by now, my career had become a nonstop odyssey—traveling from one single-year appointment in musicology to another, always in places where no one wanted to live, always for a pitiful salary. Sometimes tenure was offered as the proverbial carrot and stick, but in reality, universities periodically fired me before that could ever take place, as they did everyone else. Hiring junior faculty simply cost less. It was all a painful blur, a nightmare I needed to forget in order to go on, to survive.

Of course I had to take some of the blame for my lack of success in academia. I had refused to play the game, to treat pompous and arrogant professors the way they expected to be treated, with fawning acquiescence. But it wasn't in my nature to agree with people when I thought they were misinformed, or to hide my track record in the area of "publish or perish": everything I wrote made it into the best scholarly journals. And tenured faculty told me to my face that I was brash and tactless . . . maybe I was. And they always knew how to get back at me. Maybe it was time for me to change, to bite the bullet and be deferential at all costs. The alternative had proven ruinous.

Yet my financial difficulties could all change with the diary. Sotheby's might bring in a bundle and finally I might be able to replenish my shabby wardrobe and to afford a car instead of riding the T. To cash in the diary could mean renting a larger apartment, joining a newer health club instead of the YMCA, and even taking a date to a good restaurant for a change.

But, almost immediately, I was forced to come back to reality: the documents would first have to be scrutinized and discussed in the unbiased, disinterested forum of academia—nonprofit, nonpaying academia. Naïvely, I told myself that if the diary were authentic, the scholarly world might actually turn and notice me; it could represent my chance for acceptance, for recognition. And the most likely venue would be either the upcoming *Mozart Millennium Edition* or the *Mozart 2006.* Each scheduled for publication in 2006 (the 250th anniversary of the birth of Mozart), the two prestigious editions of the music and letters of Mozart were expected to surpass anything of their kind in the past two centuries. The director of the *Mozart Millennium Edition,* Dr. Manfred Braun in Salzburg, was unquestionably one of the most important and respected Mozart scholars in the world.

I vaguely remembered him, short and balding, with salt-and-pepper hair shooting out around his ears, a statement in gray with all the proud shabbiness of an Ivy League professor. Charming and gracious around those he felt his equal, but abrupt and short-tempered with students and younger scholars. Had I met him? I could remember his legendary, violent temper and see his metal-rimmed glasses perfectly and hear his clipped Austrian accent and his fussy, meticulous choice of words. Serious, extremely intelligent, but bitter. And I began to picture his face: petty academic humiliations had left their mark, and the rage and pain of a thousand small defeats were reflected in his eyes. On rare occasions, he was engaging, but cold, very cold. And ruthlessly vindictive. Where had I first seen him?

"So you bought them." The suave voice from nowhere startled me. Standing before me was the manicured Italian who had forced up the bidding on my folios. "Anything interesting?"

Instinctively closing the folder, I replied, "No. Useless household accounts."

"Sorry to hear that," he replied, smiling ironically. "Can I buy you a drink? Because it was my fault you lost your money."

Gathering up the folder, I replied, "It's all right. Forget it." As an afterthought, I added, "Do you work for the auction house?"

"No, I have my own business. Antiques, books, anything sellable. I'm sorry you didn't find what you wanted. In this world, one has to be a little . . . *furbo.*"

Standing up, I excused myself and said, "You're right." Unlike in English, the Italian word for cunning—*furbo*—is an acceptable, even positive characteristic. As I departed, I caught a glimpse of his expression over my shoulder: enigmatic, intensely curious, and decidedly *furbo*.

Back in Boston, in my scantily furnished single-room apartment crammed full of unpacked crates, I awaited the response from Dr. Braun. It had been a difficult decision to keep my apartment and try to make it in Boston, without a definite job prospect. But at least there were enough part-time teaching possibilities so that I didn't have to move every year, and in fact, one undergraduate music history course came through. And it was great to be back in the Hub with my oldest friends, in the city with so much university life, so much music. Opportunities to play a solo piano recital, or to accompany an instrumentalist or singer, were always there. But to survive as a freelance, I had to be flexible, so I again took up performing in bars and restaurants, mixing Mozart with Cole Porter. After a decade of university teaching, I suddenly found myself churning out requests for barfly customers interested in picking up a date, who often hardly paid attention to a note I played. But somehow the applause and occasional interesting conversation, along with the cosmopolitans and margaritas sent over by appreciative patrons, managed to sustain me.

When the response from Dr. Braun finally arrived, it was surprisingly cool, guarded, and devoid of enthusiasm. "Rumors of a diary or diaries by Mozart have been circulating for years," he wrote. "Several exemplars have emerged that proved to be fakes." He cautioned me that what I found could be the work of a clever forger whose efforts were for profit or for the mere pleasure of deceiving a gullible public, much like the Mozart "Adélaïde" violin concerto discovered in 1931 by Marius Casadesus, which turned out to be a fake that the violinist himself had apparently written.

Dr. Braun added that he strongly urged against any "race to press," as happened with the so-called Hitler diaries—later revealed to be forgeries—that were published in 1983 by the reputable West German magazine *Der Stern* and the British *Sunday Times*. He would need complete assurances that I would not make any announcements or discuss the diary with any publishers before he finished examining the manuscript. It would be necessary to see the originals, and he concluded, "Please sign the enclosed form for our records."

The "enclosed form," in German, was a legal document with a brief phrase buried in the seventh clause: "All materials submitted become the property of the *Mozart Millennium Edition*." Alarmed, I contacted a lawyer specializing in intellectual property, fully aware that, in order to pay his bill, I'd have to take on some beginning piano students—a prospect that I detested.

"I've never heard of anything like that," the lawyer told me. "The affidavit indicates that you would no longer own the documents you found. If you wanted to publish all or any portion of them, you could be prohibited from doing so. Say you wanted to sell them one day. If you sign that form, you've relinquished all rights."

The situation left me annoyed and perplexed. And suspicious, as I had reason to be: the academic world had not proven as honorable and scrupulous as I had originally thought. Just two years earlier, an Italian scholar had plagiarized three entire pages of an unpublished article I sent him. After months of expensive legal wrangling, I ended up with a few lines in a subsequent issue that attributed the material to me. It was all too complicated, as my experience with the academic world had always been. And what was Braun offering in return? Just "examining the manuscript"? My initial enthusiasm was replaced by intense disappointment.

But I had to admit grudgingly that Braun at least had a point about fakes: literary forgeries were common in every century. The "Fragments of Ancient Poetry Collected in the Highlands of Scotland," supposedly written by the third-century Gaelic bard Ossian, were actually penned in the eighteenth century by the poet James Macpherson. And in the epoch of unprecedented literary fraud—the twentieth century—Sir Edmund Backhouse had forged histories of the Chinese court, while Clifford Irving had invented memoirs of Howard Hughes. Worse, the elaborate forgeries by Mark Hofmann of Mormon documents actually led him to murder two people, resulting in his imprisonment in 1987.

So, instead of enclosing the originals, I had excellent Docutec photocopies made and sent Braun a set, with a note that I was not comfortable sending the originals, nor signing the affidavit. And at the last minute before sending them, I removed the second page from the stack—to protect myself. When I handed the packet to the Federal Express agent, I felt I had taken the right step. A quote from Ecclesiastes reverberated in my mind with the powerful resonance of a bronze church bell: "Cast thy bread upon the waters . . ." And the blue sky over Copley Square looked splendid, more radiant than I had ever seen it.

Over the next few weeks, I found myself anxiously awaiting a response, but Braun never acknowledged receipt of my packet. Exasperated, I debated writing to the editor of the *Mozart 2006,* Dr. Dennis Landry, who was locked in fierce competition with Braun. But I decided it was too much of a risk, as protocol in the scholarly world dictates that an author submit materials to one publisher at a time. And Manfred Braun had specifically stipulated that I deal exclusively with him.

Everyone knew there was bad blood between Braun and Landry, two major figures in the world of Mozart scholarship. In fact, it was an international cause célèbre. An initial mild rivalry over whether Mozart had actually written certain sections of the *Requiem* gradually deteriorated into ugly, heated scenes at international conferences alternating with nasty rebuttals in print. Perhaps the total disintegration of civility and rationality came when Landry announced he would be editing an English version of the complete Mozart letters for publication in 2006, the same year Braun's German edition was scheduled to appear.

Landry's financial resources assured a spectacular deluxe edition guaranteed to make Braun's look pitiful. But, most important, the two editions were competing on the level of scholarship to become the definitive version of the Mozart letters for the twenty-first century. And completeness was foremost, so new discoveries of authentic Mozart material could determine which edition had the edge.

Considering the potential volatility, I concluded it would be disastrous to write to Landry. Optimistically, I awaited the arrival of the mail each day, hoping there would be a response from Braun, while telling myself that everything in the scholarly world takes time, a great deal of time.

But with each passing day, I was more irritable and impatient, and it became more and more difficult to reassure myself. As I prepared my lectures for the only class I would be teaching in the fall, I found myself nervously pacing the room each time the mail was due to arrive. To compound the problem, the sweltering heat in my Boston apartment—with no air-conditioning or cross ventilation—was getting more oppressive. And I was so deep in debt that escaping to a restaurant, a nightclub, or even a film was out of the question. My nerves began unraveling like a taut, frayed cord, one thread at a time.

What had gone wrong? My future had seemed so bright. I was at the top of my class in Boston Latin, and my SAT scores in math were so high that a computer programming firm offered me—a seventeen-year-old—a yearly starting salary of $50,000.

But it had been music. And Mozart. That was all I wanted to do. At age ten, the first time I heard Mozart's great G minor symphony, something changed in my brain. From that moment, music became the principal passion of my life. Yet I never imagined things would turn out so badly. With my financial situation nearing the breaking point, I found myself obsessing on the old question: would the computer programming offer still be good after all these years?

Instead I was debating whether to take a job I had been offered at the New England Conservatory, teaching fourteen beginning piano students a day. A guaranteed paycheck, all right, but something I genuinely loathed. At least it would make my family happy, as they had begun to regard me as a loser, someone always short of money. My brother, a colonel in the army, was raising a model family, my glamorous sister earning an excellent living and traveling the world as a flight attendant. And what was I doing, my relatives wondered. With all my high aspirations, my desire to make a contribution, I was a failure to all of them, a dreamer who was never going to make it.

Waiting for the mail to arrive, I happened to catch a glimpse of the figure in the mirror: five foot seven, with broad shoulders, the result of high school training as a wrestler and years spent in the YMCA gym, aiming for a lean, toned look. As I examined my ash blond hair, a hint of premature gray in the mustache and temples caught my attention. And I knew I had to do something about it if I had any hope of dating younger women. Age thirty-five and unmarried. My most recent girlfriend had waited patiently for me to propose as I resisted commitment, and she finally gave up. By the time I changed my mind, nothing would change hers—I had missed my chance. Now I was left only with regrets, lonely and pessimistic about my chances, and dismayed to discover that the women I desired weren't attracted to me. And after the first or second date, I usually lost interest in the women who were.

People always commented how striking my blue eyes were or how young I looked without glasses, which I preferred in academic situations. But appearing younger wasn't an advantage; in practically every teaching job, I had been mistaken for a student by security guards, and now, even in my mid-thirties, I had to make sure I always carried ID, as I was inevitably carded.

As I reflected on my problems, the doorbell startled me. Looking out the window, I saw a Federal Express truck, which could mean only one thing: Braun's reply. It was only after I signed that I realized the packet was not from Braun.

# CHAPTER 2

*. . . much more invitation than command . . .*
*— Tattler (1709–11)*

Slowly, I removed a first-class airplane ticket with my name, Matthew Pierce, and a handwritten letter on embossed stationery with the gold letters "Fondation de l'Art éternel" on the letterhead.

> *Please accept my apology for this late invitation, but I would like to ask you to join me as a guest of the Fondation de l'Art éternel for three weeks. You have probably already heard about the activities of the foundation, but in case you haven't, I am enclosing some recent newspaper articles.*
>
> *If you are unavailable and cannot accept the invitation, I would appreciate if you would be so kind to call or send a fax. However, if you are able to come, I believe your visit will be both interesting and rewarding.*
>
> Vicomte René de Laguerelle
>
> *PS. Unfortunately, as you will see from the articles, we insist on complete confidentiality, and I am required to tell you that if you discuss this invitation with others, the bylaws of the foundation will require us to terminate you.*

I stared at the letter in disbelief. *A grammatical mistake,* I thought as I read the postscript. He obviously meant my consideration for a grant would be terminated. I laughed uncomfortably; for a moment, it sounded as if they might kill me.

Looking at the impressive invitation, I had difficulty believing my eyes. I had heard about the Fondation de l'Art éternel. Like the MacArthur Foundation "genius" awards, the activities of the foundation were shrouded in secrecy. The enclosed articles described various personalities in the cultural and academic world who had received awards ranging from $300,000 to $850,000 to pursue any activity they desired. Yet no information was ever given about the selection procedure, and I knew that recipients invariably declined comment since their awards were granted under express conditions of silence.

I had little scheduled for the next three weeks—nothing to do but perform six nights a week in a neighborhood piano bar and swelter during the day in my cramped apartment as I worked on the diary. The letter was a godsend; even the ephemeral possibility that I was being considered for a grant by the Fondation de l'Art éternel was enough to get me to pack my suitcases. And the language was enigmatic enough to suggest that an award was indeed a possibility. But I was astonished to see that the flight was leaving at 11:05 P.M., and that they were sending a driver to pick me up at 8:30 P.M., giving me less than five hours to rearrange my life.

Baffled by the urgency, I found myself pacing the apartment. Was this my big chance, or just another windmill I was chasing, another waste of time? An awful thought raced through my mind: *Someone else dropped out and I had been invited at the last minute.* It wasn't very flattering, but I could easily swallow my pride and just go. After all I had been through in the past few years, there wasn't much left to swallow.

When I called the piano bar to ask for three weeks off, the manager warned me that if I didn't show up as scheduled, I was fired. With no time to think, a wave of conflicting emotions swept through me, a mix of apprehension and excitement. After reflecting for a second, I did the unthinkable and told the manager I was leaving the country, hanging up on him as he yelled into the receiver. With a quick phone call, I asked my landlady to forward my mail in case the letter from Braun arrived while I was away. Then I began throwing everything I needed into my old suitcase, by now a familiar routine.

When the car arrived, I raced to close my suitcase and, laptop in hand, headed out the door. As usual, the elevator wasn't working, and I stopped for a moment to debate whether I should leave the original folios of the diary in my apartment. Since there was no time to rent a safety deposit box, I reasoned that they would be just as safe in my possession as in the apartment. After a few seconds, I went back into the apartment and deposited a single sheet—the original second page of the diary—in my file cabinet for safekeeping, placing it in the same folder with the photocopy I had removed from the packet to Braun: the page had already been transcribed onto my hard drive, and if anything happened during the trip, there would at least be an original to authenticate. With barely enough time to catch my breath, I grabbed the rest of the photocopies and flew down five flights of stairs.

In record time, we arrived at Logan. Since there was nothing to do for two hours, I calmed myself by continuing the painstaking task of transcribing and translating the folios, smoothing out archaic constructions to keep the language modern, in keeping with my musicological training.

*February 21, 1770*

*Italy. The air is saturated with music. And with amore. I have heard about this land my entire life. When I was a child, Papa rhapsodized about Italy and the world of music: expressive melodies, clear textures, lightness, passion. My earliest Italian arias, about love and duty, uncompromising honor and burning desire, helped me to imagine this land before I ever arrived.*

*And now here I am, where opera was born, in hopes of writing my first serious opera.*

*Everything is new, different. Intense. Today we saw four bandits hanged in front of the immense theatrical backdrop of the Milan cathedral. A nobleman from the order of cavaliers, wearing a formidable mask, read each prisoner a long, solemn rite and then ascended the stairs of the scaffold holding a carved crucifix before the bandit. The crowd cheered riotously after each hanging and eagerly awaited the next, shouting ugly curses in guttural voices that Papa would not translate for me. The bodies of the executed bandits will be left to rot in iron cages outside the city gates as a warning to those who commit such deeds. And Papa never flinched for a second. He approves of such displays of justice, as there have been savage crimes against travelers on the roads to Milan, and our lives have been in danger.*

*After the hangings were over, the atmosphere was festive, even exuberant. Bands of local musicians serenaded the crowds who had come long distances to see the executions, and vendors shouted nasal cries, offering all kinds of things to eat and drink. The hangman's rope was carefully removed by the cavalier because everyone here is eager to have a piece—it is said to be the most powerful good luck charm!*

*What fascinating spectacle the Italians bring to such a gruesome task, more like a memorable theater performance than an execution.*

"Air France flight three twenty-one is now boarding at Gate seventeen-C." As the loudspeaker announcement jolted me out of the eighteenth century, I typed myself a note to find out if such execution rituals really took place in Milan in the 1770s. "Hot material," I mumbled as I tried to resist being swept away by a wave of enthusiasm that could cloud my judgment. My expertise in Mozart's life and music, with an emphasis on cultural history, was clearly not adequate to evaluate Mozart's handwriting or the types of paper he used. So I had ordered facsimiles of Mozart's letters and a lengthy monograph on watermarks and paper factories in eighteenth-century Europe, all of which I had brought with me. Until I acquainted myself with this specialized literature, historical accuracy was one of the few features I could authenticate by myself. And the stuff and substance of the diary had the ring of truth.

After boarding the flight, I observed the attention and respect of the flight attendants with annoyance: on my salary, a first-class seat had never been an option. But I couldn't enjoy the efficiency and luxury as I reflected on all the years I had been living on a shoestring budget. A surprising tinge of resentment came over me when I considered the enormous difference in the way I was suddenly being treated.

The flight attendant offered me an array of American and European newspapers. I chose the *Neue Zürcher Zeitung,* to get a European perspective on what was happening around the world. Basically, there were the same news events I had read about in Boston, except for a small front-page story on a Swiss firm, the Girard Resource Development Corporation. Apparently, the company was being investigated by a dozen international agencies for ties with organized crime. But a cover-up had been exposed: the Swiss government and major banks had been denying access to crucial documents, apparently because a number of Swiss politicians and influential figures were connected with the firm. *Local politics,* I thought. *A huge mess that has nothing to do with me, thank God.*

Punctually at 11:45 A.M., Paris time, we landed at Charles de Gaulle Airport, and I felt a certain degree of uncertainty and uneasiness, accompanied by a hint of eagerness, even optimism, for the new possibilities on the horizon. Little did I know.

As I exited customs with my luggage, a uniformed driver holding a sign bearing my name descended upon me immediately. "Dr. Pierce?" he asked.

As he took my luggage and led me to a silver Mercedes sedan, I asked him if I was the last guest to arrive. "No, many other people arriving today," he replied. "From all over Europe and America."

"What's the occasion?" I asked.

"Foundation business," he answered politely, and I sensed

he didn't want to say more. When he offered to take me on a scenic detour through Paris, I immediately accepted. Through the tinted glass of the sedan, I renewed my acquaintance with the timeless architecture of the Parisian cityscape. As we sailed by, insulated from street noise and dust, I admired the sober regality of the Place de la Concorde and the size and grandeur of the Arc de Triomphe, as well as the uncompromisingly modern glass pyramid of the Louvre, bursting from within the restrained, self-consciously French baroque complex. And I glimpsed the campy playfulness of Sacré-Cœur, with its massive white dome, sprawled out over Montmartre like a white Persian cat, casually opening its eyes to what was happening below.

To break the ice, I said, "I have to admit, I'm a bit nervous about meeting so many new people."

After thinking for a while, he said, "There's no reason to worry. You'll find it's just like a big party."

"How many guests are coming?"

"Thirty-five, maybe forty," he replied, and seemed to loosen up, which helped take the edge off my nerves. "There are always a lot of important people," he added. "Some very rich. Yesterday a baroness from Germany and her granddaughter needed six men to carry their luggage. And this afternoon, a beautiful young woman from Rome received twenty large bouquets."

Leaving the city, we began our trip to Nancy on the highway, and I succumbed to the lack of sleep, eventually dozing. Several hours must have passed, because when I awoke, the monuments and skyscrapers of the Parisian cityscape had yielded to an architecture of human scale, of classical detail and light—a silent explosion of weightless baroque, refined space, and reduced proportions. In the distance I could see a splendid gate of wrought iron and gold and a cascading fountain irreverently splashing with a Dionysian exuberance. "Where are we?" I mumbled.

"Place Stanislas in Nancy," he replied.

For once in my life, I had no words. As we drove by the huge fountain of Neptune nestled under a massive canopy of delicate gold filigree, I finally said, "Amazing."

"But you really have to see Nancy at night," he continued, enjoying my admiration. "The old city is . . . well, you just have to see for yourself."

"Mozart stopped in Nancy for a short time," I said. "On his way back to Salzburg from Paris in 1778."

"Mozart liked Nancy very much," he replied. "He would have liked to live here."

"How do you know so much about Mozart?"

"The viscount is very interested in Mozart," he answered. "All the staff has to take a workshop now and then. And you should see the viscount's library. They say he has every book about Mozart ever written." Under his breath he added, "I understand he likes your book very much."

As we turned the bend, I reflected on the book I had written in graduate school: an encyclopedia of the two-hundred-plus cities Mozart visited during his short, thirty-five-year life—where he stayed, where he performed, where he wrote his immense opus of masterworks that never ceases to surprise and delight us. My professors and colleagues always managed to take potshots at it, since they hardly regarded it as an illustrious scholarly task, in comparison to "important" projects, such as calculating how much money his father earned during the great western tour, or providing a day-by-day account of what Mozart wrote on his deathbed, or speculating in excruciating detail on the possible streptococcal implications of his final illness, or whether he died of trichinosis. But I enjoyed researching and writing my book immensely, and it prepared me well for my Ph.D. dissertation on *La Clemenza di Tito,* Mozart's last serious opera. And apparently someone else liked it also.

Entering an immense gate, we passed through a courtyard leading to a complex of eighteenth- and nineteenth-century buildings, and the driver's tone changed abruptly, taking on an official color like brass fanfares announcing the appearance of royalty: "This is La Favorite, the estate of Viscount de Laguerelle and the seat of the Fondation de l'Art éternel."

Drivers were unloading luggage from identical silver sedans as a dozen or so guests ascended the staircase. Briefly, it reminded me of the *palais* of Donaueschingen, which I had visited while doing my book on Mozart's travels. I recalled the pomp and pageantry of the arriving weekend guests of the Prince of Donaueschingen. Then I had been a spectator—but now I was a participant in the colorful spectacle.

My mind was reeling as I was escorted into the Second Empire megalith, which looked more like a grand hotel than a private residence. For a moment, I felt a flutter in my stomach as I had each time I performed a Mozart piano concerto in public. La Favorite was a magnificent theater set, and I was experiencing the ineffable butterflies of a stage entrance.

With mannered professionalism, a tall, impeccably dressed majordomo greeted me. "You must be Dr. Pierce from Boston. I am Philippe. Let me welcome you to La Favorite." Nodding to the petite, reserved woman to his side, he continued, "Denise is your housekeeper; she will show you to your room and will be at your service during your stay. We will meet this evening at eight."

As I thanked him, my attention was diverted by a breathtaking pair of polychrome marble busts in the entrance foyer—wonderfully lifelike women with stylized hairdressing and shoulders draped in graceful folds sculpted in stone. For a split second my gaze was riveted on one and the majordomo noticed my admiration. "The wife of Emperor Hadrian," he commented politely. "Her name was Vibia Sabina. She was renowned for her beauty."

"Remarkably modern," I said. "But I'd guess they're at least two thousand years old. They look like museum pieces."

"There is a later Roman copy of the pair in the Metropolitan Museum in New York," he replied dryly. Sensing that it was the right moment, Denise intervened and led me and two young porters through a labyrinth of vast mirrored corridors. But everywhere I looked, I was distracted by acres of landscapes painted on canvas and wood, and colored engravings from the eighteenth and nineteenth centuries framed in antique gold. Reflecting a thousand spectrums were chandeliers and sconces—from delicate, simple Murano white glass, to massive Empire gilded bronze with glass prisms and beads. The beauty of La Favorite was a surrealistic blur of Aubusson tapestries, freshly cut crimson ginger flowers in crystal vases, and high ceilings decorated with Louis XV gold ornament.

The sound of a chiming clock in the recesses of the château was gradually joined by a dozen others, like the roar of a distant wave, carrying me into another epoch. The precious timepieces were everywhere, in hammered gold and marble, with elegant figures from mythology lounging and posing with graceful indifference. And next to them were vases of blue Sèvres and painted porcelain on splendid tables inlaid with tortoiseshell, bone, and mother-of-pearl, all nestled beneath walls covered in fabric—a thousand and one blue and peach flowers on a sea of beige silk. And there were chairs upholstered in fabrics that discreetly whispered royalty. Above them hung delicate mirrors in a cascade of carved wood and gold leaf, reflecting centuries of vanity and human posturing, and veiled eroticism.

When we arrived at my room, we were surprised to see a DO NOT DISTURB sign on my door, and Denise knocked very tentatively. The emphatic voice of a woman bellowed from within: "I asked not to be disturbed."

Denise replied, "Sorry, Miss Teal."

Could it possibly have been the voice of Alison Teal, the renowned soprano? As we continued down the corridors, escorted by men and baggage, I said to Denise, "There must have been a small mix-up."

She smiled at me politely but I could tell she was annoyed. "Miss Teal stayed in that apartment the last time she was here, and . . ." She hesitated, then continued, "I imagine she wanted the same room again. She's a great prima donna, so we have to let her have her way. Things like this happen all the time." As we walked, I had the impression Denise was carefully weighing each word. "The problem is that the viscount is too kind to hurt anyone's feelings, and guests are free to do all kinds of strange things. I'll take you to the apartment we had prepared for Miss Teal," she continued. "Let's hope nothing goes wrong this time."

With good-natured resignation, she unlocked two massive doors and smiled at me. As we entered, I gasped; the apartment was in perfect rococo style, dominated by painted panels depicting mythological frivolity. The furniture was light and delicate, in shades of gray-green and faded gold, and majestic floor-to-ceiling silk draperies hung from painted wooden valances decorated with gilded ornaments. Everything was designed to make a guest comfortable: telephone, television, and fax machine peered out from behind cabinet doors designed to hide them completely. A silver wine cooler with handles in the form of lions' heads held a bottle of Moët & Chandon, with finger sandwiches clustered under moist linen napkins on a silver tray nearby. And splendid arrangements of fresh flowers—chrysanthemums, Peruvian lilies, Oceana roses, and baby's breath—competed for attention.

Denise had been quietly watching me, curious about the new guest in her care. With a touch of theatricality, she turned and pulled open the curtains, smiling with satisfaction. Without knowing why, I suddenly found myself attracted to her. Then I realized why—she reminded me of Laura, my would-be fiancée who had given up after waiting two years for me to propose. Denise was similar to her in build, with a subtle sensuality that was hardly apparent as she wore glasses and no makeup. And like Laura, she did everything to underplay her looks.

Although Denise's light brown hair was pulled back in a style that suggested servile professionalism, with a drab gray uniform that would have made a Boston spinster proud, she could not hide her athletic, supple figure, her vitality, or the radiance of her skin. And her eyes were a sea of molten gray-green. I had been scrutinizing her absentmindedly until I noticed her face flush.

Then a rather hefty diamond-encrusted gold ring on her fourth finger caught my eye. "That's a beautiful wedding ring," I said.

"Engagement," she replied simply. "But you just arrived at La Favorite. The last thing you want is for your housekeeper to bore you by talking about her personal life."

"No, please," I insisted. "Tell me."

She hesitated. "Well," she continued, very tentatively, "all my life I've wanted to start a family, and now it's finally going to happen. After years of waiting for the right man to come along, I was sure time had run out. You know, at a certain age it becomes difficult for women to have children."

"But that's more like age forty, isn't it?" I asked. "You couldn't possibly be more than thirty."

Denise laughed aloud. "Just because you have a Ph.D. doesn't mean you can fool a woman into revealing her age. But thank you for the many years you made disappear."

"How did you know I have a Ph.D.?" I asked.

With her thick French accent, she replied, "The staff is briefed about each of the guests, *Docteur* Pierce." With a wry smile, she added, "I know all kinds of things about you."

Going about the room, checking that the apartment was in order, she turned briefly, reading the perplexed look on my face. "Please don't be offended," she said. "All very nice things." She added, apologetically, "You look like I'm going to bite you."

"What else do you know about me?"

She stopped briefly and stared into the distance. "That you come from Boston, that you are passionate about Mozart, that you . . ." She hesitated. "That you are a kind man." She continued, "The last part I just learned. When Alison Teal upset me by taking over your room, you instantly made me feel better. And here I am talking about my private life to a complete stranger . . . something I never do."

"I'm honored you told me," I said.

"Now," Denise said, reassuming a self-consciously professional tone, "you must be very tired after your trip. Just call me if you need anything. If you find any other cards that say 'Alison' or 'Miss Teal,' please throw them away." With that, she removed several handwritten cards with an embossed gold border and tossed them in the wastebasket. As an afterthought, she added, "And please don't tell anyone what I said about Miss Teal. Especially Philippe. He runs La Favorite like the French Revolution. Instead of firing people, he'd rather have them guillotined."

Changing the subject, I tried out my rusty French. *"La Favorite est vraiment extraordinaire."* She looked amused and repeated that I should not hesitate to call immediately if I needed anything. Finally alone, I closed the curtains and within minutes I was in a deep, almost comatose sleep.

*What time is it?* I wondered as I fumbled for my travel alarm on the inlaid wood side table. Five-thirty P.M. It had been such a deep sleep, I hardly remembered where I was. A waning ray of soft, filtered sunlight crept through the shutters, transforming the apartment at La Favorite into a finely drawn canvas of muted pastels and grisaille. Still groggy, I washed my face and hunted for the toothpaste. When I realized that dinner was at eight, I mumbled, "Thank God!" There was still enough time to get ready, and even to continue transcribing my diary before dinner. By now, the possibility that I was translating the candid revelations of a fourteen-year-old Mozart in Italy was irresistible.

*January 27, 1770*

*Milan is both Italian and German. Yet everything here is so much freer than in Salzburg. Such amazing things I have seen in these first few weeks alone!*

*Today, on my fourteenth birthday, Papa and I attended a church service and at the entrance there were several beggars draped completely in black with their faces covered. All were women, as men are prohibited from begging in such a manner in Milan. As we entered the church, I was astonished to see hundreds of silver ornaments of hands, hearts, heads, and feet, hanging from ribbons above the side altars. Many of them were expertly crafted—including male and female organs as well as shapely asses and well-formed breasts. With mock innocence I asked Papa what they were.*

*"Here," he replied, "the faithful thank the Lord by buying or by having an effigy made of the place they were healed. The wealthy bring silver to have it melted*

and cast into votive offerings." With annoyance, he added, "There are even services here where all kinds of poisonous snakes and vipers are allowed to run free, to test the faith of the congregation. These are just examples of superstition and license which the Italian church is slow to uproot." But during the service, I could not resist catching glances of the remarkable works of art in silver, always hoping Papa would not notice my "devotional" interest in them.

Last Tuesday was a beautiful, clear day, almost like spring in Salzburg. As Papa and I strolled through the city, we came upon a church where a great deal of activity was taking place. The spacious square in front was covered with beautiful carpets, and colorful banners were hung from the surrounding houses. Flowers, oil paintings and silver candlesticks had been mounted on outdoor tables like altars and a large choir was singing, accompanied by over fifty strings. When we inquired about the occasion, we were told it was the feast of Saint Babila, the beloved Milanese patron saint and martyr.

When the choir finished, everyone including ourselves entered the church to hear the famous castrato, Giuseppe Aprile, who sang magnificently. Afterward, we spoke with two of his pupils, Luigi and Giovanni, both my age. They were great fun, laughing and making jokes about the gruesome operation they had undergone to preserve their voices. Luigi said, "Anyone who performs the operation is excommunicated unless it was necessitated by health reasons, such as a 'fall from a horse' or 'an attack by wild pigs.'" He joked, "Italian castrati must be terrible on horseback because most of them claim to have had the same accident."

What impressed me, however, was the candor with which they spoke of their capacity to love. I was fascinated by their exploits with women (although I suspect some of their stories were exaggerated): kissing, nibbling, fondling, and much more—women of all ages,

*young and tender, older and more experienced, bored*
*wives, perfumed noblewomen, and earthy servants*
*ambitious to marry.*

*We never stopped laughing and they begged me to*
*write them some solo pieces to sing in church next week.*
*When I finish this journal, I must write down a lyrical*
*motet for Luigi that I have already composed in my*
*head; it will fit his fine voice like a well-tailored suit.*

Prying my attention away from the folio, I noticed the sun had begun its descent behind the viscount's residence in a sky of tawny rust and turquoise. Wrapping up my work, I realized that the folios were not all in chronological sequence and that I would have to put them in order another time. And I scribbled myself a note to follow up on specific pieces of information, such as whether erotic church ornaments actually existed.

Before getting ready for dinner, I rang Denise. She offered to have my dress shoes polished and my suits and shirts pressed. "And," she added, "your tuxedo, as well."

Seeing my surprise, she volunteered, "Don't worry; many guests arrive without evening dress. I can make arrangements to have one ready."

"Is dinner always formal?" I asked.

"Yes. The viscount still follows many traditions . . . he's practically the last of his generation."

"I'm a little confused." I ventured, "How old is the viscount?"

"Oh, you can ask him," she replied with a soft laugh. "But most likely he'll tell you first . . . he had his ninety-fourth birthday a few months ago."

"It sounds like you've known him a long time. How many years have you worked for the viscount?"

"Only about eight. And I don't even know how much longer I can continue—my grandfather owns a *patisserie* here in Nancy and it's becoming too much for him, so there's family pressure for me to take it over."

"Would you like doing that?"

"Actually, I wouldn't mind. I was practically raised in that shop. My grandfather was the only father I ever really knew. But I would hate to give up the world here at La Favorite—I really love all the excitement, the dinners, the people from all over the world. I don't know as much as you do about music, but I adore all the concerts."

There was a certain exuberance in her voice, in the way she moved. "You seem to be in a good mood tonight," I said.

"I'm meeting my fiancé this evening," she said.

With Denise's departure and the eventual arrival of my new tuxedo, I began to experience my usual nervousness about new people and new situations. But at five to eight, I stood ready before a full-length antique mirror, splendidly dressed in crisp, starched Egyptian cotton and the softest, finest worsted wool. The polished porphyry cuff links and studs, with the dusky color and texture of undecanted port wine, were a loan from the viscount and seemed to radiate an energy of their own.

"Damn, what a good-looking guy," I mumbled to myself as I descended the stairs of La Favorite, curious to find out what lay in store. My expectations were high: to be immersed in European culture, surrounded by charming, educated connoisseurs of art and music. But as I would soon find out, I was about to enter an intimate world where I was alone among dangerous strangers.

# CHAPTER 3

*Party-spirit . . . the madness of many for the gain of a few.*
—ALEXANDER POPE

Walking through the endless hallways, I hummed a melody under my breath that took me a few seconds to identify as "The March to the Scaffold" from the *Symphonie fantastique* of Berlioz. "The unconscious is the window of the mind," I mumbled.

In a large paneled room adjacent to the dining room, I saw two dozen people mingling around a ponderous Renaissance fireplace with stiff caryatids of carved marble. Only one or two people seemed to notice me enter, and I walked through the crowd listening carefully for any comments I might overhear.

"*. . . penso che sia americano.*" Someone speaking Italian thought I was American.

"*. . . ziemlich hübsch.*" Rather attractive. German. Whoever was speaking, I hoped they were referring to me.

"*Voici l'agneau sacrificial!*" For a moment I stopped short. Someone had said something in French about a sacrificial lamb. As I searched for an expression in the faceless crowd, I thought, *Nice welcome.* It was unnerving; in fact, it struck me as downright creepy.

No one seemed eager to speak to me, so I started a conversation with a waiter serving cocktails. "Do you know the people here?" I asked, deliberately speaking softly.

"Yes, sir," he replied with a spontaneous smile. Pointing to an elegantly dressed, obese woman in a wheelchair, he said, "Baroness Paumgarten with her granddaughter. The baroness is an old friend of the viscount. Sometimes," he whispered, "she has a little difficulty hearing. In the corner is Dr. Braun."

The man he named—with steel-rimmed glasses and an aloof, almost arrogant expression—was none other than the editor of the *Mozart Millennium Edition,* who had requested my Mozart documents. My immediate instinct was to go over and speak with him. The waiter continued, "He's talking with a music publisher from Germany, Mr. Wolff."

Scanning the room, the waiter continued, "Standing directly in front of the fireplace is Alison Teal, the famous singer." Immediately I recognized Ms. Teal, splendidly statuesque in a long white gown and draped with a pashmina shawl in muted tones of pearl gray and ivory. "She's talking to the viscount's niece," he said, referring to a delicate, slender woman, perhaps in her fifties, dressed in a simple black dress and wearing a necklace of tiny pearls. "Nadine du Pont. She's American, she used to be a ballerina."

The enthusiastic tone of the young waiter lessened my apprehension. He continued, "I'm Jano . . . from Slovakia. If you like, I'm permitted to introduce you to any of the guests." Blond and extroverted, Jano had a face that radiated eager goodwill, and I guessed he was in his late twenties. My immediate desire was to meet Alison Teal, yet I knew I had to speak with Dr. Braun.

But with the entrance of what seemed a vision, my attention was diverted. With feline suppleness, a ravishing brunette—more panther than woman—glided across the polished wood parquet toward the fireplace, where a half-dozen men seemed to awaken. "Jesus Christ," I said, with stunned admiration. "Who's that?"

"That, sir, is Miss Nicoletta Chigi," Jano replied. Cryptically he added under his breath, "It might be better if someone else introduces you."

"Never mind," I replied, dazed and trying to take my eyes off her. "Out of my league. I really should meet Manfred Braun." And within seconds, I found myself being introduced by Jano.

"Oh, yes. How was your trip?" he asked me with postured indifference.

"Very nice. Still experiencing a little jet lag."

"You'll be fine in a few days." To my surprise, he turned and glanced around the room as if we had finished our conversation.

"Did you have time to look at my documents?" I asked.

"You didn't send me the originals," he replied, annoyed. "How was I supposed to evaluate them?"

Hesitating, I replied, "I could show them to you while I'm here."

"You brought them with you?"

"Yes."

"Well, in that case . . ." he replied, with a barely perceptible gleam in his eye. Lowering his voice, he continued, "But let's not discuss it now. We have plenty of time."

I started to respond, when a gentleman in his late fifties or early sixties came over to say hello to Braun. With platinum blond hair speckled with gray, he projected an aura of importance. Yet dark recesses under his eyes and deep-set wrinkles on his forehead suggested years of indulgence. Unlike the other men in tuxedos, he was dressed in shades of gray and black with a silk polo instead of a tie.

When Braun presented me, I immediately reached out to shake his hand. Instead of responding, he scrutinized me with a fierce expression—a disconcerting combination of superiority and indifference. Then, without a word, he turned and walked off into the crowd, leaving me stunned by the brief encounter. Apparently, I wasn't worth the slightest gesture of acknowledgment.

Braun immediately noticed my reaction and said, with a patronizing tone, "Don't pay any attention. That was Prince Rudolph von Horvach. He looks preoccupied tonight."

Feeling my face flush, I mumbled, "That bastard."

Almost whispering, Braun replied, "Look, whatever you do, don't get on his bad side. He's one of the most influential men in Vienna."

Not far from us was an older man with white hair and an agreeable face that reminded me vaguely of a rustic Bavarian wood carving, speaking with another man. "Let me introduce you to Mr. Wolff, my publisher," Braun said.

When Wolff saw us, he ended his conversation, saying something that sounded distinctly like "fresh meat." As he approached, I realized that Braun and I hadn't finished our discussion about the Milan diary and tried to wrap it up. "I was wondering about the form you sent me."

My insistence angered him and he responded defensively. "It's only a formality to protect ourselves. Recently I spent months reviewing a manuscript and after all my work, the person decided to take it elsewhere. We don't want that to happen again."

"So you're comfortable making an evaluation without the form?"

Cutting me off, Braun replied in his clipped Austrian accent, "I decided we would make an exception for you. But do me a favor, Pierce, don't bore the guests here with shoptalk, as you Americans call it."

Braun's condescending tone angered me, but Wolff intervened. "Manfred, nothing this young man could say would bore me. It's so refreshing to have a new face among all the old, dissolute aristocrats. These foundation events are practically a convalescent home."

Braun bristled. "Really, Andreas, you exaggerate."

Seeing Braun's expression, Wolff backed down. "I suppose I'm being a bit too harsh. This society is really very healthy, very flourishing . . . sort of like a thriving mausoleum."

The glimmer in his eye announced that Wolff was an irrepressible brat—a large brat, in fact, in stature and girth, from his wide shoulders to his broad nose. Almost to encourage him, I looked over at the spectacular Nicoletta Chigi, surrounded by her adoring bog of attentive men, and said, "But there are a number of younger guests."

"Manfred, what shall we call Nicoletta now?" Wolff prodded, playing to his new audience. "Does she want 'Your Royal Highness' or will just 'Your Majesty' do? Should we genuflect when we do the *Handkuss*?" Wolff gestured, kissing his own hand and looking at us with mock seriousness. As he spoke, it was impossible not to notice a massive gold Jaeger-LeCoultre chronometer on his wrist, a formidable object he moved so as to best display it.

"You're really too much," Braun protested.

"Oh, come on, Manfred," he replied. "You know it's true. She's well over thirty by all recent eyewitness reports, so she'd better make use of her looks while she can. Beauty faded has no second spring."

Wolff was in the mood and his eyes sparkled with a thousand comments, all waiting to go. Caught up in the momentum, I scanned the room. "There's a fairly young guest," I continued, nodding at a slender man with thinning black hair and pale, exotic skin like translucent alabaster.

"Oh, that's Andrei Weidener, the Russian pianist," Wolff replied. "He's awfully good-looking, don't you think? But we're both out of luck . . . he's married."

For some reason, Wolff had assumed I was gay, but it didn't bother me, as I was enjoying being in his confidence. Braun immediately cut in, "Look, if you keep this up, I'm leaving."

Fully aware that we were provoking Braun, I continued, looking over at a striking, petite blond. "There's a girl who looks twenty at most."

Braun and Wolff followed my glance. "Oh, that's Ilsa Paumgarten," Wolff said. "As for her age, I don't know. I hear it fluctuates somewhere between twelve and twenty-four, depending on the circumstances. That girl should get a speeding ticket for her vagina."

Getting red in the face, Braun sputtered, "You really ought to behave yourself."

But Wolff continued, "As they say, she was born with her legs spread wide open. They'll probably need a Y-shaped coffin to bury her."

"That's it," Braun shouted. "I've heard enough."

As Braun pushed his way through the crowd, Wolff and I looked at each other. Placing his fingers over his mouth and rolling his eyes, Wolff made an expression of mock regret, like a monk who had just said a bad word. "Do you think he'll ever speak to us again?" I asked.

"He'll be fine," Wolff replied, smiling. "I'm always trying to get him to loosen up, but it's an uphill battle." In a completely different tone, Wolff continued, "The viscount happens to agree with me—Manfred needs to relax."

"Is the viscount here?" I asked.

"No. And I doubt he'll attend tonight. He never appears the first evening."

Our conversation proceeded like a grand tour, as Wolff knew something about every subject—politics, art, literature, and history. And his slightly off-color remarks and provocative viewpoints, always seasoned with zest and a flair, fascinated me. When Philippe arrived to announce, "*Mesdames et messieurs* are invited to be seated," I was genuinely disappointed to leave this congenial man of the world.

But as I looked for my place card at the table, I passed dozens of new, unfamiliar guests, and my initial sense of discomfort returned. In a short time, I had discovered that this rarefied, privileged world could also be complicated and inhospitable. La Favorite was full of people who thought of one thing alone: themselves. And the evening was just beginning.


Nothing could have prepared me for what awaited us in the dining room: the room sparkled with light cast by three massive Empire crystal chandeliers, and antique Venetian glass water goblets on the dining table reflected a bonfire of candles. As my eyes swept across the room, I saw sideboards shimmering with antique turquoise and gold Limoges porcelain and white-glazed ceramic cherubs irreverently balancing bowls of fresh peaches, figs, and grapes next to flower arrangements bursting from hammered seventeenth-century Dutch silver bowls. The guests, forty or so, generated an atmosphere of cordiality and festivity—at least it seemed so at the time.

It was a surprise to find Alison Teal seated to my right, and the thirtyish, dark-haired pianist with skin like pale veined marble at my left. Two seats were vacant, at the head and the foot of the table, so I assumed that one was intended for the host.

Miss Teal's features were chiseled perfection and her draped shawl gave her a dramatic, regal appearance. Although she was immersed in conversation with a man to her right, she smiled as I sat down. But the young pianist on my left seemed friendly and ready to talk. Immediately offering me a handshake, he said, "My name's Andrei Weidener."

With his fine features and delicate skin and hair, Andrei perfectly fit my mind's image of a great artist; his protruding forehead and receding hairline with the slightest hint of salt and pepper at the temples gave him a look of distinction. And his piercing blue-gray eyes emanated extraordinary vigor.

"Matthew Pierce," I replied. "You're the Russian pianist, aren't you?"

"Well, actually," he said, "I'm half-Russian and half-Austrian." He laughed. "And I do earn my living as a jazz pianist in Vienna—nothing too progressive. You could call it elegant jazz. How about yourself?"

"I play too," I replied. "But primarily I'm a musicologist. A Mozart specialist."

"You don't look boring enough to be a musicologist," he said, reaching for an iced bucket of huge green olives and carrot sticks. His openness broke the ice and immediately made me feel at ease. "It just occurred to me that almost everyone invited has something to do with Mozart," he continued.

"That's good to know," I said. "Because ever since I received the viscount's invitation, I've been wondering why I was asked here." Privately, I wondered if the candidates for a foundation award were ever notified that they were being considered. "Do you know most of these people?" I asked.

Andrei reached for fresh breadsticks and broke one. "Some. There are a lot of artists who play Mozart—like Hélène Benoit, the Belgian violinist. Some publishers, university professors. Several members of old aristocratic families. Our Viennese royalty is represented . . . that's Prince von Horvach, who just usurped the place of honor at the head of the table."

"Speaking of von Horvach," I continued, feeling a momentary rush of anger, "the Austrians here don't have much of a sense of humor. He and Braun take themselves so damn seriously. The one person here who seems to enjoy a good laugh is Andreas Wolff—and he's German."

Andrei chuckled. "Because von Horvach and Braun are not your typical Austrians," he countered. "In general, Austrians don't take life seriously at all. The capital of Austria is the home of the waltz, the most frivolous of all dances. There's a joke about Vienna toward the end of the war: the Germans were telling everyone, 'The situation is serious, but not hopeless.' But the Austrians were saying, 'The situation is hopeless, but not serious.'"

He seemed to be having a good time, alternating between talking and munching. "Sorry," he interjected between bites, "I'm starving. I went out for a long walk today in the park. Have you seen it? A spectacular property, stretches out forever. White deer, red squirrels, game birds stroll right across your path. Absolutely beautiful."

Suddenly Andrei mumbled under his breath, "I should warn you, the diva sitting next to you is getting rather annoyed that you haven't spoken to her."

Leaping into action, I introduced myself to Miss Teal and was about to express my admiration for her recordings, when von Horvach rose abruptly from the head of the table and came over to greet her. Although she didn't offer her hand, he took it anyway.

"Well, princess," he murmured, kissing her hand. "It's been a long time." For a second, she looked as if she had been slapped. When she didn't respond, he continued, "You look well."

"Thank you. I feel well," she said.

Returning to his seat, von Horvach added under his breath, "Try not to forget your keys."

Teal blanched. Again I began the conversation with her, but soon realized she was not listening and was on the verge of tears. "Are you all right, Miss Teal?" I asked. She placed her hand across her mouth to cover a quiver in her lip. Von Horvach was staring at her from the head of the table, awaiting her reaction. In stark contrast, the conversation around the table was animated, even buoyant.

When she didn't answer, I asked, "Can I get you something?"

With a desperate expression, she searched for my hand. "Is he still watching?"

Von Horvach hadn't stopped staring at us for a second. When I answered, "Yes," her grip tightened on my hand, a gesture of vulnerability that immediately made me feel protective of her. "What's going on?" I asked softly.

Fighting back tears, she managed to choke out a sentence. "I just don't know if I can sing tomorrow night." As she unfolded several pieces of paper from her purse, she continued, "This . . . this is unacceptable."

On one sheet, there were cutout letters of various sizes and shapes—an anonymous letter. The text read:

WEIGH THY WORDS IN A BALANCE
AND MAKE A DOOR AND BAR FOR THY MOUTH

Accompanying it was a newspaper clipping in German. Scanning it, I saw something about a disfigured body found in Lake Geneva.

Miss Teal's apprehension was followed by outrage. "It's a warning not to sing tomorrow night!" She continued, "This can't go on. I have to speak with René." We both looked to the place where the viscount should have been seated and found ourselves simultaneously staring into the eyes of von Horvach—a sensation reminiscent of looking down the double barrel of a shotgun.

"Mr. Wolff told me that the viscount never attends the first night," I said.

"That's really it, then," she said, abruptly rising from her seat. "I'm sorry to have been such poor company this evening. You've been terribly kind." With that, she glided out of the dining room, aloof and regal. And the consommé arrived with pristine efficiency.

Within seconds, I felt the faintest ripple of motion in the place where the great soprano had been: a distinct new presence had taken the seat next to me.

\*    \*    \*

Nadine du Pont, the viscount's niece and former ballerina, moved so gracefully I hardly felt her sit down. When I introduced myself, she murmured, "Glad to meet you, Dr. Pierce. How are you doing?"

"Please just call me Matthew," I replied, and added, "Actually, not too well. Apparently, Miss Teal isn't feeling well either."

Nadine breathed a heavy sigh. "I'm sorry you had to witness all of this. There's an awful lot going on tonight."

Gently, she placed her hand on my arm and looked me in the eye. "My uncle's very happy you could come." As she spoke, an army of waiters in white jackets descended upon the table, serving huge platters of striped bass stuffed with crabmeat and spinach. Nadine settled in, as if she had been sitting next to me all the time.

"I've been a strict vegetarian for years," she said. "But for this, I'll make an exception. My uncle chose the menu himself this evening."

Surprised, I asked, "Your uncle still gets involved with the preparations?"

"There's very little that happens at La Favorite that the viscount hasn't personally planned. By the way, why was Alison so upset?"

Cautiously, I explained the sequence of events, aware that von Horvach was watching us from the head of the table. Then I asked, "What do you make of it?"

"Some things," she said softly, "are best left unspoken."

The detached correctness of her reply surprised me. "Given what I've just seen, I think I have a right to know," I protested.

Nadine looked pensively into the distance. After a long pause, she answered, "All right, I'll be honest with you. The prince and Alison were together for three years. He wasn't invited here this time—he just showed up."

Her revelation caught me off guard. Encouraged, I plunged ahead. "Why did he call her princess? And what did he mean by, 'Try not to forget your keys'?"

Nadine was taking a sip of mineral water, and with my question it went down the wrong pipe. "That's pretty cruel," she sputtered. "He proposed to her and all the wedding arrangements were made. Quite a big deal when one of the most famous opera singers in the world marries a member of the Viennese nobility. That's what he meant when he called her princess."

"What about the keys?"

"Well, that's a bit depressing. Might spoil your evening."

The insistent look on my face told her to continue. Glancing surreptitiously toward von Horvach, she lowered her voice. "I'm not quite sure how to say this." Then a look came over her face, as if to say, *All right, you asked for it.* She continued, "They had a kind of love-hate relationship." Then she whispered, "He's been called a sexual sadist. His favorite pastimes are scarf bondage and asphyxiophilia."

I didn't get it. Nadine read the look on my face. "Near strangulation. It stimulates sexual pleasure through decreased blood flow to the brain. Only, it has obvious drawbacks."

Again, I didn't understand. "One woman didn't make it," she continued. "But von Horvach's lawyers convinced a magistrate that they were 'consenting adults.' Convinced, or bribed, I should say."

"Good God," I replied. "And Miss Teal?"

Nadine reflected and took a deep breath. "I understand he went over the line with her. Supposedly she started screaming for help." Nadine continued, "The servants had to beat the doors down. He saw it as a public humiliation. Yet, the next day she was ready to forgive him—"

"Why would she do that?" I asked, astounded.

"Who knows? For whatever reason, some people return to abusive relationships. But he had something else planned: when she came back to Palais Horvach, all the locks had been changed. He was smoking a cigar in his bedroom and blowing the smoke out the window. Alison thought it was a joke and started calling, 'Rudi, stop this nonsense.' She pleaded for him to open the door and after an hour of begging, she was literally down on her knees in the street sobbing, with people passing by."

Nadine's expression became very somber. "She had a complete breakdown and was in a psychiatric hospital for six months. And he got exactly what he wanted: everyone thought she was some kind of hysteric."

"My God," I said with genuine embarrassment, glancing around the table to see if others could hear our discussion. The chatter of the guests had reached a lively level and I realized that everyone was oblivious to us—except von Horvach.

"It was splashed all over the tabloids in Europe," she continued.

"How ya doin', babe?" A rich baritone voice resonating from behind us interrupted our conversation. It was a handsome giant of a man, half-black, half-Hispanic, sporting a jet-black mustache and a closely cropped goatee. Unlike most of the guests, he was wearing a dark suit and a pair of sunglasses that barely covered a deep scar under his right eye. He was obviously a serious bodybuilder, and his appearance on the scene made a striking impression.

Nadine reassured him that all was fine, and he left with all the quiet speed and intensity of a cougar. It wasn't necessary to ask her, "What's that all about?" She read my expression and laughed.

"Oh, that's Enrique. I work for an international agency that requires me to have a bodyguard."

"Sounds dangerous," I replied.

"Just a formality," she continued. "Unfortunately, some people I work with really need one."

"What do you do?" I asked.

"My agency tracks large international crime syndicates. You know, sale of chemical weapons and drugs, trading with embargo countries, money laundering."

Her response was so incongruous with the lavish dinner taking place, I found myself speechless. Finally I managed to say, "I've never met anyone in that profession. What's it like?"

"Interesting. I speak at law enforcement conferences around the world. The agency I work for, the European Council Convention on Proceeds of Crime, helps countries rewrite legislation. Basically I communicate recent developments in international organized crime and steps that are being taken against them."

Feeling generally uninformed, I repeated, "Recent developments?"

"Some crime syndicates have budgets larger than major corporations. With all their resources, they've become adept at shifting gears every time a government passes new legislation. When it becomes more difficult for them, they just transfer their operations to another country or to another scheme."

"That must keep you pretty busy," I replied.

She laughed. "Unfortunately, we're outnumbered. And there are real dangers out there: some international crime syndicates smuggle sophisticated technology and weapons, like high-tech missiles, to any country that will pay the price: North Korea, Yemen, the Middle East, the Persian Gulf. Other cartels deal in anything marketable—biological weapons like smallpox, meningitis, plague, diphtheria."

Uncomfortable about my total lack of expertise, I asked, "You said your agency also goes after drug dealers?"

"Only the wholesalers," she replied. "And investment companies, of course, because wherever there are huge profits from drugs, there have to be money-laundering schemes to cover them up. I'm particularly keen on tracking banking institutions that cross the line from legitimate high-risk ventures into criminal investments."

Nadine had been glancing around the dining room periodically, and it occurred to me that she was discreetly keeping tabs on several conversations at the table. Her momentary distraction gave me a moment to scrutinize her. Jano said she had been a ballerina and I imagined how sultry she might have looked onstage with her exotic brown eyes, dancing the role of Odile in *Swan Lake*. Guessing she was in her middle or late fifties, I noticed she had perfectly maintained her agile, petite figure. And she now wore an elegant black lace dress of the most refined simplicity. For a moment, I wondered if she could really be involved in such a hazardous profession.

As the army of waiters descended upon us again, we were distracted by the next remarkable gastronomic offering—stuffed roasted pheasant with large slices of Portobello mushrooms in red wine sauce—and by the extravagance of the presentation, on magnificent turquoise Limoges plates nestled on silver chargers. Looking around the table to see the reaction, I realized no one seemed to notice or care; everyone was immersed in lively discussion, apparently oblivious to the grandeur. Feeling overwhelmed, I concentrated on eating until a quiet, distinct voice rang out: "Speaking of crime, I've got a crime for you that you can't explain."

# CHAPTER 4

*What is life? A madness. What is life?*
*An illusion, a shadow, a story.*
—PEDRO CALDERÓN DE LA BARCA

Interrupting the tail end of our conversation, Andrei, the dark-haired pianist on my left, continued, "If you don't mind my eavesdropping, Nadine, something very strange just happened in my neck of the woods. A rare books dealer in Salzburg was found dead in an auto crash a few weeks ago, burned to a crisp. He had driven off the road into a tree and his gas tank blew up."

Andrei spoke to Nadine with a familiarity that indicated they already knew each other. Feeling somewhat daring, I asked, "So what was the crime?"

Andrei smiled. "Yesterday they discovered it wasn't his body. So what do you make of that?"

"I'd guess," Nadine said, "based on what little you've said, Andrei, that the book dealer tried to stage his own death."

"Why would he have done that?" Andrei asked.

"Dozens of possible reasons," Nadine replied. "Bad investments, unhappy marriage, gambling debts."

Andrei continued. "You know, you might be right. I heard a rumor that he had been acting strangely a few weeks before the accident ... always looking over his shoulder, jumping at the slightest noise, changing his daily route, as if he were convinced someone was going to kill him."

"Maybe someone was," Nadine replied.

"Nadine," I ventured, "doesn't organized crime run some kind of well-oiled machine to get rid of people for the right price?"

"A machine ... you could call it that," Nadine said. "But it isn't always so 'well-oiled'; there are a lot of slipups. When you hire low-life assassins and small-time criminals to kill someone, all kinds of things can go wrong. Like the wrong person getting killed, someone just going out in his yard to pick up the newspaper."

"What kind of people get involved with organized crime?" I asked. "Could I have met one and never known it?"

Andrei interrupted. "They're probably not much different from you and me, Matthew. Am I right, Nadine? On the street, I'd bet it would be hard to tell a crime syndicate kingpin, or even a paid assassin, from your typical Wall Street banker wearing a double-breasted suit and carrying a briefcase."

"Probably not far from the truth," Nadine said.

After dessert and coffee, we simultaneously opted for lighter conversation. Andrei mentioned he was scheduled to perform a Mozart piano concerto during the week and matter-of-factly added that he would be playing the fortepiano—that rare and fragile instrument distinguished by a light and clean singing tone. "The viscount wants to re-create the atmosphere of the eighteenth century," Andrei continued. "So the musicians of the orchestra are playing instruments fitted with gut strings instead of steel. The result is a softer, darker sound, unlike anything I've heard. And for those moments when the soloist is given a moment to shine—the cadenza—the viscount has asked me to improvise on the spot."

"Improvisation," I said, "now that is an art. It was so much a part of the training of every eighteenth-century musician, yet it's practically disappeared today—except in jazz."

"That's appropriate," Nadine said. "You're also a jazz pianist, aren't you, Andrei?"

He nodded, amused, and I reflected on how my own recent "career" had moved in that direction. Glancing around the room, I was surprised to see we were the last guests seated at the table. As Andrei and I walked toward the library, Nadine apologized for having to leave us and departed, with Enrique not far behind. When I saw von Horvach just inside the entrance, a renewed rush of indignation swept over me and I commented bitterly to

Andrei, "If that's who's representing your Viennese nobility, you're in deep trouble."

"I think you're judging him too harshly," Andrei answered, raising an eyebrow. "I've met him on a few occasions, and I find him, well, deliciously pathetic. In fact, I'd say he's probably the most remarkably dissolute man I've ever met."

Andrei heard his name called from the back of the library. "Excuse me one minute," he said, plowing through dozens of guests gathered in the huge paneled gallery and adjoining rooms. Already the air pouring out was a thick wall of heavy aromatic smoke from cigars and exotic cigarettes. Before entering, I hesitated for a second, then stopped. It was enough for one evening. I felt exhausted and needed fresh air . . . space. The driver from the airport had talked about the old city at night. Without a word of explanation to anyone, I made a straight line for the stairs and within minutes I was reveling in the splendid, clear night air of Nancy under the lucid, endless canopy of stars.

Calm and alone, I wandered the abandoned streets of old Nancy. An avenue of four rows of ancient linden trees led me gradually through a vast architectural playground, illuminated to highlight the purity of chiseled, classical lines. Words came to my mind to describe what I saw—calculated, refined, monumental—but they were insufficient for the eighteenth-century urban vision that stretched out before me. Unhurried, I walked the expansive pedestrian boulevard of the Place de la Carrière, admiring the flawless symmetry of massive palaces that radiated power and importance, yet with a natural lightness and grace. The deliberate theatricality of the lighting accentuated features that would have been otherwise hidden, creating an entire palette of shadows, a dramatic chiaroscuro in stone and stucco.

In the eighteenth century, Nancy became a celebrated plaything, the personal aesthetic vision of Stanislaw I, dethroned king of Poland. Together with his architect, Héré, they created an immense labor of love and imagination. And for now, it belonged entirely to me. Relaxed and at ease in this world, my mind again wandered to Mozart and to his visit to Nancy in 1778, after his desperately ill-fated stay in Paris.

Leopold Mozart had always wanted his son to experience the newest musical currents, and Paris was the logical choice, as it was one of the most vibrant musical cities in Europe. So, it was decided that Mozart would try to make his name and find a permanent position in the epicenter of French culture. In March 1778, at age twenty-two, Mozart arrived in Paris with his mother, traveling for the first time without Leopold. The relationship of Mozart and his father with their employer, Archbishop Colloredo of Salzburg, had deteriorated to such an extent that the young composer had asked to be relieved of his duties.

In Paris, Mozart again learned the painful lesson that a brilliant adult composer was far less appealing and marketable than a child genius. The trip proved to be a genuine disaster, including months of struggling to eke out a living in the expensive metropolis, hindered by the humiliation of intrigues within the artistic milieu—even performing in unheated rooms for arrogant and unmusical aristocrats. And as a final, brutal blow, his mother fell sick and died. Despite his earnest attempts, Mozart was unable to find a position as a composer and he received no commission to write an opera. It is little wonder that he began to despise the French manners and posturing he encountered.

But as usual, personal disaster for Mozart produced a blessing for posterity. Consistent with his legendary productivity, Mozart continued to create charming and congenial masterworks: the graceful, passionate Concerto for Flute and Harp, thirteen numbers for a ballet, and the *Paris* Symphony for large orchestral forces. Of course, he also published his Piano Sonata in A Minor in Paris, a tempestuous work full of dark and dramatic currents. And since Mozart never failed to fascinate people with his ability to improvise on the most recent and successful tunes, he also wrote down sets of variations on two operatic airs popular in Paris.

Alone after his mother's death, Mozart made the depressing trip back home to Salzburg through Nancy and Strasbourg. To save money, his begrudging patron, Baron von Grimm, put him on a slow coach and Mozart found himself wakened repeatedly at three o'clock in the morning to board. Some treatment for a celebrity who as a child had thrilled the greatest sovereigns in Europe!

Despite his bad experiences in Paris, Mozart loved the ten days he spent in Nancy. He wrote to his father, with mock importance, ". . . if I were well-known here, I would gladly stay, because the city is, in fact, charming—beautiful houses, beautiful broad streets and superb squares." And since few places in the world present a more untouched view of the sights and scenes Mozart saw during his lifetime, I could see that he was right.

In the distance, I heard muffled sounds of festivity and was drawn back to La Favorite. A concert had begun, but this was no conventional concert; people were moving casually from room to room in the illuminated palace. Faintly, I could hear the regal sounds of marches, cassations, and serenades by Mozart, music evoking the colorful fanfares of the past. My attention was divided between the vibrant canopy of stars and the playful exuberance of sounds emanating from La Favorite. A splendid moon, more than three-quarters full and radiant, highlighted the tops of age-old lindens, giving a shimmering, fluid luminescence to the *palais* and to the landscape. Instead of going back in, I curled up next to the stone base of a huge baroque sculpture, overlooking an expansive reflecting pool.

For a moment, I thought my ears were deceiving me: I was hearing not one but several orchestras, playing delightful, deliberate echo effects. Like a child eavesdropping on his parents' dinner party, I stood on a bench, peering through a window and saw small orchestras in all four corners of the room. Returning to my "sofa" under the huge baroque sculpture, I lay outstretched on the stone embankment around the pool and realized that, acoustically, I had found the best seat in the house.

Immediately I recognized the *Notturno* for orchestra of Mozart, and decided it was a good choice for the first night. As I absorbed the beauty of the outdoors and the spectacular concert, I heard myself saying, "Sophisticated," and for a moment I felt almost at the same level as the man who had conceived and arranged this discreet extravaganza. Norman Mailer came to mind: ". . . the wise primitive, I am indeed, in this immense jungle."

Somehow I had always known this world of brilliance and affluence existed, but I had been on the outside looking in, as I was now. Yet it was exactly where I wanted to be: experiencing the exhilaration of music of the night within the safety of a splendid solitude. Finally alone. Or so I thought.

"Oh, sorry." A voice startled me. "I didn't realize anyone was here."

Looking up, I saw a woman with reddish blond hair, not tall, with an elfin youthfulness that made her seem much younger than her forty-odd years. She was wearing a simply cut black dress and a necklace of pearls of various sizes and shapes. "It looks like we both had the same idea," I replied, craning my neck from my comfortable position, stretched out under the stars.

"If you'd like to be alone, I don't want to disturb you," she said.

"Why don't you join me?" I asked. "We can be alone . . . in the same place."

"Good," she replied, taking off her shoes as she propped herself up at the base of a sculpture. "I once read something by Rilke, that our greatest responsibility is protecting the solitude of another person. I'm Hélène Benoit." She hardly needed to introduce herself—I recognized her from a hundred CD covers and Deutsche Grammophon posters, always with her priceless Guarneri violin in hand. Wearing little makeup, she was naturally attractive, with a friendly, impish face and a kind of spontaneous, animated beauty. After only a few words, I sensed her honesty and directness.

Our conversation was interrupted by the sound of a regally somber minuet in a minor key from Mozart's *Haffner* Serenade. Neither of us spoke, as our attention was riveted by the majestic work, one of the highest and most desirable evocations of night music—tense, suggestive, and simmering in chromaticism. With a stately gesture, another minuet from the same serenade began and I commented to Hélène, "A work born perfect and whole, like Athena from the forehead of Zeus."

"And declaring its genius," she added. "Wait," she continued, "this next movement was the very first piece I played on a concert stage, when I was eight years old."

We both knew we were about to hear the first violin launch into a fiendishly difficult solo. In the frenzied, relentless sweep of flourishes and scales, it reminded me of the quest that so captivated the imagination of the eighteenth century—the search for a "perpetual motion" machine, a mechanical device that would run indefinitely. At age twenty, Mozart had perfectly captured and represented this quest in music.

Despite the elegance of our formal dress, Hélène and I were a comic duo: I was stretched out on a marble slab, silk bow tie unfastened, while she sat massaging her feet, reveling in the freedom from her shoes, all under the muscular buttocks of a huge statue of Poseidon. The sculpture, with hair, beard, and a thong in stylized seaweed cut in stone, towered above her, looking down, caught in a momentary pose as if wondering what was going on beneath him.

The atmosphere was intoxicating; between the faint scent of honeysuckle and the excitement of an occasional falling star, I decided I would never leave this secluded throne. And I asked myself why, with beauty, there always seemed to be a kind of silent pain.

The serenade over, I glanced at Hélène and realized we had not spoken for some time. She had a look of remorse, a profoundly sad expression. Occasionally, I could hear a muffled sigh. Finally, I ventured, "A penny for your thoughts."

No answer. I concluded it would be better not to press the point. Within a few minutes, Hélène spoke. "A divorce is a paralyzing event. Like something is being torn from inside me."

After several moments of silence, I asked, "Do you want to talk about it?" The festive music in the distance provided an ironic background. I could hear the gala ballroom scene from

*Don Giovanni*, a tour de force in which Mozart placed three different orchestras on the stage, each playing at the same time in a different meter.

Without answering my question, Hélène continued, "What do you do when you're in a marriage that's not good, but it's all you have? I feel like I'm destroying my life as I know it. With him, so many memories are being taken away from me, and I have so few."

It was clear Hélène was really talking aloud to herself. "He gave less and less of himself . . . I tried to ignore it for years. I was thirsty—for experiences, for life . . . for love. And he was a well running dry. Even the smallest human kindnesses were an effort for him."

"Some people control by giving," I said. "Others by not giving."

She didn't reply, and after a long pause, I added, "It sounds like you're experiencing separation anxiety." Cautiously following my intuition, I ventured to say, "That happens all the time . . . to abused wives and children."

My comment caught her completely off guard. "I've known for a long time we weren't suited for one another," she said. "But I never saw it as abuse."

Tentatively, I replied, "From what you've said, it sounds like there are elements of emotional abuse. And it becomes a simple matter of self-respect; if you stay in an abusive relationship, it means you have no respect for yourself."

A look of relief came over her face but within a few seconds she was mildly indignant. "How is it you know so much about my marriage?" As the sound of a vigorous march began, I let the question drop, and so did she. The militant sonorities emanating from La Favorite were buoyant, with all the delicacy and subtlety that only Mozart could bring to such a mundane task. It was music for the heart—and for the foot. Out of the corner of my eye, I could see Hélène distractedly tapping her toes. And watching her survey the limitless stretch of the Milky Way, I felt it was a good sign.

In the silence, I wondered what had made me go so far out

on a limb with a complete stranger. Maybe it was Hélène's vulnerability, which I sensed immediately despite her aura of competence. It was a hunch; maybe we were destined to be friends. I can't remember who left first or even how we parted. But something was right in the universe: a mutual respect, verging on intimacy, had been born.

With the huge outdoor wooden shutters closed and the heavy silk draperies drawn, my room was an impenetrable bastion against light. My sleep had been so deep, so profound, that I awoke disoriented. "Two o'clock! That's not possible," I groaned. "The day's practically over."

Within minutes after my phone call, Denise had tea sent to the room. As the waiter entered, he stepped on a plain white envelope that had been pushed under my door. "This must be for you," he said, handing it to me. After he left, I ripped it open and examined it.

### OPEN NOT THINE HEART TO EVERY MAN

Dumbfounded, I stared at the anonymous note, cut and pasted, like the one Alison Teal had shown me. Accompanying it was a folded newspaper clipping with much of the ink smudged, as if it had been read and reread. Irritated, I paced the apartment. What exactly did it mean . . . was it a threat? Was I in some kind of danger? After crumpling the two pages and tossing them in the trash, I stood and looked at them. A few moments later, I was still staring at the wastebasket. Reluctantly retrieving them, I resigned myself to reading the newspaper article. The caption, in English, read, "Grisly Execution Baffles Police: Body of 'Robber-Scholar' Found in Lake Geneva."

Alarmed and infuriated, I wondered what all this had to do with me. The account was lurid; the grotesquely disfigured body of a Canadian scholar, Arnold Schott, weighted with a block of cement, had been discovered at the bottom of Lake Geneva.

The details were so gruesome I tried to put it aside. But

within seconds, I found myself unable to resist reading it. Signs of a violent struggle. He had been savagely beaten and strangled with a nylon rope. As I read the list of events, I was sickened. The corpse had a "necktie": the victim's throat had been slashed ear-to-ear and his tongue pulled through. Body parts had been cut off and his teeth completely kicked out, as well as most of his face, perhaps to prevent him from being recognized. All probably after his death—they weren't sure.

The police were baffled by the fact that Schott's apartment had been ransacked, yet the assassin or assassins left behind dozens of works of art and manuscripts that Schott had plundered from museums and libraries around the world. And there was an international scandal brewing: many of the institutions to which Schott had liberal access did not even know the works were missing. Administrators and directors around the world whose jobs were in jeopardy were lining up to identify the stolen works.

My only option seemed to be to inform Nadine. In the meantime, I desperately needed to get out of the room. Remembering the majordomo's invitation to walk in the viscount's parks, visit his library, or play tennis, I headed for the library.

La Favorite was eerily quiet and the series of rooms called the library was essentially abandoned. A faded scent of old leather permeated the wing, mixed with the warm, inviting smell of aromatic pipe tobacco and cigars from the previous evening. Long stretches of fine inlaid wood paneling were interrupted only by the soft amber and red of antique volumes. For a moment, I was caught up in the tranquility of the setting. Then, in an adjacent room, I heard two men speaking, one of whom I recognized as Andreas Wolff, the German publisher. As I came closer, I saw that the second man was Prince von Horvach, whom Nadine had tersely described as a "sexual sadist," immersed in a heated discussion with Wolff.

As I debated interrupting to say hello, I could vaguely hear Wolff's voice: "Dammit, Rudi, we've been friends for over thirty years. This is the first time I've ever asked you a favor."

Von Horvach responded, "I won't give you a cent . . . I owe

you nothing. Unless . . . you know, that girl . . . the housekeeper, Denise—" He stopped in midsentence and I realized both men were staring at me. I had been inadvertently eavesdropping on their conversation and they were waiting for an explanation.

"I . . . I'm sorry. I didn't want to interrupt you," I stammered.

Wolff's reply was pleasant, but his voice was decidedly guarded. "Apology accepted, Matthew." It was apparent they were eager to return to their conversation. As I left the library, I glanced over my shoulder and saw Prince von Horvach glaring at me as he and Wolff resumed their conversation, almost inaudibly.

Embarrassed and intimidated, I looked at my watch and headed back to my apartment, determined to get my mind off von Horvach's irritation with me and the gruesome details of the Schott murder. But Braun's comment about von Horvach the night before continued to invade my thoughts: "He's one of the most influential men in Vienna. Whatever you do, don't get on his bad side."

Unfortunately, I had already crossed that bridge.

# CHAPTER 5

*It's only with great vulgarity that you can achieve real*
*refinement, only out of bawdry that you can get tenderness.*
—LAWRENCE DURRELL

With the crumpled anonymous note and clipping still on my
desk, a shift took place in my attitude toward the apartment; as
I watched the undulating shadows of the shutters rippling across
the walls, a sense of uneasiness took hold of me, and the splendid quarters struck me as dark, even ominous. To take my mind
off the unpleasant and embarrassing events of the afternoon—
events that I preferred to forget—I threw myself into the transcription and translation of the diary.

*October 24, 1771*
*A splendid day, of sky so radiantly blue, we could only*
*be in Italy. Papa and I now have nothing to do but enjoy*
*our freedom, as the premiere of my opera for the marriage*
*of Archduke Ferdinand was last week. For the occasion,*
*the sets and the costumes were all new, and the theater*
*painted, embellished and decorated with an infinite*
*number of candles. The music was received with great*
*acclaim, far more than the previous night for the opera by*
*Hasse, the favorite composer of the Empress. After the*
*performance, a spectacular* festa da ballo *[gala ball] was*
*given in the theater, gratis, for all who wished to attend—*
*masks obligatory.*
*We were to dine today with the archduchess at the*
*Clerici Palace but at the last minute we were notified she*
*was ill. Instead, Papa had a surprise for me, a brilliant*
*inspiration: he took me to all the most astonishing and*

*unusual places to see in Milan. First, we visited the chapel of the Brothers of Saint Bernard, where a battle was fought by the Christians, led by Saint Ambrose against the Arians (who believed Christ was not divine). The skulls and bones of those heretics slain in bloody combat are used as decoration in the chapel, with pyramids of bones secured behind an iron grate to prevent the superstitious from stealing them. Typically for Papa, there is always a moral lesson to learn from them, because, for Papa, morality is a way of life. In the chapel he reminded me, "In the war between virtue and vice, there is never a truce." Then, "Moral virtues are not endowed upon us by Nature but only through proper education." And finally, "Without religion and true doctrine to govern us, we are no more than a pile of dried bones." I said to myself that Papa must always have some noble, ethical excuse to enjoy himself. In fact, I decided he must have been having a really good time, if the number of edifying comments was any indication.*

*In the cathedral, together with four others, we were drawn up by a machine to view the most precious relic in the cathedral, a holy nail from the cross of Our Lord, preserved in a splendid case of crystal, which we were able to see at close distance. Afterward we walked up 158 marble stairs to an outside gallery where there were several gigantic sculptures of saints, martyrs, and dukes. We continued another 91 steps and found ourselves inside the roof, where, through an opening, we could see the inside of the dome of the cathedral. After four more flights, we were at the top of the dome with a view of so many statues on tall marble spires, I could not count them all. And from the cupola we had a remarkable view* [in Italian] *"of the most beautiful roofs in Milan."*

For a moment I was astonished and stopped short in my transcription. In fact, Mozart had not actually written "of the most beautiful *roofs* in Milan" (*tetti* in Italian) but, instead, "of the most beautiful *tits* in Milan" (*tette*). Could this have been a slip of the pen? Or was Mozart, at age fifteen, playing with the subtle erotic possibilities of the Italian language?

I decided to leave the question open and continued to plug away at the transcription.

> *The sacristan, who was great fun, told us there are over 4,000 statues on the inside and outside of the cathedral. As a young man, he had to stand guard every night with three other sacristans and dogs because the treasure in the cathedral is so great, it must be constantly under surveillance.*
>
> *In the cathedral and everywhere else we went today, people recognized me as the young* maestro *who had written the opera for the archduke's wedding. So many compliments—about the beauty of the arias, the magnificence of the ballet music, and, most of all, about how much pleasure it brought to everyone. It was a steady stream of enraptured Milanese who were thrilled and honored to meet me, or even catch a glimpse of me.*
>
> *After the cathedral, we visited the "great hospital," which is really like a city in itself. There are wards for the wounded and those with fever, consumption, smallpox, even a large ward for those with venereal disease, since many Milanese have been stricken with the illness.*
>
> *The hospital, with a huge courtyard of arches and marble columns, reminded me of a monastery. It has a flourishing herb garden, herds of sheep and bulls to provide meat for 1,500 patients, ice houses, and even a canal running underneath. But what intrigued me most was a copper machine that looked like a large oven. Two hours before sunset, the device is turned with the opening facing the street, and parents who cannot afford to keep their infants put them in and knock for the porter (who waits all night) to transfer the child inside to wet nurses. This remarkable invention was devised because parents*

*would often leave unwanted children at the hospital gate where they would sometimes be trampled, losing their limbs or even their lives. We were told four or five infants are placed each night in this "orphan machine," rarely less than three. But, to me, far worse than any of the diseases treated in the hospital was the condition of being unwanted, more tragic than smallpox or venereal disease.*

*Returning home, I launched into writing an aria in honor of the archduchess. In my opera, she is represented as a figure of mythology, the nymph Silvia, given by Venus in marriage to Ascanio, whose virtues are sung by a chorus of arcadian nymphs, shepherds, graces, genii, and other congenial spirits. But we learned today that the Archduchess Beatrice is very human indeed and definitely walks among us poor mortals. In fact, we heard she received a visit from that nefarious personage, Don Cacarello. In honor of the occasion, I have written an aria, "Non sò d'onde viene" ("I know not from whence you come").*

> *I know not from whence you come*
> *My Don Cacarello,*
> *This tempestuous feeling*
> *That arises in my bowels,*
> *That motion I feel*
> *Running through me.*
>
> *For such fierce contrasts*
> *to awaken in my ass*
> *Simple pity alone*
> *does not seem enough for me.*

With the light fading in my apartment at La Favorite, I had trouble reading the text, and worse, I had difficulty believing my own eyes. I knew *Don Cacarello* was an old Milanese term for diarrhea, but this parody was unquestionably more vulgar than anything I had ever read in Mozart's letters. The text, in Italian, was a perfectly crafted aria in two parts, but entirely removed from the lofty conceits of eighteenth-century opera.

Looking through materials I had brought from America, I came to the original text for "I know not from whence it comes," from the opera *Olimpiade* by Metastasio, the most important operatic poet of the eighteenth century. The model for Mozart's satirical burlesque actually read,

> I know not from whence it comes
> this tender feeling
> this motion that unknowingly
> is born within my breast,
> that chill that runs
> throughout my veins.
>
> For such fierce contrasts
> to awaken in my breast
> Simple pity alone
> does not seem enough for me.

By merely changing a phrase and a few critical words in Italian, Mozart had made a raucous, obscene parody of this paragon of stately, dignified poetry. It seemed possible that Mozart's scatological pun had been a way to let off steam after weeks of fierce pressure to satisfy singers, instrumentalists, and a fussy public. But his sense of humor was virtually guaranteed to harm the prestige of Mozart and his music. A thought came to mind: would it not be better to edit out the parody? Within moments, I realized it was the same issue that had troubled Emily Anderson in 1938 when she published the first translation of the Mozart letters into English, some of which were unabashedly smutty. But she concluded that the world would be better served if they were included. My decision was clear as well: the poem would stay, "Don Cacarello" and all.

The total absence of daylight indicated it was again time to get ready for dinner. By now I knew the routine and within no time, I was heading toward the dining room through the labyrinth of mirrored corridors, which now reminded me of an elaborate gauntlet drawing me into another volatile and unpredictable evening.

The cocktail party before dinner was again disorienting: too many people, too many rooms, too much going on at once. Walking slowly through, I again realized that I knew hardly anyone. A waiter bumped me from behind and I found myself almost thrown into the bosom of a spectacular beauty, an ebony-skinned young woman who radiated personality and energy.

"Excuse me," I mumbled. The man with whom she was speaking kissed her goodbye quickly, and I found myself directly in front of a vision of revealing embroidered lace, a confident and sensual Nubian princess. She introduced herself as Véronique Ibsen, and my heart raced as I realized I was face-to-face with a genuine celebrity, one of the most temperamental, controversial divas of the concert stage. Véronique radiated a relaxed charm and was in an exceptionally ebullient mood. On her neck, supported by a dark salmon velvet ribbon, was a heavy cameo.

"It's an honor to meet you, Miss Ibsen," I said.

"The pleasure's mine. Are you from the States too?" she asked.

"Yes, Boston."

"I just sang a concert there last September, in Jordan Hall," she said, as she gently fingered the striking cameo.

"If you don't mind my saying so," I ventured, "that has to be the most beautiful cameo I've ever seen. It reminds me of one I saw in the Metropolitan."

When she beamed and seemed eager to talk about it, I was relieved. "It's an antiquity from Roman times. I was told it comes from the greatest period of gem cutting, about fifty years before the birth of Christ."

Miss Ibsen spoke beautifully, with a refined accent that had a slight inflection from the American South, perhaps New Orleans. Her relaxed manner reassured me, and I felt genuinely flattered that she enjoyed talking with me. And the cameo—it was difficult to keep my eyes off it: a carved figure with an exquisitely detailed veil was driving two horses so delicate that the manes seemed to be painted.

"The colors are beautiful," I said, "white over salmon. Is it amber?"

"Sardonyx," Véronique replied. "It's carved from three layers of precious stone, a technique perfected in the time of Claudius."

"It looks like Apollo and his chariot of the sun," I continued.

"That's what I thought at first," she said, trying to restrain her excitement. "But it's a *woman* driving a chariot. And it's signed. The great masters signed their own work. Right here on the back," she said, tugging at the ribbon and bending over to show me.

As she leaned over to show me the cameo, she gave me a riveting view right down her dress. Two breasts of the most perfect size and proportion became forever carved in my memory: solid, unrestrained, and declaring their beauty. Her skin was tight and supple, a marvelous shade of deep mocha, and her firm, rigid nipples sat poised at attention.

"Well," I responded breathlessly, "that has got to be the most beautiful work of art I have ever laid eyes on." Quickly changing the subject, I said, "Looks like we're going to have a concert tonight."

"That's if she's up to it," Miss Ibsen replied, conspicuously not mentioning the name Alison Teal. Her change in tone surprised me. "She's upset that Rudi von Horvach is here," she continued. "And there's even a rumor she might not sing. They were lovers, you know."

"I hear he was rather cruel to her," I said, thinking my comment was common knowledge.

Clearly miffed, she countered, "Of course, they did have problems. Any relationship has things that need to be worked out. Unfortunately, she wears her martyrdom around like a tarnished war medal. I just find it so tiresome."

Attempting to be diplomatic, I asked, "What's your guess? Will there be a concert?"

"I'd almost bet there won't be," she replied with a soft, eerie laugh that I found unsettling. "I can practically read her like a book . . . a book I wouldn't care to read, that is."

Although I had only met Miss Teal, I felt protective of her and was taken aback by Véronique's mean-spirited comments. Fortunately, someone called her from the far corner of the room, and Véronique bounded off in a wake of sensual lace that delineated each of her shapely, toned curves. A few seconds later I was startled to find myself staring at a man in his late sixties, who had appeared without sound or warning. "Landry, Dennis Landry," he said with a firm handshake.

I was speaking with the renowned musicologist in charge of the *Mozart 2006* edition. "Pleasure to meet you," I managed to reply, again uncomfortable to be suddenly face-to-face with a figure of such renown. But within a minute or two of conversation, I felt more at ease, as Landry was engaging, even flattering. "I've read a few of your articles, Pierce," he said, puffing on his cigarette. "Promising work."

Landry was a formidable figure, almost larger than life with his meticulously shaved bald head. His black silk tuxedo was tailored to make his build appear more impressive. Yet I couldn't help noticing certain defects that the manicured tailoring could not conceal, such as his disproportionately short legs, his stockiness, and a huge head that seemed to sit directly on top of his torso as if his neck had been swallowed up. Pulling a small gold box from his jacket, he offered me a dark Dunhill cigarette, while scrutinizing me intensely.

"I'm curious," he suddenly said. "Why were you invited to La Favorite?"

By now, it was becoming clear to me that my invitation was in some way linked to the diary I discovered, but at the moment, I didn't feel like sharing that information. Instead, I replied, "I'm not completely sure myself."

"Maybe it has something to do with Manfred Braun," he said impatiently.

"Hardly know him," I replied, hoping to keep him off the path he was heading down. "In fact, I just met him yesterday." We both looked over and saw Braun talking to his publisher, Andreas Wolff.

"He has such a pretentious look on his face, don't you think?" Landry said, sneering, and I felt relieved he had turned his attention elsewhere. "It reminds me of a saying: 'How haughtily he lifts his nose, To tell what every schoolboy knows.'"

Hoping to stay neutral, I replied, "That's Andreas Wolff he's talking to."

"Those two. Those two," Landry said, sarcastically. "You could say they have an alliance—their hands are so deep in each other's pockets, they can't figure out how to pick their own noses." Laughing energetically at his own joke, Landry continued under his breath, "And I don't think you'd want Wolff's hand in your pocket, if you know what I mean."

I had the impression that Landry had been rehearsing these lines for years. "Pierce," he continued, with a gleam in his eye, "let's keep in touch. I have something that might interest you."

With that he left and began to circulate, leaving me feeling up in the air. Before long, I would discover that his cryptic remark was a colossal understatement.

Not far away, I could see Baroness Paumgarten, obese and somnolent in the wheelchair, again beautifully dressed, with her young blond granddaughter, Ilsa. Speaking with Ilsa was Hélène Benoit, my companion at the concert under the stars, along with an unfamiliar woman. When I approached, Hélène was exuberant and receptive. "Let me present Elisabetta von Stahl," she said warmly, introducing the strikingly tall, older woman whose platinum hair was pulled high above her head in a way that emphasized her stunning, swanlike neck. "Dr. Pierce and I spent last night together," Hélène continued with dry humor, ". . . alone."

"I want to hear all about it," Ilsa interjected.

With mock seriousness, Elisabetta von Stahl replied, "When two women are interested in the same man, it's worse than a secondhand shop."

"That's enough," Hélène protested, laughing. "We're going to frighten Dr. Pierce away."

"But, speaking of being interested in the same man," the striking platinum blond continued, lowering her voice, "look over there." The three women suddenly became dead serious and I felt drawn into their confidence as we glanced over at Véronique Ibsen.

No one spoke, and I resisted asking them why they were concerned. Looking at me, Hélène said point-blank, "Véronique was showing you her cameo."

"That's right," I replied, thinking of the beautiful view she gave me. "Why?"

Hélène said, "We all recognize that cameo. It belonged to Rudi von Horvach's mother, and now, all of a sudden, Véronique Ibsen's wearing it. There's going to be trouble . . . and I mean big trouble."

"Trouble from whom?" I asked, feigning ignorance. When no one replied, I asked, "Alison Teal?"

No one spoke. Feeling their silent accord, I continued, "She and von Horvach used to be in love, weren't they?"

"It wasn't love," Elisabetta said coolly, "it was need. That's an entirely different thing."

Hélène interjected, "Alison feels a need to rescue people."

Attempting to change the subject, I asked Ilsa, the petite, adolescent blond, "How's your grandmother doing?" Baroness Paumgarten sat quietly in her wheelchair, immovable and apparently asleep, oblivious to the discussion.

"She comes in and out," Ilsa said. "But she surprises me now and then with her comments. This morning she started telling me about her first boyfriend and after twenty minutes or so, she said, 'I love to reminisce . . . it makes me feel so delightfully old and useless.'"

"What's that on her wrist, a Medic Alert?" I asked, trying

to keep the conversation away from the issue of Alison Teal and Véronique Ibsen. But the expression of concern on Hélène's face continued unabated.

"No," Ilsa replied. "It's a talking wristwatch. The viscount gave it to her. She's absolutely in love with it. But she's so proper, she listens to it when I'm not in the room. Sometimes, after I leave, I can hear her checking the time."

Ilsa was irresistible, and I had trouble disguising my attraction to her. Just then, the same stentorian voice from the previous evening interrupted our conversation, announcing grandly, "Ladies and gentlemen, dinner is served." Locked in serious discussion, Hélène left with Elisabetta. Again, I felt a rush of relief that I had navigated through another potentially treacherous situation with people I hardly knew.

The guests gradually disengaged from their conversations and filtered into the dining room. The table was a delight to the eye, but there was hardly time to enjoy it, as I found myself seated between the hearty, entertaining publisher Andreas Wolff and the splendid Elisabetta von Stahl, the tall, platinum blond I had just met. My reaction was immediate satisfaction, as I anticipated relaxed and congenial conversation.

But tonight Wolff was more serious than the last time I had seen him, showing me a distinctly darker facet of his personality. He surprised me by asking bluntly, "What did Dennis Landry have to say to you?"

"Landry?" I asked. "He just introduced himself."

"He has a kind of prominence, don't you think?" Wolff asked dryly. "I would describe it as an aura of supreme flatulence."

Although I was determined not to get involved in their personal animosity, I sensed that the Pandora's box had already been opened. "Actually," Wolff continued, "people who call Landry a pedant and a bore are exaggerating. Now and then he stops talking and I actually find him quite agreeable."

Trying not to show any acknowledgment or emotion, I listened silently; this new game of verbal swordplay left me uneasy, since showing favor toward either of the two scholars could almost guarantee losing the support of the other. "But he's a lucky man," Wolff continued. "Musicology loves blabbermouths. It's a crazy profession anyway. All prestige and pretense."

It was becoming clear to me that the time had come to indicate just how uneasy I felt about all the simmering hostilities. "Something bothers me," I said. "There's such a thin line between private dislike and open hatred."

Wolff protested, "But Landry's the one responsible. He would do anything to ruin Manfred Braun." Emphatically, he continued under his breath, "Just don't be fooled by him, Matthew. Landry's launched a career discrediting young scholars like yourself."

His comment brought to mind a decade of painful experiences with renowned scholars known for their ruthlessness. "And whatever you do," he continued, "never turn your back on him, not even for a second."

Unnerved by the memories Wolff's comments elicited, I sat without speaking, realizing that silence was probably the best survival tack in this unfamiliar world. When a waiter appeared between us with a silver tray of smoked salmon and caviar, I was suddenly aware that I hadn't spoken a word to Elisabetta von Stahl since we sat down, and I turned in her direction. Although she must have been in her sixties, Mrs. von Stahl was a beautiful woman, her hair pulled up regally on her head. Unlike Hélène, she seemed eager to skirt the issue of Véronique's cameo and within no time, she was telling me about the program she would be playing at La Favorite, and about the incredible obstacles she had to overcome in becoming a professional violist.

"My father didn't believe young women should have a career and refused to permit me to play in public. The very first time I appeared in Salzburg, I had to arrange for a car to wait for me away from the house, and then had to climb down the roof from my bedroom window. If my father had ever found out, he would have disinherited me."

All of a sudden, she looked at my hand and exclaimed, "You're not married? Much better off. I should know—I've been married so many times. Marriage makes men insensitive and hollow. Husbands get a kind of arteriosclerosis of the soul."

Her spontaneous and irreverent sense of humor loosened me up, and I asked, "How many husbands have you had?"

"What do you mean?" she asked indignantly. "Besides my own?" Seeing the uncertain look on my face, Elisabetta laughed. "Of course, I'm joking. I've had three. Right now I'm taking a 'time-out.' So, how are you enjoying your stay at La Favorite?"

In a moment of honesty, I considered telling her about my uneasiness with the antagonism that seemed to underlie many relationships here. The anonymous notes Alison Teal and I had received were an ominous reflection of those hostilities. "La Favorite is beautiful," I said hesitantly. "Only . . ." We tried to continue our conversation between the animated movement of waiters serving roasted veal chops to the rhythmic accompaniment of wooden pepper grinders.

"Only what?" she asked.

"Only," I finally said under my breath, "sometimes it's a little hard to take. I've never heard so many cutting comments in one day. Do you know, the first day I was here, I'm pretty sure I heard someone say, 'the sacrificial lamb just arrived.' And I distinctly heard someone refer to me as 'fresh meat.'" Laughing uncomfortably, I joked, "It sounded for a second like people here want to eat me."

"Oh!" she laughed. "You're taking it all too seriously. Europeans have a much crueler sense of humor than Americans. And we're used to it; we have a tougher skin. After all, what's the point of life if you can't entertain people, wine and dine them, then ridicule them behind their backs?"

Her reassurances were entertaining, but they did little to assuage my concerns. After the arrival of coffee and a dark chocolate mousse, I could hear the sounds of an orchestra tuning. Guests were eager to leave the table to gather in the music room. With a gesture of familiarity that was pleasantly surprising, Elisabetta took my arm and led me into the salon, a decadent explosion of rococo. In the center of the room was a magnificent harpsichord painted with pastoral scenes, practically swallowed up under twenty-foot ceilings and walls covered with refined gold-leaf ornament.

But after a half hour of waiting, it seemed as if the planned concert would never begin. With the mounting cacophony of musicians tuning their instruments, I could feel rising tension in the music room. Restless guests were shifting their weight in their chairs and tapping their feet and hands with annoyance.

Elegantly reminiscent of a ballerina, the viscount's niece, Nadine, was sitting in the row in front of me, and when she looked back, I threw her a look of exasperation. Our attention was captured by the unexpected appearance of the athletic, mahogany-skinned soprano Véronique Ibsen, energetically organizing music on stands and directing musicians with the determination and skill of a general on the battlefield. "Quite a development," Elisabetta said sarcastically. "Fasten your seat belt." Although she seemed ready for anything, a wave of apprehension swept over me.

"Ladies and gentlemen," the beautiful young soprano announced confidently. "Apparently Ms. Teal is indisposed, and it would be a terrible waste to have the evening end without giving this excellent orchestra an opportunity to perform. So I have offered to sing the program. It is the least I can do to thank our gracious host, Viscount René."

The idea of another singer stepping in uninvited and taking the place of a soprano as great as Alison Teal was a shock and, like everyone else, I was tentative in my applause. Although I was impressed by her bold act, it seemed reckless, given the volatility of the situation. Véronique closed her eyes and took a deep breath. "My first aria is from *Artaserse,* an opera that Mozart never set in its entirety. It is almost incomprehensible that a ten-year-old boy could write music that touches the heart so deeply."

Nodding to the first violinist, she said, "Maestro," and the orchestra began the aria "This paternal embrace." When Ibsen entered, her voice was expressive and plaintive, supported by the rich orchestral color and warmth of horns and oboes. And the liquid, sustained quality of each note was astonishing. Her voice was more light and delicate than the powerful, dramatic sound of Alison Teal, and as she poured out her heart with elegance, tossing off rapid, difficult coloratura passages—delicate trills, light scales, and clear, rapid triplets—a rush of admiration enveloped the room.

The applause was thunderous, and she interrupted it to announce, "I would now like to perform one of the best-known vocal works of Mozart, *Exsultate, jubilate*, written at age sixteen. Although it is church music, in Latin no less, it's one of the most buoyant and effervescent pieces ever written."

Ibsen's voice was a pure delight, exuding warmth and subtlety as the attention of the audience continued undiminished, every eye and ear riveted on her. Practically sitting at the edge of my seat, I realized that an event of unprecedented beauty was taking place. But as she began a long vocal flourish on the word *Alleluia*, another sound interrupted the concert. With all the force and impact of a twenty-megaton bomb, the doors to the music room were thrown open. The concert was over, but the show was about to begin.

# CHAPTER 6

*They rushed to meet the insulting foe...*
—PHILIP FRENEAU

The music stopped, first a little at a time, then completely. A forced, uncomfortable silence replaced the exuberance of Miss Ibsen's performance. Spellbound, we watched as Alison Teal strode defiantly into the room, aware that she had an entire audience captive.

"What's going on here?" she asked, with the controlled voice of a mother who had just caught her children eating the prize cake at the fair. For a second, Véronique seemed too stunned to speak. "Answer my question," Alison demanded.

Véronique managed to regain her composure. "We were all terribly sorry to hear that you would not be able to perform this evening, so I thought—"

"You thought what? That you would perform *my* program?"

No one in the room dared to move, much less breathe, and I felt like pinching myself to make sure this was really happening. "I felt," Miss Ibsen purred, "that it would be an appropriate gift to our host, who has made so many arrangements for this concert."

Alison Teal moved closer. *"How...dare...you,"* she intoned with slow, seething antagonism.

The onslaught of open hostility triggered something in Véronique. "How dare I?" she asked, indignantly.

"How dare you try to hustle in front of all these people," Alison continued, raising her voice.

The confrontational word *hustle* left Véronique visibly outraged. Alison continued, "We're not in Philadelphia, waiting tables or whatever else you did to make a living."

Raising the stakes, Ibsen retaliated with feline *souplesse*. "Why don't you do us all a favor? Go back up to your room and have a little nip."

Like everyone else, I sat silently, not daring to move. Alison, who in fact appeared somewhat intoxicated, laughed eerily, almost as if she were enjoying the repartee. "Oh, you little slut," she said under her breath. "A friend of mine is opening a restaurant; he'll give you a job as a singing waitress. Isn't that what you do for a living?"

Defensively, Véronique replied, "When I was a student at Curtis, I sang at the Victor Café. But those are things we do when we're young. You'd have a hard time remembering."

"Waitress," Alison intoned, snapping her fingers and miming a drunken voice, "bring us a pitcher of beer and sing us an aria."

As Alison stepped in closer, Véronique looked around the room for help. "Isn't anyone going to stop her?" she whispered, and I began wondering why no one was intervening. Philippe, who had been summoned by one of the employees, strode through the main entrance and quickly looked around to assess the situation. Suddenly Alison caught a glimpse of the cameo on Véronique's neck and strained to look at it more closely. At that moment, something inexplicable happened: the world-renowned soprano Alison Teal, eyes blazing, began pushing over music stands. Arms flailing wildly, she began rapidly decimating everything in her path and lunged at Véronique. Within seconds, the two divas had landed on the floor with an explosive thud.

Véronique, too shocked to even scream, tried to defend herself. Musicians grabbed their instruments and several men placed themselves in the midst of the ferocious torrent of kicks, slaps, and punches. Like an action hero in a film, Nadine's bodyguard, Enrique, leaped into motion, opening his suit jacket to reveal a large revolver strapped to his chest as he helped to drag the two sopranos apart.

Alison was subdued by four employees of La Favorite while Véronique vented her fury at being attacked. In a violent rage, the likes of which I had never seen, Véronique pulled herself up off the floor, screaming, "Get that motherfuckin' psycho offa me." As the entire audience sat in shock, Alison Teal was literally carried out of the room, while Véronique's explosion continued. "I'll take you out, you motherfuckin' bitch. You ever touch me again, I'll beat your motherfuckin' brains out."

Like the rest of the guests, I watched in stunned disbelief. *What was I doing here?*

Completely shaken by the evening, I began to wonder how it might reflect on my professional aspirations. Silence filled the music room as the guests left slowly, whispering as they headed for the library for brandy and to smoke. One reaction to the evening's events manifested itself almost immediately: the massive silver trays covered with large snifters of liqueurs and cognac were stripped within seconds, sending the waiters rushing back to the kitchen. Still unwilling and unable to believe what had happened, I sought out Andrei, desperate to talk. Instead, he put up his hand as if to say no. "Let's try to put it behind us for now," he said. "At least, that's how everyone else seems to be handling it." To change the subject, he continued, "You've heard the expression, Music is the brandy of the damned." Without a moment's hesitation, he turned to the waiter, saying, "So make mine a double."

As the uncomfortable evening drew to a close, I climbed the stairs to my room, realizing the day's events had taken a major toll on my nerves. I began to seriously question what I was doing at La Favorite, where not a day went by without some kind of unnerving conflict. All the beauty and brilliance around me clearly had a price. And someone had to pay the check.

Awake at 11:00 A.M., I tried to sort out whether the events of the previous evening had actually happened, or if I had dreamed them. *God, that was one helluva night,* I finally concluded. Feeling testy and irritable as the full weight of the incident descended upon me, I wondered what implications it might have for my stay at La Favorite. After ringing for breakfast, I called the majordomo.

"Is there anything planned for today?" I asked.

"Just this evening, at eight, as usual," Philippe replied, in a cool, unemotional tone that avoided any reaction to the previous night's concert. "Lunch, of course, is served in the rooms adjacent to the main dining room unless you wish to have it in your apartment. By the way, you might enjoy a walk in the viscount's gardens and park; the weather's perfect."

"Thanks," I replied, "I might just do that."

But the unexpected fireworks of the previous evening left me decidedly less socially inclined; everyone's purposeful avoidance of what happened struck me as Kafkaesque. Instead of leaving my room, I decided to spend time on the Internet to determine whether the historical information in the diary was accurate. I called Philippe back and asked, "Is there an outside line in my room if I want to log on to the Net?"

"Yes," he responded. "Behind the desk. Just unplug the phone jack."

As I surveyed the room, I couldn't help being impressed by the contradictions: the idea of antique furniture, silk bedspread, and draperies—an authentic Louis XV room—completely adapted with modern conveniences for the twenty-first century. And because of the volatile events, the apartment was ideal for guests like me who wanted to remain barricaded in their rooms all day: a minibar was built inside a carefully restored commode from the period, a coffeemaker was hidden behind the door of an antique armoire, and an electric valet to remove wrinkles from trousers was concealed in the closet. La Favorite was furnished with items of priceless beauty and quality that would have been inconceivable in even the most expensive of hotels: for example, my apartment boasted a splendid Fragonard canvas, worthy of a museum, depicting a woman and a jester blowing fragile, barely perceptible soap bubbles. Yet, despite all the overwhelming beauty and luxury, La Favorite was the setting for emotional explosions and relentless backbiting and intrigues.

After showering, I felt a change of heart and decided I had to get out for a walk, postponing my Internet research. Philippe's suggestion of seeing the grounds was suddenly appealing to me, particularly if I could manage to avoid contact with other guests. And when I arrived at the entrance to the park, I was pleasantly surprised by how quiet and empty it was. Ironically, the silence struck me as ominous, and I asked myself where everyone was hiding. But this world was beyond me, and for the moment I gave up trying to figure it out.

A massive expanse of formal clipped boxwood parterres led me slowly to a remarkable jewel of a forest, seemingly wild. Yet the lack of a single leaf on the grounds indicated the great care that had been taken to maintain the park in manicured perfection. A glimpse of motion, an unhurried streak of white in the distance, caught my attention. I caught sight of two white does grazing uninhibitedly in the distance. As I drew closer, the magnificent animals looked at me with mild curiosity, then continued lunching disinterestedly.

Wild game birds dragged long feathered tails across the wooded paths and red squirrels darted playfully up and down shade trees. For a moment, I was lost in the serenity of this artificial wilderness and looked for a place to sit, where I could take in the splendid solitude. On a secluded bench, set back about twenty feet in the woods, I sat relaxed, at last. Then from a distance, several voices could be heard, coming closer and closer: two men engaged in an animated discussion.

When I recognized Andreas Wolff, my first reaction was to emerge from my secluded refuge and greet him. But within seconds, it was clear to me that the man with Wolff was furious, his tone and gestures betraying mounting agitation. *Oh, no,* I thought, remembering my inadvertent eavesdropping on his conversation with von Horvach the day before, *here we go again.*

Fairly confident they wouldn't notice me, I sat motionless. The other man was Manfred Braun, apparently in a rage, and I was suddenly curious about the nature of their argument. Since I was a captive audience, I could at least glean some insights into this insular world of which I was now a part. I could barely make out the words Wolff was speaking in German: "Look, there's no sense in creating a scene."

"Would you just shut up? Just shut up a minute and let me talk," Braun barked. "Don't you think I have a right to make a scene after what you've told me?"

"It's not the end of the world," Wolff mumbled. "What am I supposed to do, kill myself? I'm the one going to prison, not you."

*Prison?* The situation was becoming totally unnerving, since I had so much at stake with Braun. Fortunately, neither Braun nor Wolff saw me, that much was sure. As they continued into the forest, I could hear several muffled phrases from Braun, spoken in a more conciliatory tone: ". . . I know a way you could raise the money . . . could bring three hundred thousand dollars, maybe more . . . I have a key . . . certainly better than prison . . ."

After they were gone, I walked back to the château, reassuring myself that they had not seen me. When the coast was clear, I made a breathless beeline for La Favorite. All my efforts to get along with the guests of the foundation were beginning to seem futile, and the situation was getting more treacherous. Back within the sheltered confines of my apartment, I began to doubt whether I could continue to navigate such turbulent waters. In the back of my mind, I heard a tiny voice: *There's too much riding on this. You have to get through it if you want to have a shot at a foundation grant. There's much more to gain than to lose. Remember, you've experienced far worse in academia and managed to survive.*

Overwhelmed by the complicated and confrontational events, I gave up my plans to research the Net for the evening. And although the anonymous note was now securely in my suitcase for safekeeping, it was still not far enough away for comfort. Heading directly for the silver champagne bucket on my desk, I said, "God, if there was ever a time I needed a drink . . ."


Soft ashen light filtered through the thin sheer curtains of my apartment, reflecting the dusky gray-green tint of my walls at La

Favorite. As I gradually regained consciousness, my eyes moved slowly to a half-filled champagne glass near my bed and then on to a silver ice bucket holding an upside-down, empty bottle of Moët & Chandon. I couldn't believe I had finished the whole thing! Reaching for my toothbrush, I stared in disbelief at the bleary-eyed figure in the mirror. Feeling as unkempt as a skid row bum, I grabbed my watch and realized there was little over an hour before I would have to start getting ready for dinner. But almost an entire day had passed, and I still hadn't made any progress on my Mozart transcription.

As I scrutinized the date on the next page, I realized that the folio was out of place; it should have been immediately after the first journal entry.

*March 2, 1770*

*It's finally decided—in two weeks we're leaving for Rome and Naples. And we'll arrive in Rome just in time for the Holy Week celebrations: colorful processions, extravagant music in the churches, great singers. But I've hardly had time to think, as I've been busy writing arias for a private concert at Count Firmian's. He has invited over 150 guests from the highest nobility to hear my music and the evening will undoubtedly be splendid.*

*Count Firmian is the most powerful political figure in Milan. Yet he is one of the kindest men I have ever met. He is keen on music, art, and poetry in a way I have never seen in a government official; we genuinely like and appreciate each other.*

*Firmian has already entertained us in a lavish way and showed us his collection of paintings by Leonardo [da Vinci], Titian, Veronese, Rubens, van Dyck, and Claude Lorraine, which rivals anything I saw in Schönbrunn Palace in Vienna. And he has an entire library in English!*

*On our first visit, we entered a drawing room where a large number of distinguished people were gathered, first meeting Father Frisi, a mathematician, and then*

*Count Beccaria, the famous jurist whose book against*
*torture and the death penalty was even admired by the*
*Emperor. Beccaria told us that the protégés of Firmian*
*are so famous (the archaeologist Winckelmann, the*
*architect Piermarini, the scientist Volta, and the poet*
*Parini) that the count is sometimes called the "Maecenas*
*of Milan."*

*When Firmian finally entered, he radiated charm and*
*dignity, with all the spirit of an eminent person, giving*
*Papa compliments on his treatise on violin playing and*
*delighting him by speaking Italian, French, and German*
*with him. The count's health seems fragile. We had to*
*wait over a week to meet him and there are rumors he*
*suffers from an extremely delicate stomach. He is also*
*quite a character: it is very obvious that he prefers to be*
*surrounded by handsome young soldiers and clerics, who,*
*in their attention, take the role of ladies-in-waiting in a*
*great court.*

*Papa has been extremely attentive to the count as*
*well, in order to assure that I will receive a commission*
*here to write an opera. In fact, he has been more*
*charming than I have ever seen him, even more than*
*during our last visit to the Empress in Vienna.*

The diary, whether or not it was by Mozart, had captured
my attention. When I finished transcribing and translating the
folio, I glanced at my watch and was stunned to realize it was a
quarter past seven. Putting the manuscript away, I began the task
of inserting antique polished porphyry studs into a newly
pressed shirt of starched Egyptian cotton, thinking about how I
was going to get through another evening of tensions and intrigues. But I was more determined than ever to stay focused on
the reason I was at La Favorite: my career as a Mozart scholar
and the foundation awards.

Out of breath, I arrived in the library just after eight. Several dozen people were already gathered and the mood seemed
considerably more restrained and somber than the previous

evening—apparently the scene between Alison Teal and Véronique Ibsen had cooled the atmosphere. "What would you like, Dr. Pierce?" From behind, I heard the voice of Jano, the Slovak waiter from the first evening.

Taking a flute of champagne cocktail from his tray, I noticed that Andrei, on the other side of the room, was talking with a heavyset woman in her thirties with light brown hair. "Who's that?" I asked Jano.

"Caroline Weidener, Andrei's wife," he replied. "She just arrived today." A few feet away from me was Enrique, the massive half-black, half-Latino bodyguard of Nadine. Although I didn't know if it was permitted to talk to him, I decided to risk it.

"How's everything going?" I asked.

"Great, man," he said. "I feel fantastic, like a rooster who's been let loose in the henhouse. Look at all these hot women."

Enrique's irreverence immediately made me feel comfortable; it reminded me of my days as a high-school wrestler in Boston, and the decade of locker-room talk in college gyms. "Just don't forget," I said, "I saw Nicoletta Chigi first."

"Oh, yeah," Enrique answered, looking over at the svelte Italian brunette. "I've been watching her. She's the kind of woman who likes to walk all over men, just because she enjoys the sound of cracking bones. But over there, now *that's* a babe," he said, nodding toward the entrance, where Véronique Ibsen had just come in. "I would lick every square inch of her."

Checking out the women in the room, now and then undressing one slowly with his eyes, Enrique still managed to keep up his conversation with me. And on top of everything else, he was watching Nadine like a ferocious pit bull. "Nadine is an amazing woman," I said to him.

"Man, you don't know the half of it. Did you know she was a star ballerina with the American Ballet Theatre in New York?"

"How did she go from ballerina to international crime fighter?" I asked.

"During a performance in the seventies," Enrique said, "she started having pain in her feet. But she realized someone must

have done something to her ballet slippers. Since there was
nothing she could do, she danced till the end, ignoring the pain.
After her curtain calls, she ripped off her shoes and found her
feet covered with open sores. Someone had brushed the insides
of her shoes with an acid powder that was activated when her
feet started to sweat."

"Did she ever find out who did it?" I asked.

"Eventually. But the police didn't help much so she started
studying criminal investigation techniques while she was
recuperating."

"Who was responsible?" I asked.

"Another ballerina . . . a second-rate babe who wanted to
be a soloist. When the police came to question her, she jumped
out of her window on the thirty-eighth floor. Splat."

Enrique's narrative was unnerving, reminding me of the violence of the news clipping I had received. "It's such a big move
from ballet to law enforcement," I said.

"Yeah," he replied. "Back then her agency was making an
effort to recruit women, just so the numbers would look good.
But Nadine surprised them. She's one of their sharpest agents."

"She's also right in her element here with all these artists,"
I said.

"Here?" The incredulous look on Enrique's face told me I
had missed the mark. "If you let out all the prisons and nut-
houses, you couldn't find a better mix."

"Oh, come on," I protested. "This is a remarkable group of
people."

"Listen," he replied seriously, lowering his voice. "Take my
advice, Doc. Lock your doors. If you knew what I know . . ." As
he spoke, a tiny, repeated electronic tone sounded from his coat
pocket.

"What's that?" I asked. "A beeper?"

"Yeah," Enrique mumbled, lost in thought, looking around
the wall where we were standing. "I thought I shut this damn
thing off." As the sound became more pronounced and rapid, he
walked closer to a sconce of gilded bronze. Immediately he
reached into his pocket and turned off the device.

"What are you looking for?" I asked.

"Huh?" he replied. "Oh . . . nothing. What were you asking me . . . something about Nadine?"

"So, Nadine's here on business?" I asked.

"Yeah, her uncle called us at the last minute. We had to drop everything and get on a plane."

"And I understand we're finally going to meet the viscount tonight."

Enrique glanced over his shoulder. "Don't expect too much," he whispered. "The guy thinks he's Charles de Gaulle—or Napoleon."

Our conversation was interrupted by a waiter who informed me, "The young lady over there would like to talk to you." From the corner, young Ilsa Paumgarten was smiling and waving seductively.

Enrique looked over eagerly like an oversexed fraternity brother and said excitedly, "Oh, man, pinch me. Listen, when you're finished, leave me some leftovers." As I maneuvered through the crowded room, I saw Ilsa standing next to her grandmother in a wheelchair. The elderly baroness, her obesity disguised by clever tailoring, was wearing a breathtaking necklace of small natural pearls.

"You remember Dr. Pierce?" Ilsa asked, looking no more than fifteen as she bent over and lifted the hand of her grandmother toward me. As Ilsa moved, I expected her at any moment to burst out of her tailored black leather halter and skirt. Involuntarily, my imagination raced to Wolff's comment about the speeding ticket. The baroness, who seemed to be asleep, surprised me by raising her hand and greeting me, barely opening her eyes.

Within seconds, Ilsa was laying on all her seductive charm, complimenting the porphyry cuff links and my blue eyes. When I mentioned the events of the previous evening, she revealed no emotion. "Things like that happen now and then at La Favorite," she said casually. "But everyone here has seen so much. Still, I've always liked the guests Viscount René invites. It's an older crowd, but most people my age are so immature."

As she spoke, she gently fondled the soft leather strap holding up her halter top, her light hazel eyes sparkling in a way that revealed more than casual interest. They were saturated with the undertones of a smorgasbord of sexual delights. Trying not to reveal my response, I tried to keep the conversation innocuous. But below the waist there was a powerful reminder of my attraction to her. "Age is certainly an issue," I agreed. "Almost everyone is dealing with it on some level or another."

"But you don't have to worry about it for a long time," she laughed, fingering a delicate lace ruffle bordering her halter. "You couldn't be over twenty-five."

"Thanks, but not quite," I laughed. "In a few years, I'll be forty, and I'm planning to go home, lock all the doors and windows, and have myself a good cry."

With the tiny, minimal strokes of a Japanese calligraphic brush, Ilsa continued to fondle her lace hem. "Forty's not a bad age for a man," she said. "But it's harder for a woman to look great at that age."

My eyes were irresistibly drawn to the remarkable, delicate curves pressing out from beneath her black leather top, as an inner voice cautioned me: *She could be underage.* "You know my age now," I said. "But I'd have a hard time guessing yours."

Ilsa laughed as she continued to run her fingers down her neck to her shoulder and below, casually tossing her blond hair from her shoulders. "My grandmother says that women should never be too precise about their age. It's too confining. Until they're ninety, that is. That's when it's time to be candid with the world."

Ilsa continued, "Everything about age is a contradiction when it comes to men and women. But I accept the way things are; it's natural for women to like older men."

"Maybe you're right," I said, nodding toward von Horvach and Véronique Ibsen, who were locked in a tête-à-tête under a window on the other side of the room. "There's a case in point. She's not even half his age."

Ilsa turned her head to look over. "Rudi von Horvach may be in his sixties," Ilsa replied, "but he's still an adolescent." From the entrance, the strident, stentorian voice of the majordomo startled us: "*Mesdames et messieurs, s'il vous plaît.* Dinner is served!"

As she started to maneuver her grandmother's streamlined wheelchair, Ilsa glanced at my crotch and purred seductively, "I hope I'll get to see more of you," and a surge of lust swept through me. Fortunately, I was soon safely out of temptation, immersed in the task of hunting around the dinner table for the gold embossed place card with my name.

Andrei's wife, Caroline, who had been pointed out to me earlier by Jano, was seated at the place on my right near the head of the table, and I was puzzled to see several empty seats: one on my left and another next to Caroline. With her light brown hair pulled tightly back in a braided bun, Andrei's robust wife was attractive, even with almost no makeup. Eventually our respective professions became a topic of conversation and she began to explain her childhood vocation and training as a registered nurse, describing how she managed, on her days off, to run a free medical clinic for elderly immigrants living in Vienna.

Caroline's maternal aura and sheer competence helped me feel remarkably comfortable in her presence. Talking about her husband, she became more open and animated. "It's good one of us has both feet on the ground," she said. "Artists have the privilege of living in a world beyond reason or logic. Being married to one isn't easy. Andrei's head is always in the clouds, always full of music, and I have to follow him around, sorting out the disasters he leaves in his wake."

"Creative artists," I said, thinking of the two divas the previous evening, "are immersed in the beauty of their own visions, and in the enormity of their own egos."

Caroline laughed. "What can I say? Artists make terrible husbands. But if I wanted a good provider, I would have married a banker."

"There must be a positive side," I said.

"There is," Caroline replied candidly. "I love him—it's as simple as that. For one thing, Andrei's the only man I've ever met who's never lied to me. You see, ever since I was a little girl,

I've been able to tell if a person is lying." My silence encouraged her to continue. "It's minute changes I pick up in the voice, I think. Or very faint eye movements."

I recognized a subtle intelligence and commented, "Sounds similar to a lie detector. What was it like growing up with that ability?"

Caroline replied, "It caused more problems than I can begin to tell you."

Our conversation was interrupted briefly by the simultaneous appearance at opposite sides of the room of the two sopranos involved in the violent scene the night before. Their entrance seemed choreographed, as if arrangements had been made ahead of time for them to arrive at the same time and to be seated as far away from each other as possible. From the other end of the table, Andrei threw me an ironic look that asked, *Now what?*

Taking the empty seat adjacent to Caroline, Véronique immediately struck up a conversation and the two began to chat cordially. For a few seconds, I stared at the empty seat next to me and hoped someone would arrive to fill the place. Just then, the conversation in the dining room stopped. At the entrance stood a thin man with a speckled mane of gray and white hair, not over five foot five, with dark tinted glasses that covered his eyes almost completely. Although I had never met him, it was immediately clear to me who he was.

"Oh my God," Véronique murmured. "It's the viscount. And he's heading for the seat right next to you."

# CHAPTER 7

*Mankind is divisible into two great classes:*
*hosts and guests.*
—MAX BEERBOHM

The dramatic appearance of René de Laguerelle, fifth viscount of Nancy, at the entrance of the dining room, drew the undivided attention of the entire room. The reaction of the guests was spontaneous and enthusiastic, and the level of conversation immediately jumped several decibels. No sooner had he entered than he began to greet guests at the table, most of whom rose to kiss him energetically on both cheeks.

"Not bad for a man who's seen ninety," Véronique murmured.

"Ninety-four, to be exact," I replied. "And he doesn't look a day over sixty." It was flattering to think he would be seated next to me, but at the same time, a wave of apprehension swept over me.

Just before taking his seat, the viscount said, "What a pleasure to finally meet you." As we shook hands, his grip was so astounding that I had the momentary sensation my hand had been placed in a vise. Turning to Véronique, he said, "You are more beautiful than ever. How do you manage to be more *ravissante* every time I see you?"

Speaking quietly to me, he apologized for the last-minute invitation. "I'm just so honored to be here," I replied, feeling genuinely privileged to be seated next to him.

The other guests and I were treated to a stream of recollections from the viscount about world figures he had invited to La Favorite, and of great performers and temperamental conductors and composers, all described with a flair for storytelling and a remarkable memory for details. Over the course of the dinner, the conversation moved to art, history, literature, and politics, and Viscount de Laguerelle had limitless energy for narrating. "Toscanini and Horowitz were my guests at La Favorite in 1940," he said. "Sitting exactly where these two lovely ladies are now seated. Horowitz, or Volodya as he liked to be called, ate almost nothing because he was going to play after dinner. After we assembled in the music room, he embarked on one of the greatest recitals I have ever heard: it lasted over two hours and included the Polonaise-fantaisie of Chopin, the Brahms *Paganini* Variations, and the Liszt Sonata. When he sat down to play an encore, we lost our breath—he played his own arrangement of Stravinsky's *Petrushka* with a power that rivaled an orchestra. Those are moments one never forgets."

As the viscount spoke, Véronique and Caroline were listening keenly to every word, and I realized he had the uncanny ability of making a woman feel as if she were the only person in the world: "Your hands are so exquisite, Madame Weidener." "Véronique, I can't tell you how much I've been enjoying listening to the new CDs you sent me."

While I sat fascinated by the viscount's recollections, I noticed that Véronique and Caroline each took on a different character. Véronique never once tossed off her usual caustic comments in witty ingénue style, but instead demonstrated keen intellectual strengths and perceptive insights on politics and world events. Caroline, on the other hand, became somewhat vivacious, almost flirtatious, around the viscount.

And I had the opportunity of becoming a listener at the feet of a great man. When I had his undivided attention, I decided to risk asking him about the Fondation de l'Art éternel, hoping to get the conversation to move toward the "genius" awards. "The foundation is nothing more," he replied, "than what Emerson called the most serious of all occupations: the search for greatness. So that we may leave footprints on the sand of time."

It was clear he didn't want to say more about the foundation. In an adjacent room, wind instruments were warming up, and I said, "*Monsieur le Vicomte,* it sounds as if a concert is about to begin."

"Please," he replied, "you'll make me feel so old. Just call me René. Yes, it's going to be some of my favorite chamber music by Mozart." He continued, "It's informal—people will be free to circulate from room to room, as they please."

After saying goodbye, with particular compliments to Caroline Weidener and Véronique Ibsen, the viscount looked at me and his face took on a decidedly different character that surprised me: his expression was extraordinarily dark, vaguely sinister. Under his breath, he said, "We have things to talk about," and I understood he was dead serious. When I tried to respond, his finger indicated no, and he whispered, "Not now." As I proceeded alone in the direction of the library, both perplexed and intrigued, I reflected on his expression and tone, realizing that the viscount clearly had another side—one that was radically different from the charming conversationalist and host I had seen during dinner. And I was determined to make sure he would follow up with explanations the next time we were together.

The viscount's comment about people having the freedom to walk from room to room was an understatement; as waiters in white jackets offered cognac and Cuban Cohiba cigars around the massive Renaissance fireplace, animated, talkative guests circulated uninhibitedly through the endless adjacent library rooms, commenting on the viscount's remarkable gallery of paintings and books. On my way to the music room, I was stopped short by Manfred Braun, who was clearly determined to speak to me. "You know," he said, "you've asked my assistance in authenticating your diary and I've agreed to help you. But I must tell you now that I am very concerned about someone you've spoken to."

Nodding distractedly, I began to make my way to the music room before the concert began. However, the moment he started speaking, sounds began to resonate in the distance: the concert had already begun with the sublime sonorities of Mozart's Serenade in C Minor for Wind Ensemble. The rich blend of oboes, horns, clarinets, and bassoons and the dark, quietly passionate themes immediately had a profound impact on me. Braun didn't care about the music, nor notice how deeply it was affecting me. Instead he embarked on a monologue that became more vitriolic and disturbing by the minute. His target was Dennis Landry, and in the course of his diatribe, he became so agitated, he was oblivious to whether or not I was listening. "There he is, looking over his shoulder all the time, as if someone were coming to get him, just like all scholars who have had more success than they deserve and keep expecting it to be taken away from them. Listen, Pierce, I can tell you for a fact, the man's ruined more graduate students and young professors than anyone else in the field. If he needs your help, he'll be totally charming—until he gets what he wants. He's conniving and false. Completely false."

The tone of Braun's tirade and his openness surprised me and left me suspicious, annoyed; he hardly knew me, yet he had decided to take me into his confidence at this level. Gradually he pulled out all the stops: "Landry's not really interested in scholarship, just in money and power. And in seeing his name on the letterhead of an important Mozart publication."

As I focused on the wind serenade, I tried to appear interested, only catching a few phrases here and there from his torrent: ". . . a showoff . . . disgusting display of wealth, all bad taste . . . his watch, his rings . . . solid gold lighter . . . no class, no refinement."

A rush of serenity swept the room as the woodwinds began the extraordinary slow movement of the Serenade in C Minor. The smooth blend of harmonies and the endless, inspired stream of melody left me totally transfixed. And I knew I was not alone; the entire room took on a more subdued, reflective quality as guests responded to the beauty. Braun didn't seem to be disturbed by my limited attention. He continued, "His manners are a disgrace. Just look at him. He's done everything but pick his nose in public."

For a moment, the crowd opened slightly as if a sea had parted, and I saw the ravishing Nicoletta Chigi. As usual, she was surrounded by male admirers and as I gazed at her, emotion surged through my body. My temples were pounding fiercely, and the resonant timbres of wind instruments created an intoxicating cascade of sound.

Although Braun was standing directly in front of me, I could no longer hear a single word: my ears had been taken over by a "music of the sirens." But when the slow movement ended, parts of Braun's conversation began to fade in: ". . . be careful if he ever asks you to work for him . . . takes ideas from young scholars and doesn't give them credit . . . "

A sudden change in his tone captured my attention. "You're a young man with a future. Your work shows great insight." In front of me, I saw a kindly countenance offering me advice and, for a moment, I saw Braun in a new, paternal light. "Don't allow yourself to get dragged into anything that would be beneath you."

In the music room, a remarkably angular and rhythmic minuet began that momentarily and pleasantly distracted me, but my enjoyment was short-lived as Braun returned to his initial mode. "His lifestyle is so extravagant. Something doesn't fit; the silk dinner jacket he's wearing cost over ten thousand dollars—there's no possible way he could manage it on his salary."

Not wanting to offend Braun, yet determined not to respond to the wave of negativity pouring out of him, I half listened, with the beauty of Nicoletta providing my salvation. The delicate flaxen sheen of her hair, the graceful curve leading from her neck down her shoulders, the slender line of her hips, casually draped in soft folds, kept me sane in the midst of a storm.

After the expansive variations of the last movement of Mozart's serenade, the music stopped suddenly, and Braun's voice reverberated with a piercing clarity. "He's editing an edition of the Mozart letters for 2006. Something's wrong. The cost of the binding, with all the color plates and engravings, will radically exceed the selling price. Where is all the money coming from?"

In the distance, I could hear sounds of a string quartet tuning and as soon as they began to play, I realized their choice of program was eerily appropriate: Mozart's *Dissonance* Quartet, opening with some of the most modern and disquieting sounds conceived in the eighteenth century. As the disturbing and evocative music, full of stabbing dissonances and bleak chromaticism, began to swell and build, Braun's tirade filtered in and out. Although his accusations were becoming more specific, I was unable to focus on anything except the innovative, prophetic musical language of Mozart's visions.

"I have to be careful . . . dangerous to talk about these things," Braun mumbled cautiously, his voice intertwined with the relentless rhythm of the quartet. ". . . rumors . . . serious allegations . . . business associates . . . the wrong kind of people . . . a front for . . ."

The anguished opening of the quartet was followed by lighter, more animated themes. Yet long after the musicians had finished performing, the initial foreboding sounds continued to resonate obsessively in the back of my mind. A strange counterpoint took place as Braun's persistent voice began to be swallowed up by the music in my memory and transformed into the bleak, bitter sounds of the opening of the *Dissonance* Quartet, full of angst, apprehension, and pain. At the same time, I gazed at the relaxed, refined sensuality of Nicoletta Chigi and the music surging through my brain merged fluidly, seamlessly, with the supple, noble sonorities of the slow movement of the serenade for winds.

"I'm telling you this to warn you. The man is evil—worse, he's . . ." The relentless contrast and the complexity of the polyphony of the two individuals—Braun and Nicoletta—continued to ebb and flow mercilessly, first slowly, then more and more rapidly as the violent sonorities of night music raged, causing my head to spin uncontrollably. Without warning, I felt on the verge of passing out.

"Dr. Braun," I interrupted, "I have to leave you. I'm . . . totally . . . I think I've had too much to drink."

"My God, your face is completely white," he replied. "Don't apologize. You'll feel better tomorrow." Practically stumbling out, I regained my bearings by resting my weight on the carved oak banister of the staircase, where I found myself momentarily in silence.

A soft voice from nowhere startled me. To my amazement, standing behind me was Nicoletta Chigi.

It was the most beautiful sound: Nicoletta's soft, modulated voice, with her irresistible Italian accent, saying, "It's a long walk up through these corridors. I'm a little afraid to be alone in this big maze."

"Even with all this beauty?" I asked.

"Frankly," she replied, "this place frightens me. It always has. Would you mind walking me back to my apartment?"

As I accompanied her through the hallways, Nicoletta chatted with surprising familiarity. Eventually I asked her, "So, what frightens you about La Favorite?"

"You've never heard about its history?" she replied. "Maybe I shouldn't tell you; nobody ever talks about it."

"I don't think a little history will disturb me," I said.

"All right," she replied, somewhat cynically. "A little history, then. During the French Revolution, La Favorite was turned into a prison for nobles. But inmates died at an alarming rate, and it was discovered that the head of the prison was starving entire families. At least that's what an old woman who used to work here told me as a child—I think her name was Monica, or Monique. She said that at night you can hear the voices of children wailing."

Skeptical, I resisted comment, thinking, *Superstition, plain and simple.* Nicoletta sensed my discomfort and said, "Let's change the subject. What exactly do you do?"

"I'm a musicologist," I explained, "working on Mozart documents." The subject piqued her interest, and that made me eager to continue. As we arrived at her room, she asked incredulously, "After two centuries, things are still turning up?"

"You'd be amazed," I replied. "Four sheets of music in Mozart's hand were discovered recently, belonging to a horn concerto. In two hundred years, no one had even noticed they were missing from the autograph score."

Nicoletta's face revealed surprise and interest, and as she

struggled with her key, she asked, "Could you help me?" I will-ingly obliged, pushing open the door to reveal a spacious suite full of huge floral arrangements—more than a dozen spectacu-lar bouquets of yellow, red, and white roses, as well as orchids, ginger flowers, and Hawaiian anthurium in elaborate arrange-ments. She saw my amazement and laughed.

"My fiancé knows I love fresh-cut flowers, but sometimes he exaggerates."

As she glided into the room, she looked back. "Can I offer you something to drink? A glass of cognac, some whiskey?" The unrestrained opulence of the floral displays was distracting; it made the suite seem like the dressing room of a Broadway star on opening night, but I was pleased she had invited me in. "I'm quite fascinated," she murmured as she eased out of her shoes. "Where do you find Mozart materials to work on these days?"

"Archives, music libraries," I replied. "And just recently I bought some folios at an auction in Milan." My head suddenly remarkably clear, the words of the anonymous note resonated ominously: "Open not thine heart to every man," and I hesitated before closing the door.

"You're sure they're by Mozart?" she asked.

"No," I replied, "they have to be authenticated."

"My fiancé is a great lover of art and culture. If you ever want to sell them, he's exactly the person to find someone inter-ested in buying them."

Her understated offer, from someone so obviously well connected, floored me. "Perhaps I'll take you up on that."

"Really too many flowers," she continued. "I'll give them to some of the other guests. The two singers might need a little cheering up. Baroness Paumgarten might like some as well. Can you imagine, she was once one of the most beautiful women in Europe? It's a family illness that's never discussed."

"Her granddaughter seems to have inherited some of her beauty," I replied.

"Ilsa?" she asked, incredulously. Immediately I realized I had said the wrong thing. Nicoletta went on calmly, "There's only one difference between Ilsa and a whore."

As I struggled to open the new bottle of Armagnac on her bar, I resisted asking her what the difference was. She sensed I was uneasy, and I was—the last thing I wanted was to hear more vitriolic comments. With a weary laugh, she changed the subject. "Don't mind me. It's been a long day."

Nicoletta proceeded to take off her earrings and other jewelry, her face revealing an expression of relief and liberation. One of the pins she removed was a stylized gold and diamond panther, encrusted with rubies and emeralds. "I have the strange feeling I've seen that pin somewhere before," I said.

"It belonged to Wallis Simpson, the duchess of Windsor," she replied simply. "My fiancé, Maximilian, bought several pieces at the auction . . . these earrings as well. But he can't help thinking of them as a business investment." By now, Nicoletta had removed her shoes, her jewelry, and her silk scarf, and I was basking in the privilege of being with her. Curling up in the corner of a loveseat, she held a large brandy snifter in her hands. For the first time, I realized her dress, elegantly cut from pale lavender-gray silk, was identical to a slip. As she slowly began to undo her hair, a sea of reddish brown locks cascaded over her bare shoulders.

"Sit down, here," she beckoned, motioning to the place next to her. For the second time in one evening, I thought I was dreaming. "So, tell me more about your Mozart documents. It's all so fascinating."

Couching my comments in general terms, I began to talk. Nicoletta was hanging on every word, and having her complete attention stimulated me to keep going. Every time the admonition of the note came to mind, my attention was diverted by the spectacle of her breathtaking body draped on the sofa next to me. Her scarf gone, I could see she wasn't wearing a bra, and every detail of her firm nipples was highlighted by thin, gauze-like silk.

"Italians aren't very fond of Mozart," she said, her eyelids getting heavier as if she were on the verge of falling asleep. "We think of him as someone who tried to write Italian opera but who wasn't really Italian. We like our own composers best— Rossini, Verdi, Puccini."

"Nicoletta is a beautiful name," I said, changing the subject and moving closer, doing my best to keep her awake and talking.

"My real name is Nee-chay," she replied, emphasizing the pronunciation. "It's spelled N-i-c-e," she murmured, her voice drifting off. "An old Italian name from mythology. But everyone calls me Nicoletta."

"Beautiful," I repeated. She began to breathe with a rhythmic regularity and within seconds it seemed as if she had momentarily fallen asleep. It happened so suddenly, I found myself asking if it were real. Outstretched next to me, Nicoletta reminded me of an airbrushed Playboy centerfold, her delicate outline softened by the fine silk of her dress. As I sat staring at her body, I found myself violently aroused. And I questioned whether this was intended as an invitation.

Lying almost naked next to me except for the flimsy material that barely covered her, Nicoletta seemed to be saying, "Just play along." In a gesture completely out of character, I placed my hand lightly on her calf, just below the knee; if worse came to worst, I reasoned, she could always slap my face.

But she continued to breathe regularly. Somewhat drunk from the Armagnac, and swept away by the moment, I began caressing her leg with both hands in a circular motion, gently pushing her dress up. And as I continued up higher, I became more and more convinced she was awake and willing.

She didn't stop me and I couldn't stop myself either. Delicately placing a kiss on the inside of her thigh, I looked up. And for a moment I was unable to believe what I was seeing: the area between Nicoletta's naked legs was an oasis of sensual delights. Encouraged by the sound of her relaxed breathing, I continued slowly, maneuvering her dress up to her waist, and felt the irresistible urge to follow the kiss I had planted on her thigh with a thousand others leading upward, caressing the entire wide arc sweeping up before my eyes. My fingers were poised, ready and eager to run up her body, to caress the sensitive area leading to her breasts, to gently pinch her rigid, fleshy nipples, to—

Suddenly, as if wakened from a dream, I heard, *"Che cosa?"* Startled, I sat up and Nicoletta asked again, "What are you doing?" Shaken from the state of abandon that had taken over my consciousness, I didn't know what to say. Pulling her dress slowly back down around her legs as I sat back, Nicoletta seemed more miffed than outraged and I sat motionless like a deer caught in the headlights, unable to say a word. *"Birichino,"* she murmured, and I knew what that meant in Italian: You little rascal. Relieved, I watched her smile seductively as she said, "This will have to be our own little secret . . . I shudder to think what my fiancé would do if he ever found out."

Pointing to her empty brandy snifter, she said, "Pour us each another." I followed her orders and returned from the bar. Nicoletta continued, "I can't remember what you said—do you want me to talk to my fiancé about finding a buyer for your Mozart documents? He's arriving from Switzerland tomorrow."

"He could sell them?" I asked, trying to sound levelheaded.

"Yes," she replied. "And I imagine he could get you the best price."

"But they haven't been authenticated," I said.

"I don't know much about those things. But if you want, I'll ask him. He'll do anything for me." Nicoletta gestured for me to sit nearer to her. "But if Max decides to find you a buyer, he'll have to see them first." Sipping Armagnac, she stretched out her leg, which brushed gently against mine. When I didn't respond, she said, "You're acting like you're afraid of me. Don't sit so far away."

Moving in closer, I asked, "He's sold rare documents before?"

Nicoletta replied, "Sometimes in a single day." She continued, "But if he's interested, you'll have to send for them." My eyes made a quick diagonal as I tried to decide how to respond. When I didn't reply, she patted my leg and said, "It's all right. If you don't trust me . . ."

With my leg nestled directly next to hers, I felt her extend the other casually. Extraordinarily comfortable and hopelessly intoxicated, I said, "I appreciate your offer. If your fiancé wants to see them, I can show him what I have. But I didn't bring them all with me—is that a problem?"

"I'll have him talk to you," Nicoletta said. But after a few minutes, her eyes were almost closing again and she began breathing heavily. And what a sleeping goddess she was, her body highlighted by the gossamer silk that rested on her body as if waiting for the slightest breeze to carry it away. For a long, long time, I studied and memorized her face, her hands, her hair, and, most of all, those magnificent long, shapely legs stretched out in front of me.

After a few minutes of ecstatic observation, I gently removed the brandy snifter dangling between her fingers and she stirred briefly to wish me goodnight. As I left her room, my emotions raged; I understood completely that Nicoletta never was, nor ever could be, mine. In the midst of an ecstatic recollection, I was experiencing the excruciating pain of longing for a hopelessly unattainable beauty.

Walking back through the corridors that had caused Nicoletta to be uncomfortable, I stopped to see if I could hear the voices of children wailing. Instead I vaguely heard the ominous, seductive echoes of her voice purring in my ear: "I shudder to think what my fiancé would do if he ever found out."

Before collapsing into bed in a state beyond exhaustion, I headed for my suitcase to reassure myself that the diary was securely tucked away in its heavy envelope. As I tried to maneuver my key in the tiny lock, I was surprised to see that the fragile mechanism was stuck and that a deep scratch ran the length of the bronze hardware. Breathlessly, I lifted the catch with my fingernail and threw it open. Pulling out the envelope, I began to breathe more easily as I saw that the archival folder was still there.

"Twenty-one!" I said, counting the pages aloud. "Thank God!" The contents were intact, yet the broken lock was frightening; it looked as if someone had literally jammed a screwdriver into the keyhole. Glancing at my watch, I realized it was too late to do anything. But the idea that someone had come into my room was unsettling and I deadbolted the door, securing the chain. As I examined the latches on the tall windows looking out on my balcony, I glanced into the courtyard and was taken by the silent, sinister beauty of the reflection of clouds on the stucco walls below.

Stepping out onto the balcony, into the crisp night air, I gazed upward at the sky, a lunar tableau that shimmered with a brilliance almost painful to the eye. Encircled by masses of white clouds like icebound continents in an arctic map, the moon was almost completely full and luminous. Only the distinct glimmer of a lone, radiant star contrasted with the glacial celestial landscape that stretched out above me. The incessant, irreverent play of shadows on the stone ornaments of La Favorite reminded me of my solitary walk through old Nancy and I stood transfixed. And I found myself thinking that architecture is music fixed in stone.

In the surreal light, a strange reflection flickering on the cobblestones beneath my balcony caught my eye. For a second, it appeared to outline a body. But the shimmering effect of shadows of clouds, intermittently washing the pavement with sepia tones, made it difficult to see. As I strained to focus, I realized how easily lighting could play tricks on the eyes.

But no, the more I looked, the more the horrifying illusion took on the form of a body, a naked woman, one arm outstretched over her head with a mass of tangled hair.

My heart racing, I dialed the housekeeper's number. When I heard a voice answer, I automatically responded, "Hello, Denise?"

"She's not here." The abrupt, raspy voice of a woman with a thick, provincial accent in French continued, "This is Monique. You woke me up."

"I was wondering," I asked, "if someone could check the courtyard under my window."

"It's almost three o'clock," she replied, annoyed. "We'll do it tomorrow."

"Tomorrow's too late," I countered.

"No one is here," she barked angrily. "Go back to sleep, *Monsieur.*"

With the slamming of the receiver still reverberating in my

ear, I reflected for a minute. It became clear to me that I would have to go out and take a look. "It's just an illusion," I heard myself mumbling as I descended the main staircase, trying to walk softly over the ancient wooden floorboards, which creaked mercilessly despite my best efforts.

When I arrived in the huge abandoned kitchen, enveloped in thick darkness, I groped unsuccessfully for a light switch. Instead, drawn by the solitary light coming from my balcony, I scoured the courtyard with my eyes for any sign of the body. But the shifting of clouds had obliterated the pale image stretched out on the cobblestones. And suddenly I was afraid: overwhelming fear seized me with the force of a vise.

"Enough," I heard myself saying as I forced open the massive wooden doors leading out to the courtyard. In the moist stillness of the night, I stumbled slowly in the direction of the pallid shape, the sounds of my footsteps echoing from distant corners.

My foot nudged something—a wooden crucifix—sending a shudder racing down my spine. Then, under the ethereal light streaming down from my apartment, my eye moved to the form of a body, perhaps someone sleeping peacefully on the pavement. As the clouds shifted and the muted rays of the moon streamed through, I realized it had been no play of light: nestled at my feet was the body of a naked woman lying facedown, her tangled hair tossed in every direction. I reached down for her shoulder to shake her. But my hand stopped in midair as if paralyzed at the prospect of what I might uncover. As I extended my arm, I touched an unnatural skin like polished marble and a violent chill ran through my body. For what seemed an eternity, I stood debating what to do, rooted to the ground in dread. Then, with an almost superhuman effort, I turned the body over, watching in disbelief as the head fell directly back, disjointed, with the grotesque lifelessness of a rag doll. Looking directly into the icy, bulging eyes, wide in horror, I saw my housekeeper, Denise. I tried not to believe the grisly vision that flashed before my eyes. Her broken neck, held by a lifeless sheath of stretched skin, was shrouded in massive, blackish bruises, her raw features contorted in a bizarre mask of gaping horror.

Dropping the body, I stumbled backward in the dark, my vision swimming in a mist of dizzying disbelief. Disoriented and barely able to focus, I hunted for the exit, glancing over my shoulder in revulsion at the ghastly outline that disappeared with each agonizing step, into the bitter recesses of the night.

# PART TWO

# Venice, Rome

*And we forget because we must,*
*And not because we will.*
—MATTHEW ARNOLD

When I awoke, I was alone. Flimsy sheets of white curtain around my bed were drawn and the lights were dim.

"Water . . ." I tried to speak the words, but it wasn't clear if they had come out or even if anyone was there to hear them. Although I couldn't move, there was no doubt I was still alive, albeit stretched out in some kind of silent, motionless limbo, between a world I couldn't remember and another that hovered pitilessly in the distance. The face of a young woman, enveloped in white light, came in and out of a hazy focus.

". . . need a drink," I mumbled. My slurred, labored phrase sounded like the voice of a stranger. The young nurse changing my bandages immediately reached for a plastic cup with a straw and put it to my mouth. The ice water felt like a godsend to my parched lips.

A silver-blue sky cast a pale, azure tint over the linen bandages that covered my body. Around my bed, soft shadows of reflected clouds made the linen curtains come to life in a muted play of color and light.

"My shoulder . . ." I said. "Why does it hurt so much?"

She looked bewildered for a moment. "Don't you . . . remember? Oh, I see. I'll call the doctor."

"Wait," I struggled to say as she abruptly left the room.

Soon a doctor in his mid-thirties with a manicured ash blond mustache was talking to me. The difficulty I had in thinking indicated to me that I was heavily sedated. And to make matters worse, his voice began to go in and out like a radio transmission over long distances: ". . . operation on your spine . . . not allowed in your country . . . human embryonic stem cells . . . new procedure . . . cement from living coral . . . only performed once or twice . . . too soon to tell . . . if you hadn't been brought here . . . chances of walking zero."

All of a sudden, his voice seemed to bellow, echoing painfully in my ears. "Can you understand what I'm saying?"

"My chest, my shoulder," I repeated feebly.

"Try to bear withus acolleagueof mine wltalk tyou . . ."

"What happened to my chest?" I asked.

". . . removed a largeknifeblade . . . musclessevered."

From the incomprehensible stream of syllables, the words *knife blade* jumped out. As I strained to understand, his words continued to merge one with another and his voice was reduced to a nagging monotone that went up and down in pitch like a malfunctioning tape recorder.

". . . none of yrinternalorganzwrdmaged . . . yraluckymn."

As I groped for some tiny glimpse of the past, my insides suddenly began quivering violently and my hands and arms, carefully strapped in traction, shook fiercely in convulsive waves. Within seconds, the young doctor was administering a hypodermic needle with quiet firmness. As my thoughts started to recede from the conscious world, the sound of the doctor's voice reverberated in my ears, ". . . isgoing t'help yusleep . . ."

When I returned to consciousness, the same young doctor with the well-trimmed mustache was sitting attentively in front of me, wearing a crisp white coat. "Hello, Dr. Pierce," he said with a thick Czech accent. "I'm glad to see you back with us again."

"What's happening?" I asked slowly, suddenly aware that I was slurring my words.

"You've had a series of operations over the past few days, and we're going to continue this afternoon. You had some nasty internal bleeding and a shattered collarbone, and we inserted a titanium pin in your spinal column. Also four pins in your right wrist and one in your right thigh. We're going to be using a new procedure to cement one of your lumbar vertebrae. How are you feeling?"

"Awful," I mumbled.

"Do you know where you are?"

"Zaradník Clinic," I struggled to say.

"That's right. We're a private medical center specializing in new medical research and procedures. What do you remember about your, ah, accident?"

Although I tried my best, I had to say, "Nothing."

"What is the last thing you remember?" he asked.

"Something about La Favorite, in Nancy. It might have been a dream—I seem to remember a woman's body in the courtyard at night. Denise, her name was Denise. And I remember being carried on a stretcher, and seeing a knife blade in my chest. What happened to me?"

"They removed the knife in surgery. It punctured your lung, but fortunately, the blade missed your heart. The lung is functioning again and, quite remarkably, all your other internal organs are intact."

For the first time, I realized there was someone else in the room, a middle-aged woman sitting in the corner. "Who is she?" I asked.

"A witness," he replied. "We had to undertake certain emergency procedures but because you were unconscious, there was implied consent. Now that you're conscious we're going to need you to sign some forms."

In the far recesses of my mind, hours of grueling operations echoed as a painful half memory. "The longer we wait," he continued, "the more residual damage you may have."

"I'll sign," I said.

"There's also something unpleasant I have to tell you: your spinal column was severed. But you're in a unique facility. We specialize in experimental procedures that will maximize your chances of recovery."

The older woman, clipboard in hand, stood up and handed me a pen. Immediately after I scrawled my signature, she left the room and he seemed eager to leave as well. "When will I find out what happened?" I asked.

"Don't force yourself to remember," he said. "In time, it may all come back."

Alone in my room, I closed my eyes and continued struggling to remember. A sudden flash from the past startled me: a macabre dream. No, a recurrent nightmare of grim, ghastly clarity.

*In the pitch-black room, there is a palpable, oppressive sense of imminent violence. Something of unimaginable cruelty is about to be unleashed. Like a stalked animal, I wait in the silence, terrified the obsessive pounding in my temples will betray me. Incoherent emotions race through my mind: a piercing chill, the thundering bass of my heartbeat becoming louder and more rapid. With my vision spinning, I hunt frantically for a place to hide . . . in the closet, under the bed. But there is no safe place. And time is running out. Cringing in paralyzed shock, I can hear the latch on the door turning. Unable to make a sound, I try again and again to scream in a whirling of blurred images . . .*

Intense . . . too real to be a dream. Suspended between flashbacks and visions conjured up by experimental medications, I found myself immersed in a world where the borders between reality and fantasy were hopelessly blurred. Slowly, I began putting the scattered fragments back in place: the Mozart Milan diary—was it a fake? I couldn't remember. Didn't Braun tell me anything about it? Then I remembered something: Rome. We all went to Rome. For a second, I was back on course, retracing the events in the order in which they happened, the only way my brain would unshackle its secrets.

# CHAPTER 8

*Murder is born of love, and love attains the greatest intensity in murder.*
—OCTAVE MIRBEAU

My decision to head down for breakfast was more out of hunger for human solace than for food. The events that required me to be awake so early were unsettling: a police interview in the early hours of the morning revealed that Denise—whose naked body had been laid out in some kind of bizarre, ritualistic fashion with flowers and a crucifix—had been sodomized and savagely beaten before her neck was snapped.

Denise. I couldn't believe it. In the few days that I had known her, I had come to genuinely appreciate and like her. Her death in such brutal circumstances was a painful, ugly shock. When the police questioned me, it first sounded like bureaucratic formalities: Did you hear anything under your balcony last night? When did you see her last? Then an intimidating question: Why did you happen to go out on your balcony at three in the morning? The peculiar circumstances of the broken lock on my luggage came to mind and I began to narrate the whole sequence of events.

"Do you think she could have fallen from my balcony?" I asked when they finished.

The answer was curt. "We ask the questions, *Monsieur.*"

After the interview, I was politely told not to leave the country until the investigation was over. Desperate for information or explanations of any kind, I headed for breakfast in La Favorite. Arriving in the wing where breakfast was being served in a half dozen small rooms, I felt the silent but tangible discomfort in the air. While some guests sat alone reading the newspaper and nursing a cup of Viennese *Mélange,* others mingled casually in groups of two or three. Seeing Hélène Benoit seated by herself, I ventured nearer and a sense of relief swept over me when she invited me to join her.

"I know," she began, before I had said a word. "It's absolutely horrible. By the way, have you been to Rome before? We're all going, you know."

The question "What?" never made it to my lips. She continued, "Oh, so you haven't heard yet. The viscount has a friend in Rome, a cardinal who's responsible for the renovations of the guest quarters taking place over the last six years in the church of Santa Maria Maggiore. They finished two months ahead of schedule and it's been arranged for all of us to go down and stay for the remainder of the three weeks." Under her breath she continued, "The viscount is extremely upset about what happened to Denise. He also thinks no one will be able to forget what happened here, so we all have to leave La Favorite."

As I asked myself how we were all going to get to Rome, Hélène went on. "Philippe, the majordomo, explained it to everyone while you were in with the police. They spent an awfully long time questioning you."

She appeared to be waiting and I replied, "I was the one who discovered her body. In fact, they asked me not to leave the country until the investigation is finished."

"Speaking of the investigation, did you hear there's already been a change? It was quite a scene when the police arrived."

"A scene?"

"This morning around seven, when the viscount and Nadine were meeting with the chief police inspector—Clairmont, I think his name was—Elisabetta von Stahl overheard the viscount screaming. No one's ever heard him raise his voice, so it was pretty serious."

"He was mad at the inspector?"

"*Livid* is more like it," she continued. "All the French police descended on La Favorite at once—the viscount was beside himself to see them taking over his home, climbing all over his furniture, walking with muddy shoes on his Persian carpets."

"But when there's a murder, the police have to do their job," I said.

Hélène looked at me with a sly expression. "Things aren't done that way around here. The viscount wasn't going to have an army of rookies insulting his guests and tromping all over his antiques; he made phone calls to several top magistrates in the country, and I heard he even made a call to . . . I probably shouldn't say."

When she stopped in midsentence, I assumed that Viscount René had called the president of the Republic. "Suffice it to say," she continued, "Clairmont is out. There's a new chief inspector now, one who's used to dealing with people like the viscount and certain levels of society. Really, that was a bad move on their part, unleashing all those idiots on La Favorite before consulting with the viscount."

"How do they feel about everyone leaving for Rome?" I asked.

"The investigation will continue just the same," she said. "It's possible some people will be detained for more questioning, like . . ."

Again, she stopped and I sat attentively without moving a muscle or batting an eyelash. "Like Rudi von Horvach," she continued, with the slightest inflection of irony. "In fact, they've kept him in there most of the morning." The blond Slovak waiter, Jano, had apparently been listening to our conversation. As Hélène spoke, he was pouring coffee into delicate porcelain cups and his hands began to tremble uncontrollably. His whole demeanor had changed, from the extroverted young man who had introduced me with complete ease to other guests, to a pale and terrified youngster.

"Dr. Pierce," he stammered, trying to smile and appear relaxed, "there is a message for you from one of the other guests. They said to say it was very urgent. Let me get it."

Hélène and I looked at each other with surprise, our curiosity piqued. Within a few seconds, he returned, resting a folded piece of paper on the table, smudged by several greasy fingerprints, on which the word *Personil* had been scrawled. Immediately he left, with the aura of a guilty conscience. As I opened the note, Hélène watched keenly, trying to disguise her interest. The handwritten page read, "Please, I can with you later talking in privately?" It was signed "Jano."

Hélène waited for my reaction but when it wasn't forthcoming, she volunteered, "I know, you can't tell me what it's about." When I nodded, she smiled ironically.

"So tell me," I said as I inserted the note in my pocket. "Why are the police spending so much time questioning Rudolph von Horvach?"

"Who knows?" she answered cautiously, with an enigmatic expression on her face. "Unless . . ."

I waited breathlessly for her to decide whether or not she would continue. "Unless," she said, "it has something to do with his peculiar preferences when it comes to women. Unusual tastes—in bed, that is—that have caused him problems in the past."

"I heard he was responsible for a woman's death," I interrupted to say, and she nodded.

"He has an insatiable appetite," she continued. "Nannies, house servants, *au pair* girls, go-go dancers. But he also has some very good lawyers. Otherwise, he would have had to do jail time. I've already said too much . . . there's a conspiracy of silence when it comes to him. Everyone tries to pretend it all never happened. Let's change the subject."

"Tell me more," I said, "about this crazy move to Rome. How is everyone going to get there?"

"We'll be driven," she answered, "in the same fleet of sedans that picked us up from the airport. Of course, we'll have to double up. I'm riding with Véronique Ibsen and Andreas Wolff. We're all going to stay overnight in Venice to break up the trip."

"Hélène," I replied, "I don't think I'm going. The French police told me not to leave the country."

"That would surprise me," she said. "If the viscount wants us all to go, he'll take care of the arrangements with the police. By the way, have you seen Wolff today? He looks absolutely awful."

We both looked over to the other side of the room where he was sitting, and Wolff seemed to know intuitively that we were talking about him. Immediately, he rose from his seat and came over to greet us. "I can't stay long," he said, "but I wanted to wish you a good trip, Matthew. Hélène, I understand we'll both be traveling together to Rome."

The drawn, hollow figure standing before us bore little resemblance to the robust man whose vibrant personality had kept me constantly entertained. His complexion had a pale, ashen hue and his eyes, set back in dark, sunken craters, looked lifeless. Even Hélène, who had a quick response to everything, was taken aback by the gravity of his appearance. Seeing her reaction, I tried my best to fill in the silence. "So, we'll see each other in Venice, Andreas."

With glazed eyes, he replied distractedly, "Oh, that's right . . . Venice," and with his attempt to smile, the severe lines around his mouth lifted for a moment. But the strain on his face was apparent. With a bow to Hélène he said goodbye and departed silently with the slow, implacable fatalism of a solitary wave sweeping in toward the shore. A wave of ambivalent emotions came over me: confusion, curiosity, and pity. And a flash, a recollection from two days before, jarred me—the conversation I overheard between Wolff and von Horvach in the park as they discussed "the housekeeper, Denise." I considered telling Hélène about it, but immediately decided it would be unwise.

"My," she exclaimed. "He looks like hell."

"The death of Denise," I replied, "must have upset him. Apparently under that biting exterior is a very sensitive man."

"If you say so," Hélène replied brusquely, standing up and excusing herself. I sensed she knew I was concealing something but it was fortunately apparent we were still friends. "All that packing," she continued. "How I hate it."

Almost the second Hélène left, Jano beckoned me with his eyes toward a room where no guests were seated. Despite the potential seriousness of the situation, his behavior and the whole scenario struck me as some kind of Peter Sellers parody of an Agatha Christie novel. As we stood alone, surreptitiously peering out from behind the threshold of a door, I asked, "Would you mind telling me what this is all about?"

"I am doing something very, very bad," he answered, almost gasping for breath. "I am losing my job if they are finding out and I am never getting another one if I am being fired. Even my work permit is being terminated."

I started to say, "Well, it's not as if you murdered anyone." But instead I let him speak.

"I am hearing you and Ms. Benoit talking about the police and Prince von Horvach. But I know he didn't kill Denise, and I am losing my job if I am coming forward and telling the police."

Under the strain, Jano's normally polished English was disintegrating. "Please," I said, "slow down. You've lost me."

"Last night," he continued breathlessly, "around midnight I am seeing something I am not supposed to. I am bringing a camomile tea to old Baroness Paumgarten—she is in the apartment next to von Horvach—and I am hearing von Horvach's door open all at once. I am standing for a moment in the dark and Denise, she is coming right out of his room. She is looking very, very upset, and is walking very fast right by me. Von Horvach is calling her back and is saying, 'Hey you, *Nutte*'—that is terrible name for whore—'you are forgetting something.'"

Jano paused for a moment until he saw from my face that I was waiting for him to continue, and he launched back into his story. "Denise is stopping a second and looking back. Von Horvach is taking something from his wallet and he is saying, 'Hey, whore! That's for you. Pick it up.' He is crumpling a bill from his wallet and he is tossing it on the ground. They are both looking at each other, and then Denise is walking away; she is very mad. After von Horvach is slamming his door, I am going over to see what is on the ground."

"Jano," I interrupted, "hold on. I still don't understand what you did that was so wrong."

"I kept the money," he stammered. "It is one-thousand-dollar bill, U.S.! I have never seeing one before."

Jano's English was at an all-time low and I realized he was becoming incoherent, even hysterical. "So, just turn it in," I said, suggesting the obvious solution. "Report it to Philippe as a lost item."

"If I turn it in now, Philippe is asking me, 'Why you are keeping the money so long?' Philippe is suspicious and a very, very strict boss."

"Tell him you picked it up last night and were planning to give it back today, but that you were so upset by the death of Denise you completely forgot about it," I replied. "Anyone can see you're in a terrible emotional state because of the murder. He couldn't possibly fire you; if he even tries, I'll go right to the viscount. But that's not going to happen."

Jano's nervous explosion of bad English stopped. A calm, serene expression crossed his face, and his eyes radiated gratitude. As he shook my hand, I told him confidently that everything would be fine.

Exhausted as I was, there was no time to rest, as I would immediately have to begin packing my bags. As I started back to my apartment, Enrique came over with a buoyant smile on his face. "Look, man," he said triumphantly, "I've got some hot news for you. I saw the list and you're traveling to Rome with Ilsa Paumgarten and her grandmother."

"Thanks, Enrique," I replied with a weary grin. "But I'm not going anywhere. The police told me I have to stay here."

"No, man," he replied. "I just heard from Philippe that it's all set—the viscount arranged everything. The police are just going to take a few hair and blood samples from you, and then you're free to leave for Rome. But wait till you hear the best part," he continued exuberantly. "That babe, Ilsa—and I got this information from a very reliable source—she never wears underwear. Man, you've got it made."

"Enrique," I said, patiently. "We don't have a clue how old she is and that's a serious problem. Nibbling at the bait of desire isn't wise; too many times there's a hook waiting underneath."

"You're uptight, man. Listen, almost everything in this world worth doing is either sinful, fattening, illegal, or addictive. Look at it this way. What you and Ilsa do when no one's around ain't fattening, and one out of four ain't bad."

"You're attracted to danger," I replied. "Taking risks turns you on. But haven't you ever heard what happens to men our age who go to bed with fifteen- or sixteen-year-olds?"

"Listen, sex is the glue that holds this whole crazy planet together. If some politicians and cardinals had just gotten laid instead of starting wars and inquisitions, just think of how much better history class woulda been."

Grappling with his reasoning, I replied, "No, Enrique, sex is more like eating—we can't eat everything we want because if we do, we pay the price."

Enrique was having a good time expounding his philosophy on life and love. "Man, good sex is for the soul. It's like one of the ten best reasons for living. And anyway, who gives a damn about the other nine?"

Time was getting short and we both knew it. But as he looked at me, Enrique broke out in a sly grin and added, "Two days in that car, at close quarters with that scenery, and believe me, Doc, you're gonna change your mind. Talk about a room with a view. And her grandmother's completely out of it."

With his usual burst of testosterone, Enrique took off, and I ascended the staircase with heavy footsteps. "Something's wrong," I said aloud, bitterly: it all felt too short. Vaguely I recalled a saying about escaping from the tyranny of time only through work or pleasure. But for the time being, work was going to be difficult, and the precarious prospect of forbidden pleasure on the way to Rome offered little solace.

Leaving the mirrored corridors and the light, spacious civility of La Favorite, I felt nostalgic; just when I had begun to settle in, everything was over. As two young men carried my luggage, I walked reluctantly out the main entrance, where Philippe was busily directing the staff and orchestrating the event. "Your car is ready. The baroness and her granddaughter are already waiting in the car."

The entire courtyard that stretched in front of La Favorite was bustling with activity, with staff loading luggage and escorting guests into several dozen silver sedans. Despite the fact that a murder had just taken place, I was surprised to see everyone having such a good time: guests were smiling and laughing as they said their goodbyes and the entire relocation had the relaxed, carefree atmosphere of a picnic or an excursion to the beach. It struck me as genuinely macabre.

Andreas Wolff was the only exception. He was clearly not in a good mood, lost in his own personal world of demons and dark thoughts. Just as I was about to step into the car, another figure caught my eye. Enrique came over quietly with a slightly wicked smile and whispered, "Don't do anything I wouldn't do."

"Enrique," I replied, "there's not much you wouldn't do."

Once I was seated comfortably in the sedan, I realized almost everything Enrique had described in his semipornographic scenario was wrong. Ilsa was dressed in a stylish apricot-peach knit dress cut well below her knee. Her grandmother, carefully tailored, coiffed, and manicured, was attentive and alert and immediately offered me her hand, even remembering my name.

Inside, the car was arranged with seats facing one another, and I found myself with spacious leg and head room, facing Ilsa and her grandmother without any sense of feeling cramped or confined. The padded cloth seats and the streamlined, tinted glass windows gave the interior a feeling of unrestrained luxury.

"You're looking well today, Baroness," I said, speaking louder than usual. But her eyelids were now half closed, almost as if she were floating in a state between consciousness and sleep.

When she didn't respond, Ilsa spoke quietly. "She probably didn't hear you. I'm never really sure when she's paying attention." Ilsa was wearing almost no jewelry, but as she adjusted her grandmother's silk scarf, I noticed a striking art deco ring on her hand, with several large rubies encrusted in a setting of tiny diamonds. She noticed me glancing at it and responded by casually taking it off her finger and handing it to me.

"Are you interested in jewelry? Baron Paumgarten had it made for my grandmother by Cartier before they were married."

After admiring it, I handed it back and remarked, "It reminds me of the jewelry Nicoletta Chigi was wearing last night. Did you see it?"

Ilsa smiled with a certain superiority. "Those are her Wallis Simpson pieces. Her fiancé bought them at auction. That's . . . well, something no one in my family would *ever* do."

She paused for a moment. "But Max just recently came into his money. I hear he's a Swiss banker or an international developer. That's what people call themselves when they don't want anyone to know what they really do for a living."

I felt as if Ilsa were playing cat and mouse with me and decided to take the bait. "What's he like?"

"Maximilian?" she replied with a coy smile. "You'll meet him in Rome. He's coming down to see Nicoletta. She's from Rome; in fact, she comes from one of the greatest families in Italy."

"But what is he like?" I repeated.

"Have you heard of *Bunte*, the German magazine, or *Gente*, the Italian one? Both featured him on their covers as the sexiest man alive. He's tall, dark, and terribly good-looking—your typical Latin lover."

She stretched out her legs with a certain seductive flair. "For anyone who likes men, he's irresistible." And as I gazed at the remarkable legs extended languidly before me, all I could think about was Enrique's comment about his reliable source.

As we spoke, I noticed the driver looking at me in the mirror. Almost as if she sensed what I was thinking, Ilsa intoned, "Look, driver, shut the glass and the shades right away. If we need you, we'll call." Then, with a metallic, icy firmness, she continued, "And slow down. My grandmother has a heart condition."

The tinted window dividing us from the driver rose slowly, and apparently, as far as Ilsa was concerned, the incident did not even merit comment. "What do you make of the whole thing— the murder of Denise?" I asked.

"Some kind of maniac, I imagine. Her neck was snapped with such violence, the police are questioning how a man could have done it. She was practically decapitated, you know."

Unfortunately, I knew all too well.

Ilsa continued coolly, "They're doing an extensive check into her background. Who knows what she was involved in? Maybe even a satanic cult."

"Why would you say that?" I asked.

"Because there's a group that's been meeting in Nancy since the French Revolution. They celebrate Black Mass."

"Just from the brief time I knew Denise," I replied, "I can't imagine her being involved in anything like that. But . . ." For a second I hesitated. "I understand the police questioned von Horvach for quite a long time."

"I can't believe Rudi von Horvach had anything to do with it," she replied. "But unfortunately, if he did, he'll probably get off. He's bought himself out of similar problems before. Plus he's one of the most influential men in Europe and has powerful political connections: he's involved with OPEC in Vienna on the highest levels and every international committee wants him on their board."

"And I heard he has top-notch lawyers," I said.

"The law firm that represents him handles the scandals for the royal families in Europe. As you can imagine, that keeps them rather busy."

"Why do people continue to put up with him?" I asked, astonished at my own candor. "He strikes me as rude, arrogant, and presumptuous."

"That's because you're not a woman," Ilsa replied. "Rudi's really not bad once you get to know him. Don't forget that some men with the most obscene character bear the mark of greatness. Even people who don't like him admit begrudgingly that he's remarkable."

"How so?" I asked incredulously.

"His mind—it's the most fertile, inventive mind I've ever encountered. People say he's a genius. And he's a progressive political force in Vienna. Plus his charm—even though you didn't get to see it. When he's interested in a woman, he turns into a nuclear generator of pure animal passion."

"Did he ever make a pass at you?" I asked, again surprising myself.

Ilsa looked at me with a seductive, enigmatic smile. "Why, of course."

For some reason, her casual reply infuriated me. "But he's old enough to be your grandfather."

Ilsa laughed. "Well, he certainly hasn't aged well since I first met him."

"When was that?" I continued. "When you were ten?"

"You sound like my last boyfriend," she purred as she shifted her position, sliding her dress with seductive ease.

"You're willing to overlook his faults," I continued. "But what he did to Alison Teal is not very pleasant."

Ilsa was unmoved. "She might be better off as a result of what happened. For several years, she went all over Europe to excellent spas to recover from her nervous breakdown. And they say that her voice is better than ever. Not to condone what he did, but she knew what she was letting herself in for. Alison thought she could change the world by reforming one man. Of all mistakes, the worst is for a woman to think she can change a man."

Ilsa's exposed legs were capturing my attention more and more and I found myself staring at them. Every movement of her dress became the provocation of a red cape before a bull and each time she shifted her position, something inside me felt like charging. It was a transparent seduction, but unlike Nicoletta Chigi, who thrived on being admired from afar, I knew Ilsa was cooking up all kinds of wicked ideas. "When we get to Venice," she continued, "why don't you come up for a drink—after I put grandmother to bed? Just remember not to let me have more than a glass of wine. It goes right to my head."

I knew it was time to change the subject. "We must be approaching Switzerland," I said. "Can you see the mountain peaks?"

Ignoring my comments about the scenery, she stroked her leg carelessly and said, "I heard a few other things about the murder. There were some flowers taken from her room and laid out, along with an old wooden crucifix that was hanging on her wall."

The mention of the crucifix brought back a wave of unsettling memories. "I know," I said. "I stumbled across it when I found her body. It's something I'll never forget."

"Oh, yes," Ilsa continued, "and one other thing. She had quite a few—how can I say this?—hickeys and love bites all over her body. That's probably what made the police think of Rudi von Horvach."

The discussion was bringing back too many disturbing memories, and my face must have reflected it. Ilsa shifted gears abruptly. "Did I tell you I started to read your book last night?" she asked as she slid her shoes off casually, making me aware of a great deal of leg room in the car . . . and a great deal of leg. "I adore Mozart. Are you writing another?"

"Yes," I replied. "My next project—well, right now, I'm translating a document that may be by Mozart."

"Fascinating!" Ilsa answered. "You know, if you have any problems with the translation, I might be able to help you. We studied all kinds of eighteenth-century literature in high school—Lessing, Herder, Goethe. And it's always easier for a native speaker to understand the subtleties of a language."

Ilsa's idea caught me off guard. I was eager to get back to the folios, and her input was too intriguing to pass up. "There's just one thing," I replied. "You have to promise me not to discuss it with anyone."

"Agreed," she said. "Let's have a look at it."

As I reached for my briefcase with the broken lock, Ilsa's reaction was swift. "I hope you're not carrying the originals around with you."

The directness of her question made me uncomfortable. As I pulled out my photocopies of the Milan diary, I asked, "What makes you say that?"

"Oh," Ilsa replied, apparently surprised when she saw the copies. "Because I was going to tell you, in case you didn't know, that there's always a vault for the valuables of guests of the foundation, especially if they're carrying a lot of cash or jewelry. Philippe takes care of that."

I made a mental note to put the originals in the vault as

soon as we arrived in Rome. Turning to the sheet in front of me, I began to read aloud in the original German, struggling at the same time to decipher the scribbled handwriting.

*December 5, 1772*

*What madness! What a paradox to write a journal now when I still have fourteen more arias, duets, and trios to compose for my opera, Lucio Silla, as well as more recitatives and choruses. But this humble diary is more than ink and paper. It is a powerful release, even more, a liberation from the constant pressure. Since my head is so full of music and my fingers so tired from writing arias, I can only hope this stream of words will not abruptly and unexpectedly melt into one long succession of musical notes.*

*As usual, when we arrived in Italy from Salzburg, everything about the way we live our lives changed. Here in Milan, we are constantly invited out and have our main meal at two o'clock. Then in the evening, we have only bread, grapes, and a glass of wine in our apartment; it gets dark much later than in Salzburg and our simple repast in the lucid Italian light reminds me of a Caravaggio still life.*

*But the most remarkable change appears, not in external things, but in our attitudes and mores. Although he would never admit it, even Papa is overcome by a subtle metamorphosis each time we enter Italy. This is partly due to the beautiful women of Milan, renowned to be more open, with a freer way of living, than anywhere else in Italy. The shops are tended by charming women who embroider while chatting and socializing with Milanese men who stop in. In the convents, the nuns have great freedom to talk and laugh with gentlemen at the grate and are even permitted to join them during musical concerts.*

*Since Papa is still a good-looking man, women often flirt with him and he blushes whenever some remarkable*

*Milanese beauty pays attention to him. And on our very*
*first night in an inn, the clerk asked Papa if he would*
*like to have a* letto fornito, *which means "a furnished*
*bed." Papa did not know the custom and when the clerk*
*explained it to him, he declined quietly and firmly,*
*refusing to tell me afterward what it meant. But when I*
*asked Luigi, my young castrato friend, he explained that*
*a woman enters the bedroom with a mask, removes all*
*her clothing, and joins the man in his bed. And this is*
*customary in Milan for men staying in inns!*

*The freedom of women is never so evident as during*
*Carnival. The grand ladies of Milan, accompanied by*
*five or six gentlemen called* cicisbei, *host balls and*
*entertainments. And women of lesser means imitate*
*them as much as possible, enjoying freedoms denied them*
*in other parts of Italy.*

Interrupting my reading, I asked Ilsa, "So, what do you
think?"

"My!" she replied breathlessly. "I can tell you for certain
that it's flawless eighteenth-century German."

Ilsa apparently noticed that I was having difficulty keeping
my eyes open and tried to make me feel at ease. "I'm going to try
to catch a little nap," she said. "You might need one yourself after
everything that happened last night."

And she was right. My descent into sleep was a direct
plummet into an almost comalike state. What must have been
hours later, I awoke to see the pillars of a long bridge racing by
as the car sped toward the slender, serene spires of Venice in the
distance. Ilsa was sound asleep, breathing deeply with rhythmic
regularity, and I felt an unusual weight on my lap: securely nestled between my legs was Ilsa's naked foot, her leg outstretched
to the fullest. In the darkened compartment of the sedan, the
sound of the baroness' talking wristwatch announced with anti-
septic accuracy, "It is 8:47 P.M." And night fell on the next stage
of this strange journey.

# CHAPTER 9

*Let the day perish wherein I was born, and the night in*
*which it was said, "There is a man child conceived."*
—BOOK OF JOB, 3:3

After getting settled into my suite at the Grand Hotel Danieli, the intoxicating lure of Venice at night began to exert its influence on me. Within minutes, I took the opportunity to reacquaint myself with the opulent decadence of the *Serenissima*.

As I strolled past the Caffè Florian, a small dance orchestra provided an accompaniment to the real music of Piazza San Marco, the carefree sounds of laughter and clanking silverware as patrons feasted on colorful dishes of mixed sorbet and coupes of chilled *spumante*. High above the animated activity of the square, the golden domes of San Marco loomed impressively. And nearby, the four shining bronze horses of Lysippus stood, caught in a timeless pose, strutting and prancing, offering silent witness to the grandeur of times past.

An abandoned side street carried me gradually to another jeweled facet of Venice: frozen in the moonlight was a tableau of delicate wrought-iron balconies and weathered stone pillars, mutely set around a solitary arched bridge. The cool, pungent aroma of sea air and brine saturated every corner of this hidden world, where the only noise was the uninterrupted sound of a thousand tiny tongues of water lapping at the pavement's edge in a relentless rhythm.

At every turn, from every angle, Venice floated confidently above its ancient wooden pilings, more like a massive sea vessel carved of stone than a city. Silently, I took in this remarkable setting—of ornate and stylized views captured by a thousand painters, of faded pastels reflected in canals and canvases, of defiant yet fragile splendor.

It struck me that the view stretching out before me had probably not changed much from the time Mozart first walked through Piazza San Marco. During the height of festivities for Carnival, the impression it made on the fifteen-year-old genius, traveling home with his father after his first Italian experience, was powerful. In fact, the brief month from mid-February to mid-March 1771 was a treat for the adolescent composer, who could walk with his father through Piazza San Marco at eleven and twelve o'clock at night on the way to the *ridotti,* Venice's famous gambling casinos where costume balls were given. Decorated with gold leaf and colorful frescoes based on mythology and lit by lavish, ornate chandeliers, the *ridotti* were renowned gathering places for the Venetian nobility, who were required to enter wearing masks. Musical entertainment was also an indispensable feature—anything to lure the pampered Venetians to the notorious card tables, where in a single night they might lose a family fortune that had taken centuries to accumulate. And since people then were essentially the same as they are today, the *ridotti* provided the sexual allure of new faces and bodies, as well as the erotic stimulation generated by masks, and of risk, an element that attracts and unites a different breed of people within the complex world of a single confined and intimate table.

Mozart and his father were showered with proud Venetian hospitality, dining out with distinguished nobles night after night and even lunching with the Patriarch of Venice. As Leopold wrote, "The gondolas of the nobility are constantly in front of our house. At every opportunity they heap such honors on us that we are not only picked up and taken home in gondolas by their secretaries, but often the noble himself accompanies us home. And this is even true of the greatest of them."

Needless to say, Mozart and his father were also impressed by the views from the gondola as they rode on the Grand Canal every day, so I decided to join them in experiencing the inexhaustible views of the canals with Venetian Gothic windows and facades of refined stone filigree. As I climbed down worn stone steps toward the festive striped mooring poles to board the somber, black gondola, I entered a world apart from time. The splendid, stately churches of Il Redentore and La Salute stood proudly, almost arrogantly, as if to declare their immortality and, at the same time, their vulnerability.

Deftly guided by a silent *gondoliere,* we glided past the imposing classical facade of the "Hospital of the Beggars." During the first half of the eighteenth century, I recalled, these *ospedali,* or hospitals, were usually orphanages as well, and vibrant centers of the most recent, imaginative music of the time. At a time when the latest currents and fads reigned supreme, they were headed and staffed by some of the greatest composers of the continent and were famous for extraordinary performances and a unique quality of musical life.

Venice, now deceptively calm and abandoned, would soon be bustling with animated nightlife. Enjoying the peacefulness, I reflected on the lively city Mozart and his father encountered, boasting numerous opera houses where composers from all over Europe came to create new and exciting works for an enthusiastic public. And the fifteen-year-old Mozart actually landed a contract to compose a new opera for the San Benedetto opera house, a work that was never written; it is a puzzling, unresolved footnote in his biography, as no one has been able to determine why the commission was left unfulfilled. All in all, Mozart wrote that he liked Venice very much and it was not difficult for me to imagine why.

Climbing back up the worn marble entrance stairs of the Hotel Danieli, I was surprised to see a solitary figure standing outside in the dark. Wearing a wide-brimmed hat—a cashmere fedora—he was staring into the lagoon from the steps leading to the mooring site of the gondolas. "They told me you were out walking," Andreas Wolff said, pensively. "I've been waiting for you." His appearance had improved a hundredfold and I commented on how well he looked. "Thank you," he replied. But his delivery was almost mechanical.

"How's your room?" I asked.

"Beautiful . . . it's the one with the balcony right above your head. I asked for a view of the canal."

Curious as to why he was waiting for me, I asked, "What was it you wanted to talk to me about?"

"To ask a favor," he replied. "There's something I'd like you to hold for me until tomorrow."

"Of course," I replied, eyeing a ponderous, five-by-seven envelope in his hand. "But you're sure you don't want to put it in the hotel safety deposit?"

"I'm sure," he replied, as he handed it to me. "I'm very grateful to you." For what seemed an eternity, Wolff scrutinized me enigmatically, and without another word he left. It struck me as strange, but by now I had begun to expect unorthodox behavior from the guests of the foundation. Looking at my watch, I headed immediately to Ilsa's hotel room to have our drink.

As I knocked on her door, I felt as if I were doing something wrong in coming up to her room. Dressed in a short white bathrobe and a turban made from a towel, Ilsa answered the door. "Sorry," she said, "I didn't know exactly when you were coming. I just got out of the shower."

As I laid my sport coat on a chair by the door, along with the packet Wolff had given me, Ilsa eyed the envelope and asked, "What's that?"

"Something Andreas Wolff asked me to hold for him," I replied.

"Why don't you pour us both a drink," Ilsa suggested. "I'd like a perfect manhattan."

"You told me not to give you more than a glass of wine," I chided her as I went into the adjacent room, where I hunted for the minibar key and began to sort through the labyrinth of compartments and bottles. "What's the drinking age in Italy?"

Ilsa did not respond and after a few minutes, I realized there was nothing that even remotely approached the ingredients of a perfect manhattan. Finally I shouted, "How about red wine?" Returning from the adjacent room with two glasses in hand, I was astounded to find Ilsa casually perusing the contents of Wolff's packet.

"That's not fair," I protested. "He trusted me."

"You should have known you could never leave a woman alone with something as intriguing as this . . . and from Andreas Wolff, no less. By the way, he's giving you his watch."

Ilsa held up the huge, solid gold Jaeger-LeCoultre chronometer that Wolff had been so proud to display. "There's a short note here saying he was given it by an older man and he wants to do the same with you."

"You're kidding," I said, tactfully trying to get the envelope out of her hands.

Ilsa resisted my attempts and began to read aloud from a handwritten page. "'This fucking pen—couldn't it write properly, just for once?'" Ilsa read. "Nice language," she commented dryly.

"We shouldn't be doing this," I said.

"Oh, don't be so serious," Ilsa answered. "I can put it all back together—he'll never even know I opened it." She continued reading aloud:


> Pain, fear Fear and pain I'm just so sick of it And rage
> So I'd just like to say a cheerful word to all you responsible for making my life unbearable
> FUCK YOU, ASSHOLES!
> Was that too severe? I think not, considering
> Right now I have two choices To continue the rest of my miserable existence in interminable agony or to do the unthinkable and the unspeakable
> Making decisions is such a pain in the ass
> Decide, decide
> All right, I've decided
> PS. I hope everyone who's ruined my life will get what they deserve, but it just doesn't work that way, does it
> PPS. I can still hope, can't I?


Ilsa and I looked at each other in amazement. I finally interrupted the silence. "I don't want to sound melodramatic, but it almost sounds like a suicide note." The instant the words came out of my mouth, Ilsa and I simultaneously raced for the phone. After waiting impatiently for someone to answer, I decided to head directly to Wolff's room. Ilsa vetoed the idea firmly. "The front desk," she insisted with icy firmness. "Keep trying."

"No," I insisted. "There's no time." Bolting out the door with Ilsa close behind me, I sprinted toward the room facing the Grand Canal that Wolff had pointed out to me. As I raced, gasping for breath, my heart pounded with a violent thundering as if it would burst out of my chest. I slammed my body into the door to his room, snapping off the lock and deadbolt with the force of my weight.

Bursting into the room, I was stunned by the calm: sitting in a chair with his back to me, Wolff was slumped over as if he were asleep facing the window, with the illuminated Palladian Church of the Redeemer dramatically highlighted in the distance. For a moment, I stopped dead in my tracks and hesitated to approach the apparently slumbering body, afraid of what I might find. On the table next to Wolff's outstretched hand was an empty glass and a half-empty bottle of Courvoisier VSOP, along with several empty pill containers. Venturing closer, I lifted his hand and felt his pulse: it was barely discernible, but his heart was still beating. When Ilsa arrived, we began to shake him and were both relieved to hear his weak, groggy protest in German, *"Lass' mich in Ruhe."* As I continued to lightly slap his face and shake his arms, Ilsa called the front desk, telling them to order an ambulance immediately.

The subsequent quarter hour of waiting was torture. When the waterborne ambulance finally arrived with blaring lights and sirens, I was totally drained. As soon as we returned to Ilsa's apartment, she insisted, "You're completely white. I'll get you a drink." Gliding across the marble floor with a fawnlike grace and elegant indifference, she handed me a glass of Bardolino as she calmly began to untie her turban, slowly, casually letting her robe slip down around her ankles.

"What are you doing?" I asked.

Ilsa stretched out her naked leg directly next to mine and purred, "What does it look like I'm doing?"

Still shaken, I said, "How can you think of making love at a time like this?"

"Because," she replied calmly, "when you look death in the face, there's nothing like reaffirming life."

As beautiful and seductive as Ilsa was, there were too many unresolved issues, not the least of which was her age. Picking up her bathrobe from the floor, I draped it gently over her legs and planted a long, firm kiss on her forehead. "Good night, Ilsa," I said as I walked out the door, not looking back.

The chauffeured drive from Venice past acres of espalier fruit trees sunning themselves in the Italian countryside should have been remarkable—the ideal trip to Rome. Yet it was more tedious than imaginable. Despite Ilsa's determination to lighten up the atmosphere, the murder of Denise, followed by Andreas Wolff's suicide attempt, left me emotionally exhausted. I felt myself falling into a deep depression. I began to wonder what I had gotten myself into, even asking myself, *What am I doing here?*

Dressed in a flowing white linen dress that recalled her white bathrobe, Ilsa seemed in great spirits, not at all bothered by Wolff's near death. "Don't be so glum," she intoned, smiling. When I didn't reply, she reminded me gently, "After all, isn't it thanks to us he's still alive?"

"I guess you're right," I said. "I wonder how he's doing."

"To tell you the truth, I wouldn't want to be in his shoes," Ilsa replied. "I understand that when the hospital attendants pump the stomachs of attempted suicides, they deliberately make it as violent and painful as possible, so they won't see them again under the same circumstances. Believe me, he'll never try barbiturates and cognac again. In fact, I'll bet he won't even want to see another brandy snifter for the rest of his life."

"But why do you think he did it?" I asked.

Ilsa shrugged her shoulders. "Maybe he broke up with a boyfriend," she replied. "Maybe he's having a problem with getting old and having to pay young men to have sex with him."

It was clear to me that Ilsa didn't believe in mincing words.

In fact, I began to think she was doing it deliberately to keep me away from the darker directions my mind was heading. She continued, "But he'll enjoy his recovery in the hospital—being pampered by all those young, good-looking Italian interns. Convalescence is always the best part of trying to kill yourself."

Seeing my expression, Ilsa said, "You're taking it all too much to heart. Life is too important to be taken seriously."

"Suicide is a final act of desperation," I replied. "That's serious."

Ilsa refused to go along with my logic. "Even Wolff wasn't serious when he wrote his suicide note," she responded. "You know why? Because he's a man who can't resist a good joke. Some things you can do alone, like reading *War and Peace,* or *1984,* or Dostoyevsky. But if you like a good joke, you need to share it with someone. Even as Wolff was heading to his grave, he couldn't resist a wisecrack."

Halfheartedly, I replied, "Maybe you're right. A sense of humor is the best escape."

"Of course I am," she said.

Ilsa's pep talk was boosting my spirits, and my thoughts wandered far afield to Mozart's life and his raucous wit. "Whenever the pressures of life were at their greatest," I finally said, "Mozart seemed to rally his most obscene humor. Perhaps it was a way he helped his family forget the dangers of life in the eighteenth century—traveling around Europe in the days when there were bandits murdering people on the roads."

"Mozart probably used his sense of humor to escape from his disappointments . . . and injustice," Ilsa added. "With a single word, humor transforms tragedy into comedy. Like Wolff, for example. You can be sure when he's back on his feet, he'll have us all rolling on the floor, describing the perverse elements of trying to kill yourself. First the pen didn't work; then, because he never took any medication, he couldn't figure out how to open the bottle of barbiturates."

Ilsa caught me off guard. And the minute she saw me smile, she plunged ahead full-force. "Of course, then the stopper in the bottle of cognac broke. So naturally he refused to drink anything with pieces of cork floating in it, even if he *was* trying to kill himself.

"At some cocktail party," Ilsa continued, imitating Wolff's voice and delivery, "he'll say, 'Suicide is such a terrible mistake. It's never a good idea to do anything you can't discuss when they're passing the cigars and espresso.'"

From the corner of my eye, I could see the baroness, immutable and immobile, with the faintest hint of a smile. "Or he'll say," Ilsa added, "the whole experience was simply dreadful. I can endure anything except discomfort."

Ilsa's irreverence was successful: it pulled me back from a plunge into depression. When she finished, I said, "You're right that Wolff would have died if you hadn't opened his letter. So, maybe a little immorality isn't always bad."

"It wasn't immoral at all," Ilsa replied with mock indignation. "Just because I'm unconventional doesn't mean I'm immoral. In fact, I'm very moral. But all the traditional things—you know, having to stay a virgin until you're married, couples not being allowed to sleep in the same room until after their wedding, et cetera—no one believes that anymore. The whole book of rules has changed. And at La Favorite—now, *there's* a whole separate code. For example, you can talk all you want about adultery and abortion, but you can't mention indigestion or gas, or mortgage payments or barbeques or beer. Things like that are social anathema."

"Whatever the code of morality is at La Favorite," I ventured, "there's something askew."

"What do you mean?" she asked.

"Well," I said, "apart from sexual maniacs and murderers, there's far too much backstabbing going on."

For a change, Ilsa took my comment seriously. "I know what you're talking about. Sometimes it bothers me too. But it's very common among Europeans. And fortunately the guests at La Favorite are intelligent, sophisticated people who have all kinds of interesting things to say. That makes up for their faults."

Nearing Rome, we began to pass ancient cities nestled comfortably on hillsides, growing almost directly out of their barren surroundings. The names of towns reflected sun and wines and marble cathedrals hewn of teal and ochre, faded rust and charcoal black. One after another, they sped past our view: a dozen remarkable medieval fortress towns, whose names perfectly and thoroughly eluded memory.

Ilsa reminded me subtly about the folio I had begun reading to her the previous day. "You know," she said, "I've always been fascinated by Mozart. And I find his music so reflective, so immediate. When I hear Mozart, I think of light, and of blue sky and ocean."

Recalling Enrique's comment about the best things in the world, I added, "And it's not sinful, illegal, or fattening—but it can be addictive."

"And Mozart is totally sensual," she murmured. "So why don't we at least look at the rest of your Mozart letter? That will keep your mind off what's happened."

As I reached for my briefcase, I looked at Baroness Paumgarten. Again, her wardrobe reflected an inexhaustible store of remarkable jewelry, elegant fabrics, and hand-picked accessories, tirelessly alternated each day like a museum with massive holdings and limited exhibition space. And as always, I never knew whether she was listening or not, since her eyes were half closed even when she spoke. I asked Ilsa, "How much will your grandmother hear?"

Ilsa laughed. "She can keep a secret better than anyone I know."

Hardly reassured, I began to read the last folio of the "Milan diary" as Ilsa listened intently.

> *Before serious work began on my opera, Papa and I*
> *visited some new and interesting sights in the city. One*
> *of them, the Ambrosian College, has the famous*
> *manuscript drawings by Leonardo [da Vinci] preserved,*
> *including his flying machines and mechanisms for war.*
> *The accomplishments of this genius fascinate me, for not*
> *only could he paint magnificent portraits and landscapes,*
> *but he was also an expert in anatomy, optics, geometry,*

*architecture, and mechanics. Even the canal system in
Milan, we've been told, was designed by Leonardo.*

*But unfortunately his* Last Supper *is in a terrible
state, for the paint has deteriorated. And the church where
it is found, Santa Maria delle Grazie, is a very unhappy
place indeed—it is the center of the tribunal for the
Inquisition. Here those charged with a crime never know
who their accusers are, and once incarcerated can only hope
to escape from the nauseating dungeons and other dreadful
hardships by voluntarily accusing themselves. In
particular, the Jews know the severity of this tribunal;
they are never given entrance to the city without first
appearing before it. From what I have heard, there is little
that is gracious about Santa Maria delle Grazie; and she
certainly does not bestow her graces liberally on those who
enter her sanctuary.*

Ilsa was amused. "He's playing with the word *grazie* from
the name of the church. It means graces in Italian. But did
Mozart speak Italian?"

"Absolutely," I replied. "He and his sister were started on
languages by their father when they were very young: Latin,
German, French, and Italian. And later in his life, Mozart studied English, very possibly with the intention of emigrating to
England."

Through the tinted glass of the sedan, I could see the
cupola of Saint Peter's in the distance. "We should try to get
through this text before we arrive," I said as I continued.

*Today Papa and I passed Saint Vincent's Hospital for
lunatics, those inmates who lose their senses when a full
moon appears. Some wail, some howl, others foam at the
mouth. It is said that many were infants, left under the
full moon while their parents planted crops at night. The
farmers here follow the lunar calendar and have all
kinds of superstitious customs.*

Ilsa interjected, "That makes me think for a second. Wasn't it a full moon two nights ago when the housekeeper was killed?"

I nodded, but Ilsa could see I was becoming impatient. "Do you think there really are such things as lunatics?" she asked.

"Any bartender in the world will tell you that whenever there's a full moon every crazy person in town shows up." But I insisted, "Let me finish."

*January 23, 1773*

*My opera, Lucio Silla, has been a grand success: the public was jubilant and the singers ecstatic. And the most famous castrato in the opera, Venanzio Rauzzini, asked me to write a work for him to sing on the feast day of Saint Anthony to the text "Exsultate, jubilate." His exquisite soprano voice is so splendid, so smooth, so liquid, so warm. For him, I wrote something out-of-the-ordinary, a work he will never forget.*

*It makes me very sad to see Papa so discouraged, sad to see his pain, sad to see that everything he has planned for my career is going up in smoke. This is not the first time. Last year, after my opera Ascanio was such a success, Papa hoped Archduke Ferdinand would engage me as court composer in Milan. For a long time it seemed likely, there were diplomatic signals indicating all was going well. And what a dream it would have been to live in Italy with Mama and Nannerl!*

*This time, Papa is awaiting word from Archduke Leopold in Florence as to whether I will be engaged there. We were supposed to be back in Salzburg already, but Papa is pretending he has rheumatism and cannot get out of bed so we can stay longer in Milan as we await word from the Florentine court. But I sense it is a lost cause; I can feel it in the air, see it in the faces of diplomats and court officials who are our friends: there will be no appointment. Papa suspects the empress is behind our continued bad luck, that she has poisoned the*

*well. If I don't receive the appointment this time, he is*
*planning to take me immediately to Vienna to confront*
*her politely but firmly.*
    *It will be sad to leave Italy. Who knows when we*
*will ever return?*

As I finished the last word of my diary, it was strange to
think of Mozart leaving Italy, never again to return, just as I was
beginning to enjoy the translucent light of the Roman sun and
the splendid expanse of a cloudless, blue Italian sky. Knowing
that I had reached the end of the diary, I felt a certain nostalgia,
since an unusual chapter in my life was ending with it.

The drive toward Rome presented a new world, with views
of herds of sheep grazing on vast rolling hills. And the light created a limpid, lucid effect not found anywhere north of the Alps,
magnifying and enhancing the novelty of this land apart. The
proud cupola of Saint Peter's towered over an ocean of subdued
stone and terracotta *palazzi,* as if holding court amid a thousand
faithful devoted. As our car entered the city, we were suddenly
in the midst of a three-dimensional tableau of Renaissance facades and timeless monuments.

Despite the general noise and confusion of the traffic, the
city stretched out majestically, barely acknowledging this latest
intrusion into its walls. Postcard views of stone and stucco raced
past, one after another: the impenetrable fortress walls of the
Vatican, the white marble wedding-cake monument to Victor
Emmanuel III, Isola Tiberina, sculpted to make it seem a massive boat on the Tiber, and the remarkable Castel Sant'Angelo,
whose solemn circular design suggested the timeless architecture
of the Ming tombs. Almost too much to see, too much to as-
similate: the menacing walls of the Colosseum, the triumphal
arches of a dozen ancient wars, the ornate cupolas of a hundred
baroque churches.

Ilsa was in a radiant mood, basking in the excitement and
pageantry of centuries. "Have you ever been in Santa Maria
Maggiore?" she asked.

"Yes," I replied, "but only in the church, never in the guest quarters."

"We're very lucky," she said. "They're reserved for high-ranking clergy." As we drove up to a magnificent complex, I realized we could only be arriving at Santa Maria Maggiore. Two domes and a solid Romanesque campanile towered above us, and the *piazza* in front was dominated by the highest Corinthian pillar I had ever seen, topped by a metal sculpture of the Madonna and Child. We drove around the complex and I soon realized that the back, with a semicircular facade topped by four marble saints, was even more beautiful, overlooking an Egyptian obelisk and manicured lawn surrounded by brightly colored roses and bedding plants.

"When Mozart was in Rome in 1770," I said to Ilsa, "he was granted an audience here with Pope Clement XIV. From what I gather, we must be staying in what used to be the summer residence of the popes."

Ilsa smiled, listening keenly. "Mozart heard a choral work in Rome," I continued. "A *Miserere* by Allegri, that was performed only in the Sistine Chapel; making a copy of it was prohibited under pain of excommunication. After listening to it, Mozart returned to his lodgings and wrote it down, all nine voices, from memory. And instead of excommunicating him, the pope made him a Knight of the Golden Spur. When Mozart came to his audience here at Santa Maria Maggiore, he was wearing the golden star around his neck."

After the driver brought the sedan to a stop, he lowered the tinted glass partition that separated us and spoke softly. "We have to be very discreet. We were told it doesn't look good to have so many private guests in the church quarters."

As three porters began unloading the baggage, I surveyed the magnificent architecture of this splendid jewel in a splendid setting. When I looked for my briefcase, I realized the driver had already removed it from the car. "Not that one," I insisted. "It stays with me."

But it astonished me how rapidly he had managed to take

it. Under my breath, I said to Ilsa, "He grabbed my briefcase so quickly, I didn't even see him."

"You're in Rome now," she replied, "so don't *ever* leave a bag unattended."

As our luggage was carried in, I said goodbye to Ilsa and her grandmother and entered the protective walls of the residence. The massive solidity of the doors guarded a stable, reclusive world that lay behind them. Once inside, I concluded that it had been a good decision to have us all come to Santa Maria Maggiore after what happened at La Favorite. It was clear we couldn't be in a safer place.

Following the porters to my room, I suspected the remodeling of the quarters had just barely been completed before our arrival: the air was still fresh with the smell of paint, and here and there traces of powdered plaster peeked out surreptitiously from between the floorboards. But the overall effect of the renovation was magnificent, with freshly stuccoed fifteen-foot ceilings and frescoes restored so well that they looked as if they had just been painted. And the spacious reception rooms I passed, with massive mirrors in carved gold frames and imposing crystal chandeliers, confirmed that this was no monastic retreat of the popes, but a genuine palace built to indulge their luxurious tastes.

As we entered my suite, I was struck by the spaciousness of the rooms, bathed in a limpid, transparent light. Scattered about the walls were paintings of Roman ruins and landscapes and above the double bed, gazing down protectively, was a splendid gold leaf and painted crucifix.

All the elements worked together effortlessly to convey a sense of safety, as if the church provided an umbrella of security and calm. And various features—small, exquisite gifts placed throughout both rooms and in the bath—enhanced the receptive atmosphere. On the antique commode was a large basket with all kinds of dates, figs, cheeses, and crackers, in addition to several bottles of brut *spumante*. In the marble bathroom was a hammered metal box full of fragrant soaps, shampoos, and perfumed bath oil.

And an arrangement of fresh flowers brightened up the sideboard, a card from the viscount saying how much he enjoyed meeting me, with a verse he had apparently written himself:

> From earnest welcomes of first meeting,
> To undiscovered paths and ends,
> There's nothing like the quest for beauty,
> With laughter and the love of friends.

The viscount's allusion to friendship made the job of unpacking and settling into new quarters decidedly more pleasant. In the closet, my tuxedo hung, newly cleaned and pressed, and I realized that Philippe must have had it delivered ahead of time from La Favorite. And throughout the apartment, there were abundant reminders of the extraordinary organization of René de Laguerelle and his staff. A folded, gold-embossed note card from Philippe caught my eye, announcing that cocktails would be at 7:30 P.M., with dinner at nine, which would give me just enough time to take a walk and reacquaint myself with the basilica adjacent to the guest quarters.

Eager to get out and see something exceptional, I entered the portals of the remarkable church, a virtual treasure house of religious art, and my attention was immediately drawn to the massive, shimmering *caissonée* ceiling with intricate carved detail in gold, dominated by the vast coat of arms of Pope Alexander VI. Under my feet stretched perhaps the most remarkable pavement I had ever seen, of porphyry and serpentine, with delicate mosaics of such variety and detail that it seemed more like an antique Kermanshah carpet knotted by the tiniest of hands. And around the entire nave was a broad frieze of gold and green mosaic with hints of subtle reds and blues. But above stood perhaps the most splendid artwork of all: more than two dozen panels of delicate, slender figures in mosaic, silently proclaiming their sovereignty.

Two tall rows of gray-white columns carried my eye toward the baldachin, a massive canopy carved entirely of wine-red marble and emblazoned with the miter of the pope and the keys to the kingdom. As I stood back, surveying the serenity and splendor of the scene, a solitary figure in a side chapel caught my eye: Hélène Benoit, seated in front of the flame of a single tapered candle. My instincts told me not to interrupt but I was nevertheless drawn to join her.

When I knelt next to her, Hélène did not seem to notice. Staring at the solitary flickering candle, a compelling wish passed through my mind: that Hélène would make it through the turbulent period she was experiencing. After I sat back in the pew, I looked at her—she was motionless and without emotion, caught up in another world. In a gesture completely out of character, I rested my palm gently on her folded hands. Her reaction was totally unexpected. Tears began to run down her cheeks, and within seconds Hélène was struggling to hold back an outburst of sobbing. Spartanlike, she managed to regain her composure as we sat together, silent witnesses to her pain.

Hélène finally spoke softly. "I can accept that it's over," she said. "I lit a candle to say farewell forever to my marriage, and I'm waiting for it to burn out." We again sat in silence until she spoke. "What you said that night at La Favorite was a great help to me. I loved him so deeply, I always felt I could make our marriage work. But you made me realize that someone can abuse you by simply refusing to give you anything emotionally."

Watching the single taper, now almost extinguished, I was reminded of Alison Teal and the abusive relationship with von Horvach that was apparently still burning. Hélène smiled stoically as the candle went out. Sighing deeply, she said, "Enough is enough. Let's have a look around."

A tour group passed as we walked through the church and we eavesdropped on a young woman with a thick Italian accent who was leading the group. "One of the four major basilicas in Rome," she intoned. "You see an ensemble of many of the oldest mosaics in Christian art, dating from the fifth century. Fifteen centuries of the finest artists have contributed to the beauty. The ceiling is said to have been leafed with the first gold to arrive from America."

"Tour groups are not for me," Hélène whispered. "I like to

discover things on my own." I nodded and we continued in the other direction without speaking, exploring a realm that seemed endless both in size and in imagination, where every new step was a new experience. A black wrought-iron gate led us to a huge baptismal font where a golden Christ and two cherubs kept silent vigil. We wandered past a tomb adorned with translucent alabaster panels, theatrically lit from behind to reveal the subtleties of the grain, and continued past gilded angels effortlessly carrying an ideal church, a detailed fantasy of utopian architecture.

Our descent into the crypt under the marble canopy brought us face-to-face with an ecstatic marble pope, larger than life, praying on a cushioned stool, his expression frozen, looking out on a miniaturized world of tiny sculptures in tiny niches. Emerging from the cavern below, we were drawn to the focal point of the church, a dome entirely covered with mosaics of Christ and the Madonna, a work of incomparable beauty.

Bringing me back abruptly from the sublime world into which I had been transported, Hélène gently reminded me, "It's time for us to start back." Quietly, she led me toward the rear of the church, where there was a private entrance to the guest quarters. In the distance, the voice of the tour guide continued to echo, until silenced by the thud of the heavy wooden doors of the guest quarters closing behind us.

Before leaving Hélène, I said, "It's going to be pretty difficult to top the spectacular evenings we had at La Favorite. Our expectations are so high, it will be like going to the Arctic and expecting Saint Bernards to appear with brandy around their necks every time we fall in the snow."

"Believe me," she said as we parted, "knowing the viscount, we can only expect more, never less."

# CHAPTER 10

*We cannot have heroes to dine with us. There are none.*
—ANTHONY TROLLOPE

Getting dressed for dinner was a rush, partly due to the excursion through the inexhaustible recesses and corners of Santa Maria Maggiore. Finding my cuff links, studs, and cummerbund took more time in new surroundings, and occasional surprises were waiting: when I pulled open the doors of the wardrobe, I found that my tuxedo from La Favorite had been removed, replaced with a white dinner jacket and black trousers in the lightest of gabardines.

Arriving in the reception rooms barely fifteen minutes late, I was again astonished by how few of the guests I knew or recognized. In the right corner of the room was the *ravissante* Nicoletta Chigi, but this time there was a new presence with her, an extraordinarily good-looking man, who would have been as appropriately dressed in the costume of a swashbuckling pirate as in the elegant silk dinner jacket he was wearing: Maximilian De Angelis. After hearing so much about him, I realized that everything people said was an understatement. And as a couple, he and Nicoletta were electrifying, generating the kind of attention and excitement I would have associated only with Jacqueline Kennedy and JFK, or Wallis Simpson and the Duke of Windsor.

"A special cocktail for you," I heard behind me. Jano, with all his former exuberance and generosity, handed me a tall fluted glass. "Champagne, kiwi juice, gin, and grenadine."

He continued, whispering, "And tomorrow night, I heard from the sous-chef, the champagne cocktail will be with Chambord, Grand Marnier, and Sicilian blood oranges."

"You always manage to know the things I like, Jano," I said. "How did it go with Philippe?"

"Well, he wasn't convinced, but at least he didn't fire me," he said. "I explained everything just the way you told me. And it turns out that Prince von Horvach is lucky, because I'm his only alibi. It would have been pretty bad for him—the samples of body fluids they found could be identified because he doesn't believe in using condoms."

"Based on his past," I said, "there would have been a very strong case against him if you hadn't come forward."

Our conversation was interrupted by the splendid appearance of Elisabetta von Stahl, who dismissed Jano icily. "I'd like a glass of champagne," she said. "*If* you don't mind." He snapped into action and I found myself staring at a remarkable older woman who had been transformed by the Italian air and light. The hair that had once been lifted up around her head was now falling freely in a remarkably modern cut. Her previous elegant, dignified evening dress was replaced by a gown of soft coral that cascaded around her shoulders, draping her like a Hellenic goddess. And her neck, once adorned in pearls, was bare, with a scalloped V neckline that seemed to descend almost to her navel. But in particular, the suppleness of her face and skin made her look infinitely younger.

When she realized I was astonished, she laughed. "I had an Italian husband for eight years. Every time I come to Rome, something wonderful happens to me."

Elisabetta tactfully broached a sensitive issue. "I know you like Andreas Wolff a lot. You'll be happy to know he's doing fine and will be rejoining us tomorrow evening."

A sigh of relief spoke volumes to Elisabetta. "But what should I say to him?" I asked.

She smiled. "Act as if nothing happened."

Her advice floored me, and I was annoyed, particularly after having discovered Wolff practically dead in his hotel room. Regardless of how the guests of the foundation behaved, I had to know what drove Wolff to such a desperate act, and why he decided to drag me into it by handing me his suicide note.

Looking over at Nicoletta and Maximilian, Elisabetta said, "It looks as if they're holding court."

"A spectacular couple," I replied.

"Frankly," she said, "I don't envy either of them. Everyone says he's mixed up with organized crime. And although she comes from one of the wealthiest families in Europe, she's penniless. *Penniless.* Her brother inherited everything and cut her out of his will."

"Why did he do that?" I asked.

"Well, he was always rather fragile—precarious mental health. And he adored his sister, that's the irony. But as beautiful and fascinating as she may be, she's capable of unbelievable cruelty. Her vanity and selfishness emerge with such ferocity, most men never recover."

"It amazes me," I continued, "because I spoke with her one evening and didn't get that impression at all." But I recalled Jano's manner when he hesitated to introduce me to Nicoletta that first night, and Enrique's comments, suggesting a darker side.

"A real paradox of a personality," Elisabetta replied. "She's warm, spontaneous, and genuinely kind to others; I've heard it said she would give you the shirt off her back. Yet at the same time, she has a kind of pathological coldness toward men."

"And her fiancé—Maximilian De Angelis—how is he going to handle her?"

Elisabetta smiled knowingly. "He'll manage."

An unexpected surge of disappointment swept over me. "What I don't understand," I said, "is how Nicoletta, coming from such a distinguished family, could get involved with someone notorious."

"Many people think it's to spite her brother," Elisabetta replied, flashing a smile. "But the simple truth is that criminals are fascinating people."

For a second, my attention wandered to the other side of the room, where von Horvach was deep in discussion with Braun. "You can always judge a man by the company he keeps." The deep, nasal voice of Dennis Landry resonated in my ear, as he caught me looking at the two men. "Oh, sorry," he said with a slightly wicked smile, "did I startle you?"

Looking around quickly for Elisabetta, I realized she had departed as soon as she saw Landry coming. "I've been thinking about you," Landry continued. "My editorial committee could use a consultant with your expertise. When can we talk privately?"

"Any time you like," I replied, trying not to appear too eager. It sounded like my big chance.

"After the concert tonight, then," he said. "Come up to my apartment. I have something interesting to show you. But don't let Braun see you leave."

On that cryptic note, Landry smiled and departed as suddenly as he had appeared, leaving me uncomfortably eager and curious. But there was hardly time to react as Philippe, speaking Italian with an unmistakable French accent, announced in a stentorian tone, "The distinguished gentlemen and ladies are requested to take their places at table."

The atmosphere was different from La Favorite: less stiff, more playful—totally Italian. The night air, imbued with the scent of Roman pines, was intoxicating, and the sound of cicadas provided a resonant background to the animated chatter of the guests. And in the dining room, candlelight began to replace the waning light in the sky, which was taking on deep tones of Pompeian rust and Mediterranean blue.

Seated at my left was Nadine, wearing the softest pastel aquamarine silk in a simple cut, her shoulders veiled in transparent voile, as if inspired by the costume of a ballerina. On my right, I was astounded to see Maximilian De Angelis—impressive and debonair—nodding a greeting to me before returning to his conversation with the woman beside him.

"There's something I've wanted to ask you," Nadine began almost immediately. "I'll tell you why later. Can you tell me the kinds of things Mozart did during his concerts when he toured Europe as a young boy?"

"Well," I said, "they were a bit of a circus—more like a sideshow than what we would call a concert today. Often they would open with one or two movements of a symphony he had written and end with the remaining movements. In between, he would do all kinds of things to astonish people, like playing scores in different clefs, transposing compositions at sight, and improvising on themes suggested by members of the audience. Once, I believe, they picked up a second violin part and turned it upside down to make a melody for him to improvise fugues. But why do you ask?"

Nadine laughed. "Because Andrei was rather upset the other day and told me the viscount had asked him to re-create a typical Mozart concert. Andrei was obliged to turn him down— something that's not very easy to do—and protested, 'Unfortunately, Mozart was one of a kind!'"

I looked around the dinner table quickly to see where Andrei was seated, but there was no trace of him. "He's not here," Nadine volunteered. "He's performing tonight and didn't want to eat beforehand. By the way," she continued, "I'm sorry you had the terrible experience of finding Denise's body in the courtyard."

As the gruesome memory flashed through my mind, my face reflected how disturbing I found the event. Nadine continued, "The police told me what happened at La Favorite with your briefcase. My uncle said to let you know you're welcome to leave your diary in the safe if you wish."

"To tell you the truth, it's beginning to sound like a good idea."

"If you need help authenticating it, I just heard about an excellent optical laboratory in Chicago. The scientist who runs it uses polarized light and scanning electron microscopes to identify the molecular composition and then compares it with the century in question. In fact, he was the man who proved that the Vinland map of a flat world was a twentieth-century fraud."

When Nadine saw that I was interested, she added, "I can get his name and address from my colleague Ingrid, in Munich, who told me about the lab—I met her at a conference where I was giving a paper."

Our conversation caught Maximilian's attention, and he looked over casually and smiled. "How are you doing these days, Nadine?"

She laughed softly. "I'm doing well. Thanks, Max. But you just saw me ten days ago in Berlin. In fact, I was surprised to find you in the audience, uninvited, in the midst of all those crime enforcement officials. Don't you think it was a little like the devil attending the pope's election?"

Maximilian flashed a good-natured, slightly guilty smile. "You flatter me, Nadine."

Sensing a hint of hostility brewing between the two, I interjected, "Hardly anyone believes in God anymore, so I imagine that goes for the devil as well."

With an ambiguous smile, Maximilian looked me directly in the eye and said, "I believe in the devil, don't you?"

For a moment I didn't know if Maximilian was serious or joking. He continued, "It's certainly more reliable than believing in God." Point-blank, he asked me, "Don't you believe in the devil?"

I didn't know what to say. Finally, I replied, "I suppose if the devil were to exist, he would fit Shakespeare's description in *King Lear*: 'The Prince of Darkness is a gentleman.' What do you think, Nadine?"

"I imagine he would be someone rather attractive," she replied. "Like Max, except completely without morals."

Maximilian apparently enjoyed sparring with her. "What is a moral person, anyway? For me, there are only two kinds of people in this world—interesting and boring. And interesting people are full of all kinds of nasty ideas."

"What are you implying, Max? That you don't believe in morals?" Nadine asked.

"Why should I?" he replied with a cavalier grin. "I can afford not to."

To my surprise, Nadine laughed at his bon mot and continued. "And I imagine the devil today would be a very clever, imaginative criminal."

"Well," Maximilian replied, "that leaves me out. A criminal

is someone without a clever accountant and good legal council, and I have both."

We were interrupted by the commotion of a dozen waiters descending on the table with plates of green and white linguine in a sauce of salmon, topped with caviar. "Food comes first, then morals," Maximilian quipped.

With that, Max resumed the conversation with the woman on his right, and Nadine looked at me, a little exasperated. "Well, it's good to know at least one person will benefit from my paper in Berlin."

Curious, I asked, "What was your talk about?"

"In rem proceedings," she replied. "A tool that's being used against international crime syndicates."

When she realized I wasn't familiar with the term, she explained, "It's a legal device that makes it possible to confiscate property—cars, boats, houses, planes—anything involved in illegal activities. We've been using it in America and we're trying to convince other countries to pass legislation allowing it. But to tell you the truth, it's all a bit discouraging. In Louisiana, policemen were arresting law-abiding citizens for offenses like failing to signal a turn, then selling their cars for a college fund for their own children."

"That's outrageous," I said.

"Plus, despite all the things we're doing, we never seem to get the kingpins, the ones who are running the show." She nodded toward Max. "Lately, criminals have gotten a big jump on all the new technology—you know, money laundering using mobile encrypted phones and the Internet. But I'm convinced it's only going to take one unexpected little slipup on their part and we'll see an entire house of cards come crashing down."

Again our conversation was broken off by a flurry of waiters, this time descending on the table with plates of sliced roulade of pheasant and white truffles. The man on Nadine's left diverted her attention and I looked over to Maximilian, only to find him looking me directly in the eye, as if he had been waiting. "I'm afraid my sense of right and wrong is a little more avant-garde than Nadine's," he said. "But she's never really understood the totally unacceptable realities of capitalism. International finance today is an intellectual dance, and legal loopholes are the musical accompaniment. If I wanted to be controversial, I might even say that criminality is the drumbeat that keeps everything moving. You don't have anything against someone being a little controversial, I hope?"

"It depends," I replied.

Max continued, "In my opinion, when a person ceases to be controversial, he ceases to live."

"Playing devil's advocate makes for good conversation," I replied. "But it sounds like you're defending crime."

Maximilian smiled as if he had spent a great deal of time thinking about the subject. "It's a simple matter of terminology. If you define crime as breaking the law, then everyone on this planet is a criminal. But crime to one person is simply good business sense to another. And regardless of what you call it, it's something that requires all the things people want to have: intelligence, daring, skill, even courage. Of course, everything's relative. We immortalize figures like Hannibal, Julius Caesar, and Napoleon. They broke the law on a grander scale than all the criminals in our prisons today. But they were successful, and our society idolizes success."

"To tell you the truth," I said, "I don't have much experience with the world of finance. I've spent a lifetime in the world of artists and academia."

"Well," he continued, "then you probably understand what I'm saying better than anyone. An artist will beg, borrow, or even steal from anybody in order to finish his work. So you could say that artists are criminals at heart. And on the other hand, I imagine, criminals can be artists, with crime becoming a form of creative expression—an aesthetic activity, a stimulation of the intellect."

Nadine had been listening to our conversation, and as the dessert arrived her expression gave me the distinct impression she had heard enough. Maximilian must have sensed her disapproval, yet he continued his eulogy of vice. "The society we live in is totally hypocritical. Everyone admires wealth and success, but those things don't just happen without having to take risks,

risks that can sometimes be construed as immoral, or even illegal."

Nadine responded coolly. "But certainly there are more essential things in this world than wealth and success—like fairness, trust, honesty. Self-respect."

Maximilian replied bluntly, "The most essential element in this world is money, and all morality should proceed from that fact."

"You're saying it's irrelevant how money is made," Nadine continued, visibly angered. "That prostitution and drugs are just another business venture."

Disguising his mild annoyance with a smile, Maximilian replied, "We'd all be better off if people like you stopped trying to save the world from crimes it doesn't want to be saved from."

Nadine countered instantly, raising her voice. "And what if the prostitutes are eight years old? And sale of AK-47s to street gangs? Where does it all stop? Biological and chemical weapons for dictators? Nuclear technology to terrorists?"

Just when it looked like Max and Nadine were about to embark on overt hostility, I stood up abruptly. My gesture succeeded in shaking both protagonists from their mortal stance of fight or flight and each instinctively retreated to a more casual social posture, narrowly avoiding a scene that would have marred the carefully planned evening. Without a word to either of them, I turned and headed immediately into the music room, not looking back.


Hushed anticipation swept through the music room as the electric lights were extinguished, leaving hundreds of candles flickering in antique Murano glass sconces and mirrors. The intense silence that ensued was almost out of character for a roomful of guests who never seemed to stop talking. But the narrowly averted altercation with Nadine and Max made the atmosphere feel more disturbing than evocative, and I was already preoccupied with slipping out unnoticed after the concert, in keeping with Landry's peculiar request.

As the first violinist signaled the orchestra to tune, I glanced at the simple gray and gold program to see the music for the evening: an animated piece by Mozart, the Symphony in A Major, K. 201, would begin, followed by the Piano Concerto in A Major, K. 488, a buoyant masterwork with a profound, dark slow movement.

The lively opening symphony was full of high spirits and wit—exactly what I needed. After the symphony, Andrei arrived on the platform with his dark and distinguished good looks and launched the ensemble immediately into the dazzling virtuosity of the first movement of the A major concerto. The rapidity and lightness of his scales were exciting, but the unique attribute Andrei brought to this occasion was the personal fire he managed to generate on the fortepiano.

Before the beginning of the slow movement—the famous *Sicilienne*—the unrelenting flickering of candles seemed even more somber and melancholy than before, as some of their flames, reflected in facets of glass chandeliers and sconces, had finished burning and were swallowed up, diminishing the light almost imperceptibly. After a brief moment of silence, Andrei began his eloquent solo on the fortepiano and within the first few notes, we were immersed in a world of exotic places and distant perfumes. The stately rhythm of the dark, brooding movement evoked a vast microcosm in a universe full of turbulent emotions suspended between despair and hope, with all the sublime resonance of night music. The title evoked faint echoes of Sicily, a land apart, conquered and dominated in succession by cultured Greeks, dark, esoteric Arabs from the coast of Africa, blue-eyed Normans, and swarthy Spaniards.

With his warm, sultry tone, Andrei transformed the instrument into a singer gifted with the agility of large vocal leaps, and the plucked notes of the strings became the solitary accompaniment of a guitar under an expansive canopy of stars—a serenade on a cool summer night as a desperate lover made a final plea to his beloved: "Come, the boat is ready." Each time the haunting melody returned, Andrei added a delicate variation, as had been done in the eighteenth century, an era when singers and instrumental artists were also composers trained to embellish each performance with their own personal touch and flair. The young pianist became an active partner in Mozart's conception, taking us on an excursion into penumbral tonalities ideal for darker visions and inflections of mood.

Plaintive, seductive woodwinds and muted strings followed, renewing a pathos of smoldering passions and tragic eloquence, and I understood that Mozart had used a formal courtly dance to disguise an interior world of Latin passion, jealousy, and desire. And with turbulent waves of sound, Mozart, the classicist, was again revealing himself as an unrepentant romantic.

At the conclusion of the concerto, the applause reverberated with approval, admiration, and even gratitude. It soon became a stampede, with guests applauding with their feet as well. The women in the audience in particular did not want Andrei to leave the stage and each time he returned, he was met by new and more approval. With each bow, his face radiated with the satisfaction of an artist whose outpouring of passion had found resonance in like souls.

As guests gradually began to move toward the library for cordials and espresso, I waited cautiously for the right moment to escape from the crowd for my appointment with Landry. My heightened apprehension made it seem as if eyes everywhere were watching. When the time was right, I ducked into an adjoining room. Heading up to Landry's apartment, I reassured myself that my departure had been undetected. But it hadn't. As I would find out, nothing in the foundation ever went unnoticed.

# CHAPTER 11

*. . . the devil took [Jesus] to a very high mountain, and*
*showed him all the kingdoms of the world and their*
*glory; and said to him, "All these things will I give you,*
*if you fall down and worship me."*
—BOOK OF MATTHEW 4:8–9

The silent labyrinthine corridors leading to the deserted upper
floor contrasted with the sounds of distant chatter coming from
the music room, resonating in the summer air. My initial muffled knock did not bring Landry to his door, but after a second
one, the door opened slowly.

"Oh yes. Good evening," he said, as if he had forgotten our
appointment. Shaking my hand firmly, he closed the door behind us. "You're much younger than I realized," he said. "Do you
mind my asking your age?"

"Thirty-five," I replied, not knowing what to expect.

"A good age to finally experience some of the success you
deserve. I imagine it's hard for a junior colleague like yourself to
make a name in a tight, closed field like Mozart studies."

"Well," I replied, "as you know, younger scholars have to be
around for decades before anyone takes them seriously."

"Where did you go to school?" Landry asked. Immediately
I recognized the tiresome game he was playing: trying to establish some kind of pecking order. "Boston College," I replied,
playing along with his script. "And Brandeis for my doctorate."

A smug expression spread across his face, which I assumed
meant he had studied at Yale, Princeton, or Harvard. "It's about
time you joined the ranks of the major players. I have a list here
of the members of the editorial committee of my new *Mozart
2006* and I'm sure you'll recognize some of them." The sheet he
handed me was the actual printed cover page of his edition with
twelve of the most distinguished Mozart scholars in the world,

a virtual celestial hierarchy. It was overwhelmingly flattering to be considered to join such illustrious company but the nagging suspicion persisted: Why me?

I tried to probe Landry without insulting him. "It's an honor to be considered, but does it have anything to do with the diary I recently purchased?"

"Well, actually, yes. I like your directness. Your name had come up before, but when the librarian of the Mozarteum informed us about your discovery, we decided we might try you out."

"The diary has already been submitted to another editor. Is that a problem?" I asked.

"Not really. You'll have to withdraw it, but that can be done easily when the time is right." Turning his back to me to open his briefcase, he said, "But we're jumping the gun." For a second, my attention was diverted to several crumpled pieces of paper in his wastebasket and I found myself glancing at them out of the corner of my eye, dumbfounded. With the same pasted letters of various shapes and sizes, one sheet was identical in style to the anonymous notes Alison Teal and I had received at La Favorite, while the other was unmistakably a newspaper clipping. Barely I could make out most of two large words, "EGG——" and "PARTRI——."

Not noticing my reaction, Landry flipped through papers and continued, "I have something here I'd like you to look at. It purports to be a diary from 1770 by a Neapolitan noblewoman and mentions Mozart. Examine it for a few days and give me your conclusions about its authenticity. Since I'm only giving you a photocopy, you'll have to base your decision solely on style and content. And I'll have to insist on strict secrecy. Are you in agreement?"

"I certainly am," I replied. "But what do you mean by strict secrecy?"

"There have been some interesting discoveries made lately," he answered, lowering his voice slightly. "And our profession is fiercely competitive, so I wouldn't want this information to fall into the wrong hands. No one else is to see or hear about it."

"Agreed," I said.

Landry continued, "Of course, I want you to know that, if all goes well, this will not be a token appointment. The *Mozart 2006* is supported by a corporation that has substantial financial assets and they're willing to invest considerable sums to guarantee that it will be the premier work of its kind in history. If I'm satisfied with your comments, I'm planning to offer you ninety thousand dollars a year—I'm sure that would be a nice supplement to your salary as a junior professor."

For a split second, it felt as if my hearing had shut down. I was not able to respond, and the recollection of my last eight scholarly articles flashed before my eyes: thousands of hours spent researching and writing for which I had not received a cent. It had seemed as if musicology would always offer that kind of financial compensation.

Landry interrupted my silence. "I believe professional consultants in musicology should be paid just as well as in any other field of business or finance."

"Totally honored," I finally blustered. "It would be a privilege to examine your documents." As we said good night, Landry escorted me to the door and I caught a momentary last glimpse of his wastebasket with my peripheral vision.

Back in my apartment, I opened a chilled bottle of dry Cartizze *spumante* and stretched out comfortably in an armchair to reflect on the day's events. Landry's proposition was thrilling, but the day exhausted me far too much to begin an examination of the new diary. And it was not the prospect of being a member of the board of the *Mozart 2006* that held my attention: I was at a loss to put out of my mind the anonymous note in Landry's wastebasket. As I climbed into bed, I decided I would ask Philippe for a Bible in English with a keyword index and try to make sense out of all the quotations. As sleep began to overtake me, the same question returned obsessively to my mind: Who exactly was sending the notes . . . and why?

Waking up rested at eight o'clock was a genuine novelty. Visiting Landry, instead of burning the candle at both ends and drinking cognac with the viscount's guests until two in the morning, had guaranteed I would be in bed at a reasonable hour. For a change, I prepared myself for breakfast without having to rush.

But the crisp oversized envelope with Landry's "Naples diary" was too tempting to resist, and I carefully removed the eight photocopied pages. A brief note from Landry indicated that the writer of the diary was the Duchess Bianca di San Felice, who had lived from 1734 to 1785, and the handwritten date on the first page read June 10, 1770.

Seventeen seventy. According to my calculations, that would make her thirty-six years old, and Mozart, fourteen. Her handwriting was remarkably legible, even artistic, and I scanned the pages rapidly for the name Mozart. Immediately, on the first page, a lengthy passage began in which the composer's name, spelled "Mozzart," could be found again and again.

As I returned the pages to the envelope and buried it in a drawer, I considered the possibility that Landry was setting me up to be taken in by a fake. Just before leaving my apartment, I remembered the Bible with the concordance and called Philippe. Cold and professionally aloof as always, he assured me he would find one. "Such a strange request," he added ironically before he hung up, barely disguising his curiosity.

Locating the rooms where breakfast was being served was easy, as the unmistakable aroma of freshly ground Italian espresso beans saturated the corridors. At a table near the window, Manfred Braun was absorbed in reading a newspaper, the *Neues Salzburger Tagblatt*. Seated at a table near him were Andrei and Caroline Weidener in the midst of an animated conversation with Véronique Ibsen. Wearing his tails, and with a bow tie dangling around his neck, Andrei was feasting on poached eggs with salmon and red caviar. The ladies were still dressed in gowns from the previous evening, and I concluded that they had not gone to bed after Andrei's concert.

"They had me playing until five A.M.," Andrei said, sipping a glass of champagne with a splash of orange juice. "Slave drivers."

He was clearly the man of the hour after his extraordinary concert. Véronique was ecstatic about his performance. "I've never heard anything like it. And around 3:00 A.M., after everyone had gone to bed, Andrei began to improvise in the style of Mozart—rondos, variations, andantes. Caroline and I sat for hours listening—it was pure genius."

"That's too much," Andrei protested. "I'm just too lazy to learn all the notes from memory. It's much easier to make up new ones."

"Typically humble," Caroline replied.

"Sometimes an artist has a right to be proud, even arrogant," I said.

Véronique added, "And after last night, Andrei, it's not your right but your duty."

Braun folded back his newspaper from Salzburg, oblivious to our conversation, and Andrei noticed an article on one of the pages. "Another Austrian in the news," he said. "A forger murdered in Munich."

Braun looked distractedly for the story Andrei had seen and his face showed a radical transformation. Suddenly serious, his eyes scanned the article with a fierce intensity. "Anyone we know?" Andrei asked. Completely ignoring him, Braun stared into space as if he had just seen a ghost. Then, with a surprising burst of energy, he stood up, overturning his chair.

"I have to leave," he mumbled and rushed out of the room, newspaper in hand.

"What happened?" Caroline asked.

"Something in that article," Véronique said. "Is there another copy of it?"

"Let's see," Andrei replied. He returned in a minute with the same paper and hunted for the article. Translating into English, he summarized it aloud: "An Austrian, Peter Arneis, one of the most renowned forgers of modern times, was found murdered in his apartment on Lake Starnberg outside Munich yesterday. An anonymous tip alerted the police, who arrived at the scene too late to save him.

"Apparently a gangland-style execution," he said. "His

wrists and ankles were bound behind his back and there was a cord leading to a noose around his neck that tightened each time he moved until he strangled."

"Why would they kill someone that way?" Caroline asked.

"Who knows?" Andrei replied. "Let me finish this." Scanning the article, Andrei continued, "The police recovered examples of his work from his apartment, left behind by the killers. All very interesting: whoever killed him didn't have much time to get away, so the police have a lot of clues."

"So why was Braun so upset?" I asked.

"Maybe it was someone he knew," Andrei replied. "Austria is a small country—they might have come from the same town, or gone to school together. In any case, Caroline, it's about time for us to start heading back to get some sleep."

"What are your plans today?" I asked Véronique.

"Catnaps and reading," she replied, smiling demurely. "I'm singing tonight, so nothing too strenuous for me. Some light scales and vocal exercises, *mezza voce*. And of course a manicure and a hot bath. Maybe I'll use that beautiful bath oil the viscount had sent to my room. I've been saving it for a special occasion."

Leaving the weary trio, I climbed the staircase to my apartment, where I discovered Philippe had gotten to work immediately: a reference Bible in English was waiting on my desk. Thumbing through the index, I searched first for "egg——," and in the long list of quotations that followed, the meaning of the second word, "partri——," became clear: "As the partridge sitteth on eggs, and hatcheth them not, so he that getteth riches, and not by right, shall leave them in the midst of his days." The quotation from the Book of Jeremiah was clearly referring to Landry's newly acquired affluence.

Fortunately Philippe had sent me a Catholic Bible, as the quotations for Alison and me—"Weigh thy words in a balance and make a door and bar for thy mouth" and "Open not thine heart to every man"—were from the Book of Ecclesiasticus in the Apocrypha, not part of the Protestant Bible. I began to make a mental list of what the quotations had in common.

All three anonymous notes had been taken from the Old

Testament and shared an intimidating moral tone. But the messages to Alison and me from the Apocrypha were radically different from the admonition to Landry from the Book of Jeremiah. In fact, the first two were strangely similar, as if we were both being warned not to talk too freely about something. Immediately, the thought occurred to me that no one had known Alison was going to take my apartment. Was it possible that the note that so upset her had been intended for me?

But the "Naples diary" was going to take some serious work, so I put aside my reference Bible and rolled up my sleeves, reaching for the envelope Landry had given me. Within seconds, I was being transported into a world that was centuries removed from the events and the situations surrounding me.

*June 10, 1770*

*A remarkable flurry of activity began today with the arrival of the coach of Princess Belmonte, who sent her valet along with an excited note. She and Mrs. Hamilton, along with Princess Francavilla, are sponsoring an academy in the home of Imperial Ambassador Kaunitz that is to rank among the most dazzling receptions ever seen in Naples. The occasion is a concert of the miracle of nature, Mozzart, a Salisburghese, to which the most illustrious and influential members of Neapolitan society are to be invited.*

*Princess Belmonte enlisted my help to create the impression of an indoor garden in the ballroom, filled with huge blooming hydrangeas and splendid potted orange and lemon trees heavy laden with fruit. All the streets leading to the palace are to be illuminated with torches, and large colorful banners will be hung from the windows of the surrounding houses.*

*June 17, 1770*

*After a feverish week of preparations, the long-awaited day arrived. Mozzart entered with his father who walked behind him like a chamberlain to a great personage. Each guest, regardless of how great and distinguished, pressed in breathlessly to catch a glimpse of him. The young prodigy, dressed in an elegant coat of maroon velvet with embroidery and lining in gold, looked like a child prince as he was received by Prime Minister and Marchesa Tanucci and by each of the grandees present.*

*Weeks prior to the reception, fire and smoke had begun to burst forth from the center of Vesuvius, gradually building each successive day to create a remarkable spectacle. But on the night of Mozzart's concert, Vesuvius chose to surpass all expectations, producing a brilliant display rarely before seen. Foreigners and scientists have been coming to the city for months in great numbers to study the unusual phenomenon, and it was taken by all as a great sign of Providence that it would occur the same night the other wonder of nature, Mozzart, gave his concert. A huge flaming pillar of smoke, accompanied by explosions like fireworks, caused a sensation among the guests, as the crater of Vesuvius began throwing out rocks and gases with a brilliant illumination that was both wonderful and terrible at the same time. Mars and the gods of destruction forged their thunderbolts, delighting in the fearsome and breathtaking spectacle.*

*And Mozzart delighted his audience of musical connoisseurs and dilettantes by directing new symphonies and concert arias. But it was his ability to improvise at the keyboard that most astonished us. One after another, professors from the conservatories sang him a theme, to which Mozzart immediately played fugues and canons, some very learned and difficult, inverting the themes and playing the melodies backward. Fantasies, fugues for three voices and for four and five, double fugues: each of his improvisations sparkled, not with the somber and archaic sounds of the academic contrapuntalists, but with the resonance of modern music. The young Mozzart even played variations on a popular Neapolitan street song,*

*with an elegance and brilliance that left everyone*
*charmed and astounded.*

Intrigued by the wealth of detail in this supposed eyewitness account, I tried to recall what Dr. Charles Burney, the
eighteenth-century English music historian, had written about
Vesuvius when he visited Naples in the summer of 1770. Vaguely
I remembered that, together with Hamilton, the British ambassador, Burney had walked to the upper limits of safety of a Vesuvius threatening to erupt, so his account supported the credibility
of Bianca di San Felice's handwritten memoir. And the names in
her diary lent an aura of truth as well: Belmonte, Francavilla,
Tanucci, and Kaunitz were all mentioned in Leopold's travel
notes as people they had encountered during their trip.

Glancing at my watch, I had to make a decision to get
ready immediately or to run late and miss cocktails. But the
diary was too compelling and it was impossible for me to put on
the brakes. Under time pressure, I embarked on translating the
long, florid verse, written in poetic meter, that concluded her
"Mozzart" memoir.

Precocious gift of Nature,
Responsive to the delights of Aphrodite,
The charm of his youth concealing
Vibrant maturity beyond his years,
And the torment of unfulfilled manhood.

Sequestered in the chains of innocence,
His desire locked as if in a prison,
My embraces were his key to freedom.
With candid intimacy he savored my caresses,
Grazing on the fields of passion.

Evanescent and fleeting his innocence, a splendid lily,
Fervent his ardor, a burning fire.
And with the wings of a turtledove
I offered my oblations on the altar
Of the gods of song, the gods of love.

With passionate gratitude he accepted
The soothing intimacy of my offering,
Deepest union of the sublime and the sacred.
Appeasing the raging torrents of manhood,
And abandoning himself to the mystical arts of love.

I began to wonder if I were dreaming. Behind all the florid prose, surprisingly erotic by eighteenth-century standards, it appeared that Bianca di San Felice was suggesting something that would send shock waves throughout the world: that she had given the young Mozart his first sexual experience.

The implications made my head spin. *If the* New York Times *hears about this,* I thought, *it will be instant front-page news around the world.*

My only means to pull up any biographical information on the duchess would be the Internet, but I couldn't find the phone jack, as the telephone cord was disguised beneath wooden moldings. After a brief call to Philippe, I was informed that the jack was hidden behind the draperies. "But you won't be able to make or receive telephone calls while using the line," he admonished me. "And," he continued icily, "you don't have much time before dinner."

Quickly beginning a Net search, I pulled up several obscure biographical references to Bianca di San Felice from Italian articles. Her achievements were particularly remarkable for the eighteenth century, given that women had been excluded from the world of science, politics, art, literature, and music. As a child, Bianca di San Felice had shown enormous religious zeal and later entered the convent of Saint Mark as a novice. She began to have ecstatic visions that alarmed her superiors and ultimately never took her final vows, instead marrying the older Duke Federico di San Felice to whom she bore three children. When she was a young widow, her salon in Naples attracted the most renowned foreigners of the time, including artists, archeologists, painters, scientists, and important statesmen and clergy. Also an accomplished harpsichord player, she composed vocal duets and canzonets found today in manuscript in various Italian collections. In 1785, at age fifty-one, she died in a hospital for wealthy aristocratic ladies with neurasthenia, a term for mental disorders.

There was hardly time to react, as I knew I would have to leave almost immediately for dinner. Yet I suspected more searching on the Net would turn up more information. My hunch proved correct: a recently published newspaper article mentioned her name. The complete Naples diary from which my pages were taken had sold for an astonishing record price at Christie's—over $11 million to an anonymous buyer. But the controversial contents were well documented because potential buyers had been able to examine it before the auction.

Wondering where I had been when all this happened, I scanned the article. Not only had Mozart been initiated by her into the arts of love—according to the Duchess of San Felice—but also Emperor Joseph II of Austria, Prince Anton Kaunitz, Count Firmian of Milan, the famous archaeologist Winckel-mann, and a dozen other renowned figures of the period.

"Damn," I mumbled as I started preparing for dinner. Another disconcerting thought began to challenge the credibility of the revelations of Bianca di San Felice's memoir. Recalling that Winckelmann had been a confirmed homosexual who had been stabbed to death by an Italian man in the context of a sexual encounter, I realized an intimate experience with the duchess would have been highly suspect. And Count Karl Firmian, the plenipotentiary minister of Milan and great patron of Mozart, had never been married and was once described by a contemporary as "organically insensitive to women."

My initial exhilaration about the diary rapidly faded, as I realized that her suggested relationship with Mozart was unlikely, considering that Mozart's father vigilantly guarded his fourteen-year-old son and controlled his every move. Plus, over ten years later, before marrying Constanze Weber, Mozart had written to his father that he had no prior sexual experience. Lost in thought, I had just finished buttoning the studs in my shirt, when a knock on the door startled me. Opening the door, I found a young Italian woman in a housekeeper's uniform staring at me. She informed me that I had a long-distance phone call, but that I would either have to take it downstairs at the major-domo's office or unplug my computer from the telephone line.

"I'll take it up here in a second," I replied absentmindedly. "I forgot to log off." Seconds later, I heard the voice of my land-lady in Boston on the line.

"How are you?" I asked, a bit surprised.

"Well, not so well. I'm afraid I have bad news. Your apart-ment had a break-in early this morning. In fact, the door was just replaced and I'm waiting for the locksmith now."

"What did they get?" I asked.

"Looks like your television and video. Oh, yes, also your computer."

I remembered the diary folio I had left in Boston. "Could you take a quick look in my file drawers?" I asked. "There's a large manuscript page filed under M."

After several painfully long minutes, she returned to the phone. "There are no files. The cabinet drawers are all gone."

I stood in stunned silence. Incredulous, I asked myself if the burglary of the electronic equipment had been to cover up the theft of my diary. And the broken lock on my briefcase the night Denise was murdered returned to haunt me. A torrent of paranoid thoughts raced through my mind, while the admoni-tion of the anonymous note rang out ominously, almost as if to say, *I told you so.* Only Nicoletta Chigi had known that I didn't bring the entire diary with me, and now the folio I left in Boston was gone.

After gathering up the remaining twenty-one folios of my diary, I headed rapidly through the corridors in search of Philippe: it was urgent that I deposit them where they would be absolutely safe—in the viscount's vault.

# CHAPTER 12

*Italia! oh, Italia! thou who hast*
*The fatal gift of beauty.*
—LORD BYRON

As I carried the original diary to Philippe's office, my suspicions returned to Nicoletta Chigi. I decided I was going to have a little chat with her—or more likely, an all-out confrontation.

Philippe led me past ancient cobwebs, through dimly lit basement corridors, to a musty wine cellar containing what looked like a portable bank vault with dozens of security deposit compartments. Explaining that it was commonplace for guests to arrive with valuables, he said, "The ladies who come with many pieces of jewelry feel better knowing there is a place to keep them protected." With the diary safely locked away, Philippe placed the key in my hand and said, icily, "We should go upstairs immediately. Dinner has begun."

It was not difficult to find my place at the huge table, as the only seat remaining was between Andreas Wolff and a young man whose face I did not recognize. Wolff gave me a friendly nod and I tried my best to smile, realizing it was going to be difficult if not impossible to disguise my frayed nerves and bad mood. Instead of picking up my spirits, the animated chatter in the dining room and the amusement on the faces of the guests irritated me. And despite the fact that the windows were wide open, the evening air felt uncomfortably heavy.

The young man seated next to me was talking to Ilsa Paumgarten, and both smiled at me before resuming their conversation. Looking around the table, my eyes fell on Nicoletta, more seductive and radiant than ever, seated not far from her fiancé. Seeing her and Maximilian gave me an uncomfortable jolt as questions raced through my mind and conflicting emotions began surging within me. Feelings of betrayal, and even jealousy.

Andreas Wolff, despite his recent suicide attempt, seemed in surprisingly good form. "I'm sorry for all the problems I caused you," he said immediately. "Will you accept my apology?"

"Of course, Andreas," I said. "But what drove you to do it?"

"If you don't mind," he replied, looking remorseful and un-characteristically humble, "I'd rather not talk about it here. Suffice it to say, I've had some financial problems."

I agreed to respect his wishes and let the matter drop. Despite my dismal mood, it was impossible not to notice the festive dinner table: braided breads with toasted sesame seeds and loaves shaped like roses had been placed around it with a calculated effect. As an army of waiters in costume began to circle the table, Andreas informed me, "We're having a rustic eighteenth-century meal tonight." As part of the pageantry, the waiters distributed large ravioli into soup dishes and began ladling steaming broth from hand-painted *maiolica* tureens.

Dressed in a colorful eighteenth-century costume, the waiter announced as he served, "A broth of capon and quail, with tortellini stuffed with veal and beet greens, ricotta and pine nuts."

As I glanced distractedly at Nicoletta a second time, Wolff observed me quietly and smiled. "She moves a goddess, she looks a queen," he said, reciting some obscure poem.

"But a colder fish was never seen," I responded cynically. Realizing what I had said, I immediately apologized.

"You're not the only one who feels that way," he said. "Sitting next to you is her ex-fiancé, Roberto. He's an architect, and I rather imagine he shares your view. He's been camping out here uninvited, in a sleeping bag on the floor of Ilsa and her grandmother. We all know him. When he and Nicoletta were going together, they were guests of the viscount."

Glancing at Roberto, I was reminded of a lovesick puppy who had followed his master to school. "How did he manage to get in?" I asked.

"God knows," Wolff replied. "Maybe Ilsa let him in

through her window. But it wasn't good for security, and when the viscount got word of it, he invited Roberto to join us."

As I again looked over at Nicoletta, I wondered whether it was possible that the most beautiful, desirable woman in the world could be totally unfeeling, opportunistic, and calculating. Wolff continued, "Well, Nicoletta and Max are certainly center stage tonight. Just look at them. On the outside they appear to be the happiest couple in the world. But nothing could be farther from the truth." I listened in amazement as he went on candidly. "I'll tell you one thing, she hasn't a clue what she's letting herself in for."

"His business dealings?" I asked.

Andreas looked at me with a cryptic smile. "Much more. I know something about Maximilian De Angelis that if she ever found out, there would be no marriage."

Wolff seemed to be playing with my curiosity. And in a perverse way the conversation was pulling me out of my state of mind. "Tell me," I insisted. Just as he leaned over to confide in me, the multicolored army of costumed waiters carrying huge platters interrupted our discussion. Unusual types of roasted fish were carefully served with a vivid green sauce, and almost immediately the sound of silver on porcelain plates began. Before I could resume my conversation with Andreas, Nicoletta's former boyfriend reached over to shake my hand and introduce himself. Although he must have been in his early thirties, his longish ash brown hair and slight beard gave him a more youthful appearance.

"This fish is what Italians call *branzino*," he said. "There's also turbot and sweet water pike. Interesting choice."

"Where are you from?" I asked.

"Rome," he said simply. "How about you?" As he spoke, his blue-gray eyes shimmered with an astonishing intensity.

"Boston," I replied. "I haven't seen too many Italians with blond hair and blue eyes," I continued.

"My mother is from Sicily," Roberto said, smiling. "The Normans conquered Sicily in the eleventh century, so people with blond hair are not at all uncommon."

"Have you known the viscount long?" I asked.

"Several years," he replied. As he spoke, I tugged at my collar without thinking. Roberto noticed the humidity was making me uncomfortable and said, "Women are much luckier than men in weather like this—to be wearing dresses with bare shoulders. But we get back at them in the winter, when it's freezing and their legs are uncovered. Hopefully this humidity won't last long. Can you see how black the sky is over there? We're going to get a real summer storm that will cool everything off."

Several times as he spoke, I noticed his eyes wander to where Nicoletta was sitting, and I wondered what he was thinking. At one moment he stared at her and sighed, "Thou art to me a delicious torment."

"What?" I asked.

After a long silence, he spoke. "I was planning to marry her, but she broke it off. I don't even know what I'm doing here. Sometimes I feel like I'm walking around in a dream."

"Is it too personal to ask why you broke up?"

"I'm still not sure," he replied. "When she moved into my loft in Rome, it was the happiest day in my entire life. Then a few months later, I returned home and she had packed up and moved back into her brother's *palazzo* without a word, without a note. And she never returned my phone calls."

Glancing briefly at Nicoletta, who was smiling with cool confidence as Maximilian charmed the guests near them, I sensed she knew she was the subject of our conversation and wondered if she was feigning indifference. Or worse, maybe she really *was* indifferent.

It was time to change the subject, and I asked Roberto if he liked classical music. "All kinds of music," he replied. "It doesn't matter whether it's a symphony with huge forces, or a funky jazz trio, or the monks of Solesmes, or street groups from Ecuador. For me, music is immediate—it makes me want to go out and act, to accomplish something, to build a cathedral."

His comments were interrupted by the entrance of costumed waiters in pairs, bearing unwieldy platters holding a remarkable assortment of roasted game birds and meats cooked on the spit. As they offered thrush and pheasant, then rabbit, wild boar, and stag, stewards followed with carafes of a wine that appeared black, revealing an intense dark ruby hue when caught by an occasional reflection of light. "From Maiolo," I heard a wine steward say as he carefully and deliberately poured a glass.

A faint suggestion of thunder rumbled in the distance and I complained, "This weather is really insufferable," as I adjusted my starched collar, which was becoming more confining than ever. "It's a shame air-conditioning never caught on in Italy."

"Even with all the clever architectural design to keep this building cool," Roberto said, "on evenings like this there's absolutely nothing that can be done."

Wolff had been listening to us and turned to join our conversation. "What kind of architectural design are you talking about?" he asked.

"This was the summer palace of the popes," Roberto replied. "Built with marble floors to keep the interior cool and hollow walls to transfer air up from the basement. I understand it costs a fortune to heat in the winter."

As he spoke, the waiters served sorbet garnished with ripe figs, apricots, and blackberries as glasses of sparkling Moscato wine were poured. "Do you know what we're going to be hearing tonight?" Roberto asked.

"You haven't heard?" Wolff replied incredulously. "It's the first time Alison Teal and Véronique Ibsen have ever sung together on the same program."

As he spoke, the candles in the music room began to flicker; air currents were sweeping more forcefully through the residence. It was clear that we were in for a full-fledged Roman storm. But the thunderclaps approaching from a distance were not the only violent tempest about to strike. In the music room, another storm was brewing.

Astonished and uneasy, I asked, "Who arranged for both of them to sing on the same program?"

"The viscount, of course," Wolff replied. "He smoothed out

their ruffled feathers and decided that the best way to put everything in the past was to have them cooperate, with music as the focus."

Completely skeptical, I felt sure something explosive was going to happen, and that the whole idea of the program was a colossal mistake. I asked Wolff, "Are we going to have more fireworks?"

He smiled and shrugged his shoulders. "I take all these things philosophically. After all, as Robert Browning wrote, 'Who knows but the world may end tonight?'"

Guests began to rise from the table and move toward the music room. Since the concert was bound to be memorable, Wolff was anxious to go right in, and hurried me in a good-natured way so we could sit together. As I looked around the room, I continued to have questions about why on earth the viscount mixed all these complicated and talented people. After all, not an evening went by without something unexpected and outrageous. Perhaps the music was not the real purpose for our being invited here, but rather that we were participating in some kind of theater of the absurd.

As we entered the music room, a faint lightning bolt flashed in the distance, followed by muffled sounds of thunder. Enrique, always prepared for any event, saw me and came over. "Storm's moving in," he said. "I just counted twenty-two seconds between the lightning flash and the thunderclap."

A wire running from his ear to inside his coat caught my eye. "An electronic detection device?" I asked. "That you won't tell me anything about?"

He flashed a mischievous grin. "No," he said. "My little secret." Motioning for me to look inside his jacket pocket, he revealed a tiny MP3 player.

"Toni Braxton, Luther Vandross, salsa," he said. "Now that's music."

"Don't you ever listen to classical music?" I asked.

"I hate classical music," he said with a wicked smile. "Especially Mozart. This Walkman is the only way I can make it through one of these concerts."

Wolff had found two seats in the front row next to Andrei and Caroline, and motioned for me to sit between him and Elisabetta von Stahl. "I wonder how Rudi von Horvach will react to seeing Teal and Ibsen singing on the same program," I asked Elisabetta. Briefly, we scanned the audience and both realized he was not there.

"I'll bet he's up in his room hiding for dear life," Elisabetta said with a sly smile.

The members of the orchestra had been warming up, and when the concertmaster, violin in hand, walked vigorously to the front of the room, applause broke out. With the orchestra tuning, I glanced at the embossed program, dominated by gold letters in German: *NACHTMUSIK*. The evening was to be a mixture of instrumental serenades and vocal nocturnes by Mozart, with the voice parts sung by Ibsen, Teal, and an unfamiliar baritone.

Almost without warning, the orchestra broke into the extroverted *Eine kleine Nachtmusik* (A Little Night Music), an engaging instrumental piece written by Mozart in the course of a single day. The well-known, buoyant four movements still managed to convey a fresh and spontaneous spirit. When the orchestra finished, enthusiastic applause broke out, masking the increasingly insistent and violent rumblings from afar. Within a few seconds, Alison Teal and Véronique Ibsen strode majestically onto the stage from opposite directions, each looking splendid and self-confident. Alison, as always, was dressed in subdued shades of ivory and pearl gray while Véronique wore pastels— salmon and muted peach—that emphasized the erogenous beauty of her dark mocha complexion.

But the colors they were wearing were not the only difference between them: Alison's classic, draped simplicity contrasted with Véronique's evocative translucent lace that clung to each of her well-defined curves. And there was still another difference—Alison had several delicate white flowers woven into her hair, while Véronique boasted a showy wrist corsage of rare fresh orchids nestled in soft folds of ribbon.

Followed immediately by the baritone, they were to sing some rarely performed Mozart trios with the unusual accompaniment of basset horns and clarinets. The baritone spoke first. "The opera texts of the Italian poet Metastasio provided the inspiration for an entire continent, to such an extent that the eighteenth century has been called the century of Metastasio. But he also wrote intimate love poems that stimulated the imagination of composers to write introspective chamber duets and trios like the ones we will sing tonight. We will open with *Ecco quel fiero istante,*' or 'The dreaded moment has arrived,' when the poet realizes he is about to be separated from the woman he loves."

The brief *notturno* was fascinating in its conciseness, purity, and sophisticated vocal and instrumental color. The three singers projected the beauty of the words and the nuances of the harmonies with extraordinary feeling. But after they finished singing, in the midst of the applause, our attention was abruptly drawn to the frenetic play of light in the music room caused by drafts of air sweeping through the windows, splattering hot wax onto polished wood furniture and floors. Staff members ran around trying to protect the antiques and drapes and to prevent objects from falling.

Véronique stepped forward to recite the poetry of the next nocturne with calm eloquence. "If you are far away, my beloved, the days are endless. My days spent with you, my idol, are but moments." While she spoke, she looked briefly around the room, perhaps to catch a glimpse of von Horvach. And as the music began, the thought occurred to me that, before our eyes, art and poetry were fusing with the complicated passions of real life.

At the conclusion, it was Alison's turn to speak. Looking at Véronique, she smiled coolly and said, "According to the poet, making fun of the most treasured virtues is what young people do today. Metastasio writes, 'Everyone speaks of fidelity. Yet even among a thousand lovers, there cannot be found two who are faithful.'"

It was clear that Alison, with a controlled tone, was using the text to give the younger singer a lecture. Elisabetta whispered, "And they had been acting so diplomatically until now." During their performance of the *notturno,* an abrupt breeze caught the light undercurtains, throwing them back and forth in disorder. Suddenly, as if by a single breath, a violent gust of wind tossed the heavy drapes aside and the candles in the room were extinguished simultaneously.

The effect was unnerving, sending a shudder through me. Despite the unexpected turbulence, dim electric lighting permitted the singers to continue. For a moment, I thought Véronique did not look well; her color had taken on a pallid cast and her gaze was glazed and distant. At the conclusion of their number, I mentioned it to Elisabetta, who replied, "It must be her diet. I've heard she's anorexic."

Before the next piece, Ibsen suddenly looked annoyed and I heard her say to the baritone, "This damn corsage just stuck me again." As he untied it from her wrist, he said under his breath, "There must be a thorn on one of the flowers." Reaching into his dinner jacket, he pulled out a handkerchief to dab a few drops of blood on her wrist and they both smiled to reassure the audience that nothing serious had happened.

In the diminished light of the music room, the baritone stepped forward to speak. "As a special treat, we will perform an orchestration of a fragment left by Mozart in the style of his *notturni*. The text is again Metastasio and reveals amazing candidness; he is openly hostile, taking aim at the woman he once loved. Her name, pronounced Nee-chay in Italian, is rarely used today, perhaps because it figured so often in the poet's work in such a bitter context. She was apparently a great beauty with a superficial and self-centered character who did not return his feelings—feelings that run from intense attraction and fascination to total despair and finally to scorn. The poet writes:

Thanks to your many deceptions, Nice, at last I can breathe.
Finally the gods took pity on a miserable man.
And don't be offended if I make a candid observation,
But I now see defects in your attractive appearance that I once
   mistook for beauty."

The sarcasm of the text was met by a burst of laughter from everyone but me, as I was reminded that a beautiful and captivating woman of the same obscure mythological name had probably misused my confidence and betrayed my trust. Ironically, Mozart's effervescent music, performed with élan, magnified the bitterness I felt.

In the middle of the performance, the full fury of the storm descended on us and the alarmed staff attempted to close the huge wooden outdoor shutters. But closing the shutters had a disconcerting effect: in a sense, we were walled in. And the crescendo of violence unleashed by the storm was mirrored by the heightened level of apprehension among the guests.

The unpredictable events were apparently taking a toll on Alison Teal's nerves and her voice began fading in and out. At the conclusion of the piece, she reached frantically for a glass of water and whispered something to the baritone. As she scrambled to remove a small lozenge from a cloisonné pill box, the baritone announced, "Miss Teal is experiencing difficulties. She will try to continue the concert, but asks for the patience and understanding of the audience."

The rousing applause competed with the steady momentum of the storm, mercilessly pounding the walls and roof of the residence. Despite everything, the singers were determined to conclude the concert with the famous trio *"Soave sia il vento"* from Mozart's opera *Così fan tutte*. Again the baritone spoke, barely able to project his voice over the fury of the tempest, mounting with each second. "The poetry that inspired Mozart's sublime music is for lovers: 'May the wind be gentle, the water tranquil, and may every favorable element respond to our desires.' It is to lovers that we would like to dedicate this piece this evening."

The orchestral accompaniment oscillated gently like the waves and winds of the poetry—a murmur of muted strings and wind instruments with a spacious melody soaring above—eerily contrasting to the pandemonium of the storm around us. Soon the calm beauty of the work was swallowed up by the jarring bursts of raindrops, followed by hailstones that began pounding the windows like gunshots. And with each fierce bolt of wind, the banging of a shutter that had broken away from its latches caused guests to jump in their seats.

Despite the chaos around us, the audience was wildly appreciative. Guests compensated for the tempest by showering their enthusiasm on the performers, pounding their hands and feet energetically in rhythm. While the other singers acknowledged the thunderous applause, Alison again grasped her cloisonné pill box.

Ignoring the storm, the guests continued clapping, forcing the singers to return again and again to acknowledge their applause. With each bow, Véronique looked more disoriented; her once vibrant complexion was now ashen pale and she was staggering. "Something's wrong," I said to Caroline. On the final bow, Véronique grabbed for the shoulder of the baritone to maintain her balance and said, "Help me." Caroline turned to me and shouted, "She's about to faint."

As we lunged for her, Véronique's legs collapsed, and we were barely able to catch her as she went down. "Bring her over there," Caroline ordered as the cacophony of wind and hail pounded above. As we carefully extended Véronique's unconscious body on the floor, Alison Teal clasped her throat and began to gesticulate wildly. My hands full with Véronique, I was forced to watch as Alison staggered erratically, unable to speak. Without warning, a horrifying series of shrieks and guttural screams erupted from the corridors in the distance. Interspersed with barely intelligible words, I heard a breathless torrent of repeated phrases in Italian with one word echoing above the others with grisly clarity: *"morto."*

In an explosive burst, the doors of the music room flew open to reveal a young woman with a frenzied look in her eyes, shouting incoherently, *"É morto . . . Orvake."*

"Jesus Christ," I said, startled.

"What is she saying?" Standing next to me was Andrei, demanding a response.

"Dead," I replied. "Whatever that means."

Burying her head in her hands, the young woman shrieked

over and over, *"Orvake é morto."* Sobbing, she continued, *"Il principe Orvake . . . nel bagno . . . insanguinato."*

Andrei looked at me uneasily for help in understanding. "It sounds like she's saying 'in the bath,'" I said. "And something about blood." Then, for the first time, I realized what *principe Orvake* meant. "Prince Horvach," I blurted out. "She's talking about von Horvach."

"I'll be right back," Andrei mumbled before taking off in the direction of von Horvach's apartment.

"Wait!" I replied immediately. "I'm coming with you!" Together we began a breathless dash through the seemingly endless corridors leading to his room.

Arriving at his door, Andrei shouted, "It's stuck." Together, the two of us began ramming the door until it burst open. As we crossed the threshold of his apartment, a wave of searing, moist air billowed from his bathroom. Stopped in our tracks, we found ourselves face-to-face with a sight that resonated with all the ghastly clarity of a high-resolution color photograph: von Horvach, bloated almost beyond recognition, was floating faceup in a bath of water and blood that threatened to overflow the sides of the tub. The veins on his monstrously swollen arms and legs looked as if they had been outlined in streaks of crimson black ink. And his head continued to bob up and down sardonically in a regular, perverse rhythm, his bloated tongue a grisly shade of blackish burgundy.

*"Il faut partir immédiatement!"* The voice of Philippe behind us shook Andrei and me out of our riveted state of shock and disgust. Not far behind Philippe were the viscount and Nadine.

"Everyone should go back and stay in the music room," she said quietly. "With Enrique."

With the grotesque scene still in my mind, Andrei and I returned to the music room. The frenetic activity made it seem like a beehive. The housekeeper was shrieking incoherently as staff members attempted to calm her down. When someone began to question her, she misunderstood, thinking he wanted to lead her back to the scene, and began to struggle and flail her arms. Occupying herself with the unconscious body of

Véronique stretched out on the floor, Caroline was desperately shouting commands to a waiter who did not speak English: "Call an ambulance . . . an ambulance." Jano arrived immediately and quickly began translating into Italian: "Telephone, first aid kit, blankets."

Hélène Benoit frantically grabbed for seat cushions to prop up Véronique's head, while Elisabetta von Stahl loosened her tight waist snaps. As several dazed guests began to leave, Enrique shouted, "Stay here! No one leaves this room." Other guests pushed in closer to see what was happening with Véronique, while Caroline, increasingly frustrated, ordered them to keep back.

Suddenly, Landry began to bellow, "Do you mean we're supposed to just sit and wait in this room? This is outrageous! We might all be in danger."

Braun, his face flushed with anger, shot back with a vengeance, "The last thing we need in a crisis is an obnoxious loudmouth! If you're such a coward, get out!"

Bumping and pushing the surprised guests blocking his way, Landry charged out of the room. As Andrei and I joined Caroline next to Véronique's lifeless, outstretched body, Caroline scrutinized Andrei, whose face was completely blanched. "What's going on?" she asked.

"It's von Horvach," he mumbled in a strange, distant tone. "He's dead . . . drowned in his bathtub."

The ear-splitting siren of a Roman ambulance squealed in the distance, and I tried to put the image of von Horvach out of my mind. As the impatient sound reached the courtyard, Caroline showed me Véronique's upturned wrist and grimaced. "Look at this," she said somberly. "Blood poisoning going right up the vein. If it reaches her heart, she's dead."

Within minutes, an eerie diagonal beam of light pierced the shutters of the music room. Glancing around the room, I caught a glimpse of Maximilian, who seemed calm, despite the bizarre events. His arm was stretched protectively around Nicoletta, whose porcelain features were strangely serene.

The piercing squeal of the siren stopped abruptly, but the

rotating blue lights continued, creating shadowy reflections through the slats of the shutters. Slowly and cautiously, men in white coats transferred Véronique's body onto a stretcher, then through the corridors into the waiting ambulance. Soon the shrill, relentless wail of the ambulance again filled the air, punctuated by the occasional high-pitched accompaniment of brakes on rubber, as the grim procession sped off into the distance. When the ambulance was gone, the rhythmic rotation of the blue lights from a police car in the courtyard continued to wash the interior walls of the music room with a surreal glow, illuminating the residence with a strangely hypnotic iridescence.

PART THREE

# Vienna, Salzburg, Munich

# INTERLUDE

*The dream is the small hidden door in the deepest and most intimate sanctum of the soul.*
—CARL JUNG

"Feel like eating something?"

Her face, so youthfully unselfconscious and at ease with the world, was lit by soft morning light filtering through white linen panels. As she fed me warm spoonfuls of mashed banana and oatmeal, I looked around the room. Several striking bouquets of fresh flowers caught my eye.

"Who are they from?" I asked.

Casually, she stood up and drew the cards, first reading them quietly to herself. "René de Laguerelle and Nadine du Pont," she responded. "And Brother Cyril. Suzanne. Hélène Benoit. Lord Nigel Sackville Williamson . . . there's more."

"I don't remember anything about the brother," I said. "Or the first woman you named, or the long name you said. Do you know who they are?"

"Sorry, I'm new on this ward, taking over for my friend whose baby is sick. By the way, I was working when they brought you in. They said there was nothing they could do. But just look at you now!"

"I'm not doing that well," I mumbled.

"Well, you're better off than the two men they brought in with you."

Holding my breath, I waited to see if someone was finally going to tell me. "My boyfriend is an emergency medical technician," she continued. "He had to keep doing CPR on one of them and bagging him, the one in fatigues."

"Bagging?" I asked.

"Squeezing the bag valve mask to give him oxygen because they aren't allowed to pronounce anyone dead unless they're decapitated—like the other one was."

A vivid image pierced my consciousness with the swift precision of a dagger: a picture, brutally clear, of the man in fatigues.

"Good morning." My conversation with the new aide was interrupted abruptly by the appearance of a tall, dark-haired doctor with a solid Roman nose and a full, thick mustache that bristled above his lip. "Who are you?" he asked her.

"Voršila Pilková. Taking over for—"

"That's enough for today," he interrupted. "Please drop by my office."

After she had taken the tray and left the room, he smiled at me and said, "I am Král. Vlastimil Král. I'm here to help you. I'm a psychiatrist."

"A psychiatrist?"

"You're suffering from traumatic shock. It's a miracle you're even here today." Scrutinizing me, he continued, "Sorry I interrupted your chat. What were you talking about?"

"About the two men brought in with me."

We looked at each other for a few moments, each waiting for the other to speak. Finally, I interrupted the silence: "For a moment, I vaguely remembered him: jet-black hair and eyes, dressed in guerrilla fatigues."

As I waited impatiently for an explanation, he stood silently. Finally he replied, "I'm amazed at how the mind reconstructs lost images. I've read your chart and it's clear to me that the dreams and flashbacks you've been reporting are the theater in which your memory is unfolding. Trying to recover what you've lost, but always with a buffer of symbols to protect you."

His answer struck me as evasive and I asked him point-blank, "Who was the man with the knife?"

"Let your mind work it out in its own time, without forcing it," he replied. "Otherwise we might reactivate your trauma. Have you read any of Carl Jung's works on the mind? He wrote that we can train the conscious mind how and what to think—like a parrot, so to speak. But not the unconscious mind."

"When will I be able to remember what happened?" I asked.

"In cases of amnesia caused by traumatic shock," he replied, "there is no single recipe for treatment. The glove that fits one hand is too tight for another. Each patient carries his own problems and solutions."

"But I'm ready," I protested.

"Then follow the emotions associated with an image," he said. "They may turn out to be the means of regaining your memory. The knife you mentioned, for example. What kinds of feelings are associated with it?"

First I remembered it protruding from my chest when I arrived in the emergency ward. Then gradually I began to picture more of it: a shiny, new stiletto with a six- or seven-inch blade, glistening in the darkness. As I visualized it, fierce pain gripped me and my chest muscles began to tighten into a knot. My lungs immediately became taut and constricted and a feeble panting replaced my breathing. Foreign-sounding intercostal gasps were coming from my mouth: "Ahh . . . ah . . ." Watching me implacably, without emotion, the psychiatrist took a syringe from his jacket pocket.

"Don't try to do too much too fast," he admonished me, plunging the hypodermic needle into my arm. The last words I heard were swallowed in a gauze of filtered light and sound, gradually disappearing. "Slow down and take it easyonnyourrselllf . . ."

# CHAPTER 13

*Art is long, and Time is fleeting,*
*And our hearts, though stout and brave,*
*Still, like muffled drums, are beating*
*Funeral marches to the grave.*
—HENRY WADSWORTH LONGFELLOW

Von Horvach's funeral was scheduled to take place in Vienna with all the pomp and regalia due a head of state, and again I found myself on the road, luggage packed, not knowing what to expect. The first-class flight to Vienna International Airport and my accommodations in the Hotel Sacher were extravagant, just like everything else I had come to expect from the viscount. Yet, alone in my suite, the isolation was particularly keen, as I was aware the party was coming to an end.

The uncomfortable question of what was going to happen after the funeral was followed by a more unpleasant one: What am I going back to? My brief stay at La Favorite and Santa Maria Maggiore had helped me realize that I didn't fit into the larger fabric of mainstream America: watching game shows and football, arranging day care and rides to after-school practice, planning birthday parties for the children and saving for their college educations. And I would probably never fit in the world of academia either, with all the petty politics and passive aggression of tenured professors against younger colleagues. I was detached from the stream of society, a bystander at the window of life. That was the sum total of my existence and I was afraid.

Dressed in a black suit and overcoat, I walked through Vienna's Old Town toward St. Stephen's Cathedral, where a performance of Mozart's *Requiem* would provide a farewell to von Horvach and a final curtain for that intense, sophisticated world I had barely come to know. But as much as I tried to get into the mood of respect and mourning for von Horvach, I couldn't help thinking, *Good riddance.*

The pale blue of the Viennese sky stretched above me, creating a pastel canopy over the delicately chiseled facades, giving me the sensation I was immersed in a colored engraving from the eighteenth century. Only the people walking in the streets— some in sneakers and casual dress, carrying packages or with cameras dangling from necks and wrists—reminded me that I was still very much a participant in the present.

*Worry about existential issues and the course of your life later,* I told myself. *You're in Vienna now.* With no preparation or anticipation, I was walking through the city of Mozart, where the staggering opus of masterworks from his last ten years was born. Vienna—the city where the six-year-old Mozart had been received with extraordinary graciousness at court by Emperor Francis I and Maria Theresa, performing for them on a covered keyboard and even jumping into the lap of the empress and kissing her soundly. The city where Mozart moved permanently after his turbulent break with his employer in Salzburg, Archbishop Colloredo. And where he courted and married Constanze Weber who, contrary to her modern reputation as a scatter-brained playmate, was a devoted wife whom he loved dearly, a real partner in decisions, a companion who shared his life.

For several years, Mozart's career as pianist and composer in Vienna had taken off rapidly. But despite the sublime flights of fancy of *The Magic Flute,* the eloquent Clarinet Concerto, and the monumental last symphonies, Mozart's final years in the city were marred by a less-than-enthusiastic aristocratic public and by debts that were increasingly difficult to pay. At the age of thirty-five, Mozart died prematurely and abruptly in the city that had so attracted and inspired him.

Arriving in St. Michael's Square, I stared in admiration at the Hofburg, the vast imperial residence in the middle of the Old Town, and reacquainted myself with the imposing view that had impressed countless generations of visitors before me. Towering above me on all sides of the square were sweeping curves of stone, dramatic arches leading to distant perspectives, and flamboyant baroque sculptures staring down from the heavens. Monumental was the word for this architectural complex. It proved that tons of stone could be light, carrying the eye effortlessly past graceful Corinthian pillars, through taller to tinier windows and balustrades, and upward to sculpted eagles and angels spreading their wings majestically. Sweeping higher, my attention was drawn to delicate vases with flames of stone and elegant verdigris copper domes whose weight was suspended casually above. Side by side with more pompous nineteenth-century architectural additions, the square conveyed a conception of the world in which Vienna, the Hapsburg capital, was still solidly and splendidly in the center.

Across from the Hofburg, I found myself admiring the golden archangel of St. Michael's Church, poised effortlessly above a mélange of classical ornaments, guarding the church where two of Mozart's six children were baptized. Adjacent to the church I saw the austere St. Michael's House, where the twelve-year-old Mozart was said to have been tested by the court poet, Metastasio, to prove that he, and not his father, Leopold, was writing his compositions.

From the Kohlmarkt, the aroma of light Vienna roast coffee and chocolate truffles led me past elegant shops and cafés into a world stamped with the original Viennese baroque: theatrical and frivolous with a calculated hint of superficiality imitated throughout Europe. As I continued along the elegant avenue of the Graben toward the cathedral, my eye was captured by a massive gold-leaf and marble monument, the Pestsäule, erected in the seventeenth century to commemorate the deliverance of Vienna from the plague and barely completed one year when an army of 300,000 Turks arrived at the border and attempted to capture the city for the Ottoman Empire. Now the monument stood proudly before me, climbing upward in a visual *Te Deum* toward drifting cumulus clouds and vast blue washes of Viennese sky.

Soaring in the distance was the powerful spire of St. Stephen's Cathedral, covered with delicate beads of stone like costly embroidered brocade. As I approached the church where von Horvach's body was lying in state, the fragility and brevity of life again became a painful reality to me. The results of the autopsy and the initial police investigation had already been leaked to the press: someone very knowledgeable in chemistry or herbal medicine had removed the contents of the bottle of bath oil in von Horvach's apartment, replacing it with a mixture that would have killed a horse—an ether compound activated in water, mixed with monkshood and other yet undetermined herbal extracts. It was a brilliant and perverse concoction. The ether made him drowsy in the bath, while the monkshood relaxed his muscles to the point of paralysis. But this expert left little to chance: some unknown substance so dilated his blood vessels that they burst; hence the gruesome scene Andrei and I found.

The poisons used on Alison Teal and Ibsen were equally diabolical: arsenic and quirori from the poison dart frog, used by natives of Central America to anesthetize their prey, had been applied to the thorns hidden in Véronique's wrist corsage. And the toxic throat lozenges delivered to Alison's apartment were made of the concentrated extract from dieffenbachia, or "dumb cane," a common but poisonous houseplant.

There was a happy end for Véronique, whose young Roman doctor immediately initiated emergency treatment for blood poisoning using micronized activated charcoal, and managed to save her life. After a few days of intense mutual flirting, he proposed, no less. It also turned out that an innocuous event on the day of the concert may have saved Véronique's life. She had complained to Philippe about a painful swelling in her ankles and several times during the day he sent her a tea made from butcher's broom. The tea, with natural steroidlike compounds, not only relieved her symptoms of joint pain and swelling, but also contained antidotal properties, apparently enough to keep her from dying before she reached the hospital.

Alison Teal was also fortunate, because she had resisted the temptation of taking more lozenges when she began to lose her voice. The essence of dieffenbachia from which they were made would ultimately have killed her. But within a day or two, she had recovered and, to my amazement, was even scheduled to sing the solo soprano part in the Mozart *Requiem* for the funeral.

The murder and the two attempted homicides generated interest that far surpassed any recent news in Vienna, and as I approached the cathedral, I could sense a carnival-like atmosphere looming in the distance. A horde of newspaper reporters and paparazzi swarmed over the street along with police, security officers, and curious bystanders. St. Stephen's Square, normally dwarfed by the enormous weight of the cathedral towering above it, now seemed even more miniature because of the mass of bodies crowded within it. After checking to see that I had my ticket, I waded into the confusion, finally having to push my way forcibly through an immense sea of humanity.

As I reached the huge portal of the cathedral, the Giants' Doorway, I glanced up at the minutely detailed carved stone sculptures of Christ and the apostles gazing benevolently on the confusion below. Taking a deep breath, I entered and within seconds was swallowed up in a world of Gothic spaciousness.

Sternly formal ushers escorted me wordlessly toward the first twenty rows of reserved seating, where I noticed much calculated posturing from European politicians and their wives and from dignitaries and friends of the von Horvach family, all demonstrating their entitlement and importance. But after walking past crowds fighting to get in, the experience of being treated like a guest of state was refreshing.

As I moved down the central aisle, the magnificent works of art in the cathedral competed silently for my attention: a splendidly carved stone pulpit with busts of the four fathers of the church announced that this was no ordinary church, and a dramatic carved red marble sepulchre reminded me that many important figures had been honored here when they died, just as von Horvach was about to be. The welcome faces of Andrei and Caroline jumped out at me immediately, and very soon I realized many other representatives of the La Favorite crowd were in attendance. Taking my seat next to Andrei, I whispered, "It's good to see so many of the guests made it."

Andrei responded dryly, "My father always used to say, 'If you don't attend other people's funerals, they won't attend yours.'" When I realized he was pulling my leg, I let out a muffled laugh.

The world of the foundation had actually turned out in full force. As my eyes wandered, I couldn't help remembering the animated conversations and newly made friendships, as well as the violent outbursts. When the cardinal arrived before the splendid painted and gilded wooden altarpiece to speak, my mind continued to wander from guest to guest, in a stream of consciousness, interrupted by snippets of the eulogy fading in and out. "He lay like a warrior taking his rest, with his martial cloak around him" resonated in the cavernous side altars as the cardinal spoke, and with that, my mind returned to the business at hand.

Remembering the arrogant sadist who had abused Denise the night of her death, I knew that the eulogy was a whitewash. But as it went on, I instead heard of a man with staggering achievements, someone who had been a tireless advocate of new hospitals and schools, who had pressured city planners in Vienna to create adequate housing, pedestrian zones, and underground parking ten years before the need was urgent.

The mayor of Vienna walked to the lectern and read, "We carved not a line, and we raised not a stone, but we left him alone with his glory," as he recalled a man who had pioneered the preservation and renovation of the Old Town at a time when unchecked urban renewal was laying waste to the precious architectural patrimony of Vienna; someone responsible for skillfully negotiating with OPEC when it looked as if the Western nations were on the brink of being held economically hostage; and someone who had intervened to supply clean needles to drug addicts to prevent the spread of AIDS when only Zurich was providing such programs.

Incredulously I asked myself if von Horvach could really have been a monster and national hero at the same time. My head spinning from the drastic new direction things were taking, I listened intently as von Horvach's own wishes for his funeral were read: "Let no one pay me honor with tears, nor celebrate my funeral rites with weeping."

"I think I'm going to be sick," I mumbled to Andrei, who for once had nothing to say. Gradually I began to recall the surprisingly tame tone in the recent tabloids; nothing had been said about von Horvach's defects of character or his peculiar "tastes" when it came to women, and there were only discreet, subtle allusions to Alison Teal's nervous collapse after their breakup. The conspiracy of silence surrounding von Horvach was not limited to La Favorite.

The newspapers and tabloids were generous when it came to Alison Teal, digging up photos from her years of celebrity with von Horvach, when they were publicly linked in a high-profile love story. The sordid details of their split and her breakdown were avoided, with the emphasis given instead to her desire to sing at his funeral, a final tribute to the man who had been the greatest love of her life.

The entrance of the orchestra in concert dress brought a welcome sense of relief. And the arrival of a chorus in formal black, followed by four distinguished soloists, made it clear that the performance of the Mozart *Requiem* would be elaborate and memorable. But at the time, it wasn't clear just how memorable it would turn out to be.

With somber urgency, the orchestra began the slow, legato introduction, plaintive and foreboding at the same time, setting the tone for an excursion into the darkest recesses of human despair, tragic resignation, and bitter, reluctant release. Mozart's dark ensemble of mournful basset horns, bassoons, and trombones began to unveil the world of unsettling passions that he experienced while writing the masterwork, in the last months of his life.

With dramatic fatality, the chorus entered on the ominous Latin word *Requiem,* voices building relentlessly in an uncompromising dialogue with the eternal. In this temple saturated with so many associations, the sonorities mounted as I reflected on Mozart's funeral, held that bleak day in December 1791. Constanze did not attend, as she was both pregnant and ill, and two of Mozart's pupils who had planned to walk to the distant St. Marx Cemetery reportedly had to turn back because of unfavorable weather. Covered only with a sack, Mozart's corpse was unceremoniously dumped in a row grave. Ironically, Mozart's abrupt death took place at the height of his artistic powers, just at the time he had been appointed music director in St. Stephen's, a position that would ultimately have granted him more financial stability and peace of mind.

*The same, recurring destiny for artists,* I thought. I could imagine Mozart fainting repeatedly from physical and nervous exhaustion as his last creative energies dwindled away, composing and sketching with almost superhuman determination to create new and luminescent sound palettes, pouring out his life energies even until the last moment of consciousness to create something of incalculable beauty—fueled to the end by the obsession to embody perfection and prove that something is right in the world.

My thoughts were interrupted by the glorious sound of Alison Teal's voice soaring upward in a solo of impalpable translucence on the words *Te decet hymnus.* Her silhouette was illuminated from behind by an uncanny play of light streaming in through the towering stained glass windows, and she appeared to shine with an angelic radiance. The movements of the *Requiem* unfolded as powerful outbursts alternating with moments of calm reflection, creating musical visions of transcendental luminosity. In an explosion of power, a thunderous chorus announced the *Dies Irae,* the fateful "day of wrath," to the furious accompaniment of trumpets and drums.

As stately, pompous rhythms proceeded, a desperate call to the judge of mankind was evoked by the chorus with the three-fold cry of *"Rex,"* transformed at the close into an intimate plea on the words *salva me.* Amid the surreal beauty, Alison's voice, usually a model of controlled perfection, cracked, shattering in the middle of a note.

Without warning, she sailed off the platform, the long

black trail of her dress gliding silently behind her. Andrei and other members of the audience looked alarmed, and I wondered if something else had happened to her. Waiting in hushed silence, we were greeted by the appearance of a younger soprano, and the conductor launched breathlessly into the expressive lyricism of the *Recordare*.

The performance continued as if nothing had happened. Extremes of mood and passion followed as the dramatic *Confutatis* chorus began, evoking with locomotive force the frescoed images of hellish horrors by Giotto and Luca Signorelli. Angular accents of tenors and basses were followed by the ethereal sound of women's voices imploring, "*voca me.*" But as a series of exquisitely beautiful tonal shifts began, my mind wandered, and I asked myself what had happened to Alison Teal. And how the concert organizers knew she would not finish the performance.

The *Lacrymosa,* the movement in which Mozart broke off writing his *Requiem* on the climactic words *Homo reus,* followed. Seamlessly, other movements unfolded: the propulsive energy of the fugue on the words *Quam olim Abrahae,* the placid reverence of the *Hostias,* and the remarkable eloquence of the *Benedictus* quartet. Ending the *Requiem* was the music from the opening, leaving the audience with a sound that was pure Mozart at his most sublime. After a final prayer by the cardinal, the audience began to rise to leave, the compelling beauty of the performance still resonating in the voluminous vaults of the cathedral.

As the crowd began to move slowly toward the exit, I asked Andrei, "Do you think Alison Teal is all right?"

"Someone will find out what happened," he replied. "They'll tell us soon. Anyway, we're all staying here in Vienna until the viscount decides what to do." He added, "But no more concerts now. It would be bad form so soon after the funeral."

"We're not all just going home?" I asked.

"Heavens, no," Andrei said. "The invitation was for three weeks, and the viscount hasn't even presented the foundation awards for this year."

The mention of the awards set my thoughts in motion, and I again wondered about the likelihood of a grant for me. Although it was an unreasonably high expectation, I had come to understand that, in this rarefied and unpredictable world of the foundation, anything was possible. Andrei interrupted me in midthought. "I'll tell you when I hear about Alison. But I'm leaving in a few hours . . . I'm going to Salzburg for a day. Some business that has to be taken care of immediately. Caroline can't travel—she has to see her doctor here in Vienna."

"I hope she's all right," I replied.

"Couldn't be better. We just found out she's pregnant."

Enthusiastically, I grabbed Andrei's shoulder and shook his hand. He responded to my congratulations, showing his own quiet excitement, although his eyes revealed a piercing vulnerability. "It's our first," he said.

"Would you like some company on the train?" I asked him. Andrei was surprised.

"Sure. You want to go to Salzburg?"

An idea had occurred to me, something related to the Mozart diaries, and Andrei seemed to sense it. But it was only a hunch, and I wasn't sure if I wanted to share it with anyone. "Yes," I replied. "When do we leave?"

"There's a train in two hours. Is that cutting it too close?"

"No. I only need about ten minutes to throw an overnight bag together."

"All right!" Andrei said. "We'll meet at the track." As we nodded in agreement, we were drawn with the flow of the crowd from the central aisle to the area before the huge exit doors, where guests were more eager to exchange a few words than to leave. Within seconds, Enrique joined us, his dark glasses making him look suspiciously like a character from *Men in Black*.

"Too bad your job keeps you here," Andrei said to Enrique. "We're going to Salzburg for a day, and I know a great stripper bar."

"Bring it on, man," Enrique replied with a carnal gleam in his eye. "My motto is, Love means never having to say you're horny. Speaking of which, that Ibsen babe is looking hot. Looking and cooking and hanging all out of that Frederick's of Hollywood dress."

The three of us looked over at Véronique, whose strikingly provocative attire—sheer, suggestive black lace covering her well-toned arms and shoulders with a vertiginous plunging line in back—confirmed Enrique's comments. Ibsen looked over in time to catch the three of us staring at her, and without a second's notice, she started toward us. "Uh-oh," I mumbled. "We're in trouble now."

"Yo, babe. You looking great," Enrique said, and to my relief, Ibsen melted immediately.

"I'm glad someone thinks so," she answered demurely. "I've been getting the distinct feeling everyone here is going out of their way to ignore me. Did you know I didn't even get an invitation to the funeral? Philippe said it was an oversight but I'm not so sure now, seeing how everyone's acting."

"Look, babe, you hold your head high," Enrique said. "Don't you take *nothing* from nobody here." As he spoke, he noticed Nadine summoning him with her eyes, and in the time it takes a beeper to go off, he left with two clipped words: "Gotta go."

As Enrique departed, Elisabetta von Stahl sailed by us. Dressed in a simple black silk gown that delineated her tall, chiseled figure, she was restored to the glacial elegance of her pre-Rome appearance. "She ignored me," Véronique whispered resentfully. "Walked right by me." Taking my arm with a vise-like grip that defied resistance, she insisted, "Come with me, Matthew. I'm not taking this anymore."

Endowed with a muscular strength that far surpassed her size, she escorted me firmly, leaving me little hope of getting my arm free. Within seconds we were standing directly in front of Elisabetta, who was aloof and distant, and I found myself an unwilling spectator to an impending disaster. With assertive sweetness, Véronique began, "Hello, Elisabetta. I'm completely recovered from my little case of blood poisoning, in case you were worried."

Elisabetta acted casual. "I'm glad to hear you're better. But don't you think you should cover up a bit?" Seeing Véronique's indignant expression, she added, "I mean, you wouldn't want to catch a draft right after being in the hospital."

"No danger of that," Véronique responded, holding her head high, as Enrique had counseled. "When you're my age, drafts aren't a problem."

Elisabetta's expression was restrained, concealing any emotion. "Well, I'm glad you're back on your feet," she replied. Turning to leave, she added under her breath, "For a change."

Véronique was clearly not to be dismissed. "Wasn't the eulogy beautiful? Tears kept welling up in my eyes. I couldn't help it."

Looking straight through her, Elisabetta replied, "I really must go now."

Ibsen plunged ahead, forcing herself on someone who did not want to speak to her: "What a brilliant mind he had. And so many remarkable achievements. Look at all the ambassadors and members of the press here."

Elisabetta interrupted her and told her directly, "You know he also had a rather twisted side."

"He would never have shown that side to me," Véronique declared. "With me, he was always a complete gentleman. So cultured, so charming. Perhaps there were things he did in his life that he regretted—people often do those kinds of things when they're unhappy in a relationship."

With a glacial tone, Elisabetta replied, "That's where you're a bit confused. He did those kinds of things when he was *happy* in a relationship." Again trying to leave, she added, "But after all, you didn't know him very well."

Again Véronique refused to be dismissed. "There are people you feel you've known all your life," she replied. "In the short time we were together, we became—how can I say it?—soul mates."

Elisabetta bristled. "Excuse me for saying so," she replied, "but that's absurd. It's impossible to know someone as complex as Rudi von Horvach in a matter of one or two days."

"I hate to disappoint you," Véronique said, lifting her hand triumphantly, "but Rudi had other plans for us." With that, she displayed a striking diamond ring surrounded by a dozen tiny amethysts.

Elisabetta blanched. "I'd put that out of sight if I were you," she managed to say, looking uncomfortably around the crowd.

Enjoying her newfound leverage, Véronique began playing with the ring provocatively, turning it in the light and stroking her finger coyly. "So you see, Rudi and I had begun a new chapter."

As a bead of sweat started an excruciating journey down my temple and onto my cheek, Elisabetta, now completely flushed, snapped and began raising her voice. "I'm sorry to have to tell you this—in case you had some adolescent idea about becoming the next Princess von Horvach—but frankly, he was just using you to torture Alison Teal."

Véronique stopped short as Elisabetta continued furiously, "And excuse me for being so blunt, but you meant absolutely nothing to him—*nothing*. No more than any one of his nannies or babysitters, or anyone else stupid enough to fall for it. You were merely a plaything to be used and discarded when he got tired, like the call girls and escorts he hired by the hour."

The muscles of Véronique's arm and elbow tensed in violent preparation for a right hook, and I planted my feet firmly on the ground. Instantly, and with the silken sweep of a black cougar, Enrique appeared, sliding silently between the two totally engaged femmes fatales and blocking their view of each other. "Sorry to interrupt you, ladies," he announced, "but Miss Ibsen's limo's leaving for the cemetery. *Like right now.*" Practically lifting her with his arm around her waist, he escorted the outraged diva firmly toward the exit, saying, "Big honor, babe. The viscount's car."

Without a moment to react to the narrowly averted cataclysm, I heard a voice from behind me and caught a glimpse of Dennis Landry looming near, more dark and Mephisthophelean than ever, in his somber attire. As I turned, I heard him say from the side of his mouth, "I need to talk to you, Pierce. Right now. I'll be waiting in my car behind the cathedral on Domgasse."

Guests were leaving the cathedral, and I could see Elisabetta from behind—her blond hair lifted high above her long, slender neck, like a sculpted bust of Nefertiti—and still fuming. Looking nervously at my watch, I was worried about how much time Landry would need, since the train for Salzburg was scheduled to leave in less than two hours. But I was intensely curious as to what lay in store.

# CHAPTER 14

*At every word a reputation dies.*
—ALEXANDER POPE

After climbing into Landry's formidable black Mercedes limo, I responded to his questions about the Naples diary in what amounted to an impromptu evaluation of my abilities. "Consistently credible handwriting and style for the eighteenth century," I said. "The content is surprising and has the ring of truth, as if the Duchess Bianca were, in fact, an eyewitness to Mozart's performance in Naples. Names cited are accurate and the description of the eruption of Vesuvius is consistent with the date. If true, her account has significant implications, suggesting that she had a sexual experience with the fourteen-year-old Mozart as a kind of offering to assist his creative genius. My conclusion, very preliminary, is that the diary is authentic and that she was present for Mozart's gala performance. However, her suggestion of sexual intimacy would appear to be the product of an active fantasy life; in fact, she died in a hospital that specialized in mental disorders, possibly even with a basis in sexual dysfunction . . ."

"Good work," Landry said. "Your first paycheck will be deposited tomorrow after my assistant gets your bank account number. But there's something more pressing I have to talk to you about. I'd hoped it could wait but, as it turns out, I'm going to have to proceed right away. It's your first official duty as part of the *Mozart 2006*, so I'm assuming I can count on you."

Landry's manner struck me as peculiar. It was now clear he had no interest in my evaluation of the diary, and I suspected I was being used. My face must have registered a moment's hesitation. Immediately picking up my reaction, he scrutinized me and asked, "Did I mention that half of your salary would be paid up front, in one lump payment? That would be, let's see, forty-five thousand. How does that sound?"

"Great," I said, doing my best not to reveal my concerns. At that moment, I decided it would be better to avoid antagonizing him. Although it could backfire, I would at least have time to sort things out, and stay privy to any information Landry might disclose. But it was becoming apparent that I was getting enmeshed in intrigues of the foundation; playing along with Landry while pumping him for information was clearly the most dangerous game.

"So, your first task," he continued, "won't be pleasant. But we've all had to do something or other that wasn't easy at least once in our life. You see, that other edition, the *Mozart Millennium Edition*, is also scheduled to come out in 2006. We made an offer to buy it, to incorporate it as the official German version of our edition, but there's an obstacle."

He stopped and waited for me to respond. Incredulously, I asked, "Braun?"

"Yes," he replied curtly. "I don't want that vile little worm on our team. He's not a very good musicologist, you know, and his personality makes it impossible to work with him."

Weighing every word, I replied, "But, it's his edition."

"Well, not for long. You see, he's had a checkered career. Some major mistakes in publications, a history of psychological problems, administrative mismanagement, disgruntled graduate students and employees. I'd rather not go into detail; you can read about it yourself in three days. A major exposé on him is coming out in the *Times*."

"How did you find out about that?"

"The article in the *Times*? A colleague of mine is writing it as a personal favor."

Stunned, I asked, "That will make Braun change his mind about selling?"

"He'll never change his mind—that's the problem. He's a very disturbed and disturbing character. It's going to take a more drastic approach to get rid of him. Ultimately he'll have to sell out whether or not he wants to. His publisher, you know, that, uh—that 'gay,' Wolff? He's been embezzling money from the firm for years to finance his gambling debts. That's why he tried to kill himself in Venice. My assistant is going to break the news to Braun that his publisher is broke, the same day the article comes out."

"So," I replied cautiously, retracing the thread of his logic, "with the news about his financial backing and the article in the the *Times*, Braun will relinquish the *Mozart Millennium Edition*, and you'll be able to buy it?"

"Yes. Only . . ."

Returning his stare, I waited, thinking, *Only what?*

"Only, I don't want to take any chances this time. The stakes are too high and Braun is a hard nut to crack. That's where you come in."

With a sudden lump in my throat, I stifled an urge to swallow. "Me?"

Landry slowly began to rotate the massive diamond-encrusted gold ring on his finger, staring off into the distance. As if watching a film scenario illuminating an imaginary screen, he began to smile—an odd mix of fascination and pleasure—as his eyes took on a luster and animation. "On that same day," he said slowly, "you'll tell him you've decided to withdraw your diary from his consideration. When he demands an explanation, you'll hold him off. Let him twist in the wind for as long as you can. Finally, when he insists, you'll look him straight in the eye and tell him, 'I would have preferred not to say this, but I've been hearing bad things about you and your work. Everyone I've spoken to has told me you're a tenth-rate musicologist, and I've been warned about your competence and even your personal integrity.'"

Stunned and revulsed, I looked at Landry, whose face beamed with an expression of perverse ecstasy, reminding me of depictions of Salome gazing at the severed head of John the Baptist. He was expecting me to reply and I said, "Except I've never heard that from anyone."

With my comment, Landry returned from his reverie,

and the abrasive, nasal tone came back to his voice. "I didn't say you have to repeat it word for word," he barked. "You can say something like, after speaking to other people, you've had doubts about him. At least that's true, isn't it? And believe me, after you've read the article you will. You'll thank me for getting your diary back."

Landry was not going to take no for an answer and I knew it would be useless to argue with him. I was imagining the shrill sound of the whistle announcing the departure of Andrei's train, so I tried to come up with something quickly. "I'll have to think" was all I could muster, but the instant expression of outrage on his face told me I had said the wrong thing. ". . . about exactly how I'm going to say it."

With that, a reluctant smile settled over his face, and I knew I had reassured him enough, while giving myself room to sort things out. Quietly, I said, "My train's leaving for Salzburg and I haven't even packed."

"Salzburg?" he asked incredulously. "You're going to Salzburg?"

"Only for a day," I replied, realizing I was handling him with kid gloves.

"I'll give you a ride to the hotel," he said, motioning to the driver. "So, you'll practice what you're going to say to him?" he continued, more command than question. "I'll fill you in on the details, when and where, et cetera. And when you get back from Salzburg, don't forget, *everything is depending on you.*"

As we arrived at the Hotel Sacher, I said goodbye with all the false enthusiasm I could muster. Safely inside the main entrance, I saw his sedan disappear as he sped off into the distance, and realized the frightening moment was over. All that remained was a deep, aching pit in the bottom of my stomach and an overwhelming sense of emptiness.

"Andrei," I whispered in an almost inaudible dialogue as I ascended the stairs to my suite, "not a moment's waste. Bring on the strippers."

\*  \*  \*

Settled comfortably in the padded cloth seats of the air-conditioned first-class compartment, I looked at Andrei and took a deep sigh of relief. The streamlined Intercity had been ten minutes late—an unusual occurrence that allowed me to climb aboard moments before the train departed.

"What takes you to Salzburg?" I asked him.

"My aunt's cousin died a week ago, and my aunt asked me to help her with some red tape about her inheritance. You'd be surprised how much bureaucracy there is in Austria. Plus, she needs my help to blow open a safe."

Again I wondered whether Andrei was pulling my leg. He added, "But we can still have a good time. That is, if musicologists can ever have a good time."

Too tired and upset to take the bait, I humored him with a patient smile. Andrei continued, "What exactly do you musicologists do anyway?"

"Well, we spend our lives researching esoteric subjects in music history—things the rest of the world hasn't the slightest interest in."

"And then," he replied, "you tell people about it, whether or not they want to hear it."

"You've got it," I said.

"Finally! It's remarkable to hear it presented so clearly for once. Well, you musicologists are certainly well represented at the foundation this time. Braun, you—and the viscount is some kind of amateur musicologist himself. The only other musicologist I know is someone in Salzburg, a crazy Englishman, a Ph.D., who works in a music store in Salzburg, Tom Carlyle. You should meet him sometime. By the way, he knows Dennis Landry."

The name I had temporarily succeeded in putting out of my mind jolted me. "If he has a Ph.D., then what's he doing working in a music store?"

"A bit of a strange story," Andrei replied. "In the eighties, he was traveling through Switzerland and happened to see a manuscript about to be sold at some small auction house in Zurich. It was supposed to be a diary written by Mozart during the last year of his life, but it was full of all kinds of errors: things like Mozart dictating his *Requiem* to Salieri on his deathbed. So Tom concluded it was a fake."

"Sounds like the kind of modern myth that originated with *Amadeus*," I replied. "Everyone who spent time with Mozart when he was finishing his *Requiem* is documented, and Salieri was certainly not among them."

"Exactly," Andrei continued. "Well, Tom met Landry when this diary was on view before the auction. Apparently they were the only two musicologists who saw it."

"Did he ever talk to Landry about it?"

"Yes, but that's what's so peculiar. Tom didn't stay for the auction but read in the newspapers a few days later that a valuable Mozart document had been sold to an anonymous Swiss buyer for an astronomical price, something like eight hundred thousand dollars. He didn't believe it, so he wrote Landry, saying the manuscript was a fake."

"Did Landry reply?"

"Yes, and he attacked Tom on every level, challenging his credentials, his motives, his honesty. It was such an abusive response, Tom went into a total depression for weeks. Shortly after that, he was turned down for tenure by his university and began to find his articles being refused for publication."

"And he thinks there's a connection?" I asked. "That Landry wields that kind of power?"

"According to Tom, it's a simple matter of a phone call or two by Landry, or a few words spoken under his breath to colleagues at conferences. Now Tom feels he's been ostracized. And he sells sheet music for a living—the man who's writing the definitive work on Mozart in Salzburg!"

"Creepy," I said, thinking to myself how unwise it would be to get on Landry's bad side. A hallucinating scenario began to pass through my mind as I envisioned myself struggling to make ends meet selling pop sheet music and electronic keyboards.

"But Tom's kind of paranoid," Andrei continued. "It's hard for me to know how much of what he says is true."

The conversation was making me extremely uncomfortable, and I finally asked, "Could we change the subject?"

"Yes," Andrei continued, "but just one more thing, then we'll drop it. Back then Tom told me something that stuck in my mind. The forged diary made references to a lawsuit against Mozart by Prince Carl von Lichnowsky and at the time it sounded like total nonsense to him. But some years after the diary was sold he saw in the newspaper that a man had discovered a court record showing Mozart had actually been sued just before he died by Lichnowsky. So the fake diary was right. It's all very peculiar."

Switching gears, I said, "By the way, remember the rare books dealer from Salzburg you mentioned—the one who disappeared?"

"The one whose car burned up, with the wrong body inside?"

"That's the one. Does he have family in Salzburg?"

"I know he has a mother. She's taken over his shop, trying to sell what's left. Why?"

"Could you arrange for me to meet her?" I asked.

My request caught Andrei off guard and he looked at me with a peculiar expression. "The people of Salzburg don't trust strangers. But I'm sure my aunt Traute and I can find someone who knows her. I'll make some phone calls in the morning."

When I started to thank him, Andrei smiled and put up his hand as if to say, *It's nothing.* "Do you mind my asking what it's all about?" he asked.

"Just a hunch," I said. For a moment, I considered taking Andrei into my confidence, but decided against it. "I'll tell you afterward."

Andrei gave me a pained expression that indicated he was not satisfied. But he let the matter drop. "So what did you think of the funeral?"

"A very moving performance," I replied.

"Which performance?" he asked, deadpan. "The mayor's or the cardinal's? Or Alison Teal's?"

"Why, do you think Alison Teal was acting?" I asked.

"Not really," he said. "But she certainly got great mileage out of it. Did you hear what they're saying on the news? Commentators are dripping with sympathy toward her, about how she collapsed with grief in the middle of the *Lacrymosa*."

"Only it wasn't during the *Lacrymosa*," I said.

Andrei gave me a puzzled look. "I just heard it," he said. "And I'm sure they said, 'During the performance of the *Lacrymosa*, Miss Teal was overcome by grief and had to be replaced by an understudy.' They called it a 'living monument' to her lifetime devotion to Prince Rudolph von Horvach that she would sing at his funeral so soon after a near fatal attempt on her life. And I specifically heard them say, 'At the same point in the score where Mozart left off writing his *Requiem*, Miss Teal's eloquent voice became silent.'"

"All well and good," I replied, "but it wasn't during the *Lacrymosa* that she stopped singing. It was at the end of the *Rex tremendae*, on the words *salva me*. The music is so ethereal at that point—like a tiny, solitary voice crying in the wilderness."

Playing with the Latin translation of *Rex tremendae*, Andrei mused, "King of tremendous majesty."

"Fountain of pity, save me," I added.

"Is it at least true that Mozart stopped writing during the *Lacrymosa*?"

"The score of the *Lacrymosa* cuts off after the eighth measure," I replied. "After Mozart's death, Franz Süssmayr finished it."

"So Alison Teal actually stopped singing on the words *save me*?" Andrei asked, and I saw a spark in his eye. "Do you think she feels she's in some kind of danger?"

Thinking for a second, I answered, "Maybe. But I have another question: how is it that two people have been murdered and none of the guests is leaving? Isn't anyone worried about safety? Or am I the only one who's considered the possibility that the same thing could happen to any one of us?"

"To tell you the truth," Andrei replied, "I'm not worried. Very competent people are handling the investigation. Plus, the simple fact is, I'm not rich, like other guests of the foundation. This is the best-paying gig I've ever had. What makes you think you should be concerned?"

"Well," I said as I tried to make sense out of the threads that tied events together, "whoever killed von Horvach tried to kill Ibsen and Teal as well. Denise's death could have been related to von Horvach, since he was the last person to see her before she was murdered."

Silently, I reflected on the anonymous notes Alison Teal and I had received a few days before someone tried to kill her; there was even a possibility I would be next. The persistent image returned of the messy rows of distorted pasted letters: "Open not thine heart to every man." And as much as I wanted to confide in Andrei, I knew the consequences of talking too much. Breaking my silence, I said, "I was thinking . . ."

"Yes?" he replied, waiting.

"I was thinking . . . " I said. "I don't know. Tell me about this strip joint."

Andrei's eyes took on an animated glimmer as he embarked on a detailed, colorful account: firm nipples glistening with soft, translucent beads of sweat and moist breasts being passionately liberated from their aching confinement, all to the pagan accompaniment of ecstatic breathing and muted gasps of rapture. And his description gradually assumed a rhapsodic, almost poetic, quality as he described the exquisite beauty of supple, muscular buttocks in motion and the Dionysian pleasures of flimsy negligees being ripped from steamy bodies bursting with the abundance of ripe fruit.

As he spoke, I was amazed how full of surprises Andrei was. Somehow, with all his intensity and seriousness at the keyboard, I'd never imagined him to be a libertine. Andrei's description carried him on, in a paean to the symbolic delights of firm poles straddled by well-developed thighs, locked in a frenzied ballet of hypnotic abandon, evoking the cobra's erotic and lethal seduction. His voice became more passionate as he described the building momentum of legs and breasts in motion, spilling over to the indescribable excitement of lap dancing. Finally, almost as if exhausted, he collapsed back into the plush upholstery of his seat.

"Whew," he said. "You know, I'm beginning to feel the

weight of this entire day crashing down on me. Do you mind if I try to catch a little sleep?"

Almost as soon as I said, "No problem," Andrei began to doze off, a contented expression lingering on his face. Andrei not only improvised like Mozart, but he shared a keen appreciation of the erotic. Evidence of Mozart's libertine tendencies sprang to mind, and I quietly pulled open my suitcase to retrieve my dog-eared, tattered copy of the Mozart letters. Taking out the volume, I leafed through the correspondence of the twenty-one-year-old Mozart to his young cousin, nicknamed the Bäsle, in Augsburg, whom he called "a little wicked, like me." She had inspired him to write letters of such scabrous and scatological wit that succeeding generations of music lovers, who wanted to imagine Mozart as pure and otherworldly as his compositions, were left bewildered and dismayed. As I leafed through letters to the Bäsle abounding with bathroom humor and Mozart's invented phrases, such as "spuni cuni," I came to an animated comment he wrote in French, dated November 12, 1777, that suggested he had amused himself a great deal with his cousin: "I kiss your hands, your face, your knees and your [illegible], enough, I kiss everything you permit me to kiss."

Skipping through the pages, I came upon the earthy prose Mozart wrote his wife from Berlin in May 1789, another letter that someone had later made almost unreadable by deliberately scratching out parts of the text:

> Put your dear, lovely nest in order because my little
> rascal has earned it, since he's behaved himself and wants
> nothing more than to possess your most beautiful
> [illegible]. Just imagine, as I am writing, the little
> rogue is crawling up on the table and shows himself to
> me inquisitively. Not being indulgent, I've given him a
> firm little smack on the nose, but the little fellow is only
> [illegible]. Now the brat is burning even more and
> refuses to be restrained.
>
> Your faithful tomcat,
> W. A. Mozart

As the train approached Salzburg, the lights of the Old Town shimmered in the distance. Thinking about the freedom of Mozart's creativity, I concluded that his playful sexuality was just another colorful facet of his personality and his genius—part of the whole picture of the man who left the world such a staggering musical legacy.

Andrei's regular, deep breathing indicated he was sleeping soundly, and I reflected on the many sides of this other libertine as the illuminated fortress of Hohensalzburg, nestled high on the hills overlooking the city, came into view. The shrill train whistle resonated into the cavernous darkness of the surrounding countryside as I put away my ragged copy of the Mozart letters and prepared for a visit to his hometown, to be guided by an insider with a taste for life on the wild side.

## CHAPTER 15

*God Almighty first planted a garden. And indeed,*
*it is the purest of human pleasures.*
—FRANCIS BACON

A walk through the Mirabell Gardens after a light summer rain captured all the splendid luminosity of an oil painting on wood, with palatial facades and vast boxwood parterres spread out like embroidered quilts on a background of varnished green. With more than a half hour to spare, there was time for me to enjoy the exceptional vistas and the pools, arbors, and pathways of the spacious formal gardens, all designed by Fischer von Erlach with calculated rococo playfulness to delight and astonish the eye. A delicate mist rose from the warm earth as sculpted grotesques of stone smiled seductively from their vantage points overlooking fleurs-de-lys parterres. Alongside mothers with babies and toddlers, older, well-dressed natives of Salzburg reemerged from the rain and were strolling in a bucolic setting of relaxed, old-world life and style.

Across the river, the towering fortress of Hohensalzburg looked down from lofty heights upon the Old Town, its onion-domed spires climbing upward like newly sprouted seedlings. Crossing the bridge to the old town, I entered a world of baroque facades in soft beige and pastel pink, with rustic fountains and sedate portals hewn from rough stone.

Andrei and his aunt had made a few calls to locate someone who knew the mother of the rare books dealer, and she had agreed reluctantly to meet me in her son's shop on Getreidegasse. I arrived at the picturesque street abounding with elaborately gilded and painted wrought-iron signs and realized the shop was on the same street as the house where Mozart was born.

Andrei apologized for not coming with me to ease my introduction to the mother, but he needed to arrange some details and sign some contracts to assure that the safe would be blown open on schedule. The hand-painted sign on the door in old German script read OPEN and immediately upon entering, I could see the silhouette of Frau Pahlmann waiting amid the dust and disorder of the dismal, half-empty shop. In her late sixties or early seventies and with her gray hair in a bun, she was exceedingly drab, dressed in a dreary brown skirt, sweater, and shawl.

When I introduced myself, she looked somewhat tense and suspicious, but after I described my work in the field of Mozart studies, her attitude softened. "My daughter is playing Mozart to my new grandson every day," she said. "They've discovered it increases intelligence in children."

"And in college students as well," I replied. "It's been called the Mozart Effect." But as there was little time for small talk, I immediately brought up the subject of her son's disappearance.

"You read about it in the newspaper?" she asked. "Outside of Salzburg? Which newspaper?"

"I don't know what newspaper," I replied. "Someone sent me a clipping."

"And who was that?" she asked suspiciously. "Someone from Salzburg?"

Realizing I would get nowhere unless I leveled with her, I replied bluntly, "They sent it anonymously."

With an incredulous edge in her voice, she asked, "Why would anyone do that?"

"Perhaps because I bought some papers at an auction that appear to be by Mozart."

She took a few steps away from me, stunned. "Traute and her nephew wouldn't have sent you if you were someone I shouldn't talk to. But I don't know. My son Georg found something. He told me about it, but I forget exactly what he said, except that it was about Mozart. It was so long ago. I didn't mention it to the police because it didn't occur to me. I've been here in the shop for months and haven't found anything like it."

"How about business correspondence, or records or receipts from the time he disappeared?" I asked.

"Nothing out of the ordinary," Frau Pahlmann replied.

"Would you mind if I took a look?" I said. "It never hurts to have a second pair of eyes when you're hunting for something."

My question disturbed her. "But it's my son's private correspondence. I don't really have a right to show it to anyone. Why? Do you think there might be something in it?"

When I nodded, she replied, "We could look at it together, but you have to promise me not to talk to anyone about it, especially here in town."

As she began to bring out boxes of unfiled letters and receipts, I rolled up my sleeves and took a seat. "Sales of books," I said, "and purchase orders for editions, repairs of old volumes, restoration and coloration of prints, binding orders, even receipts for rare stamps." She stood poised over my shoulder like an eagle as I leafed through page after page. Something familiar caught my eye: the letterhead of the *Mozart Millennium Edition*.

Completely lost in thought, I rapidly scanned the typewritten letter. The text was almost identical to the letter Dr. Braun had sent me. He would need complete assurance that no discussions with publishers would take place before he examined the document. And he would need to see the original.

Suddenly I looked up and saw Frau Pahlmann scrutinizing me carefully. "Did you find something?" she asked suspiciously as she lifted the letter from my hands and arranged her reading glasses on her nose. Holding it under the light, she read it to herself and handed it back to me. "What does it mean?" she demanded.

"Perhaps Dr. Braun of the *Mozart Millennium Edition* has the original copy of whatever your son found," I replied.

She looked bewildered. Finally she asked, "What should I do?"

"Do you know a good lawyer?" I replied. "Have him write to Dr. Braun and insist on the immediate return of your son's property. The veiled suggestion of legal action might scare him into returning it."

Frau Pahlmann was visibly shaken. "First to lose my son without any explanation," she said. "Then this. I just don't know what to make of it."

"Do you believe Georg is still alive?" I asked.

"My honest feeling?" she answered, reflecting. "In my heart, yes. But not hearing anything, not knowing . . . it's all so difficult for me." For a moment, I thought she was going to burst into tears.

"Trust your feelings then. Maybe he had to find a safe place for a while. We all have to do that at some time in our lives, don't we?" She smiled for a brief moment as if a weight had been temporarily lifted from her. As she led me to the door, she asked me to keep in touch, and I agreed I would.

Outside in the square, I checked my watch and realized it was quarter of three, almost the time I was scheduled to meet Andrei and his aunt for the blowing open of the safe. As a warm drop of summer rain splattered on my cheek, I picked up my pace through the narrow side streets, trying to stay protected from the shower by keeping under the broad wooden cornices above.

One thing was certain: Braun knew far more than he was saying. I began to wonder what role he might have played in the disappearance of Pahlmann. Then for a brief second, I remembered the coup de grace Landry expected me to deliver to him on that critical day approaching. All kinds of deadly games were taking place behind the scenes, and I heard myself saying, "Careful where you tread."

In the noisy waiting room of what resembled a huge welding factory, Andrei introduced me to his aunt Traute and we sat without speaking as a half-dozen men worked intently amid fountains of golden sparks cascading from acetylene torches. Over a drone bass louder than an army of dental drills, punctuated by ear-shattering shrieks of metal on metal, pneumatic pumps and hydraulic jacks darted in and out, eerily suggesting a modern-day Vulcan's forge.

"Come with me," the chief technician said with a congenial look on his face. "We're set up in the back. All the holes have been drilled into the safe and the charges placed."

As we walked through a rustic courtyard to the back of the complex, hidden behind what would otherwise have been just another sedate eighteenth-century facade, Andrei said to me, "The owner of this workshop says the safe is over two hundred years old."

"Let's hope the contents are not destroyed with the explosion," Aunt Traute said with an expression of both concern and controlled excitement. Dressed in a coarse-knit brown sweater, the heavyset, well-groomed woman appeared to be the quintessential Austrian hausfrau, with both feet solidly on the ground.

Andrei added, "If they're not, we could get quite a look into the past. Like opening a time capsule."

"How is it that no one ever opened the safe in all those years?" I asked.

Andrei's aunt explained, "It wasn't easy to find anyone to do this kind of work. My cousin asked around town for years but no one could get it open. And I never would have known where to look, if Andrei hadn't found this place that just opened last year."

"Unfortunately, it's a rather expensive procedure," Andrei added. "They're charging us over seven hundred dollars and they don't guarantee anything. Even if they blow up the contents, we still have to pay. That's how it works in Austria."

Traute interrupted, "But if we don't try, we'll never know. I used to see the safe all the time when I was growing up. My grandfather used it as part of a desk and my cousin and I invented all kinds of stories about what was in it. So when she died a few weeks ago, I decided I was going to try to get it open. It might just be empty or full of worthless papers."

"Who knows?" I said as two men prepared to detonate the explosives. Peering through a thick Plexiglas window with barely enough room for one person, we heard a muffled sound in the next room and saw a pale gray puff of smoke shoot out forcefully, then rise slowly to the ceiling. If there was anything left inside, we would soon find out.

*   *   *

"That's it?" Andrei asked, dumbfounded. Leaving us in the shielded room, the owner of the workshop joined another man at the safe and gave the handle a firm twist. Returning with a satisfied smile on his face, he held out a cloth sack wrapped in paper, covered with a fine coat of black soot.

"A packet of documents," Andrei said, examining the contents. "And this." Handing the papers to his aunt Traute, he held up a magnificent pocket watch encrusted with diamonds on a long gold chain.

"Amazing," I said as Andrei tried to rub off a tarnished spot from the watch.

"Must be a family heirloom," Andrei said. "I'm happy the papers made it intact."

"What kinds of papers are they?" I asked.

"Hmm . . . two different letters," Andrei replied. "Not official letters, personal ones."

Traute unfolded the heavy writing paper and examined the first letter. "The envelope reads, 'To be delivered personally into the hands of Frau Hofdemel,'" she said.

"That name rings a bell," I said. "Mozart had a piano student named Hofdemel."

"Yes," Traute replied, smiling. "In fact, my name is Hofdemel. She's an ancestor of ours. Didn't Andrei tell you?" Examining the pages intently, she continued, "The first letter is dated April 10, 1792 and it's signed—"

Traute put her hands down at her sides and looked at us in disbelief, as if debating whether or not to tell us. "It says Constanze Mozart. What would it be doing in the safe? I hope this isn't some kind of joke."

Andrei shook his head skeptically and I remarked, "If no one's opened the safe for two hundred years, it would have to be a pretty old joke."

A little impatiently, Andrei added, "Aunt Traute, aren't you going to look at the other letter?"

Leafing through the pages, she replied, "It's dated May 5, 1792, and addressed to 'My dearest Theresa.'" Jumping to the end, she continued, "And it's signed, 'Your devoted and loving Mama.' It looks as if these are tearstains where the ink has run."

"May I look at one?" Andrei asked. Completely engrossed in reading, Traute handed him the second letter. As they pored intently through the pages, I watched their expressions, feeling like a third wheel.

"This is a very long letter," Traute finally said. "She tells her to destroy this letter after she reads it."

"Tell me again," I interrupted. "Who is 'she'?"

"Constanze Mozart," Traute replied. "She writes to Magdalena Hofdemel about rumors circulating that Mozart was poisoned by Magdalena's husband, Franz."

Andrei interrupted a little distractedly as he read the second letter. "This one's pretty long, too. Whoever wrote it basically says that the letter from Constanze Mozart must be kept as a legal protection in case anyone claims her husband poisoned Mozart."

"Then it must have been written by Magdalena Hofdemel," I said. "And that would make Theresa her daughter."

Andrei continued reading. "She says she deliberately had the lock damaged on her husband's safe so that no one could read Constanze's letter, but so she would still have it if she ever needed it."

Traute's attention returned to her own letter and she continued reading. "Constanze writes that Franz Hofdemel came to visit her in Baden and told her he was sterile, so he believed that Mozart was the father of his children."

Andrei went on reading from his letter, stunned. "This takes my breath away. Magdalena says that the real father of her two children is 'the most tender and brilliant of men, the great Mozart.'" Excitedly, he continued, "And she says the watch was given to Mozart at Versailles when he was seven years old by Madame Adélaïde, the daughter of Louis XV."

With equal intensity, Traute read from her letter. "She says here she doesn't believe Magdalena's husband poisoned Mozart and that they both have to be silent in the face of rumors that might ruin their families."

With the two of them tossing out comments at an accelerated rate, the content of the two letters was becoming jumbled to the point where I was totally confused. "Now *this* is heavy stuff," Andrei continued. "Magdalena describes a gruesome scene the day after Mozart died. Her husband went berserk and slashed her with a razor, screaming, 'No one else will ever have you, woman, you will die with me!'"

It was suddenly apparent to all three of us that the owner of the workshop was standing a few feet away, waiting to close up for the day. Traute and Andrei looked at each other, and Traute finally said, "Why don't you come over tonight and we'll read through the letters without rushing."

For a second, Andrei did not reply, and I realized he was debating whether or not to relinquish our night on the town. It was soon apparent he could not decide and seemed to be looking to me for help.

"Sounds good to me," I said. "What time?"

"If you come at eight, I'll have time to prepare dinner," Traute said. "And if your train leaves at half past midnight, we'll still be able to read through the letters."

Andrei's quixotic expression suggested he was thinking of the strip club. Finally, he capitulated and asked, "Venison with black currants?"

"We'll see," Traute replied, smiling.

"In the meantime," Andrei added, "I'll make some photocopies of the letters." Seeing Traute's apprehensive look, he added, "Don't worry . . . I'll be careful."

After we left Traute, the two of us went in search of a photocopy machine and Andrei apologized. "We'll have to make up for the strippers when we get back to Vienna. But we're in for a great meal. My aunt's making her specialty."

As we walked under the splendid, colorful wrought-iron signs of the narrow Judengasse, I marveled at Andrei's concern that I would be disappointed to lose our night on the town; the letters could be among the most exciting Mozart discoveries of recent memory and he was apologizing to me for missing a strip show.

"By the way," he continued, "how do we go about finding out if the letters are authentic?"

My mind began to trace the long, circuitous route to authenticate my own "Mozart diary" and I realized that, after months, there was no apparent progress. "Sotheby's," I replied flatly. "Wouldn't do it any other way."

The old apartment building was immaculate and well lit, and as we climbed the steep staircase, I caught a glimpse of Aunt Traute standing at the top. "This is how she stays in shape," Andrei whispered, trying to catch his breath. "Up and down three or four times a day is better than a StairMaster."

As we entered, I presented Traute with my house gift, a respectable bottle of Sekt (the Austrian version of sparkling wine) and complimented her on her impressive dinner table. Everything, from the fine china to the sparkling lead crystal and linen, had been calculated to create an imposing effect, without being showy. As Traute poured glasses of sherry, Andrei mentioned my work on Mozart. "Then I imagine you know all about the Hofdemel affair," she said, smiling.

"What I recall," I replied, "is that Mozart had a beautiful piano pupil, Magdalena Hofdemel, whose husband, Franz, was in the same Masonic lodge as Mozart. And that, as one of your letters describes, the day after Mozart died, her husband attacked her with a razor, disfiguring her, before killing himself. Also, I remember that years later, Beethoven hesitated to play for her because he believed she had been Mozart's mistress. So, tell me more about how you're related."

Traute responded with animated interest. "Once, some years back, my cousin became very interested in doing a family tree and she found that Magdalena Hofdemel was a member of our family. I managed to find the chart today, so we can look at it."

As she spoke, Traute opened a bundle of large pages, carefully written by hand, with all the familiar features of a home-made genealogy. "So, you're her descendant?" I asked.

"Actually, no," Traute explained. "Her daughter, Theresa, married a man named Weidener—that's Andrei's family name.

My cousin and I are related to the main Hofdemel branch, but we're not actually descended from Magdalena."

"So, wouldn't that make Andrei her descendant?"

"Yes," Traute replied. "In fact, you can see it right here." Slowly her finger passed upward from Andrei's name through the generations, to rest on the name Theresa Hofdemel Weidener. The three of us stopped and looked at each other, stunned, having simultaneously arrived at the same conclusion. At that moment, Andrei's life would be changed forever.

# CHAPTER 16

*A man falls in love through his eyes,*
*a woman through her ears.*
—WOODROW WYATT

"If the letter is authentic," I reasoned, "Andrei is a direct descendant of Mozart."

Traute was speechless. "Damn it," Andrei replied, laughing. "If I had only known this all those years I was trying to convince my father to let me study music. He was determined to have me become an accountant or a banker—anything but a musician."

"Quite a turn of events," I said with astonishment. "This sounds like the right time to open the bottle of Sekt."

Traute insisted, "But first let's look some more at the chart. Magdalena had two children, Theresa and Johann Alexander. Was Magdalena pregnant when her husband attacked her?"

"Yes," I replied. "According to your cousin's chart, Johann Alexander was born on May 10, 1792, so that means Magdalena was in the fifth month of her pregnancy when she was slashed, because it was on the day after Mozart died. And it looks like Johann Alexander died around 1804, which would have made him about twelve or thirteen."

Andrei returned from the kitchen with three champagne glasses and the chilled bottle. As he slowly twisted the cork, Traute placed the original letters safely at a distance. "To our discovery," she said, raising her glass.

"And to our new descendant of Mozart," I added.

"That's assuming the letters are authentic," Andrei replied, to the delicate sound of glassware clinking. He reached for the first letter and said, "Let's get right into the letter, signed Constanze Mozart, with the envelope that reads, 'To be delivered personally into the hands of Frau Magdalena Hofdemel.'" As he began to read aloud in German, Traute and I sat back and listened carefully.

*April 10, 1792*

*Dear Magdalena,*

   *Please allow me the liberty of again addressing you by your first name, as a friend with whom so many memories of happier times were shared, swept up in the beauty of my late husband's music, so tastefully and sensitively performed by you. Alas we have both lost so much that such memories are now even more precious.*

   *When word arrived of your miraculous recovery I praised God. And although I attempted to visit you the doctors would not allow it, nor would your family. Unfortunately, the urgency of my entreaty does not permit me the luxury of waiting even another day. So serious is the nature of my request that I must ask you to destroy this letter immediately after reading it.*

   *Since the death of my husband and the tragic injuries to you, there have been rumors circulating from unseemly voices, the malice of which is almost unspeakable. When I first heard of them, I was speechless that anyone could contemplate such diabolical slanders, particularly given the state in which we both find ourselves, widowed with children to guide and nurture in this cruel world, without the help and protection of our husbands. Yet, painfully, I must put them on paper to prevent them from destroying what little hope is left for my family and for yours.*

   *The message of the evil tongues is that your husband, Franz, out of jealousy, poisoned my beloved husband with acqua toffana and that, realizing his guilt and fearing the inevitable consequences, turned his hand upon himself.*

"Sorry to interrupt," Traute said, "but I've never heard that expression before—*acqua toffana.*"

"Poison, isn't it?" Andrei asked, looking at me.

"It's a colorless poison," I replied. "Made from white arsenic. It could be slipped into someone's glass when they weren't looking. It's well-known to scholars of the eighteenth century. A Sicilian woman, Teofrania di Adamo, and her daughter invented it back in the seventeenth century. Kills the victim gradually, with symptoms that resemble natural causes."

After reflecting for a second, Andrei continued reading with his original momentum:

> Voices have also begun to circulate (and forgive me for acknowledging them, but I must) that my departed husband's relationship to you was of a more intimate nature than teacher and pupil. I can only say that, in the past, my husband did confess to Galanterien with other women, but it did not cause me to cease loving him, for I understood his genius and the terrible demands it made upon him, demands that would destroy even the strongest of men. And for the past two years, my health has been precarious, so that I have spent many weeks away from him with the result that his needs and desires could not be met.
>
> I am not interested in hearing these rumors and was relieved to see that the Empress Maria Luisa has shown her disdain for them by the interest she has demonstrated in assisting your recovery. We need never again acknowledge them, neither to one another, nor to the world.
>
> But what alarms me most—and this must remain of the greatest secrecy—is that your late husband came to me one day unannounced when I was at Baden for a cure. Franz was in a most agitated state and asked urgently to speak to me in private. He confided to me that he had, some years prior, experienced a brief illness, outwardly benign and harmless, yet one that, according to his doctors, led to his inability to produce offspring. He told me he never wanted to alarm you by telling you, but

*that when you became pregnant, he began to believe my husband was responsible.*

*I reassured him such a thing was impossible and that you and my husband were both driven by a great love for music, an overwhelming and consummate passion, and that was all. But the discussion with Franz has continued to disturb me. He was violently convinced of it, and if he spoke of it to others, it could seriously harm both our families. The incoherent jealousy that led him to inflict such unspeakable injury on you, dear Magdalena, would thus give credence to the malicious voices circulating that he poisoned my husband.*

*I must also alert you to a disturbing matter that would give credence to such a false and injurious lie. My husband himself believed he had been given a dose of* acqua toffana, *and although I tried my best to dissuade him, he insisted this—on a number of occasions—to friends and to my family. But I must say unequivocally, I do not believe his death was caused by poisoning. And I believe, no, I* know *that his delusions were due to exhaustion and his deteriorating condition during the last months of his illness. If we are to come out from this threat imposed by false voices, we dare not give credence in any way, nor acknowledge even the possibility, lest we be ruined and our families with us.*

*The sympathy granted us by the highest in the land has prevailed until now in the face of indescribable tragedy. Our silence is the only weapon that can defend us against the tides of calumny:* EVEN THE SLIGHTEST WORD *spoken in innocence is capable of igniting a fire that could sweep through and destroy everything in its path.*

*My fervent prayers are with you and your children.*

*Constanze Mozart*

Finally, Traute and Andrei looked to me, waiting for my reaction. "It corresponds with what we know about the situation.

But it would be unwise to jump to conclusions. We shouldn't make a judgment without first consulting a specialist who can identify Constanze's handwriting."

Traute, apparently moved by the letter, had a distant look on her face as she folded it carefully and reinserted it in the envelope. "I'll do what you say—about consulting specialists," she said. "But right now, I know the letter is genuine. I can feel it." Suddenly remembering dinner, she said, "But if we don't go to the table right away, I'll be guilty of sending you both off to Vienna hungry."

Within minutes a blend of piquant aromas and seasonings began to pour out of the kitchen. "We'll read the second letter in the train," Andrei said. "In the meantime, let's try to put Mozart aside and enjoy some real Austrian cooking."

Stretched out comfortably in the train with no other passengers to disturb us, Andrei pulled out a small bottle of Asbach Uralt brandy and two plastic cups. "Since we didn't have time for an after-dinner drink, Aunt Traute sent this along with us."

"By the way," I said, "what should we expect when we get back to Vienna?"

"I called Caroline early this evening," he said. "Get this, the viscount has another friend, a lord or something who has an estate near London. We're all invited there, and we'll fly out the day after tomorrow. Also, she said something about a costume ball being planned to get our minds off all the unpleasant events."

"Unpleasant events," I repeated distractedly. "That's a nice way of putting it." The thought of returning to the foundation again made me wonder, *What have I gotten myself in for?*

As the scent of aged brandy filled the compartment, Andrei took out the photocopies of the second letter and I kicked off my shoes. "Are you comfortable?" he asked as he began to read the letter from Magdalena Hofdemel to her daughter, Theresa.

*February 5, 1793*

*My dear Theresa,*

*You may read this letter many years from now, perhaps after you have become a woman, perhaps even after I am gone. Since my accident and the death of your father, the very survival of our family has been a miracle and I have been forced to resort to extraordinary measures and precautions, all for one reason alone: to protect you and your brother.*

*With this is a letter from Constanze, the wife of Mozart, with whom I studied piano. In it, she states without question that she does not believe my husband poisoned Mozart. Although I planned to destroy her letter as she asked, at the last moment I was persuaded by an inner voice not to do so. She writes, since the time of the ghastly tragedy that almost took my life and that of your brother, a specter has loomed in the distance that threatens to destroy us, namely the rumor that Mozart was poisoned by Franz Hofdemel. If evil tongues result in formal charges, the letter from Constanze Mozart may be the only document that will serve to clear our family name.*

*I have thus kept it carefully protected from the eyes of others for over a year with great concern. Finally a solution became clear to me: I would place it alone in your father's official court document safe, and then have the lock damaged, thereby securing the contents until such time as I might need them. But as I write this letter to you, I have come to a decision about another matter and realized that the silence I have faithfully maintained in the world is too heavy to conceal from you, my beloved daughter.*

*Having assured a means to preserve the privacy of my letters, I have decided to unburden my heart of the secret that has been an unbearable ordeal and responsibility, yet at the same time an unspeakable joy. Your father, and the father of Johann Alexander, was not that possessive,*

controlling bureaucrat who disguised his cruel nature to
everyone but to me, but rather the most tender and
brilliant of men, my adored teacher, the great Mozart. If
there was ever any glimmer of happiness in my
unbearable life after my marriage, it came from that
man whose heart sang in continuation, whose thoughts
overflowed with melody and beauty, and who showed
me gentleness and kindness beyond measure.

It was heartrending for me not to be able to comfort
him in his despair at his deathbed for fear of reprisals
from that raving and cruel madman to whom I was so
unhappily married. And although I was forced to destroy
each of Mozart's letters, I could not bring myself to part
with his gift to me, a watch presented to him by
Madame Adélaïde, the daughter of Louis XV. Again
following the judgments of my heart, I am enclosing this
last remaining memory of him so that you may have it.

Like Mozart's widow, I cannot believe Franz
poisoned Mozart before killing himself. His suicide was
not a result of guilt or fear of being found out, but was
precipitated by an event on the day after my beloved
Mozart died. Franz continued to taunt and heckle me,
insisting I was in love with Mozart, until I could take it
no more. During his deluge of cruelty, I finally broke
down in a torrent of grief that would not stop, a
complete outpouring of my unhappiness and sense of loss.

At first Franz was alarmed, totally surprised to see
me lose my composure for the first time, to see me
incapacitated and inconsolable. But after a few minutes,
he began to raise his voice, then to shout, "You see, you
loved him. What greater proof can there be?"

Not fearing him, nor death, nor anything, I looked
him directly in the eye and replied, "Yes, I loved him." At
first he did not know how to react. But then he began to
scream, "It's over for me. This is the end. I have been
betrayed by a man who was a guest in my home, my
lodge brother." As I watched in horror, he raced out of the

*room and returned with a razor, shouting, "No one will
ever have you, woman, you will die with me!" I
remember only the first blows to my face and throat, and
then nothing. My next memory was waking with my
father sitting next to me, holding my hand and
reassuring me over and over, "Everything will be all
right, my child."*

*My beloved Theresa, you and your brother were born
of love, of a union that surpasses time and reason. Please
do not judge me too unkindly.*

*Your devoted and loving Mama.*

"Well," Andrei said, "that certainly explains the gold watch."

Moved by the contents of the letter and the abundant tear-stains visible even on the photocopies, I had difficulty replying. After a while, I thought of Hélène Benoit and Alison Teal: *Abuse. Even in the eighteenth century, it was part of the fabric of human existence.* "Unfortunately," I said to Andrei, "Theresa never saw her mother's letter."

Andrei replied, "Nor the watch."

With a sigh, I continued, "The watch could probably help authenticate the letters. Just about every one Mozart received is in a catalogue—the missing ones are noted."

"Can it be proved if Mozart ever played for the daughter of Louis XV?" Andrei asked.

"We know that he performed at Versailles when he was seven. But an astute forger would have known that, because forgers are exceptionally good liars."

"How about the other information in the letters?"

"It's pretty consistent with what we know about Mozart. Constanze went frequently to Baden for a cure during the last two years of Mozart's life. We also know he wasn't always faithful to his wife. After his death, Constanze said he had confessed several sexual escapades to her, with maids, for example."

"How about the part about Magdalena Hofdemel being slashed by her husband on the day after Mozart's death?" Andrei continued. "The whole thing sounds like an eighteenth-century soap opera."

"Truth is stranger than fiction," I replied. "They barely saved her life by pumping air into her lungs with a pair of bellows." Seeing Andrei's look of astonishment, I continued, "The reason truth is stranger than fiction is because fiction has to stick to some kind of reality check or no one would ever believe it. But real life is permitted the luxury of being totally unbelievable."

"Neither of the letters rules out the possibility that Mozart was actually poisoned," Andrei said. "It almost sounds like Constanze is in denial and that the two of them are involved in a kind of cover-up."

"It's always been pretty clear that there was a cover-up after Mozart's death," I replied. "The Austrian court was definitely involved; there are documents that court censors did not permit to be published even decades later, like the one explaining the mysterious circumstances surrounding the anonymous patron who commissioned the *Requiem.* And the lawsuit by Prince von Lichnowsky a few months before Mozart died was apparently totally hushed up, just like all the implications of the Hofdemel affair."

"Do you think we'll ever know the truth?" Andrei asked.

"Truth is a pretty big bill to fill," I replied. "These letters may be all we'll ever have, yet they're full of all kinds of ulterior motives and subjective points of view and agendas. A couple of years ago at the Harvard commencement, Václav Havel said, 'The truth is not simply what you think it is; it is also the circumstances in which it's said, to whom, why, and how it's said.'"

Annoyed, Andrei said, "That sounds to me like a bunch of relativistic crap. Mozart was either poisoned or he wasn't."

"I guess what I'm saying," I replied, "is that we may never know for sure."

Andrei was unconvinced. "Speaking of poisoning," he added, "we still don't know who poisoned Teal and Ibsen, or who murdered von Horvach and Denise." Clearly, Andrei wanted me to confide in him what I knew. By now, I felt comfortable enough to do so. But there were no clear leads in my mind, just vague suspicions about a satanic cult in Nancy, and outside po-litical enemies of von Horvach. And of an elusive mystery boyfriend.

When I voiced my thoughts, Andrei replied, "I'd be more likely to suspect someone at La Favorite. If it is a single killer, that is. I'm not even sure of that. Look at von Horvach—the death of Denise points directly at him, based on his past. But then he was murdered."

"No, because he had an alibi," I answered. "Jano saw Denise leaving his apartment before she died."

"Hmm," Andrei said, lost in thought. "I hadn't heard that. Well, von Horvach certainly had his share of enemies. Like Al-ison Teal."

"And Andreas Wolff, I might add. Von Horvach turned him down for a loan."

"I hadn't heard that either," he said, dumbfounded. "Well, the person responsible for poisoning the two singers had to be damn good at mixing. Did you know that Philippe spent the first part of his career as a chef? And that one of his employers died? The pathologist's report cited death by unknown causes."

"Interesting," I replied, reflecting on Andrei's new informa-tion. "Plus, Philippe knows something about herbal medicine. Did you know about the butcher's broom tea he sent to Véronique Ibsen?"

"Yes, I heard that," Andrei continued. "In my book, that puts him under an umbrella of suspicion." When I nodded in agreement, he smiled with satisfaction. As our train began to enter the suburbs of Vienna, our attention was drawn to the vast expanses of night-lacquered valleys, gradually replaced by end-less rows of city streetlights and elegant facades. Our return to Vienna signaled a hint of tension. Andrei had called his stay with the foundation "the best-paying gig I've ever had," and when I thought about my own financial possibilities, I had to agree with him. But a voice in the back of my mind, increasingly louder and more insistent, was urging me to leave, to get out of the whole sordid mess before it was too late.

Perhaps Andrei shared my apprehension about returning

to Vienna more than he wanted to admit. Probably even more so, since his universe was changing to include the responsibility of bringing a child into the world. And in particular, a child with a remarkable lineage.

As the train glided slowly under the extensive arched canopy of Vienna's West-Bahnhof, an image flashed through the window. "I must be dreaming," I commented wearily. "For a second, I thought I saw Nadine and Enrique."

Andrei chuckled as we pulled our luggage down and wrestled our way through the narrow corridor of the train. "The mind plays tricks on you when you're tired."

But the minute we climbed down the iron grate steps to the platform, the boisterous resonance of Enrique's voice sounded behind me: "Yo, Doc, over here."

Incredulously, I asked, "What's going on?"

Nadine stood next to him with a calm, detached smile. "I need your help," she said. "Enrique and I are leaving for Munich right away. Will you come with us?"

As I sorted through the possible reasons why I had to stay in Vienna, I remembered that Landry was counting on me. "Dr. Landry wants me to do something for him the day after tomorrow," I replied. "It's urgent."

"We're only going for a day," Nadine said, reaching for my arm as Enrique took my overnight bag. "I promise I'll get you back in time."

"Then I guess we'll meet again in London," Andrei said, as the three of us waved goodbye. As we walked toward the parking area, I felt like I was being escorted away.

"You must be tired," Nadine said as we approached a white American-style stretch limo. Whispering, she continued, "Please try not to make fun of the car. Enrique's absolutely in love with it."

The "car," as she called it, was an ostentatious fantasy of polished chrome and white lacquer, entirely surrounded by a flashing ribbon of white lights. And on the hood, holding the world with the broad, muscular shoulders of a Herculean sculpture by Giambologna, stood a massive silver ornament of Atlas. It was so totally incongruous with Nadine's style that I finally yielded to the urge to ask.

"Unfortunately," Nadine replied, "it was the only thing available at the last minute. It belonged to a rich sheik in OPEC who was living here in Vienna. I think it gets about two miles to the gallon."

"Man, this is my kind of car," Enrique said, stretching out his legs as we settled inside the capacious interior. "Cellular phone with fax machine and twenty-one-inch high-definition color TV with DVD. And wait till you see this." Pressing a remote control device, Enrique demonstrated his favorite feature: mirrored panels glided effortlessly to the sides, revealing a padded wall enclosing a built-in ice machine and a well-stocked bar, replete with cut crystal tumblers.

Reaching for silver art nouveau ice tongs shaped like voluptuous mermaids rising out of lily pads, Enrique poured himself a Glenlivet on the rocks. "Man, this guy really knew how to live. What're you having?"

"I see a nip of Rémy Martin over there," I said.

"Pretzels?" Enrique asked, comfortably playing the host in this adult playground. "This is a regular museum on wheels. Look at that painting—now that's what I call art."

Nadine and I looked behind us to the small oil canvas in a heavy gold-leaf frame depicting a naked farm girl outstretched amid tawny haystacks, her hand suggestively placed between her legs, two fingers tucked away out of sight. "Early twentieth-century primitive," I said. "Could be American, or even French."

"Feel this," Enrique gushed. "The upholstery is the real thing—zebra skin."

"How did you know when Andrei and I would be arriving?" I asked.

"Caroline spoke with Andrei at seven," Nadine replied. In her pale gray knit outfit, she looked beautiful and ambiguous as always, but for the first time she reminded me of a shadowy, understated Ingrid Bergman, with all her splendid film noir undertones.

"What's going on in Munich that's so urgent?" I asked.

Nadine replied, "A Sicilian hit man named Bruno Abruzzese jumped from the south tower of the cathedral, the Frauenkirche. It's hard to believe, but he's still alive; a mountain of mulch that had just been brought for the flower beds broke his fall."

"What does that have to do with us?" I asked.

"He's been in and out of a coma for about three or four days. A young Bavarian doctor who understood Italian heard him raving about teaching a forger a lesson and getting information out of him. Earlier, there had been an anonymous tip from someone who directed the police to the forger's apartment—someone who spoke Italian. They think it was Bruno Abruzzese."

I remembered what Andrei was reading in the newspaper article that morning at Santa Maria Maggiore: the forger's death, and the unpleasant impression the news had made on Braun. "I heard about the murder of a famous forger," I said. "But what did he forge, counterfeit bills?"

Nadine shook her head slowly, her eyes lit by a barely perceptible gleam that said *Try again.*

"Paintings?" I continued.

"No," she answered with the same elusive smile. "Diaries."

Finally understanding the tantalizing thread of her logic, I asked, "Mozart diaries?"

"That's why I asked you to come."

"They found him murdered in his apartment in Starnberg, didn't they?"

"That's right, less than a week ago. The two killers got away, barely, but they left interesting things behind. That's where you come in. You're the only Mozart scholar who's going to see them. I'd tell you more, but I honestly don't know anything else. Ingrid, a colleague of mine in Munich, called me."

"Speaking of your colleagues," I said, "I've been meaning to ask you about the investigations into the deaths of Denise and von Horvach. Are they keeping you up to date?"

"The French, Italian, and Austrian police each have their respective forensic teams working," Nadine replied. "But they're not telling me much. My area is international money laundering and proceeds of crime, remember?"

"So, why did your colleague call you?"

For a moment, Nadine debated what to say. My look of annoyance at her hesitation must have convinced her to reconsider. "There's a record of a private account of the forger with a holding company that might be linked to Syndicat International."

Although her last two words were not familiar, I felt an immediate, violent shudder. Seeing my reaction, Nadine repeated, "Syndicat International. We call it SIN for short. If the forger's linked to SIN, it could be the big lead we've been waiting for."

"But Mozart diaries?" I asked, dumbfounded.

"It wouldn't be the first time a large criminal operation sought out a money-laundering scheme that gave an impression of legitimacy," she replied. "About one hundred billion dollars of criminal income has to be laundered each year in the United States—and that's only one-third of the worldwide figure."

"It's all so complicated," I said as an abrupt spray of rain splattered over the roof and the windows. I noticed that Enrique had been unusually quiet. Suddenly and brusquely, he pulled himself up in his seat and said, "Shit, this guy's listening in on the intercom." Pounding on the glass partition separating us from the driver, he shouted, "Hey, man, shut that thing off."

Immediately, the driver rolled down the tinted glass as he apologized.

"It's the second driver I've had who was eavesdropping," I said quietly to Nadine as the glass partition rose again.

"They get bored," she replied. "In a way, you can't blame them. It's human nature."

As Enrique twisted open another Rémy Martin and poured it into my glass, I asked him, "So, what's your slant on the two murders?"

"I'm glad you asked, because I've been taking the best criminology course in the world—reading Sherlock Holmes. Whoever killed that von Horvach dude—you know, Prince Vicious—is an expert in herbal medicine. They still haven't figured out all the things von Horvach went skinny-dipping in."

Looking at Nadine and baiting her, I said, "It was lucky for Véronique Ibsen that Philippe sent her a tea made from butcher's broom on the day she was poisoned. He knows something about herbal medicine."

Nadine was not impressed. "Yes, but just because someone knows about butcher's broom tea doesn't make him a murderer. And after all, if he were trying to poison anyone, he wouldn't have sent Véronique a tea with antidotal properties."

A flash of lightning in the distance was followed by a violent thunderbolt that rocked the limo with an almost visceral force, reminding me of the ill-fated night of the concert in Rome. "According to Sherlock Holmes," Enrique continued, speaking softly and covering his legs with a blanket, "when you have eliminated the impossible, whatever remains, *however improbable,* must be the truth. So, this is how I figure it: every night, when the lights go out, all the locks on the doors are secure, except the locks on the doors of Baroness Paumgarten, whose room is next to von Horvach's."

"Wait a second," I said. "The locks on the doors of Baroness Paumgarten?"

"She always has to have the doors and windows unlocked," Nadine said. "Her fear of being locked inside during a fire. It's pretty clear the killer went through her room, because all von Horvach's other doors and windows were bolted from the inside."

"So," Enrique continued, speaking even more softly, "after a waiter brings her up a cup of camomile tea, while everyone else is having cordials in the library, something inexplicable happens." Slowly pushing the blanket down around his knees, Enrique continued, "The shawl covering the legs of the old baroness drops from the wheelchair to the floor. For years she's led everyone to believe she can't walk, but all of a sudden she begins to stand up . . ."

Lowering his voice to a nearly inaudible level, Enrique continued, "Then . . . she begins to walk around the room, looking . . . looking . . ." Opening his eyes wide, Enrique suddenly thrust his hand through the air, as if plunging a knife, and shouted, "For her next victim."

His explosion evoked the climactic scene in Hitchcock's *Psycho.* My heart racing, I managed to say, "Bravo, Enrique."

Nadine said quietly, "Now that you've solved the murders, Enrique, can we please move on?"

Enrique settled back in his chair and poured himself another Glenlivet. "You know," he said, "we all think of killers as monsters or psychos, but whoever's doing the killing probably thinks he's an ordinary kind of guy, just doing what needs to be done."

"I wouldn't necessarily assume it's a *he,*" Nadine countered. "In fact, I'm trying not to assume anything at this point."

"But tell me frankly," I asked Nadine. "Who do *you* think did it?"

"They say, Look close to home," Nadine replied. "But in this case, I'm guessing von Horvach made some enemies in his business dealings or politics."

"What about Teal and Ibsen?"

"Apparently whoever hated von Horvach decided to get rid of the women in his life as well. Something like what the 'ndrangheta does in Calabria, killing the families of those who cross them—even children, five- and six-year-olds."

There were other possibilities, such as Braun's involvement. I wondered if a scholar could be capable of killing. Of course, academia, fueled by so much bitterness and disfigured by so many deadly rivalries, was the setting for all kinds of savage politics and dirty tricks. The impending Armageddon between Braun and Landry struck me as a case in point. *Somehow Braun was involved,* I thought. *Up to his ears.*

The rush of associations led me to my friend, Andreas Wolff, who had an enormous ax to grind: despite von Horvach's wealth, the aristocrat had refused him a loan. And they had a common bond: the housekeeper, Denise.

My eye caught Enrique's, and I tried to imagine what he would say if he were ever serious for a second. "If you ask me, Doc," I imagined him saying, "it's the viscount. After all, he brought all these weirdos together—no offense intended. And two people got murdered. You know, I never trusted that guy."

Enrique caught me looking at him and smiled mischievously. Stretching broadly, he yawned and said, "Big day tomorrow, guys. Better catch some sleep." Nadine and I sat silently as the rain pummeled the glass roof, a sound soon joined by Enrique's deep breathing. Reflecting the oncoming headlights, phosphorescent droplets on the windows dissolved into shimmering silver threads, then reemerged as if magically beginning the cycle again.

"You don't mind that your bodyguard drinks whiskey and falls asleep on the job?" I asked.

Nadine could barely restrain a laugh: "It's a little comical, isn't it? But over the years, I've come to realize something about Enrique: he would step in front of a bullet before he'd let anything happen to me. I trust him more than anyone else on the planet. Except for my uncle, of course."

"Am I wrong or do I detect a hint of antagonism between the two of them?" I continued.

Surprised at my candor, she replied, "Whenever Enrique and Uncle René are in the same room, you could call it *When Worlds Collide*. The viscount is from the old school—you know, racial attitudes from another generation. Plus he has bad eyesight, so when Enrique's around, he'll say things like, 'Do we have a Haitian working for us?' You can imagine how that makes Enrique feel."

"There's an expression I once heard," I said. "Prejudice is our mistress. But reason is our wife; we hear her all the time, even though we seldom pay attention to her."

"Don't worry," she continued. "Enrique can take care of himself. He never fails to take a potshot at my uncle when he gets a chance."

"I've also noticed that when Enrique's around women,

there's an aura of admiration in the air. That must stir up all kinds of jealousy among the guests."

Nadine nodded. "Some treat him like a cabdriver or a waiter. But others are worse. Von Horvach acted mercilessly superior toward him, and lately I've noticed Maximilian bristle whenever Enrique's near Nicoletta. Landry looks right through him, and Braun finds it amusing to bring up the story of Soliman whenever Enrique's within earshot. Do you know who Soliman was?"

"Angelo Soliman. Yes, he was a brilliant black man—very much admired by Emperor Joseph II—who was in the same Masonic lodge as Mozart. He spoke five or six languages and was highly regarded by the great artists and scientists in Vienna. Then when he died—"

As I stopped short, I realized why Braun liked to tell the story: after the remarkable Soliman died, the emperor had him stuffed and placed in an imperial collection along with wild birds and other taxidermic curiosities. As late as the nineteenth century, the macabre trophy was still on display before a curious public in a wing of the Hofburg Palace, until it was destroyed in a bombing attack on Vienna.

"It's practically impossible for us to imagine what Enrique is feeling when he's around the world of the foundation," Nadine murmured, tucking herself under a long cashmere blanket. "The petty insults, the deliberate sneers and insinuations. That's why I look the other way when he unwinds with the Glenlivet."

Nadine nestled under her blanket, as if ready to sleep, but my mind was completely alert and there were too many things I wanted to ask her. "This crime organization—Syndicat International. Who's in charge of it?"

Immediately focused, she sat up and asked, "Why would you possibly want to know that?"

"Just idle curiosity, I guess."

"When it comes to Syndicat International, there's no such thing as idle curiosity. You lose a certain innocence when you begin to understand the level of corruption that exists on this planet."

"I guess I'm just interested because it's so removed from my own world and my own profession."

"You'll be sorry you asked," she said.

For a moment, I reconsidered. Then I plunged ahead. "Tell me more." And without realizing it, I had opened a Pandora's box.

# CHAPTER 17

*Truth has rough flavours if we bite it through.*
—GEORGE ELIOT

Nadine began to speak slowly. Her cold, unemotional tone unnerved me. "One of the members is Eladio Marquez—Mexican Mafia. Two years ago a journalist named Perez wrote a carefully documented biography of him, one that cited an unpleasant detail: Marquez was gang-raped in prison at age fourteen. Marquez set him up with the exclusive television interview of a lifetime, one that no journalist could ever turn down. And in the course of the interview, two men dressed as television crew members came in and stabbed Perez—a total of eighty-three times, to be exact—on camera and in full view of Mexican policemen and security personnel. When they got Perez to the hospital emergency room, his corpse was drained of blood. He might have survived; when they got him in the ambulance, he was still alive. But everyone was in on it, including the medics who transported him in the ambulance."

Noting the expression of shock on my face, she continued, "When you learn about Syndicat International, in a way, you become part of it. That's why you're better off not knowing."

"It's a little too late now," I replied. My curiosity was overwhelming. As I reached for the Rémy Martin, emptying it into Nadine's snifter, I continued, "So, who else is running Syndicat International?"

She spoke slowly and deliberately. "Alberto Bordone is the Sicilian board member," she continued, "for lack of a better word. If someone ever double-crosses Bordone, he prides himself in slaughtering every living member of that person's family:

brothers, aunts. Recently even children of cousins. That's very new. In the past, they left children out of it."

I felt my question had taken me farther than I wanted to go, but something made me continue. "Who else is on the board?"

Nadine hesitated, then gave me a look as if to say, *You're asking for it.* "Yakov Rubinov, Russian Mafia. Thinks nothing about blowing up an apartment building and killing three hundred innocent people just to make a statement to the government to lay off their investigations."

Taking a deep breath, I asked, "Who else?"

Nadine continued, "Adrien Hajjar, a Lebanese supplier of arms to Afghanistan during the war with Russia. Regardless of what he does, the CIA looks the other way. And he picked up a trademark from his dealings with the Afghan guerrillas—when he gets rid of someone, he has the man's genitals sliced off and sewn into his mouth. That's how Arnold Schott was found when his body was fished out of Lake Geneva. Curious coincidence, don't you think? But you can imagine, when Hajjar's name comes up, people think twice about cooperating with us."

Suddenly sick to my stomach, I struggled to lower the window and let in some air, wondering why I had insisted on asking. But Nadine had answered my questions. And she seemed completely unmoved—to her this was nothing out of her normal routine. Settling in for the night, she curled up in her blanket, and the sound of her light breathing began almost inaudibly to lapse into a slow, sustained pitch. Gradually I felt myself succumbing to the hypnotic accompaniments, which now resonated with a new, unfamiliar bitterness.

The intense conversation with Nadine fermented in my brain the rest of the night like yeast in a warm kitchen. My restless dreams were a vivid, endless safari of rampaging zebras, plumed waterfowl, and other exotic African wildlife, culminating with a surrealistic exposition featuring a life-size figure of Enrique, exhibited in taxidermic splendor. After a night of traveling in our padded cell of zebra skin, the prospect of a deluxe suite in the Königshof Hotel made me almost delirious. And a three-hour nap followed by a steaming bath was the ideal prescription for recovery. When I left my room to meet Nadine, I was a new man.

"Where's Enrique?" I asked as she appeared alone at the door of her suite.

"At the dentist," she replied. "He broke a tooth about an hour ago."

"Can we go without him?" I asked.

"Of course," she said, locking her door behind her. "Enrique provides a little added insurance but, unfortunately, there are never really any guarantees of safety in this world. Our appointment isn't until five. Why don't we walk?"

The cosmopolitan pedestrian zone leading to Marienplatz was a wash of colorful umbrellas and blue-and-white-checkered banners, with local residents and tourists sitting outdoors reading and sunning, savoring the local brew, or eating a meal of white sausages with sweet mustard and stone-ground bread while watching the endless parade of humanity. Everywhere along the route, the air was saturated with the acrid, pungent perfume of ivy geraniums in immense planters that stood like boxed corsages, bursting with fragrant lobelia, white asters, and the tart silver tones of dusty miller. "Isn't this exhilarating?" Nadine asked. "This morning, the Alps were visible from my room, still covered with snow and so crisp and near, I felt I could reach out and touch them."

Gilded clocks and statues, narrow neo-Gothic turrets, and pristine facades painted with multicolored architectural details captured our attention as we strolled. As we arrived in Marienplatz, the massive gray stone and brick edifice of the town hall towered above us, draped in riotous cascades of crimson hanging geraniums. Crowds were already lining up in front of the facade to see the costumed mechanical figures of the glockenspiel perform the coopers' dance high above on a miniature stage of tarnished copper. Instead of waiting, we continued around the corner, where an elegant dragon in bronze was perched, stretching his webbed wings while waiting to astound the unprepared visitor.

"Did Mozart ever make it to Munich?" Nadine asked.

"No less than eight times," I replied. "In fact, one of the very first trips Leopold Mozart made with Mozart and his sister was here, in hopes of having them play for the Elector Maximilian III Joseph. The event was such a success that Leopold embarked on an ambitious three-and-a-half-year trip to the major courts in Europe."

"Happy memories of Munich, then," she said.

"Yes and no," I continued. "Mozart had some critical disappointments here. On the way home to Salzburg from Paris in 1778, he was rebuffed by Aloysia Weber, an opera singer who was perhaps the most serious love of his life. Of course, he ended up marrying her sister, Constanze, a few years later."

"Did he ever settle down here?" she asked.

"He was commissioned twice to write operas for Munich so he stayed for the months required, but when he tried to get a permanent position in 1777, the Elector told him it was too soon. And nothing materialized. Actually, his chances had probably been ruined years before by the Empress Maria Theresa, who viewed the concert tours of the Mozart family as running around the world like riffraff, begging money from the nobility."

Looking at her watch, Nadine said, "I can't believe we made such good time. There's over a half hour before our appointment. What else is there to see?"

With a sudden stroke of inspiration, I took her arm. "If we're in luck, we can see my favorite place in Munich, just before they close the doors."

The disgruntled Bavarian cashier looked first at his watch and then at the clock on the wall before admitting we had arrived in time. Within minutes, Nadine and I found ourselves alone, surrounded by one of the most remarkable stage sets of all time, the Cuvilliés Theater, shimmering in all its rococo opulence. Standing inside the theater, surrounded by carved crimson and ivory heavily laden with gold leaf, felt as theatrical as being on the stage itself. Here generations of Bavarian woodcarvers had elevated their art to the sublime, the intricately chiseled pillars and ornaments of wood and cascading drapes cleverly imitating delicate creases and casual folds of costly fabrics. Designed to overwhelm with regal splendor, the theater at the same time presented an irresistible warmth and vigor on a delightfully human scale.

"Can you imagine?" I said. "This theater only exists thanks to a remarkable stroke of planning: during the Second World War it was dismantled piece by piece and removed from the site, saving it from a fiery end in 1944 when the Residenz was bombed. So we get to enjoy the beauty of the theater where Mozart's opera *Idomeneo* was first performed. A huge success, by the way. In fact his father and sister were in the audience to witness Mozart's triumph."

Nadine's face radiated in the amber reflected light from the crystal chandelier and the sconces of gilded bronze as she examined the beauty of the details above and around us. "Who could have imagined anything this phenomenal?" she asked.

"Believe it or not," I replied, "a dwarf—François Cuvilliés. He was a court jester to Max Emanuel and was so talented, the Elector sent him to Paris to study architecture. After he returned, he became chief architect to the Bavarian court." Glancing at her watch absentmindedly, Nadine suddenly realized that our excursion into a timeless world had come to an end.

As we made our way toward the police headquarters at a brisk pace, the distinctive outline of the dusty twin towers of the Frauenkirche loomed in the distance. With every line chiseled in broad strokes and without marble ornaments or decoration, it was a monument to aesthetic essentials. The towers, each capped by a dome of verdigris copper and topped with a shimmering golden bead, reminded me of exotic headpieces like Ottoman calpacs. But the vertiginous height of the worn brick towers sent an involuntary chill down my spine. For a gruesome second, I could visualize the free fall of the Sicilian assassin through his eyes, and sensed what he felt the moment he began his descent, plunging downward with terrifying speed. And I thought of him lying in a coma in the intensive care unit, holding on to life by a fragile thread—his body mangled, every internal organ crushed, his brain occasionally triggered by some surge of guilt or remorse.

In the shadow of the cathedral, not far from where Bruno Abruzzese landed, I could see the plain facade of the police station. We made our way to the third floor, where a woman appeared at the door, and within a few seconds I knew immediately that she was Ingrid, the colleague who had telephoned Nadine to come to Munich. There was something strikingly similar about them: intelligent eyes and understated attractiveness, and a demeanor of "no frills, no nonsense" softened by a relaxed friendliness.

"Thank you for coming all this way," she said. "Nadine, it's been about ten months since the Naples conference, hasn't it?" They embraced enthusiastically, but afterward did not waste a minute getting to the issues of the case. As Ingrid described the recent developments, I listened intently, somewhat intimidated by her clarity and precision and afraid to miss a single word.

"If it had not been for the Sicilian, Bruno Abruzzese, we would never have gotten these leads," Ingrid said. "The downside is that the police were probably responsible for the forger's death."

"How so?" Nadine asked.

"The Sicilian kept saying that they weren't planning to kill Arneis."

I interrupted, "I read that Arneis had been executed Mafia-style, with a noose around his neck."

"Yes," Ingrid answered. "They stretched the rope behind his back and tied his ankles and wrists to his neck. Every time he moved, even with the slightest involuntary motion, the knots tightened. But that was only to scare him into talking. Unfortunately, when our officers arrived, the two hired thugs didn't have time to cut him loose. After they left, it was probably the sound of the police breaking down the door that caused him to jerk and strangle himself. He'd only been dead a short time when they found him. And his death opened a can of worms."

"How?" I asked, feeling fortunate to be privy to this high-level information.

"He had a cache of manuscript folios and photocopies of handwritten pages, and even my colleagues were able to read the signature on one: Wolfgang Amadeus Mozart. Would you like to see them?"

"Yes," I replied, trying not to appear overeager. "But to tell you the truth, I'm already suspicious, because Mozart practically never used the middle name Amadeus. He usually signed with the French form, Amadé, and it was only after his death that historians christened him with the Latin name Amadeus."

Ingrid smiled cryptically and led us into a room with tables set up like exhibits in a court of law. One displayed writing instruments and inks, another various shapes and sizes of old paper, still another bank statements and canceled checks. She continued, "Peter Arneis was a meticulously organized man. I've laid out some things taken from his apartment that we'd like you to look at."

Reaching for a handful of unkempt feathers, I surmised aloud, "Quills used for writing. Some have been sharpened with a knife, you see? Then there are various shades of ink and pigments and a variety of solvents." On the table full of oversized leaves of heavy paper, I also recognized blank pages similar to those of my own manuscript diary. Leafing through the stacks, I was amazed at the variety and extent of the collection of individual sheets and folded folios, separated by dividers indicating "Nineteenth century—Bavaria," "Sixteenth century—northern Italy," "Eighteenth century—Switzerland," and so on.

"These must be authentic blank pages from different centuries and countries. I guess it's logical—they're a necessary part of every forger's work." As I spoke, I noticed that one of the pages was not blank, but instead covered with writing.

"Oh, that," Ingrid said. "It's in French. Looks like a trial run or a practice page of something Arneis was working on."

Covering the page were meticulous scrawlings in different shades of ink, with letters of differing thickness and several blottings where too much ink had been applied. Scanning it, I had difficulty making any sense of the first few dozen words, but I immediately recognized the characteristics of Mozart's elegant penmanship:

*September, September 1766, lodging, stories, adventurer, adventurer, silhouettes, Lake, Lake Geneva, Niton's, Niton's, Niton's, Niton's Rock, Treille, Treille, Treille, Celtic gods, gods.*

As Nadine and Ingrid waited for my reaction, I continued scanning the page, trying to understand the jumbled text. Finally I said, "I'm guessing it's a forgery made from an early example of Mozart's handwriting. But I'd like to look it over more carefully. Could you make me a copy?"

Nodding, Ingrid announced with a smile, "Here's something more substantial." She headed for another table and removed a glossy set of photographs of manuscript sheets covered with writing from a stack of large manila envelopes. "What do you make of these?"

Leafing through the pages, I made a discovery that had a devastating impact. In my hands was something I recognized, in every minute, intimate detail.

As I began to recognize sheet after sheet, the revelation made my vision spin until it was an unfocused blur. Almost choking, I blurted out, "This is my Mozart Milan diary. How did it get here?" Immediately, I hunted for the second page, which I had deliberately left in Boston. But it was nowhere to be found. "These must be photographs of the photocopies I sent Braun months ago," I continued.

In midsentence, I stopped short. "Wait. Something looks a little different." Examining the first page carefully, then jumping from page to page, I began to notice more and more subtle variations—extraordinarily subtle differences—from the pages of my diary. The words were identical, the lines spaced exactly the same, but visually something did not match up. "Perhaps it's in the conformation of the letters," I said as I began to formulate my own conclusion. "I'd have to compare these with my originals, but I'm pretty sure these are not photographs of my document. They would have to be . . ."

The conclusion was so logical, so elegantly simple, I was surprised it took me so long. "These are photographs of a forgery made by Peter Arneis, using my diary as the basis."

Ingrid was brimming with satisfaction at the speed at which things were moving. "Would you like to see what else we have?" she asked. Taking out another envelope, she reached in and pulled out a photograph of a small text in German that took up a mere fraction of the page. "We don't have the slightest idea what to make of this."

The photograph showed that the scrap had distinctly jagged edges on the bottom, as if the remainder had been ripped off. And as I read, I made note of the handwriting, which was again the characteristic penmanship style of Mozart I had come to know so well:

> *August 24, 1791*
> *Alas, sorrow takes up the pen more willingly than joy.*
> *Once again grief and despair inspire my hand to produce*
> *these wretched scribblings on an empty page, and for*
> *what avail? Inside my heart, a potent rage is*
> *simmering, having returned home today after a total*
> *humiliation in court, sued by my friend, Karl*
> *Lichnowsky, one of the richest men in Vienna, for a*
> *pathetic pittance of a loan made in the time of my*
> *greatest need. What princely conduct! What noble*
> *superiority of character! Kindness to inspire even the*

My intensity provoked their curiosity. Nadine's gentle hand on my arm shook me out of a trance. "This makes reference to a lawsuit by Prince Carl von Lichnowsky a few months before Mozart's death," I said. "It's something musicologists have only known for the past decade. I don't know what to say.

Maybe it's a fragment from a Mozart diary, written in the last year of his life."

"Then wait until you see this," Ingrid continued, lifting out a sheaf of photographs from another envelope.

Here, the set of pages opened with the identical lines of the fragment, but the date was different: December 5, 1791. "Strange," I said. "Mozart died on the fifth at one o'clock in the morning. I find it difficult to believe he wrote a diary in his last hours, particularly since he was in and out of consciousness before his death."

Then I found myself laughing aloud. "Ridiculous," I said. "This must be a joke. First, it's signed with that spurious signature, Wolfgang Amadeus Mozart, and second, it talks about Salieri helping him write down the *Requiem,* with Mozart, ill and bedridden, singing the various parts to him."

"Why is that so funny?" Ingrid asked.

"Because the idea of Mozart dictating the *Requiem* to Salieri on his deathbed is a myth created by Peter Shaffer in *Amadeus.* This diary is a hoax."

"What else does it say?" Nadine asked, a little impatiently.

Scanning the pages, one after another, I said, "Quite a bit about a stranger arriving with a commission to write a *Requiem*—but that's a well-known fact." Again, I found myself chuckling. "All these details about Salieri visiting him while he completed the *Requiem.* Whoever wrote this must have watched the film a dozen times, but unfortunately, he believed it."

As I spoke, I suddenly remembered the discussion with Andrei on the train about his friend, Tom Carlyle, and the diary he had run across in a small auction house in Zurich. Looking at Nadine and Ingrid, I asked, "Have you ever heard about the Mozart document that sold in Switzerland about ten years ago for eight hundred thousand dollars?"

Seeing their blank expressions, I continued, "I can give you the name of an English musicologist who examined it. Sounds identical to what we have in our hands now."

"So what would you say about the fragment?" Ingrid asked.

"I'd be inclined to guess that it's genuine," I replied. "Apparently Arneis came across this small piece of a diary—controversial—written during Mozart's last year in Vienna, and then proceeded to make a longer, more substantial diary on his own, adding all that nonsense from the film *Amadeus.*"

"In the world of art fraud," Ingrid said, "that's what's called a pastiche—when a forger incorporates something authentic into the fabric of a larger counterfeit work. But what makes the diary fragment controversial?"

"Look here," I replied, showing her the photographed page. "The jagged edges on the bottom of the original indicate it was ripped off, and someone obviously crumpled it up as well—all the wrinkles could not be pressed out. My guess is that the negative references to someone as important as Prince Lichnowsky would have been politically embarrassing if this fragment had ever come to light."

"Well, we certainly know more now than we did before," Ingrid said.

"What's next?" I asked.

"Give me an hour or two," Nadine said. "That will give me time to look into money trails. There's no reason for you to sit around while I go through canceled checks and bank account numbers—we'll meet back at the hotel."

"And in the meantime, I'll make the copies you wanted," Ingrid said.

My job accomplished, I again found myself on the wide, paved pedestrian street leading through the perfectly restored and painted model city of Munich, glistening in the fading light like an extravagant dollhouse. The somber bell towers of the Frauenkirche were just beginning to take on silhouettes of indigo and cobalt against the last filtered light, under a canopy of Marian blue. Echoing in the recesses of my mind, I could hear the fragile, nasal lyricism of Mozart's Oboe Quartet, written in Munich, and revealing the composer at his most tuneful and spontaneous. Yet there was something bittersweet in the plaintive, haunting sounds in my mind of the oboe floating above waves of undulating strings—the resonance of a kind of deathless music. As darkness crept in, a poem by Coleridge came to mind: "About, about in reel and rout, the death fires danced at night." And I thought about Bruno Abruzzese and Peter Arneis, again experiencing a kind of shudder rising inside me, from deep within. Now there was a new scent in the air, the undeniable odor of death, faint and smoldering but inescapable. It was now part of the vast landscape stretching out before me, seamlessly woven into the fabric of the city along with the vague reverberations of music of the night.

# PART FOUR

# London

# INTERLUDE

*The unconscious is the ocean of the unsayable,*
*of what has been expelled from the land of language . . .*
—ITALO CALVINO

"Night terrors, that's the clinical name for it. You've been waking in the middle of the night and experiencing your nightmares as if they were actual events. Anyone on the staff trying to help you just becomes one of the terrifying figures in your dream."

In contrast to his words, the face of my psychiatrist, Dr. Král, was calm and reassuring, his mustache meticulously trimmed as always and the aquiline slope of his nose more prominent than ever. "I forgot to mention," he continued, "your mouth guard will be ready later today—you've been grinding your teeth violently at night."

Weeks of retracing the past had yielded detailed memories of what happened before my accident, but I was impatient to know the events that had brought me into the emergency ward of the Zaradník Clinic. My words, *I want to know now what happened . . . what happened . . . what happened!* reverberated with an insistence that surprised me.

"The problem is figuring how to do it without incurring more trauma," he replied.

"Isn't there a way to bring back memory using drugs?" I asked.

He stared at me. Then he said, simply, "You're already taking a huge list of medications."

"Then maybe one more wouldn't make that much of a difference," I said. "Isn't there a kind of truth serum that makes people remember?" I continued. "Sodium pen-tothal?"

"We don't do that anymore," he replied bluntly. "Or amobarbital—that's a barbiturate used about twenty years ago. My concern is that you could be permanently retraumatized."

It was clear to me that he was running the show, so I asked, "Then what do you suggest?"

Rather tentatively, he continued, "In the past, I've been successful a number of times with a therapy that uses anxiety-reducing drugs, coupled with a mild form of hypnosis."

"When can we begin?" I asked.

Reaching for my chart, he thought for a second and replied, "In about ten days. We'll cut back on some of your present medications and start you on the new ones today. But let me know right away if you start to feel any unusual reactions."

After he left the room, I lay back in the bed and closed my eyes. Slowly, my hand explored the raised surfaces on my chest where the skin had been sewn: an inch-and-a-half-long rough gash under my left collarbone. Struggling to remember, I felt enormous resistance in my mind. Frustrated, I tried to let my mind wander freely as a blur of images began to ebb and flow: sumptuous food and wines in abundance under shimmering light reflected in prisms of glass, costumed figures in a frenzy of color and movement buoyed by lively music. And powerful and confusing erotic drives mounting and swelling in a torrential surge, racing uncontrollably to the breaking point. Gradually, I let my mind return to the narrative thread that was leading me slowly, like Ariadne's line, through the labyrinthine corridors of my past.

# CHAPTER 18

*The last temptation is the greatest treason:*
*To do the right deed for the wrong reason.*
—T. S. ELIOT

"Would you care for champagne?" The Lufthansa flight attendant, her hair carefully arranged and every fold in her uniform perfectly creased, poured a flute of Taittinger Brut. I marveled at how a sparkling aperitif could soothe ruffled nerves, but couldn't resist the calculation of how much that refreshing first-class perk cost the Fondation de l'Art éternel.

Nadine, alert and buoyant, sat next to me, and I glanced back to see Enrique stretched out behind us, in a blissful state, his eyes closed, headphones in place. "I take it you're satisfied with our whirlwind visit to Munich," I said.

"Very satisfied," she replied.

"Tell me again how you met Ingrid," I asked.

"We're members of the same organization, which unfortunately has a rather cumbersome name: the European Council on Laundering, Search, Seizure, and Confiscation of Proceeds of Crime."

As the flight attendant began to clear glasses for takeoff, I asked Nadine about her hunting expedition through the mountain of bank statements and receipts. "Arneis had a deposit slip for a check deposited in a Swiss account from an investment company called Girard Resource Development—GRD," she replied. "They're known to do business with Syndicat International. Already a big step toward proving SIN is involved."

"Now we've got two organizations with easy names," I said. "Sin and Greed."

Nadine smiled. "GRD is mostly involved in selling and

trading with embargo countries—Cuba, Yemen, and Iraq, for example—and in finding third-world and former communist nations willing to accept the dumping of toxic waste. But something more interesting: one of the members of the board of GRD is a friend of Maximilian De Angelis's. In fact, they both belong to the same yacht club."

"Speaking of Maximilian," I said, "Nicoletta said he might find a buyer for my diary. How does that strike you?"

Nadine looked intrigued. "We could give Max some rope and see what he'll do with it. If he asks you for a price, why don't you suggest a huge figure, say seven hundred and fifty thousand."

"Seven hundred fifty thousand dollars? If he said yes, I'd take the money and run."

"Whatever happens," she continued, "just don't sign anything. We'll take it from there."

As the takeoff jolted us, I thought about Nadine's proposition. It struck me as far-fetched, but by now Nadine had enormous credibility. Within minutes, the sound of clinking crystal resumed as fresh glasses of champagne appeared. "We both know the diary's not worth that much," I replied.

"Well, whether it is or not, someone believes it has enormous value. Who knew that you left a page in your apartment in Boston?"

"Braun could have figured it out from the copies I sent him," I replied. "And unfortunately I told Nicoletta Chigi that I didn't have the whole diary with me. I'm debating how I'm going to confront her about it."

"That could make her defensive," she said. "Plus, it's possible she doesn't know anything about the break-in. But tell me, what do you think of my idea about making Max a suggestion of seven-fifty?"

Such a radical approach made me hesitant. But I took a daring leap. "I'll give it a try."

"Could you wear a microphone?" she continued in a very discreet tone. "That would be even more helpful. We can plant a tiny one—you wouldn't even know it was there."

"Sorry, but that's not my style," I said firmly. "Is that legal?"

Nadine laughed. "My colleagues and I are fighting one of the most ruthless organizations in the world, which has absolutely no regard for human life, and you're worried whether it's legal? If the information hasn't been obtained legally, it just means we can't use it in court. But when we're trying to track down what a crime syndicate is up to, we don't always follow the rule book."

Her frankness caught me off guard. "And Maximilian?" I finally asked. "It sounds like you're determined to nail him."

She smiled. "Max is a slightly perverse archangel—but his time will come. Right now he thinks he's smarter than anyone else. And you know what they say about pride."

Returning her smile, I asked, "Did you learn anything after I left you last night?"

"Just some background on the Sicilian, Bruno Abruzzese, who leaped from the Frauenkirche. An Interpol computer search turned up his police record as a mercenary and hit man involved in everything from the Mafia to freelance drug smuggling to extortion. But I also went through recent police reports and found out something interesting. When he was first seen in Munich, he was covered with cuts and bruises—literally black and blue—and apparently his teeth had been kicked out. Plus, he was acting very strangely. Several priests reported seeing him hanging out around churches, hovering near confessionals, but never going in."

"Is he still in a coma?" I asked.

"He died last night."

Even though I had somehow had an inkling as I walked through Munich, the news of his death jarred me.

"But before he died," she continued, "he asked to say confession to a Catholic priest."

"What did he say to the priest?" I ventured.

"That's a confidence a priest won't break," Nadine replied.

"Too bad," I said. In the distance, I was able to make out the faintest outlines of the British Isles.

But Nadine's matter-of-fact approach to everything from

illegal surveillance to Abruzzese's death left me unnerved. The machinations and inner workings of her world were nearly incomprehensible to me, and I began to question the wisdom of my involvement in her high-stakes game, the lethal ballet she was choreographing with Max, and the potentially volatile consequences for me.

En route to the baggage claim of Heathrow Airport, I looked around for Enrique. As if she had read my mind, Nadine said, "I sent him on an errand. He'll meet us back at the residence." When our luggage arrived, we headed toward the exit, where I recognized one of the silver sedans from the viscount's fleet through the sliding glass doors.

"All the way from Nancy?" I asked.

"It's not even a long trip from France anymore," she replied, smiling. "The car-train takes them right through the Chunnel." As we climbed in, Nadine asked, "Did you see the *Times* today?"

"No," I replied. "Where did you find a copy?"

"On the plane," she said. "Quite a terrible article about Braun, beginning on page four, no less. I almost wonder if he's all that bad."

"What does it say?" I asked, not wanting to divulge what I knew.

"That he's totally disorganized, eccentric, and irresponsible, and not a very good scholar to boot. And it asks whether the historic task of editing the Mozart letters should be in his hands."

As I anticipated my unavoidable "chat" with Braun later in the day, my attention was diverted by an imposing view through the tinted glass of the sedan: the black and gilt wrought-iron fences surrounding Buckingham Palace, protected from tourists by guards in vivid red jackets and tall black hats. "Are we taking the scenic route?" I asked, remembering my drive through Paris.

"Apparently," Nadine replied, "because this is a very indirect route from Heathrow to Chelsea."

Our informal tour carried us past the splendid Gothic spires of Westminster Abbey and the familiar complex of the Tower of London. "Something I remember," I said, "is that the little eight-year-old Mozart was frightened by the roar of lions when his family visited the Tower of London. The royal menagerie was kept there in the eighteenth century."

"I imagine London's changed so much since then, there's not much left of what they saw."

"Things have definitely changed," I replied, "but some places are still around: Lincoln's Inn Fields, Westminster Abbey, St. Paul's Cathedral . . . also The Monument. And Mozart and his sister performed in The Queen's House, which is still part of Buckingham Palace, hidden inside the building toward the rear. By the way, where are we staying?"

"In an estate outside the center of London, in Chelsea," she replied. "A friend of my uncle's, Lord Williamson, offered it to him when he heard about von Horvach's death. Uncle René has done the same with La Favorite, when his friends needed a place for their guests at short notice. I've heard this residence is particularly beautiful, almost like being in the country."

"Interesting," I said, "because Chelsea was countryside in the eighteenth century. Leopold Mozart went there for a number of weeks to recuperate from an illness." As we turned into a sheltered driveway leading to a courtyard guarded by a formidable wrought-iron gate, the chauffeur announced that we had arrived. Neither of us moved or spoke as we examined the estate; although quaint in comparison to La Favorite, Lord Williamson's home was framed in one of the most refined rustic settings imaginable, with an ivy-covered facade of russet brick and moss-coated columns in Portland stone, nestled in the shade of ancient oaks and chestnuts.

"There's not going to be quite so much space here as at La Favorite," Nadine said. "Only one room per guest, plus bath, of course. But Philippe told me the rooms are large with very high ceilings."

After our bags were unloaded, Nadine was escorted inside by a tall young man who hoisted her luggage onto his shoulder as if it were papier-mâché. I watched in disbelief as a tiny waif of an elderly man began struggling to lift my bag. First he gripped the handle and began to walk, but the suitcase refused to budge even a fraction of an inch. With his other arm, he repeated the ritual but again the bag remained obstinately in place. Stepping back, he scrutinized it intently and was about to try again, when I intervened. "Let me carry it. I can use the exercise after sitting so long on the plane."

Through the corridors on the way to the room, his pace dragged interminably, but I could admire the architectural features and abundant decorative details of the residence. We passed large rooms on the first floor, through what seemed to be acres of frescoed ceilings in the theatrical, grandiose style of Tiepolo, and my eyes scanned paintings of imaginary ruins with mythological figures who always seemed to be having a good time. In contrast to the severe delineated architectural lines, the decoration displayed a touch of playfulness, making the whole effect less intimidating, more human. I caught a glimpse of a collection of Georgian and Regency furniture worthy of a museum, with exquisite chairs and semicircular tables ornamented with detailed wood inlay of draped garlands and slender classic urns, and sideboards with graceful bow curves and fluted wood columns. Again softening the effect of somber refinement, examples of chinoiserie were everywhere: black lacquered screens inlaid with ivory depicting chrysanthemums and cranes, cloisonné clocks and vases in turquoise and gold, and countless blue and white Canton bowls and Rose Medallion lamps of remarkable age and beauty, creating an atmosphere of established refinement.

"Here we are, sir," the old butler said as he struggled with the key to my room. "There's no central heat, but each bath has recently been equipped with its own heater and hot water unit. Plenty of extra comforters and quilts, as this old building gets chilly at night. Air gets in around the sills."

He was certainly right, as the remarkably tall windows, original from the time the residence was built, were considerably warped. Looking around at what resembled an extremely elegant version of an English bed-and-breakfast, with damask curtains and bedspread and original pieces of porcelain and silver scattered around the room, I mumbled, "Charming."

"Very well, sir," the butler replied as he walked around the room to check that everything was in order.

"I'd like to make a phone call," I said, hoisting the suitcase on a chest apparently designed to hold luggage.

"Very well, sir," he repeated, and I thought to myself that he must have seen so many guests come and go that hardly anything registered with him. "If you need anything, sir," he continued, pointing to a long thick cord with a tassel, "ring here. Tea is served downstairs at half past five."

No sooner had he left than I heard a muffled knock on the door. "Who is it?" I asked, without opening the door.

"It's me, Jano." His appearance, exuberant as always, was a welcome note in strange surroundings. "Just wanted to tell you that you can always count on me while you're here. I'll give you my extension number . . . I had the feeling Jeremy wouldn't be much help."

"He did his best," I said. "But I get the impression he doesn't pay much attention to what anyone says."

"He's completely deaf," Jano replied. "That's why he keeps saying, 'Very well, sir.' I heard a rumor he's over ninety, but nobody has the heart to tell him to retire." Jano was his old confident self. "Something else I have to tell you," he continued. "Dr. Landry's been leaving messages all day that he wants to see you as soon as you get in."

"Oh, no," I mumbled, annoyed, as I recalled the coup de grace Landry had devised for me to deliver to Braun. The ominous entrance of Mozart's chorus on the word *Requiem* began to play itself out in my mind. Trying to escape the invasive sounds, I asked, "How's everything going here, Jano?"

"Very well," he replied. "More or less. Some of the guests are upset because there've been a number of anonymous notes."

Jano quickly picked up on my chagrin. "What did they say?"

"All kinds of alarming things, quotes from the Bible. Like 'Woe to her that is filthy and polluted' and 'The love of money is the root of all evil.' Oh yes, also something like 'He that toucheth pitch shall be defiled.' You can imagine how outraged some of the guests are."

"Some of the guests?" I asked, hoping he would say more.

"Well, Maximilian is furious about the one Nicoletta received. She took it as a kind of veiled threat not to go ahead with their marriage."

"Heavy," I mumbled.

"And newspaper clippings," he continued. "About a scholar dumped in Lake Geneva and a forger strangled in Munich. A couple of others too . . . I can find out more if you want to know."

"I'd appreciate that. By the way, could you do me a favor and tell Dr. Landry I'll meet him as soon as I unpack?"

"Sure thing, sir," Jano said, with a gesture reminiscent of saluting and clicking his heels. "He's staying in the room right above you. Oh, one other thing. They're coming to measure you for your costume today at three thirty. Is that convenient?"

"It's fine," I said.

"Philippe doesn't want the other guests to be alarmed about the anonymous notes," he added, smiling. "So don't let him know I told you, or I'll be guillotined."

As he headed for the door, a peculiar thought occurred to me. "Do you know," I said, "the night before she died, Denise said almost exactly the same thing." On hearing her name, Jano's expression saddened. "Have you found out anything more about her death?" I asked.

"I've been talking with other members of the staff and I did hear something. It turns out Denise had a boyfriend; she might even have been engaged to him, because she showed up one day at work with a big, flashy ring."

"Yes," I said, "I saw it when I arrived at La Favorite."

"Well," he continued, "she never talked about him and they were never seen together. Except once, about a month before the guests arrived, one of the maids saw her talking to him. She thought he was a contractor working at La Favorite."

"Did she say what he looked like?" I asked.

"She didn't pay much attention and now, all of a sudden,

the police want a description. All she could tell them was that he was a few inches taller than Denise and dark haired and dark complexioned—sort of swarthy, she said. And extremely good-looking."

"Interesting," I said.

"I'll go tell Dr. Landry you're here," he said, smiling. "He'll be quite relieved, I think." Knowing Landry was waiting, I plunged into the task of reordering my life in a new space. As I unpacked, I kept trying to sort out the news about Denise's mystery boyfriend. With the trip to Munich so recent in my mind, certain coincidences stood out: Whoever killed Denise had been obsessed with ritual and religion in a very superstitious way, laying out her body with a crucifix and flowers. And in Munich, Bruno Abruzzese had been acting strangely before he jumped, hovering around confessionals as if guilt-obsessed.

This was really a far-fetched theory. Nancy and Munich were hundreds of miles apart and only connected in my mind because I just happened to spend time in each place. But the link was there—the Mozart diaries. The broken lock on my briefcase remained unexplained, and Denise had a key to my room. Abruzzese was connected with the diaries, at least peripherally, because of his involvement with the forger's death.

But Landry was probably fuming, and it was time to get moving. As I struggled with the lock on my door, I decided to confide in Nadine about my conjecture about Abruzzese.

Heading through the corridors breathlessly, I felt dazed. So much had already been set in motion prior to my arrival, it reminded me of a play in which the curtain opened before all the characters had arrived at their places. I was rushing to get onstage, and I still hadn't learned my lines.

# CHAPTER 19

*History, Sir, will tell lies, as usual.*
—GEORGE BERNARD SHAW

As I knocked on Landry's door, I knew my fears were not unfounded; this was the long-anticipated "day of demolition." It would be the last time I talked with him before my encounter with Braun. Landry was relieved when I arrived, but annoyed. "Cut it pretty close, didn't you? You had me really worried. Well, you're here now, that's what matters. And there isn't much time."

Landry's heavy-handed tactics emerged as I had come to expect. "So," he said, with a commanding tone, "your check has been deposited in the account you told my assistant. Forty-five thousand dollars, isn't that what we said? Plus I added a little bonus, five thousand. Now that everything's on schedule, I don't have to remind you how much I'm counting on you. Remember, your objective is to teach Braun a good lesson—to put him in his place. Tell him how everyone thinks he's a tenth-rate musicologist and that he does bad work—you can say it in your own words. Mention that people have warned you about his personal integrity and his competence. All right?"

Landry waited for my reply. I acknowledged him with the faintest nod. Sensing it would be unwise to push me any further on this issue, he moved on. "I really had to pull some strings, but I managed to have his son turned down by Harvard, Berkeley, Yale, and Princeton. And I made sure he found out about it today—his son's been too afraid to tell him."

I couldn't believe my ears. How could Landry muster such astonishing power—to do evil?

"Braun is not really even a musicologist," Landry continued. "We need a new title for someone like him—maybe 'specialist in essential bibliography' or something like that. If you ever need help on footnotes or paragraph indentation signs, he's probably the best person for that."

"But are you sure this isn't going too far?" I blurted out.

"Too far?" he repeated. "Look, Pierce, I don't pretend to be a saint. But I know for a fact there are very few saints in this world. The ones we read about are just sinners who were reshaped and revised by some editor. You might as well listen to this, since you're about to embark on a new direction: more than any historian, it's the editor who holds the supreme position of power in this world of ideas. That's what it's about—power, pure and simple."

Landry flushed as he spoke. "Editors are the ones who ultimately decide what's true and what's not. We have the ability to shape—no, to create—history. No one ever reads what really happened, they just read the editor's slant. Heroes and villains: sometimes they're the same person, depending on who's revised and edited them."

Trying to hide my apprehension, I said, "You don't think Braun might do something to harm himself, like Wolff did?"

"Look, Pierce, goodwill is all right to a point but then it becomes stupidity. Don't let it get in your way and, especially, don't get sidetracked. You don't owe him a thing. And Wolff is nothing but an old faggot who's better off dead."

Landry must have suddenly gotten an inkling of the revulsion I was trying to hide. His tone softened considerably. "Braun'll be fine. Old codgers like him eat rusty nails for breakfast. By the way, you're going to like the other members of the board. We get invited on two or three private yachts a year, and we always attend the same events together: the America's Cup, Royal Ascot, the tennis tournaments at Gstaad and Wimbledon. Have you ever been to a royal wedding? The board is invited to practically every major event in Europe—christenings and funerals. Something tells me you'll like your new lifestyle."

Trips on yachts and royal weddings were the last thing on my mind; my concerns for Braun were overwhelming. But it was patently clear to me that arguing with Landry was pointless. And that it would have swift and irreversible consequences for me. Landry scrutinized me intensely and said, "There's something strange about the way you're acting, Matthew, something that doesn't inspire my confidence. My assistant, Margot, now *she* does exactly what I tell her and never flinches. I hope you're not going to fall apart on us."

When I didn't reply, he became antagonistic. "Look, if you're going to do this half-assed," he barked, "the deal's off and you can give me back the fifty thousand. And if it turns out you've been playing games with me, I'll make sure you never work again in this field. Are you with me all the way or not?"

Being tongue-lashed by Landry left me speechless. With as much conviction as I could muster, I replied, "Yes."

He continued to scrutinize me with his intimidating stare, and after a tense moment, said, "Good. I'll be waiting to hear how it goes." Opening the door, he gave me a powerful handshake and slapped me vigorously on the back, pushing me out of his room. "Talk to him this afternoon during tea. Just don't pussyfoot around—the stakes are too high."

I was nervous and angry, having allowed myself to be bullied and manipulated. Unfortunately, I now knew all too well the consequences of antagonizing Landry. *Is there any way I can pull this off?* I wondered. *And still somehow be able to look at myself in the mirror?*

I began to sort out the possibilities. If Braun didn't demand an explanation when I asked him for the diary back, I could let it drop right there. But if he persisted, I would have to go ahead with Landry's script. After all, he would clearly be asking for it.

No. I was lying to myself; it was all a cruel charade. As I wandered through the halls, variations of the imaginary dialogue with Braun kept playing in my mind. I'll tell him I'm concerned because he's kept the diary for so long. Or maybe that I've been warned about him by others. If he really insists on hearing more, I could say I no longer have confidence in him and would rather have the diary examined by people whose work I trust. But as hard as I tried to rationalize what I had to do, the truth was plain and simple: I wanted Landry's ninety-thousand-dollar job and the rest was all a lie.

As I resigned myself to following Landry's agenda, I realized how tired I was of allowing others to push me around. Lonely and furious with myself, I found the staircases and long corridors confining, more oppressive than I had remembered.

Crossing the threshold of my room, I stumbled upon a note with the immediately recognizable gold-embossed letters of the Fondation de l'Art éternel. Opening it quickly, I read, "May I have the pleasure of seeing you in my apartment before tea this afternoon? Shall we say 4:30?" It was signed René de Laguerelle. Glancing quickly at my watch, I realized I'd have to catch a quick shower immediately if I wanted to be on time to be measured for my costume, then to meet with the viscount. But the news thrilled me; the viscount might tell me that I was going to receive an award from the foundation.

No sooner had I stepped out of the shower than the phone rang; the tailor and the seamstress were on their way. A knock on the door startled me, a wooden sound as if someone were beating the door with a stick. A heavyset man wearing a white vest and scarf came in, followed by a slender wisp of a woman dragging a wheeled trolley overstuffed with period costumes.

"*Bonjour, Monsieur.*" Their amicable voices echoed in the corridor as they steered the unwieldy cart through the narrow door.

"What do you think, Dominique?" the man asked. "Something amusing like Papageno with bird feathers?"

"No," the woman replied. "He's too serious for that. Let's make him someone romantic like Tamino or Figaro."

"If you ask me," the man continued, "he's not quite the romantic lead type," and I listened silently, surprised to hear myself being evaluated while I stood there.

"We could make him an Austrian gentleman," the woman continued. "Or how about an Englishman, a young Dr. Burney?"

The man retained an unconvinced expression on his face as I recognized names they were tossing about, obscure to anyone but historians and Mozart scholars: Dr. Burney was a prolific writer and critic from the time of Mozart, who published detailed observations about famous musicians and the musical scene in the important European cultural centers.

"How is it you know so much about the eighteenth century?" I asked.

The man responded immediately. "Dominique did her master's degree thesis on how people dressed in the eighteenth century. And I have been designing costumes for operas since I was nineteen—I won't tell you how long ago that was," he said.

"Henri, how about Joseph II?" Dominique interrupted.

"Maybe," he replied. "He wore those flimsy white trousers. I think the *docteur* would fill them quite nicely."

Ignoring his comment, Dominique said to me, "You know, Joseph hated all the pomp of the court of his mother, Empress Maria Theresa. He was all austerity and reform. I don't quite see you as Joseph II—you strike me more as someone who enjoys the good life."

"But men in uniform are sooo sexy," Henri insisted. "Generals, naval captains, army officers." He sprang into action, saying, "Let's take his measurements and we'll decide later."

"Don't I get any input into what I'm going to wear?" I asked.

"I guarantee you'll like what we choose," Henri replied. "It's more fun this way, it's a surprise."

"But what if I don't?" I asked.

"If you don't like it," Dominique countered, "we'll make you something else."

"So, what do you do when you're not here?" Henri asked me as he measured my waist. "I take it you're not married?"

"Not married," I replied, not interested in saying more.

"A girlfriend, at least?" he continued.

Dominique interrupted. "So many questions, Henri. You'll make him uncomfortable."

Henri was engaged in taking my inseam measurement, and as I watched Dominique write down the numbers, I felt a quick squeeze where I least expected it: Henri had taken an unconventional measurement. He smiled as he stood and draped the tape measure around my shoulders. "Such a large chest. Try this jacket on for size."

Dominique caught my reaction and intervened. "Don't let him frighten you. He's harmless. This kind of costume event makes us all a little crazy. A week's work and only two days to do it."

Measurements taken and recorded, they were soon packing up and heading out the door as quickly as they arrived. "When will it be ready?" I asked.

"Tomorrow at five," Dominique replied. "If you need any changes, we'll still have plenty of time."

Henri laughed. "But that rarely happens."

Costume taken care of, my next order of business was an appointment with the viscount, whose requests, despite their politeness, were more command than invitation. By now I was burning with curiosity as to what he would say. And it looked like I would finally get answers to my questions.


A tall, distinguished butler showed me into the viscount's antechamber, with bookshelves full of ancient leather volumes, and soon returned to announce, "The viscount will see you." As I was led into his chambers, I passed Queen Anne and Georgian furniture in a near-perfect state of preservation and an abundance of decorative objects: miniature busts of Roman emperors mounted on pillars of gray-veined marble, impressive urns of black and gilded bronze and porcelain Veuveperrin hand-painted boxes with Italian landscapes. After several minutes of polite conversation, the viscount launched into his reasons for asking to see me. "This relatively sudden appearance of Mozart diaries like the one you found concerns me. Why, after two hundred years, are they turning up now?"

I had been completely taken in by the viscount's aura of omniscience, his having so many friends and connections in high places. But his puzzlement made him suddenly seem like just another person grappling with the complexities of the situation. "Perhaps scholars are combing libraries and archives in greater numbers and with greater care," I surmised. "Or the increasing awareness of Mozart and his music in the general population makes it possible for amateurs to recognize clues in documents that were once overlooked."

As he listened, the viscount's face took on a more serious expression and the tone of his voice darkened. "If the diaries are authentic, their value to scholars is inestimable. But they shouldn't be attracting the huge prices they're getting at auctions. It makes no sense to me whatsoever. And all these, well, unusual events surrounding them."

"When you say 'unusual events,'" I asked, "are you talking about the homicides linked with the diaries?" Seeing his agreement, I continued, "Someone here among your guests or staff is also aware of a connection and is slipping newspaper articles and anonymous notes under doors."

"It's very disturbing that my guests have to go through this unpleasant experience. But we're taking measures to find out who's responsible, and I've been personally keeping an eye on the various newspaper clippings. What do you know about Arnold Schott?"

"He's the Canadian art scholar who stole a page of the *Book of Hours for the Duc de Berry* from a museum in Italy."

"That's the one," he replied. "After he was apprehended, they discovered he'd been stealing and selling manuscripts and artworks for decades. He was out on bail, but a few weeks ago, before he came to trial, his body was found in Lake Geneva."

"That newspaper clipping was slipped under my door at La Favorite," I replied. "His face was unrecognizable." Remembering a gruesome detail, I added, "And he was found with his male organ sewn into his mouth."

"I know," he mumbled. "Ghastly."

"Nadine would probably be the person to ask," I replied. "She knows far more about those things than I do."

"Nadine's invaluable," he continued. "But the situation is complicated, and it's hard to get a perspective of what's going on."

Feeling secure enough for the first time to probe him, I

asked, "Is that the reason you invited so many people connected with Mozart?"

"One of the reasons," he replied.

"It's still not clear to me what the connection is between Schott and the diaries," I continued.

"I've just learned that Schott was trying to sell a Mozart diary he found in Geneva. So it appears there's a risk associated with the diaries. Something you should perhaps keep in mind."

"The thought has occurred to me," I said quietly.

"Nadine has been keeping me filled in and she mentioned her suggestion that you offer the diary to Maximilian for a large sum. Since the time she told me that, I've been worried she may have initiated a chain of events that will be impossible to stop once it's set in motion. You see, Max can be quite persuasive and might even tempt you to sell the diary on the spot. After all, it's your right to sell it for whatever price and to whomever you wish."

"Excuse me, viscount," I replied, "but the figure she wants me to suggest—seven hundred fifty thousand dollars—is so high, there's little likelihood he'll accept."

"Just in case he does," the viscount continued, "I hope I can persuade you to wait before committing yourself. A number of them have been sold within the last few years—probably more than you're aware of—and under much less sensational circumstances. But whenever a diary is sold, it disappears from circulation, permanently. If there are no plans to publish them, it's a terrible loss to the world."

"How about Braun and Landry? Aren't they including some new diaries in their upcoming editions?" I asked.

"Neither one will say," he continued, "and their reticence is making me fear the worst. Perhaps we'll never get an opportunity to look at them."

"So let's say Max actually finds a buyer at that price. You're suggesting I turn down a once-in-a-lifetime opportunity? Wouldn't the foundation be prepared to make a counter offer?"

The viscount was shocked by my question. "The bylaws of the foundation are restrictive," he replied. "And there are no provisions whatsoever for that kind of expenditure. We deal with disinterested scholarly and artistic pursuit, which is the very cornerstone of culture. As a scholar, you must understand this. Everything you've done with your career has been true to those ideals. It seems obvious that earning a lot of money did not play a role in your choice of profession, or you never would have gone into a field as unlucrative as musicology."

The viscount's comments brought me back to the way things were before I entered his world, where the stakes were so high. "I hear what you're saying and I'll certainly keep it in mind," I said. But I was going to keep my options open.

"There's no question in my mind that you have a clear choice before you," he continued. "You're standing at the crossroads between profit and conscience."

The viscount rekindled a spark of idealism in me, but I was disappointed that he had not broached the issue of the foundation awards. I assumed our discussion was over and stood up, ready to shake his hand. Instead, the viscount remained seated. "There's another matter I wanted to discuss with you," he continued, and I again took my seat. "Something I've been keeping under wraps for a few years until I could find the right person. Nadine told me how much you helped her in Munich, and I'm beginning to think you might be perfectly suited to the task."

My curiosity apparent, he forged ahead. "A very dear friend of mine has some damaged manuscript pages with a text that was completely illegible. His librarian read about Büchner's play, *Wozzeck*, and decided to try to recover the text. Do you know the circumstances surrounding *Wozzeck*?"

"Yes, for the most part," I said. "Büchner left it in the form of a preliminary draft that remained unknown for forty years after his death. Then a man named Franzos was able to have the unreadable pages chemically treated and deciphered the text. After the play was performed, it became the subject for the opera by Alban Berg."

"Precisely. Well, my friend took his cue from Franzos and treated the manuscript pages with a special solution, then examined them under ultraviolet light, and now he's convinced he has a Mozart diary on his hands. But he's an extremely private person and doesn't care to get Braun or Landry involved. He doesn't trust them—and I can't say I blame him. I've been keeping my eye open for someone discreet. Which brings me to the point: would you be willing to take a look at it?"

"I'd be delighted." But immediately I hesitated and asked, "But when?"

The viscount replied firmly and matter-of-factly, "In a day or two." Flabbergasted, I listened as he continued. "Let's see . . . tomorrow is the costume ball. You can leave the following day."

I replied, "You really want me to leave in two days? I'm not so sure I want to leave so soon . . . all the concerts and events. And what about the awards of the foundation?"

The viscount spoke quietly, and from the somber tone of his voice, I suspected he was about to give me bad news. "There will be other foundation events and concerts in the future, but this is something unique, an opportunity that may never present itself again. Can I count on you?"

I hesitated. Although I was completely keen on the prospect of examining a new Mozart diary, I felt my hopes of receiving a stipend from the Fondation de l'Art éternel were jeopardized. Taking a risk, I decided to speak up. "What about the awards of the foundation?"

The viscount looked genuinely disarmed by my directness. Bluntly, he replied, "They were decided long before you received my invitation to La Favorite. But if all goes well with the diary, who knows. Maybe next year's awards."

I reflected on my present options: the viscount was playing a game of carrot-and-stick with me, but my only chance of success lay in cooperating with him. He wasn't giving me much choice. My disappointment about the award was offset by the appeal of being the only outside expert permitted to see the newly discovered document. "I'll do it," I replied and the die was cast.

"Good," he replied, beaming. "I'll tell you who and where, but you must not write it down or repeat it to anyone." With great formality, the viscount said, softly, "Abbot Cyril . . . Benedictine monastery, Lesní Klášter . . . outside of Prague." After I was sure I had memorized it, I nodded, and he leaned back in his chair. "Now you understand why discretion is so necessary. The serenity of that place must be preserved. I'll give you a card to use in automatic bank machines around Europe to cover your expenses. But don't mention to anyone where you're going or write or call from there. Take all the time you need. I'll see you back in Nancy when you're finished."

"Why do you want me to leave so soon?" I asked.

"There's urgency surrounding the diaries. That's why I'm asking you to leave tomorrow, after the costume ball. It's a great deal to ask, but I consider it a personal favor."

As I reflected on his requirements for strict secrecy, I resolved to follow every precaution to the letter; the whole scenario relating to the diaries now clearly warranted it.

Apparently delighted with the resolution, the viscount said, "Shall we head down to tea?" After escorting me out the door, he stopped short and said, "And I trust you'll stand firm about not jumping at any offers to buy your diary. We hear a great deal of rhetoric today from young people about improving the world, but I've learned one thing: it can only be achieved with a single act. Anything else is just grandiose idealism."

*Jesus,* I thought as we walked downstairs together. *This frail, fragile little man in his nineties just negotiated me right off the table.* But another urgent matter was about to demand my complete and immediate attention: Landry wanted the last nail driven into Braun's coffin and I was the designated driver.

## CHAPTER 20

*For a crowd is not company; and faces are but a*
*gallery of pictures; and talk but a tinkling cymbal,*
*where there is no love.*
—FRANCIS BACON

When the viscount and I arrived in the library, he was engulfed by old friends greeting him with a display of affection I had rarely seen elsewhere. Without an opportunity to say goodbye to him, I found myself pushed to the sidelines by enthusiastic well-wishers. The magnificence of the crowded concert room where guests were gathered for tea caught my attention. The unusually high frescoed ceiling was surrounded by an elaborate white plaster frieze of cherubs and overflowing fruit baskets. And tall, remarkably detailed portraits of the ancestors of Lord Sackville Williamson, perhaps painted by Gainsborough or Joshua Reynolds, gazed down with composure.

A concert was planned, and chairs and music stands for several players had been set up in a circle around a rare but unmistakable instrument, the glass harmonica. Set within a fine case of inlaid wood, the instrument consisted of glass bowls of different sizes, one mounted inside another on a long horizontal shaft stretched out above a shallow trough of water.

I tried to distract myself from the unpleasant task ahead, but after a few minutes I saw Braun. There he was, standing by the fireplace, alone, glassy eyed and ashen, looking shell-shocked. But this time a new element revealed itself in his face: rage, unadulterated rage. There was every good reason for me to keep my distance, but I had a job to do.

"Dr. Braun?" I said softly.

With an annoyed look on his face, he snapped, "What is it?"

"May I have a word with you?"

"It's not a good time," he replied, and turned away from me. The intimidating presence of Landry seemed to be hovering over my shoulder, and as I remembered his firm slap on my back, I winced involuntarily and plunged ahead.

"I'm afraid it can't wait," I responded. "I've been waiting months for word on the diary I submitted to you, and finally I've decided to withdraw it from your consideration."

To my surprise, Braun turned and looked me directly in the eye. His complete attention startled me; his eerie expression sent a shudder racing down my spine. "Do you mind telling me just what prompted your decision?" he asked with a sly tone. In that brief moment, Landry's script raced through my head. I took a deep breath and started to speak. But I stopped. Despite all his arrogance, the man who had just been the subject of one of the most brutal articles ever written about a musicologist looked so pitiful and devoid of spirit that I was momentarily speechless.

I decided I would not kick a man who was down, regardless of the consequences. Switching gears completely, I replied, "It's just that I've waited for months and have decided to get it authenticated elsewhere."

"Is that all?" he asked incredulously.

"Yes," I responded.

"Isn't there anything else you'd like to say to me?" he asked, almost prodding me. With the slightest hint of a smile and a knowing look in his eyes, he continued, "Like, maybe you've had some doubts about my competence?"

Unprepared for the turn, I replied, "Not really."

"I hope it's not because you've heard rumors about my personal integrity or the quality of my work?"

Braun's precise choice of words shook me and I stared at him, bewildered. He raised his voice. "The incredible nerve, running around chasing offers like an opportunist. You Americans have no shame whatsoever."

"Keep your voice down," I said, but Braun got louder.

"If you're getting involved with Landry," he barked, "you're in way over your head."

After two weeks of trying everything within my power to get along with the guests of the foundation, something inside me snapped. "If you can't keep your voice down . . ." I said, clenching my teeth.

But Braun interrupted me and his voice became more high-pitched: "Let's face it, the only reason Landry is interested in *you*, a tenth-rate musicologist, a *nobody*, is because he wants to get his hands on your diary."

Our discussion had drawn the attention of the entire room. Raising my own voice, I said, "Look, I'm just asking for the return of my diary. If that's not acceptable to you, my lawyer will handle it from here."

With an enraged look on his face, he stared at me until he shattered the silence. "Just who do you think you are?" Turning abruptly, he continued, "You disgust me," and walked away, leaving me standing alone in front of a room of riveted guests.

Within seconds the full impact of his tirade hit me. Replaying the conversation in my mind, I went over the phrases Braun had used, and made a mental comparison with the script Landry had concocted for me: "doubts about my competence," "rumors about my personal integrity," and "the quality of my work."

More than anything, "tenth-rate musicologist" stung. The striking coincidence raised suspicions in my mind and I found myself debating whether Landry and Braun had concocted the whole thing. Embarrassed and angry, I arrived at a decision: this was absolutely the last time anyone connected with the foundation would walk all over me.

Jano arrived with a single flute of champagne. "I thought this might be a good time to switch from tea to cocktails," he said, beaming as usual, pretending not to have noticed my heated exchange with Braun.

Thanking him, I gulped it down and walked on, feeling the weight of whispered comments and critical eyes. From my solitary stance in a corner, I saw Andreas Wolff approaching, looking like his old self, extroverted and confident. He immediately gestured for two more glasses. As he handed me one, he asked softly, "Braun playing hardball? Don't take it seriously. And especially don't worry what anyone thinks. Every single person here has a past. Just do what they all do—smile, chat, and pretend. Act like nothing is wrong."

Eager to talk about anything that would deflect attention from my argument with Braun, I looked at the chairs around the glass harmonica and said, "It looks like we're about to have a concert."

"Yes," he said. "There's a virtuoso on the glass harmonica today. She's performing Mozart's Adagio and Rondo with flute, I think, and some other instruments."

"Oboe, viola, and cello," I said almost automatically. As we spoke, a woman took her seat at the instrument and began to play, but it was difficult to hear as the sound did not project well. To make matters worse, I was temporarily distracted by Nicoletta Chigi, without Maximilian, surrounded by three or four attentive men. Wolff saw my eyes move in her direction and could not resist his favorite target. "If you ever want to study morons," he said, "look for a beautiful woman in a crowded room. They're usually surrounding her like flies to—"

"Ripe fruit?" I asked, finishing his sentence.

"That's not what I was going to say," he continued. "But I'm trying to behave myself tonight."

"Where's Max?" I asked.

"Good question," he replied. "Max, the man with the Midas squeeze. Those two certainly have their hands full."

"How so?" I asked.

"When Nicoletta loves someone, she isolates him and demands his full attention, eventually obliterating every trace of his spirit, absorbing his energy and dragging him like a helpless star into a gaping black hole. Take Roberto over there. Since their breakup, he's been a wreck."

"Andreas, you never finished what you were saying about Max that night at Santa Maria Maggiore."

"Someone should slap a deadbolt on that man's penis," Wolff said, unflinching. "And her—what she's looking for is simple: a huge cock with a huge checkbook attached to it. Poor

Roberto, such a nice kid, getting caught up in a mess like that. What can I say? The heart searches in quiet torment."

He smiled as the faint sounds of the glass harmonica wafted in our direction. "I really should stop this maudlin philosophizing, I'm even depressing myself. Thank God for music."

"And for Mozart," I added.

"I'll drink to that," he said, beckoning to a waiter. "In fact, lately I'll drink to anything." Holding a fresh glass to mine, Wolff made a toast: "If life is pain then Mozart is morphine."

"Let's go over and try to hear the glass harmonica a little better," I said. And as we approached, I was able to recognize the pieces she was performing, an andante and a fantasia that Mozart wrote for mechanical organ, followed by some unfamiliar music by Mozart. The artist, in a black dress that covered her from head to toe, was immersed in her performance. With her brown hair in a bun and wearing thick glasses and an old-fashioned white lace collar, she looked like a frumpy spinster.

As she finished, Wolff said, "Beautiful," and we both applauded.

"I didn't recognize the last piece you played," I said.

"It's a work Mozart never finished," she replied. "A composer I know tried his hand at completing it."

"Do you get many calls to perform?" Wolff asked.

"Not really," she said, smiling. "Mostly, I perform as an organist."

"Where are you from?" I asked.

"Iowa. I'm a librarian at Iowa State."

"We've both been fascinated with your performance," Wolff said. She smiled and began shuffling pages for her next piece. Roberto, who had been watching us from the other side of the room, came over with a look of fascination on his face as he examined the exotic-looking instrument.

"Wow," he said, "this looks new. Did you have someone build it for you?"

"Yes," she replied. "A harpsichord maker in Germany."

"You're creating sound by rubbing the rim of the glass with wet fingers," Roberto continued. "Basically like the trick everyone's done at least once in their life in a restaurant with drinking glasses."

"The same principle," she said, "except these glasses have all been cut and polished to a specific pitch, then mounted on a shaft—Benjamin Franklin's idea."

"Like nothing I've ever heard," Roberto said. "Almost like a reflection, or a shadow, of a sound. And it's a contradiction, because the sound is both mellow and piercing at the same time, very calming, yet very unsettling."

"Doctor Mesmer," I said, "the man who invented hypnotism in the eighteenth century, used the glass harmonica to put his patients into a state of relaxation. But it was also said to upset people's nerves and was banned by the police in some towns in Germany."

"You're kidding," Roberto said, eyes wide-open. "The effect is like a bell or a Chinese gong; sometimes it reminds me of a dark, breathy whistle."

"For me," Wolff added, "it's distant voices in a cathedral, angelic, almost supernatural."

"Many people hear sounds in terms of colors," I said. "So this would have to be the light blues of delphiniums and lavender."

Wolff, waxing poetic, said, "It's darker, more somber shades, evoking moonlight and distance—forest green and midnight blue."

As we spoke, four musicians carrying their instruments moved into place around the glass harmonica and we stepped back to give them room. After arranging their music on the stands, they began their performance with a clear, brisk attack that surprised the guests and caused a hush in the conversation. The haunting sounds of Mozart's Adagio in C Minor began to fill the room with a suggestion of brooding fatality. In this quintet, written in the last year of Mozart's life, the composer had progressed to an advanced sound world, using an economy of instruments to create unparalleled subtlety of orchestration, colored by the haunting, unearthly timbre of that near-extinct eighteenth-century species, the glass harmonica. The somber adagio was succeeded by a spontaneous rondo boasting one of the most refined and courtly melodies ever heard, and as the work concluded, polite applause was followed by a return to conversation. From a distance, Wolff and I saw Nadine walking toward us and he said to me quickly, "I really should go over and smooth Braun's ruffled feathers. In case you haven't noticed, he's having a bad day."

Surprised at Wolff's abrupt departure, Nadine said, "I hope I didn't scare him off."

"He's got some business to take care of," I said. "So, how's my favorite crime fighter?"

"Not bad," she replied. "Wasn't the quintet beautiful?"

"Splendid," I said. "Did you hear about my fight with Braun?"

Nadine nodded. "How are you feeling?"

"Like I was run over by a tank," I said. "But let's not talk about it now. I've been meaning to ask you about something else, Nadine, just don't tell me I'm crazy. I heard Denise had a secret boyfriend, a kind of dark, swarthy guy."

"I heard that from the police," she answered. "But who told you?"

"I'd rather not say," I replied, for once not confiding in Nadine. "Because I don't want to get anyone in trouble. And I want to keep that line of communication open." My reticence apparently didn't bother her, so I plunged ahead. "Here's what I wanted to ask you. It's a long shot, but there are some peculiar things that make me think of Bruno Abruzzese. The bizarre, ritualistic way Denise was laid out, with the crucifix and flowers, almost as if the person who did it was very superstitious in a religious way; Abruzzese's behavior before he jumped. Also, Denise's boyfriend supposedly was seen by almost no one, and that would make sense if he were a hit man." I held my breath.

"What else did you hear about the boyfriend?" she asked.

"That he was a few inches taller than Denise."

"I heard that too." Nadine's eyes darted upward diagonally as she made a quick mental calculation aloud. "Denise was five foot five, which would make her boyfriend around five eight. Abruzzese was five foot nine. That's in the ballpark."

"Could you find out more?" I asked. "DNA testing?"

Nadine reflected. "I've been planning to make a trip to police headquarters in Nancy and bring myself up to date on Denise's murder. It's always better to go in person because the French police won't say much on the phone. This might be the time."

"All the way back to Nancy?" I asked incredulously.

"Why not?" she asked. "It's not such a long trip now that the Chunnel's operating."

"And leave us here all unprotected?" I continued, with a forced smile. I was alarmed at the prospect.

"If you're worried, I could leave Enrique here. In fact, that might not be a bad idea."

"Probably not necessary," I said, downplaying my concerns.

The stentorian announcement, "Ladies and gentlemen, dinner is served," interrupted our conversation and sent us in the direction of the huge table. After saying goodbye to Nadine, I ran into Max, who had just walked in the door.

"How's it going?" he asked with his usual confident charm.

"Not bad," I replied, lying through my teeth.

"Nicoletta told me you were looking for a buyer for your diary. Why don't you come by my room tomorrow and we'll discuss it?" When I nodded, Max added, "How's three o'clock?"

"That's good for me," I replied nonchalantly. But I was eager to meet with him: Max was my ticket to finding the best possible price for my diary.

I remembered Nicoletta's comment about Max's ability to sell a document: "Sometimes in one day." Overnight, I could become a rich man. Then we were engulfed in the confusion of guests filling a small area and were soon swallowed up in the commotion of the madding crowd.

Surrounding the surprisingly long table, expansive seventeenth-century Flemish tapestries depicting scenes of the hunt hung majestically along the walls. I hurried to find the place card with my name on it until I reached the head of the table, where I least expected it to be. An unfamiliar guest, whom I assumed to be Lord Williamson, was also seated at the head of the table, immersed in conversation with Alison Teal on his right. There was an empty seat between him and a half-dozing Baroness Paumgarten, which put me directly in the center of a great deal of age and establishment.

The baroness did not respond to my greeting, nor did Ilsa, seated next to her, already deep in conversation with the guest to her left, so I turned to Lord Williamson. Looking to be in his late seventies, he still sported a full head of auburn hair, showing signs of white. Alison Teal, whose theatrical eye makeup made her seem more exotic than usual, had begun to chat with Roberto on her right.

"It's good to meet you," Lord Williamson said. As he spoke, an army of men wearing white jackets and gloves began to remove the seat plates.

"A butler for every guest?" I asked.

"It's a tradition in my family," he replied, pleased that I was enjoying the novelty of the situation.

I made a quick mental count—more than forty guests—and noticed that each waiter remained standing behind the chair of the particular guest.

"In case you'd like anything, don't hesitate to ask them." With that, he gestured to the waiter behind my chair, who arrived with an attentive smile.

"Yes, Lord Williamson?" the waiter asked.

"Dr. Pierce needs a fish fork," he said calmly, and I was amazed he could discern that a single piece was missing from the intricate rows of Georgian silver extending from both sides of my plate. "Terribly sorry, Lord Williamson," I heard, as the waiter scurried to retrieve a replacement.

Speaking with a distinguished accent and a mellifluous voice, Lord Williamson was engaging. And his informal style put me immediately at ease as he began discussing novels and novelists, showing great familiarity with literature ranging from

Petronius's *Satyricon* to Proust's *Remembrance of Things Past*, as well as twentieth-century authors from Eco to Steinbeck, Marguerite Yourcenar to Robert Graves and John Berendt. Trying to remember the name of a particular author he had read several years back, he surprised me by saying, "My memory is not as good as it used to be. One of the disadvantages of growing old, I'm afraid. But, as the Chinese say, everyone wants a long life, but no one wants to grow old."

"I also remember that Strindberg said something like growing old may not be pleasant, but it's interesting," I replied.

"Well," he said dryly, "if nothing else, it certainly is that."

"But I have to admit," I added, "these days I find older people more interesting."

"On the contrary," he replied, "I tend to enjoy the company of younger people. But I have to . . . there's hardly anyone my age left." As Lord Williamson launched into a discussion of cinema and recent plays on the London stage, classic courses presented with understated elegance arrived one after the other: lobster bisque topped with vintage sherry and *crème fraîche,* followed by terrine of fresh foie gras, then delicate salmon quenelles.

"In the past week, I've moved from Italian cuisine to Austrian and Bavarian," I said. "But this is all classic French."

"Thank you for noticing," he replied. "Our cooks have to begin with a French cookbook we have in the kitchen—it's over two hundred years old—and they start by learning to prepare everything exactly the way it's described."

"Your cooks have to know how to read classical French?" I asked, astonished.

He laughed. "Yes. It's always a shock at first. And initially preparations take them a long time, but after a while they get used to it, and soon they figure out how to prepare the dishes in less time while still maintaining the integrity of the recipe."

An incongruous sound, a flat, nasal voice, rang out, "It is now eight thirty P.M." Looking around, I realized it was the talking wristwatch of the old Baroness Paumgarten. The sound aroused her from her semiconscious state and she turned her head to me, eyes still half-shut.

"That man who was shouting at you at tea," she said. "Is he a minister?"

"No," I replied. "He's a musicologist. Why?"

"Because he speaks like he has a marble pulpit in his mouth," she answered, chuckling softly under her breath. Her unconventional sense of humor caught me off guard, but her implicit support was appreciated. With eyelids suspended, she appeared half-asleep, but her comments made it clear she was taking in far more than one would imagine.

"The last time we were together," I said, "was on the ride to Rome."

"Of course," she replied. "We began the trip at two-twenty and you were wearing a canary yellow polo shirt."

The baroness' memory for time and details floored me. Trying to account for it, I attributed it partly to her sleeping disorder, which limited the number of things for her to remember, and partly to the talking wristwatch that somehow jarred her awake and registered in her memory. As the waiters again converged on the table en masse, carrying a dish that looked like coq au vin with wild game birds, I commented to the baroness about the uniqueness of Lord Williamson's table.

"His family's been part of the English nobility since the time of the Norman conquest," she replied, again chuckling. "They regard the present royal family as brash newcomers." As she spoke, I noticed Alison Teal was already immersed in conversation with Lord Williamson, her voice projecting effortlessly thanks to her flawless diction.

"It was a blow when our relationship ended so abruptly," I heard her tell him.

"What is Alison Teal saying?" the baroness asked me softly, almost as if she were taking me into her confidence.

Listening more carefully, I replied, "She's talking about how she went to thermal spas all over Europe after her relationship with von Horvach ended. She now believes she's a better, stronger person than before it all happened."

*"Ach, ja,"* the baroness said. "Her nervous breakdown, a terrible thing. I'll never understand why the von Horvach boy acts

that way. If he doesn't change, he's going to meet a bad end."
Now it was clear to me that Baroness Paumgarten had distinct
gaps in her knowledge. "What is she talking about now?" she
asked, enjoying making me her partner in crime.

Listening for a moment, I replied, "She's saying it turned
into a kind of spiritual journey for her, consulting healers and
learning all kinds of alternative medicine. As a result, her breathing and even her voice have improved considerably."

"It's been many years since I've spoken with Miss Teal," the
baroness admitted. "She doesn't like my granddaughter. It's a
shame—I've always liked her."

The entourage of waiters served glazed pieces of apricot
and pear tarte Tatin, as bowls of unsweetened whipped cream
were carried from guest to guest. To extricate myself from my
new role of eavesdropper, I changed the subject. "Are you enjoying your stay here?"

"Yes, very much," she replied. "Only I didn't sleep very well
last night. A bad dream kept me awake."

Ilsa, who had ignored us until then, overheard her grandmother and said, "Now and then grandmother has a dream
about being locked in during a fire. That's why we always keep
the doors and windows unlocked wherever we're staying."

"A recurring nightmare," I said, thinking for a moment. "I
have one myself from time to time. I'm always in a dark room
and something is coming to get me, so I hunt frantically for a
place to hide, sometimes for what feels like an eternity. Just as
the door to my room opens, I wake up in a sweat, never knowing what it was."

"How often have you had it?" Ilsa asked.

"Only about ten times, but it always leaves a deep impression. Have you ever dreamt anything similar?"

"Yes, but nothing as dramatic as yours," Ilsa replied. "I
dream I hear people talking about me, and one after another,
everyone is saying something vicious. I always wake up upset."

"But I'm sure you find ways to take your mind off it," the
old baroness interjected. While I guessed she was referring to
Ilsa's frequent exchange of bed partners, I decided not to go there.

The aroma of freshly ground coffee filled the air as espresso was served, accompanied by tiny walnut wafers and intricately decorated chocolates. Smiling wryly as she passed over her grandmother's comment, Ilsa said, "Hélène is playing two very difficult Mozart concertos tonight. She's such a powerhouse."

"Which concertos?" I asked.

"The Third Violin Concerto and the Symphonie Concertante."

"Who's the other soloist in the Symphonie Concertante?" I asked.

"Elisabetta von Stahl," she replied. Noticing that guests had begun to rise from the table and move toward the music room, Ilsa stood up and we followed them. Standing next to Hélène Benoit on the platform stage, informally leafing through musical scores, was Elisabetta, wearing a sensational low-cut, strapless evening dress of vivid scarlet. As we took our seats, Andrei remarked under his breath, "I'm certainly going to enjoy this concert."

Taking a quick look around the room, I realized that male guests of all ages had maneuvered themselves quickly to the first four rows of the room, capturing the seating nearest the stage. Enrique, instead of standing and keeping an eye on the room, was firmly ensconced in the first row next to Roberto, both eagerly awaiting the start of the concert.

"I see you're getting to like Mozart," I said sarcastically.

Enrique beamed. "Someone'd better be ready to help her out in case she falls out of her dress."

The program began with Mozart's Symphony No. 1, written in London in 1764, when he was a mere eight years old. The three light movements again confirmed to me that Mozart's genius and style, his personality and character, were stamped indelibly from the earliest beginnings. At the conclusion, Hélène Benoit strode onto the platform with the complete confidence of an experienced artist.

After the extroverted orchestral opening of the Third Violin Concerto, Hélène attacked the rich double-stops on her legendary Guarnieri with fiery bowing and dynamic tone.

As introspective muted violins and flutes soared over an accompaniment of plucked strings, the Adagio second movement grew darker, with moments of excruciating tension
created by a repeated two-note accompaniment with the uncomfortable insistence of a water drop. At the conclusion of
the work, applause roared throughout the room and Hélène
glowed with satisfaction. When she returned, she was followed by the spectacular Elisabetta von Stahl, who took her
place on stage left.

"Hey, man, that's not fair," Enrique protested. "I picked
this seat specially, and now she's on the wrong side." Almost immediately, the orchestra began Mozart's unparalleled masterwork, the Symphonie Concertante for Violin and Viola, an
excursion into unexplored worlds. Each performer executed an
endless stream of echoed motives in rapid-fire succession, using
their bodies to convey the motion of the music and the sweep of
their conception.

In the slow movement, Elisabetta's eyes were closed as she
made the viola sing, especially on the lowest string where her
sound was never lacking in refinement and elegance, and Hélène
also shut her eyes during the rhetorical dialogue. Despite the
technical difficulties, Hélène and Elisabetta made the music
sound effortless, propelling the melodies of the third movement
upward rhythmically, like dancers springing higher and higher
with each jump. They carried the work to an exciting conclusion
before a room full of appreciative listeners and as applause broke
out, Enrique turned to me and commented quietly, "I think I
could get into this."

After the concert, the library was soon overflowing with
guests and with the aromas of exotic tobaccos and unusual
liqueurs. We awaited the appearance of the celebrated artists,
who arrived and needed little encouragement to throw themselves into the festivities. Before I knew it, two A.M. had passed
and, sated and satisfied on every level, I dragged myself back to
my room.

As I turned the key, I noticed a white envelope. Ripping it
open, I read the distorted text in grotesque, pasted letters:

I SHALL WIPE JERUSALEM AS A MAN WIPETH A DISH,
WIPING IT, AND TURNING IT UPSIDE DOWN

Paralyzed, I tried to stop the chaotic bass that was thundering in my ears. I understood the reference to Jerusalem to be the foundation, and I knew that some kind of imminent cataclysm was being prophesied. But the newspaper clipping, from an Italian *cronaca nera*—a crime tabloid—struck closer to home: it described the murders of Denise and von Horvach in ghastly detail.

Reading it, I began to wonder, *What kind of people continue to band together despite all the deaths? And move from city to city while members of their ranks disappear one after another?*

They were legitimate questions. But in my case, the reason was clear: money, plain and simple. An enormous amount of money, far beyond anything else I could ever hope to earn in a lifetime. And I was ashamed.

# CHAPTER 21

*The selfish spirit of commerce, which knows no country,*
*and feels no passion or principle but that of gain.*
—THOMAS JEFFERSON

In the morning, I drew open the weighted damask draperies on my window with a firm tug, to reveal a splendid sun-drenched view of lush shade trees and lawn, framed in the distance by eighteenth-century brick row dwellings in soft tones of burnished russet. Before meeting Max, I decided to clear my mind by indulging my passion for walking. And it would be on the unhurried, quaint walkways of Chelsea where so much of previous centuries had been carefully preserved. After a quick call to Jano, a late breakfast was dispatched to my room, leaving me with a block of time to explore my new surroundings.

In the eighteenth century, Chelsea had been a calm suburb of London, and although it was now part of the city, I observed everywhere an unhurried lifestyle, reminiscent of a time when the air was filled with the muted sounds of horse-drawn carriages on unpaved streets. Immersed in a tapestry of manicured lawns and tiny lots bursting with perennials as only the cool English summers can boast, I found my way to Cheyne Walk, a secluded world permeated with the pungent musk of ornamental pines.

As I walked, I distracted myself, reflecting on what an extraordinary chapter in Mozart's life his stay in Chelsea at the age of eight must have been: it was his first opportunity to turn himself exclusively to composition. It arose after an evening performing at the London home of Lord Thanet, when his father, Leopold, contracted a serious illness requiring more than seven weeks of recuperation. During that time, Mozart and his sister were not permitted to play the keyboard or make any noise, and Mozart used the "down time" to write his first symphony and to put a great number of keyboard works and sketches on paper.

Prior to Leopold's illness, the family's visit to London had been an unqualified success. The children had been received with great warmth and enthusiasm by King George III and Queen Charlotte, who treated the Mozart family with what Leopold called "easy manner and friendly ways." Twice before Leopold fell ill, and once after, the children performed for the royal couple at Buckingham Palace, Mozart playing works by Johann Christian Bach and Handel at first sight, accompanying the queen as she sang an aria and demonstrating his uncanny, precocious musical abilities on the king's pipe organ. And the amount of music Mozart wrote during their stay in London and Chelsea—from April 1764 to July 1765—was prodigious, including a sacred madrigal for four voices, several symphonies, a tenor aria with orchestra, and six sonatas for violin and keyboard dedicated to the queen.

As I walked past the charming brick facades of Ebury Street toward the house where they stayed, I managed to put the recent developments at Lord Williamson's estate out of my mind and recalled how Mozart's mother began to cook for the first time during their stay in Chelsea, with the enthusiastic encouragement of Leopold, since the food prepared for them had been so dreadful. After a long stroll, I arrived at the "physic," or botanical garden, where carefully edged and labeled rare plant specimens were thriving in a tranquil setting protected by walls of aged stone. Calculated to delight and awaken the senses, the garden was saturated with the reassuring aromas of ancient boxwoods, fragrant lavender, and bitter rosemary.

I continued toward the Royal Hospital, an imposing structure of classical lines and symmetry designed by Christopher Wren. Grand stretches of intense green lawn led me through the imposing pillars designed to dwarf the surroundings and astound visitors, then on past spacious courtyards to the remarkable frescoed Great Hall. As I strolled to a distant vantage point, it was easy to imagine what Leopold meant when he described the place outside of Chelsea where he had been carried in a sedan chair to enjoy the fresh air: "It has one of the most beautiful views in the world. Wherever I turn my eyes, I see only gardens, and in the distance, the finest castles."

Invigorated and renewed, I returned to the residence ready to deal with whatever was in store for me. Promptly at three o'clock, I knocked on Max's door and stood waiting, looking at my watch repeatedly to reassure myself I was on time.

Max took his time to answer and then greeted me casually. A quick glance around the room revealed distinct differences in Max's style: his desk had been placed strategically near the center of the room with two facing chairs, and on it, arranged with professional precision, were a fax machine, external modem and disk drive, a cellular phone, and a sophisticated laptop. His open briefcase of carefully stitched padded leather was unlike any I had ever seen, with metal compartments reminiscent of a safety deposit box and a handle wrapped with a formidable metal electronic device. And a striking desk set of sleek black marble gave me an impression of sophistication and luxury.

As he motioned for me to sit down, Max noted my silent admiration of his black marble desk set. "A gift from the president of the Ivory Coast," he said. "He commissioned Gianfranco Ferré to design it, and I understand they only made one exemplar. I'm rather fond of it." No sooner had he spoken than Max received a call on his cell phone.

After apologizing, he stood up, then walked into the adjacent room and shut the door. "Goddamn it," I heard him suddenly shout in Italian, "didn't I explain all that to him yesterday?" Speaking more softly, he continued, "What the fuck am I supposed to do? Jesus Christ, tell him I'll call him later, I can't talk now."

With a calm, composed smile on his face, Max returned as if nothing had happened. Unnerved by the explosion I had heard, it was not easy for me to appear pleasant and casual. Immediately, he launched into business. "Nicoletta mentioned you might be looking for a buyer for your diary and, as you've probably figured out, I'll do anything she asks me."

Feeling immediately suspicious at the mention of Nicoletta's name, I said, "That's very kind of you."

"So, what kind of figure are you looking for?"

It was time to get down to business and I replied, "Roughly speaking, around seven hundred fifty thousand."

Max sat motionless, with his mouth half-open. Finally he said, "You're mad." Laughing cynically and looking away in disgust, he continued, "And you don't even know if it's authentic. You astonish me."

Resolute to follow through with Nadine's plan, I looked him directly in the eye and sat in silence. He added, "And I thought you musicologists weren't interested in money," hoping to prod me into saying something. When he understood that I wasn't going to budge, Max walked over to the window and looked out for a few moments. Then turning back, he softened his tone. "Well, I guess it's understandable. It's no disgrace to be poor, but it's a hell of an inconvenience."

He sat down and scrutinized me. "All right, I'll ask around and see what I can come up with. I just hope you're not playing games; the buyers I deal with are high-stakes players who don't like it when someone fools around with them." With a peculiar, sinister tone in his voice, he continued, "In fact, I've just been reading about some unfortunate characters I suspect were trying to double-cross their clients. Like that forger in Munich."

"Good God," I said immediately with an uncomfortable laugh. "Are you implying your clients might kill me?"

"Come on now, of course not," Max said, turning on the charm with a smile that failed to reassure me. "Don't take me literally, we're just having a little man-to-man chat."

"So the forger double-crossed his clients?" I asked, refusing to let the matter drop. "Is that why he was killed?"

"I'd have to find out who he was working for and why they took him out," he replied. "But I got the distinct impression he was playing games with the wrong people."

"So he deserved what he got," I continued doggedly.

"I have to admit," he said with an ambiguous inflection in

his voice, "I take a more pragmatic view of these things than most people, based on my experience in global finance. International business is no different from the criminal justice system, or war, or even the church, where getting rid of someone is sometimes, well, you could call it an unavoidable evil. But it's always an option, something indispensable and occasionally even necessary."

I couldn't believe what I was hearing. "I take a more traditional view of these matters," I replied, trying to decide if Max was actually threatening me or just trying to intimidate me.

"Look," Max protested, "I'm sorry I even brought it up in the first place. After all, we're both on the same side, aren't we? You're looking for big bucks for your diary, and I promised Nicoletta to find you a buyer who's willing to give you what you want. Are you happy with that?"

"Sure," I replied, trying to muster up some conviction.

"Good," he continued. "Then let's shake on it." As he reached his hand over the desk, my immediate reaction was to pull back my hand. But to avoid appearing hesitant, I extended my arm. Dwarfing my own in size and stretch, his huge hand encompassed my fingers, and I was astounded by his sheer physical strength.

"You're a man who knows how to do business," he said as he led me to the door, draping his arm around me. "I like that."

As I left, I wondered what I had gotten myself into and tried to remember why I even agreed to it in the first place. "Nadine," I realized immediately and decided she should be brought up to date about the conversation, and in particular about Max's veiled threat. I returned to my room filled with conflicting emotions and headed straight for the telephone. "I'd like to speak with Nadine du Pont," I said to the operator.

"She's not here, sir," she replied politely.

"Would you have her call me when she gets back?"

The operator replied, "She's gone. She left for Nancy an hour ago."

Putting down the receiver, I suddenly felt nauseous. Nadine was an anchor in the midst of the intrigues and outbursts.

And now I was totally alone, dealing with a situation that was out of control.

And there was no time. In less than a half hour, the costume was arriving, and I hadn't washed or shaved. With the pounding of the running bathwater in the background, my thoughts moved to my next inevitable and imminent chore, packing for my trip to the Czech Republic. How would it be to give up the world of luxury and convenience for a cloistered monastery in the middle of nowhere? Stretched out in the bath, I was overcome by a delayed reaction to Max's mixture of cajolery and intimidation. As mental and emotional fatigue set in, my mind wandered further, to Munich—seeing a forged copy of my diary, missing a page, among the personal effects of a murdered man. I tried to sort out how it could have happened: Someone could have taken the diary out of my room at La Favorite and made a copy, which would explain the broken lock with nothing missing from my briefcase. Or Braun's copy could have been taken from the piles of papers on his disorganized desk and then returned without his knowledge.

Sorting out the threads, I felt my eyelids begin to lower, and my body sinking slowly into the bath foam. I relaxed, half-suspended in the bath, and allowed my mind to float aimlessly. Suddenly, with the intensity of a camera flash, a vivid image snapped into my mind—von Horvach's naked, bloated body floating in the bloody bath.

Gasping, I shot up from the bath and scanned the room quickly for any sign of bath oil or other unusual paraphernalia. *Paranoia,* I thought, settling back in the steaming water. Making an effort to push away the grotesque image, I lectured myself: *Try, just for once, to forget everything and have a good time tonight.* And I focused on the intriguing possibilities of a masked ball, a gigantic party where no one knows anyone else's identity, everyone free to act out any role for a night, to become someone they've secretly wanted to be. The eroticism of the situation sent a rush of anticipation through my body.

As I toweled off, a knock on my door reminded me I was

behind schedule. Wrapping a towel around my waist, I peered through a crack in the door and saw Dominique and an unfamiliar woman standing outside with a brass clothes rack on wheels loaded with costumes in black liners and several hatboxes. "I'm sorry," I said. "I'm not dressed yet."

"Don't apologize," Dominique responded, pushing her wheeled clothes rack through the door without waiting for my reply. "I don't mind naked men, do you, Dolly?"

"Not at all," the woman replied, smiling. In her hand was a large wooden box that looked as if it held artist's paints. The costume, enclosed in a thick black plastic liner, was unveiled with deliberate pomp and ceremony, and I stood gaping in front of a splendid velvet officer's uniform with a jacket of dark navy blue, ornamented with intricately hammered gold buttons and a long ivory vest.

"Henri had his way," Dominique said, smiling. "I hope you like it."

As I tried on the jacket, I managed to say, "This lining looks like pure silk."

"But of course it is," Dominique said. Closing the door of my bathroom behind me, I put on the knee-length stockings and climbed into the white trousers—a remarkable fit. Next, a linen shirt with a minute lace ruffle and new boots of black leather, and I knew without a doubt that Henri had made a brilliant choice.

When I came back out, Dominique and her colleague were standing ready with a red-and-gold ribbonlike sash and a powdered wig of tightly bound hair that just covered my own. "My, it suits you," Dominique said.

"I would not have recognized you," the other woman added. "It makes you look . . ." She stopped, searching for the appropriate expression in English.

"Like such a hunk," Dominique said, and the two women giggled like adolescent girls. Immediately, the second woman began making energetic touches of theatrical makeup, discreetly outlining my eyebrows and mustache and adding gold medals of different sizes and a final unexpected touch—a black Venetian mask that covered the upper half of my face. Within seconds, I was staring at a figure in the mirror I scarcely recognized.

"So dashing," Dominique cooed.

"The women will be fighting over you tonight," the other woman said.

Dominique became dead serious for a moment. "But no one is to reveal his identity until one o'clock. Are you in agreement?"

"Absolutely," I answered.

"Some of the women are going to be dressed as men," Dolly added.

"Sounds kinda kinky," I said to myself under my breath as I looked in the mirror, realizing I was beginning to think and talk a little like Enrique. The two women placed several heavy rings on my fingers, finally adding a heavy gold-handled sword to my belt.

"As far as I know, none of the men are going to be dressed as women," Dominique continued. "Dolly, Henri is not invited, is he?"

"No," the other woman replied, smiling as if enjoying a private joke.

As they wheeled out their equipment, both women continued to examine my costume for details, nodding their approval. I was unable to take my eyes off the splendid uniform I saw in the mirror. But soon I became aware of just how revealing the costume was. "Jesus," I mumbled, realizing that I had better keep my mind on pure thoughts over the course of the evening. After removing the heavy rings from my fingers, I took off the heavy sword and set my wig carefully aside to take a nap, realizing that dressing and undressing was no small matter in the eighteenth century. Stretched out on the bed in full costume, I slept for an hour.

When I awoke, the light in the room had begun to take on the burnished tones of tawny amber and salmon. After one last look at the figure in the mirror, I opened the door to leave. An unassuming white envelope captured my eye, apparently slipped under the door while I was napping. In the unlikely event I would see the person responsible disappearing down the corridor, I surveyed the hall in both directions.

"All right," I said aloud. "Let's get this over with." Ripping it open, I found a page with the now familiar format of pasted letters of peculiar shapes and sizes:

THE NIGHT COMETH WHEN NO MAN CAN WORK

Anger rose in my throat in a thick wave. But I tried to focus my attention on the logic behind the quotations, looking for clues about the identity of the person sending them. This time, the clipping came from a German-language newspaper and described details surrounding the investigation in Salzburg into the disappearance of Georg Pahlmann, the rare books dealer whose mother I had met.

Whoever was sending them knew I could read Italian and German. The clipping, written in an unadorned, factual style, described how police had been able to link the carbonized body found in the car wreck outside Salzburg to a cadaver missing from a medical school. But there was still no indication whether the disappearance of Pahlmann was staged by him or by someone else. Or whether he was still alive.

Crumpling each page separately and shooting the first in a tall arc in the direction of the wastebasket, I said, "This is what I think of your little notes." The second missed the mark and instead of retrieving it, I ground it with the heel of my black leather boot as if crushing an insect. Demonstrating my disgust for the anonymous tipster, I kicked it across the floor, adding, "Take that." By now the costume had begun to exert an influence on me and, feeling light-headed and cavalier, I strode out of the room.

Dismissing the implications of the note, I imitated Enrique's deepest baritone drawl, "Tonight ahhm ready for lo-o-o-ve." Darkness had begun to fall, and subdued light enveloped the corridors in a gauze of dusky ocher. The seductive sounds of an orchestra could be heard in the distance. The novelty of the experience of remote music began to sweep me into a state of elation, and the metaphor of night music captured my thoughts—a counterpoint to the dark complexities of human relationships, acted out on a stage with plots and scenarios, intrigues, pursuits, and love triangles, all played out with relentless passion during the hours when erotic drives reach their most ferocious and irrepressible peak.

Perhaps influenced by my costume, my mind had begun to move in uncanny directions, as if an unfamiliar, eerie presence had taken charge of my reasoning: *Human existence is played out over a huge, cavernous drum used to beat primitive accompaniments for tribal rituals, enacted over and over. The night propels us endlessly to tap out crude rhythms with savage regularity, to abandon ourselves to the primal, the instinctual, the inner self that lies just beneath the surface* . . .

For a moment I tried to account for the peculiar direction of my thoughts. Like Ulysses under the spell of the sirens, I was overwhelmed by the sounds of music in the distance, and I again drifted back into my abstract monologue, as if an unknown voice within me were speaking: *When darkness falls, the essential world begins, and another nature emerges—the stalking instincts, the predatory search for love, the irresistible urge to violently possess and to be possessed.*

The full descent of night was under way and my disturbing stream of consciousness continued full force: *The moment has come to relegate the oppressive veneer of civility to the shadows, to explore the instincts from within.*

"Denise," I whispered, wondering why her name had suddenly sprung to mind with such urgency. I could visualize her as she bent over to smooth the wrinkles of my bedspread, her supple figure almost hidden under her deliberately drab uniform. My mind continued to wander: *Ritual requires sacrifice—someone must always be destroyed upon the altar of the gods.*

Completely shocked by where my own train of thought had led me, I stood rooted to the ground. Almost inaudibly, I said, "God. There are parts of myself I scarcely recognize." And I tried to remember whether I had ever seen Denise bending over my bed, or if my imagination had just concocted it. There were unsettling gaps in my memory. But as I approached the ballroom, the sounds of an exuberant orchestra captured my full attention and I was drawn silently, irresistibly into the magnetic pulse of an invitation to escape.

## CHAPTER 22

*On with the dance! let joy be unconfined;*
*No sleep till morn, when Youth and Pleasure meet*
*To chase the glowing hours with flying feet.*
—LORD BYRON

As I strode around the corner and across the massive oak threshold, the full impact of sight and sound swept over me with explosive force, and I was temporarily blinded by the dazzling light of gilded bronze chandeliers, reflected in immense and elaborately carved Georgian mirrors. The orchestra had just begun the triumphant triadic opening of Mozart's ballet *Les Petits Riens.* And my head swam as I tried to take in the lively chatter, the scent of sophisticated perfumes, and the brilliance of the ballroom, bustling with color and motion as dresses of pastel silks and lace brocade swept across glistening hardwood floors.

On both sides of a parquet dance floor that stretched in front of a low platform stage, an orchestra divided into two parts was playing with a rhythmic propulsion that immediately set my foot tapping. And behind the platform, a stage set had been constructed with large painted flats depicting the interior of a sumptuous mirrored rococo theater in the predominant colors of silver and blue, like the Amalienburg in Munich or the Maryinsky Theater in St. Petersburg. Cascading from the top and sides were valences and floor-to-ceiling draperies of the same azure-colored material as those on the windows in the ballroom itself, with identical swag tassels of cobalt blue, creating a merging of reality and illusion, as if the entire room were an opulent extension of the eighteenth-century theater set.

As I attempted to get my bearings, I noticed four couples at center stage, all professional dancers costumed as figures of Italian commedia dell'arte, performing stylized courtly eighteenth-century dances. Arms moving in graceful gestures, they strutted and postured in the traditional costumes of Harlequin, Colombina, Pantalone, Scaramouche, and Pierrot, bowing and stepping gracefully like colorful porcelain figures come to life. In the midst of all the activity, waiters in ruffled shirts and powdered wigs whisked glasses of punch and champagne and trays of tempting hors d'oeuvres through the room.

My habitual urge to scan the room for attractive women kicked in immediately, leaving me with an eyeful of coral pink cleavage and shapely curves bursting out of tightly bound dresses, and I mumbled, "Damn." In vain, I continued to hunt for a single person I knew. But the costumes, masks, and makeup had successfully eliminated all identifiable features. Passing slowly through the room in search of clues, I caught only fragmentary bites of conversation, thick with accents in German, French, Italian, and even Russian: "My, don't you look splendid." "Henri's a genius when it comes to costumes." "Let me guess, you're Madame Pompadour." "My dress is pulled so tight, I can hardly breathe."

As I strolled through the room, the splendid costumes fascinated me: a dignified older man in the full ecclesiastical regalia of a cardinal, a couple as Papageno and Papagena from *The Magic Flute*, each resplendent with exotic feathers and colorful artificial birds resting on their hands and shoulders, a tottering figure with a cane, horn-rimmed glasses, and a white beard, aged prematurely with the aid of makeup and powder. Yet I couldn't find anyone I recognized, and continuing my stroll, I listened more intently to the conversations as I passed.

"Were you at La Favorite for the Elisabethan ball?"

"Careful of the punch, it's potent."

"I never would have recognized you in a million years."

"We sent him an offer last night in writing. He'd better take it while he can." The nasal sound of Landry's voice caught my attention, and I realized he was talking about his projected takeover of Braun's edition. Looking in the direction of the voice, I saw an Oriental despot with long flowing robes, a silk turban, and a menacing goatee speaking to a shepherdess holding a long cane with a plush stuffed animal, a baby sheep, in her arms. It was Landry, costumed as the Pasha from *The Abduction from the Seraglio* and talking with his assistant. I immediately headed in the opposite direction.

Continuing to scan the room, I finally caught a glimpse of a familiar figure: Baroness Paumgarten, who appeared to be dressed as some kind of Spanish princess, draped from head to toe in black and seated in a wheelchair, miraculously transformed into a carved wooden throne. With an elaborate black lace shawl covering her legs and a dark gossamer scarf tied around her head, she was accompanied by a remarkably tall beauty with a tiny waistline and a plunging neckline—Ilsa, I assumed, normally petite, but now wearing impossibly high heels. Their costume identities suddenly leaped out at me: the baroness was a stunning likeness of the dowager Empress Maria Theresa in somber black as she had dressed for years after her husband's death. And Ilsa, with a rose in her hand and two delicate necklaces of oblong pearls around her neck, was her daughter, Marie Antoinette, who married the king of France, Louis XVI, in the worst of times. A broad striped bow strategically placed around her neck drew the eye toward Ilsa's vertiginous neckline, and her hat with several extraordinary plumes called to mind the famous portrait of the unfortunate queen by Madame Vigée-Lebrun.

The choreographed ballet had ended and the dancers were casually going through the steps of the minuet and contredanse on the dance floor with adventuresome guests as others looked on amused. Strolling through the room, waiters offered canapés of caviar and crabmeat and sparkling punch in delicately etched crystal coupes. One person at the far end of the ballroom stood out from the crowd because of his extraordinary size: Enrique, covered from head to toe in black body paint, and decked out in a purple vest with extraordinary pointed shoes topped with golden bells. He wore an elaborate turban held together by an emerald-and-diamond-encrusted brooch.

Guessing he was the Moorish slave from *The Magic Flute*, I had started to walk in his direction when, out of nowhere, a woman appeared and asked, "What have we here? An Austrian officer? Would you care to dance?"

"Thanks, but not now," I replied. "Nice costume, by the way. Barbarina from *The Marriage of Figaro*?"

"No," she replied, "I'm Colombina."

Recognizing her as one of the dancers who had just performed onstage, I replied, "I enjoyed your performance a few minutes ago."

"Now," she continued, "I'm helping guests learn the dance steps."

Holding out her hand with a gesture that was more than an invitation, she said, "Please indulge me. That's why I'm here."

Gently, she led me through the steps, first of the minuet, then of the contredanse. "Sorry," I mumbled. "I'm not very good at this."

"You're doing fine," she insisted. "You'll have it in no time." And to my amazement, within minutes the logic of the dance and the music set in and I found myself responding without thinking. "Now keep it up," she said. "It's time for me to look for some other bewildered guest."

Sipping a glass of champagne, I looked around the room, trying to decide where to begin. Not far away, a strikingly attractive woman caught my attention, her hair mounted up around her head in an intricate hairstyle with a broad ribbon entwined. Standing alone with a gold and ivory mask on her face, she smiled as if she knew me and began lightly fanning her neck and ample bustline, which aptly fit the French expression *Il y a du monde au balcon*; in fact, her balcony was clearly overcrowded. While I debated striking up a conversation, she smiled again, and I drew toward her slowly.

"We know each other," I said, hoping she would take the bait and tell me her identity. Instead of responding, she smiled and took out a lace handkerchief, lightly touching her temples and under her ear, from which intricate earrings of small diamonds dangled.

"One o'clock," she said, delicately chastising me, as we had agreed to keep our identities secret until that time.

Although I was listening carefully for any hint of an accent that would reveal who she was, the few words she spoke brought nothing to mind. "We're at least allowed to say we know each other, yes?" I asked, trying again.

Ignoring my question, she opened her fan again. "I saw you dancing with Colombina. You picked up the steps very quickly."

Her comment sounded like a hint, so I extended my arm and asked her, "Would you care to try?" Without answering, she smiled and took my arm, and we were soon walking through the steps, first slowly, then with more freedom, allowing ourselves to be swallowed up by waves of sound. As we danced, I scrutinized her smile and her splendid bosom, the only visible features by which to identify her. Noticing a glistening bead of perspiration as it disappeared slowly down into her cleavage, I made a mental comparison, one by one, with Elisabetta von Stahl, Nicoletta Chigi, and the other female guests I had met, eliminating virtually everyone as a possibility.

From the far corner of the room, Philippe, the majordomo, dressed as an eighteenth-century French ballet master, stamped his stick energetically and announced it was time to find a partner. As the professional dancers began pairing up guests in a long line and choosing partners for themselves from among the guests, my elusive partner and I joined the line. With the orchestra playing a rousing series of numbers, the stage dancers led the long line of couples around the ballroom, up and over the mirrored stage, and through the adjacent rooms. "The dancers come down into the audience, and the guests become part of the ballet," my partner whispered. "It's hard to tell where the stage ends."

"They're re-creating the *festa da ballo*," I realized, remembering the similar spectacle that took place in Venice and Milan during opera performances. With the professional dancers setting the tone and style, we stepped to the accompaniment of lively music in a comfortable mixture of rhythmic walking and occasional dance gestures. A kaleidoscopic blur of faces and costumes passed by as guests chatted with their new partners, trying to catch a breath because of the brisk pace. Passing through the doors of the opulent stage set and continuing through festively decorated rooms, I watched my partner out of the corner of my eye, catching glimpses of her radiant skin tone, her bosom that glistened from excitement and exertion, and the suppleness of her long, naked neck stretching down to the limit of her plunging neckline.

As the walk concluded, she took my hands and quickly led me to a quiet corner, where she began to fan herself, trying to regain her breath. Noticing beads of perspiration glistening on my forehead, she took her wrist handkerchief and patted my face, carefully blotting a thin line running from my left temple to below my earlobe, then slowly down the side of my chin to my neck. The light, mildly erogenous touch of her lace caused electricity to race through my body, and when she cupped my right cheek with her hand, I stepped in closer.

I heard a slight moan as she continued stroking my neck and cheek, and I realized the sound was rising from the back of my throat. Releasing myself into her touch, I relaxed as she began moving her hand in slow, circular strokes, continuing toward the back of my neck.

"You have a piece of thread caught in your wig," she murmured. "Hold your head up straight and look over toward that portrait." Positioning my neck as she stood closer, I complied, and she extended both hands over my shoulders, tugging gently to remove the tangled thread. A quick involuntary reflex took my eyes to where a glimpse of firm, youthful breasts and soft, coral nipples flushed with color held my attention.

"You won't find it down there," she said, deadpan, not even looking at me. As she continued trying to extract the stubborn thread from the tightly bound hair, I found myself intensely aroused by this mysterious figure. Both arms draped around my neck, her weight shifted, and to maintain my balance, I placed my hands on her waist, where I felt a firm, responsive body. Standing so close to her, I felt my own breath rebounding off her cheek, and I lowered my lips almost to her neck. When she didn't resist, I continued slowly stroking the nape of her neck with my breath, caressing the contoured line from her ear to her shoulder without touching her as she inclined her head in response.

Suddenly stopping short, she said with surprise, "Some people live for love. I've lived my whole life avoiding it." Momentarily dazed, I tried to return to the slow caress of her neck and felt myself grabbing her waist more violently to draw her closer. Her briefest gesture of surrender was followed by resistance as she stepped back, holding her arms straight out to regain control of the situation, and bringing me abruptly back to my senses.

"All kinds of feelings can come out at a masked ball," she said. "Some we didn't even know we had."

The familiar voice of Philippe announced a group contredanse and I reached for her hand. Instead, I felt an empty space and realized she had disappeared.

In the distance, I could see her gradually being swallowed into the crowd. Watching her disappear, I continued gasping for breath, experiencing light-headed elation and the burn of violent sexual arousal. Still disoriented, I noticed several small groups of guests talking near a splendid buffet table. Making my way toward them, I understood for the first time why eighteenth-century masked events had been so carefully regulated by the government: in an anonymous, sexually charged atmosphere like this, emotions were triggered and once they erupted, it was impossible to rein them back in.

Colorfully costumed guests were standing and chatting around the buffet table, which displayed miniature tall ships of elaborately carved wood and was decorated with multicolored roses intricately carved from vegetables. Next to huge, iced lobsters overflowing with caviar, and ice sculptures depicting commedia dell'arte figures, were trays of finger-sized hors d'oeuvres glistening in tawny gelatin: rounds of melba toast and thin focaccia topped with fresh foie gras, tiny shrimp, and avocado, paper-thin beef with fresh asparagus tips and wedges of Roquefort, and aged Camembert with dark grapes and walnut halves.

After helping myself to a sampling of the miniature culinary artworks, I drew in near a small group of three women and a man chatting amiably. A striking, statuesque woman dressed as a noblewoman—perhaps Donna Elvira from *Don Giovanni*— was explaining to her small audience, "My first husband was a simple man, which is another way of saying he was cheap and had no imagination. Life with him was a crash course in poverty. When I left him, I said goodbye forever to the world of perpetual need."

A petite woman dressed as a young boy—perhaps Cherubino from *The Marriage of Figaro*—responded, "The problems of my marriage were very different—money didn't play much of a role. In the beginning my husband was warm and considerate, but in the end he had become *un homme glacial,* a man of ice. I've since learned that people who stay in bad relationships aren't noble; they're cowards."

"Ah, ha," I mumbled, remembering our brief but poignant conversations at La Favorite and Santa Maria Maggiore— someone I recognized: Hélène Benoit.

"But you both want to fall in love again, am I right?" It was a slender young man with a half-beard of dark blond hair, dressed in a rustic costume—a virile peasant, possibly Masetto from *Don Giovanni*—with an open shirt showing off a full chest of ash blond hair. "As far as I'm concerned," he said, "the only antidote to love is to love more."

"You're refreshingly naïve," the taller, more statuesque woman replied. "We always remember what it was like the short time we were in love and forget the eternity we spent breaking up."

"No," the young peasant protested, "I remember that well. Nicoletta and I were always breaking up and getting back together. Sometimes I couldn't even remember which of the two states we were in."

Laughing to myself, I realized Roberto had just given himself away. As they spoke, each sipped punch or champagne freely, and it was clearly helping to loosen the tongue. "By the way, where is Nicoletta?" Hélène, as young Cherubino, asked.

"I haven't been able to pick her out," Roberto said. "Maybe she's not here yet."

The heavyset woman in the remarkable feathered costume as part of a Papageno and Papagena couple replied, "I did see Max, though. He's easy to recognize. He's Don Juan tonight, or I guess I should say Don Giovanni, since that's what he's called in Mozart's opera. There certainly are enough good-looking men here tonight. For once I wish I weren't married." As she spoke, she looked toward me and asked, "Is our young officer looking for his troops? Why don't you join us awhile between battles?"

I stepped in closer and they continued their discussion. Hélène directed her comments to Roberto. "You're much better off without her. Some people are better suited as friends than as lovers."

"If only we *were* friends," he replied. "But she hasn't spoken to me since she left. I just wish I had been prepared for the end. When it happened, I was completely caught off-guard. That's what's so painful."

"You've got to look for the signs," the tall woman said. "I've come to know a relationship has run its course when the happiest moment in your day is hearing the sound of his key in the door as he leaves in the morning."

The woman dressed as Papagena followed her lead. "A relationship is ready to end when you start to envy the last person who broke up with him." Laughter broke out and she asked me, "What does our lost army officer think?"

"A relationship is over," I replied, "when you realize your lover's a complete stranger, but that's exactly the way you want to keep it." Their enthusiastic laughter encouraged me, and for the first time I felt like part of the group.

Roberto continued, "But there must be something positive to say about love, right? Otherwise, why do we all want so desperately to be in love?"

"That's what is so incredibly illogical about the whole thing," Hélène replied. "Being in love is the most agonizing state a human being can experience. Yet time after time we choose it above all else. Does that make any sense?"

By now, I had eliminated Alison Teal as a possibility for the statuesque beauty, whose accent and unabashed cynicism instead suggested Elisabetta von Stahl. She continued, "Nothing about love makes any sense. It's always too much or too little, there's never anything in between. The fact is, love is an exquisite, sublime waste of time."

"And I bet you can't wait to be in love again," I ventured.

Without flinching, she replied, "Of course, how did you know? I shudder at the thought of men . . . I'm due to fall in love again," quoting the famous poem by Dorothy Parker. In the midst of their laughter, I looked up to see the splendid figure of Marie Antoinette, arriving with Maria Theresa on her elaborate throne on wheels.

"Are you going to tell our fortunes?" the tall blond I suspected was Elisabetta von Stahl asked.

"Actually," I said, "this is not a fortune-teller, but none other than the illustrious Empress Maria Theresa herself."

Ilsa, as Marie Antoinette, replied, "But I know what she's referring to. She's heard that my grandmother can see things no one else can." Absolutely no one spoke, as her modest comment had riveted everyone's attention. The baroness, apparently sleeping, was oblivious to our conversation, but Ilsa continued, smiling, "If she's in the mood, she can give a glimpse into a person's future. Usually not very far, just a little around the corner, as she likes to say."

The stately Elisabetta von Stahl continued, "I've heard about her talent for years. Isn't she related to Queen Elena of Montenegro, famous for the same thing?"

Ilsa replied simply, "Queen Elena was her aunt."

With a certain insouciance, Elisabetta asked, "Would you ask her to do it for me?"

Ilsa looked at her grandmother, who appeared to be stirring, as if coming out of sleep. "Grandmother," Ilsa whispered, "this magnificent lady would like you to look into her future."

"*Freilich*," the dowager replied cordially, and Ilsa took Elisabetta's hand, placing it delicately in that of her grandmother. Gently, Baroness Paumgarten began squeezing her hand, holding it next to her face. Suddenly, she laughed and asked, "What do you want to know? About the next man in your life?"

Elisabetta smiled and the baroness chuckled. "Yes, I see a man, but I don't dare to say who it is."

"Why?" Elisabetta asked, delighted by the novelty of the entertainment.

"He's a young man," she continued, with a quiet laugh. "Much younger than you. It wouldn't be right to say his name."

"Will we be married?" Elisabetta asked.

"That's up to you," the baroness replied. "Oh, it's such a gift to be young."

Everyone seemed willing to play along and Ilsa suddenly reached for my hand. "Why don't you be next?" she asked. When I didn't resist, she asked, "Grandmother, what do you see in the future of this young Austrian officer?" Gently massaging my hand, the baroness looked off into the distance. She remained silent as we watched, amused. Suddenly, the baroness sat erect in her wheelchair. As if struck by lightning, she locked my hand tightly in her grip, her gaze fixed on some distant event, with a disturbing expression frozen on her face.

When no one dared to speak, I cleared my throat and asked, "Is she all right?" Again, no one spoke. We watched in silence as she continued to sit upright in her chair, immobile except for her eyes darting back and forth in sporadic, rapid movements. I tried to withdraw my hand but she continued to clutch it with the ferocious tenacity of a vise. With all my force, I finally yanked it out of her grip and her head slumped down as if she were asleep.

For a second, I didn't know how to react. Finally I managed to say, "I never liked party games."

Elisabetta spoke up. "Whatever you do, don't put your hand in the Bocca della Verità," referring to the famous sculpture in Rome reputed to bite off the hand of anyone who is lying.

"Is your grandmother all right?" Hélène asked Ilsa.

"She seems to be," she answered. But I knew Ilsa was avoiding reacting to what had just taken place. She continued, quietly, "It's a mild form of narcolepsy."

The pastime that had suddenly turned violent left me uncomfortable and I realized, *People here constantly avoid anything unpleasant, like a communal sense of denial. If anything disturbing happens, everyone automatically jumps away from it.*

A familiar figure suddenly appeared next to me, diverting my attention away from the group: Enrique, in his brilliant disguise as Monostatos, the Moorish slave from *The Magic Flute.* Looking larger than life, he sported an open vest revealing muscle-bound pecs, making me aware for the first time of just how massive he was. "Yo, Doc," he said softly, apparently not interested in introducing himself to the group. As we turned away, I asked him quietly, "How did you know it was me?"

"Have my sources," he said, smiling cryptically. "To tell you the truth, I saw your costume when Dominique was sewing it."

"So how are you making out?" I asked.

"Great," he replied. "There's a ton of hot numbers here. By the way, saw you dancing with the watermelon cart." In midsentence, Enrique stopped and his head swiveled in the direction of a woman whose impressive cobalt blue dress shimmered with a thousand sequined stars. As she glided gracefully through the crowd maneuvering a mountain of petticoats and holding a magic wand topped by a crescent moon, I had little doubt which character her costume represented.

"Wow," Enrique mumbled. "Who's that supposed to be?"

"The Queen of the Night," I said, "from Mozart's *The Magic Flute.*"

"The Queen of the Night," he repeated distractedly as he admired her, mouth open. "What's that, some kinda witch or something?"

His comment made me think for a second. "Now that you mention it, at the beginning of the opera, we're led to believe she's a poor mother whose daughter's been kidnapped. But in the last act, we find out she's an evil sorceress. She vents her rage in one of the most hair-raising arias ever written, full of all kinds of vocal fireworks. In fact, Alison Teal is famous for singing it."

Enrique flashed his pearly grin and we understood immediately that this extraordinary figure could be none other than Miss Teal herself. "Man," he sighed, "she just looks so . . . so . . ."

Seeing Enrique at a loss for words, I suggested, "How about, lickable?"

"You really know how to read my mind, Doc. By the way, how'd you make out with that hot babe you were dancing with? Get her room number?"

"I don't even know who she is. But I'm keeping my eye out for her when one o'clock rolls around. How about you, found the perfect woman yet?"

"You know how it is; you search your whole life for the perfect babe and then you find her, only to learn she's not interested." Enrique sighed and I wondered what woman had captured his interest.

"I know," I replied. "As they say, the heart is a lonely hunter."

"That's exactly what I always say, Doc. The hard-on is a lonely hunter. So who do you think your hot number is, Nicoletta Chigi . . . Ilsa Paumgarten?"

"Maybe someone I haven't met yet," I replied.

"Want me to find out?" he asked.

"Sure, if you can." Without another word, he took off into the crowd, and I had the feeling he would soon be back with the mystery solved. The festivities were becoming louder and more boisterous; I closed my eyes and felt myself pleasantly swept away by the rich resonance of the music.

As if from nowhere, a voice interrupted my listening. "This is a good time, let's talk business."

# CHAPTER 23

*. . . and luxury is the forerunner of a barbarism
scarcely capable of cure.*
—PERCY BYSSHE SHELLEY

Opening my eyes, I saw the swashbuckling figure of Maximilian, smiling with a charm that seemed almost Arabian. As he put his massive arm around my shoulder, his cape gave me the momentary sensation of being draped under the folds of a huge statue. "Let's go over there," he said, leading me through several rooms lined with books. As we arrived at a quiet, semidarkened alcove, he continued, "We can talk here without being disturbed." Patting me on the abdomen, he observed, "You go to the gym a lot, I see."

His familiarity caught me off-guard and I replied, "It's hard to tell with this costume."

"You're right," he laughed. "It's easier with this one." With that he tugged open his shirt, cut above the waist, displaying a chest with chiseled pecs and abs, delineated with contoured waves of black hair like iron filings over a magnet. "Look, I've got good news," he continued. "I found just the client we're looking for, someone who wants to buy your diary. I've been authorized to write you a check tonight . . . it'll be transferred to your account tomorrow."

In his enthusiasm, Maximilian was standing closer to me than felt comfortable and I made a gesture to move out of the corner. A sudden shift in the pressure of his weight indicated he wanted me to stay put. "Would you just relax for one minute?" he said, mildly annoyed.

Staring directly into my eyes with an intense, deep gaze was a man who perfectly fit the role of Don Giovanni, someone who would clearly not take no for an answer. "I just need a little time," I managed to utter. With that, I again attempted to move out of the alcove but he stretched out his arm to block me, moving in closer, the weight of his body pressing me to the wall.

"Look at me," he insisted. "Jesus, what's your problem?" It occurred to me that we were in a compromising position, and I was afraid to imagine what people would think if anyone saw us.

Practically face-to-face with him, I asked, "Can I get back to you tomorrow?"

"Why do we need to wait till tomorrow?" he asked. "What's holding you back?"

At a momentary loss for words, I finally said, "Something the viscount said to me."

"The viscount," he replied cynically, increasing the weight of his body against mine. "It's easy for him to talk. People who've never had to work a day in their life can afford to have high standards. So what'd he say?"

"Something about making the world a better place," I answered.

Maximilian chuckled aloud, and for the first time I realized he was heavily intoxicated. "Of all mistakes you can make, there's none more stupid than trying to improve the world. It's a shark pool out there, in the midst of a massive feeding frenzy. Don't look so shocked. You're a big boy, aren't you?"

As Max said the words *big boy*, he smiled inexplicably. Literally nose-to-nose with him and pinned against the wall by the full weight of his six-foot-plus frame, I was unable to move. "Why can't we take care of this right now . . . right here?" he asked. His thick black mustache was almost touching my face and his breathing was becoming more rapid, as if the cat-and-mouse situation was exciting him.

"I need to think about it . . . just for one day," I mumbled.

"I'll pay you whatever you want," he said in a seductive tone. "Just say yes. Now."

For the first time, I felt his heart pounding powerfully against my body and detected the musky scent of bourbon on his breath. But within seconds I realized the pounding wasn't coming only from his chest—it was from below the waist. His mouth started moving in a circular path around mine and, as I tried to turn away, I felt his hands holding my head firmly like a vise.

"This little game you're playing is really turning me on," he murmured. "That's what you're trying to do, isn't it?" His half-whispered erotic stream of consciousness continued: "Or maybe you're one of those guys who gets turned on by rape fantasies, so you don't have to admit you like it. If that's what you want . . ." The weight of his body pinning me to the wall left me with little choice but to stay put and listen and I remembered, as from a distant dream, what Ilsa had said of von Horvach: when he's interested in someone, he turns into a nuclear generator of pure animal passion.

As his mouth moved slowly and rhythmically around my mouth without touching, I found myself looking into his intensely dark eyes as if captured by the hypnotic stare of a cobra. With the sounds of faraway music echoing in my ears, lulling me in unfamiliar directions, Max's raw sexual magnetism and undisguised desire were strangely persuasive, and I found myself succumbing to a vague, euphoric state. Caught up in the broad, slow movements of his rotating pelvis and the relentless rhythm of his breathing, I was locked into his insistent gaze. In an unexpected moment of release, a dark, primordial moan of passion escaped from my mouth, and I heard the sound of my breathing echoing simultaneously and seamlessly with his. All at once, with a single broad stroke of his hand, he ripped open the buttons leading from my chest to my navel, tugging forcibly with his other hand at the flimsy snaps holding up my trousers.

For a second that felt like an eternity, he stopped short, absolutely still, staring in disbelief. Looking down at the hem of my jacket, he asked, "What's this?"

When I didn't reply, Max said slowly, one word at a time, "You're wearing a microphone."

In an abrupt return to reality, I straightened myself up and replied, "A what?"

In his hand, Max was holding a small, unobtrusive device, examining it carefully. "It's Korean made." Surprised, I stared at my lapel, but no words of explanation came to my rescue. "This is all a setup," he said, angrier by the second. "You've been playing me for a fool the whole time."

In the darkened distance, I could see the costumed figure of Enrique approaching. "So there you are, Doc," I heard him saying. "You've got an important phone call that won't wait." As an afterthought, he added, "You guys are getting pretty chummy, I see."

Max and I looked at each other, stunned, as Enrique placed his arm around my shoulder and led me off with firm pressure. "Look, it's none of my business, Doc," Enrique said as we walked off. "Live and let live and all of that. But really, you guys coulda at least looked for a bedroom." Behind me in the distance, I could make out Max's expression of disbelief, exasperation, and a rage on the verge of exploding.

Some distance away from Max, I stopped in my tracks and snapped at Enrique. "You're responsible for this, aren't you?"

As I spoke, I noticed that my trousers and shirt were suspiciously open, with several buttons missing, and began fumbling to put them back in order. "Better pull your pants back up, Doc."

"You and Nadine planted a bug on me."

"Wait, wait, before you start blaming Nadine," he protested. "This was all my idea. It's like this, man. I got this big budget for sophisticated electronic wizardry with no place to use it. Thought what you didn't know wouldn't hurt you. But he's a pretty clever dude, a lot smarter than I thought. I didn't expect it to backfire like this, but after all, I couldn't have predicted you'd start ripping each other's clothes off the very first minute you were alone."

Infuriated beyond my limit, I clenched my teeth. Enrique interrupted me. "Hey, I found out who the babe was you were dancing with . . . that is, before you decided you like guys so much."

Enrique was enraging me so much, I could hear the hissing of air through my teeth and felt the rushing of blood pumping in my temples like a geyser. "Look, damn it, I don't give a goddamn who—" I said before stopping abruptly. Momentarily snatched out of my rage, I asked, "So who is she?"

"The glass harmonica player," he replied triumphantly. "It's amazing what a tight dress'll do for a frumpy babe."

Returning to my anger, I barked, "You've really gotten me into a serious mess."

"Sorry, man," he muttered. "Yeah," he continued apologetically. "You're definitely right about that. I wouldn't want to be in your shoes for nothing."

"Well, you'd damn well better do something about it—and now," I said, raising my voice.

"Yeah, gotcha, Doc," he replied, with an almost patronizing tone. "Don't worry, I'll take care of it. Look, I'm really sorry about this, man."

Too exasperated to even talk, I gritted my teeth and walked off abruptly, leaving Enrique standing with an apologetic look on his face. Within seconds I figured out exactly what had to be done and started searching for Max, rationalizing the gravity of the situation by telling myself that a few words of explanation would straighten everything out. The boisterous enthusiasm of Jano's voice calling my name from directly behind my ear startled me, and I unleashed the full wrath of my pent-up anger on him. "Don't ever do that to me again," I said. "You scared me half to death."

Jano bowed and whispered, placing his forefinger over his lips. "Sorry, sorry," he mumbled apologetically. "Just brought you some reinforcements," he continued, whispering and offering me a fresh glass from his tray. An angry shake of my head told him I wasn't interested, and he continued bowing and walking backward with his finger still pressed to his lips, reciting in a whisper, "Sorry."

As I returned to my unnerving hunt through the rooms, Maximilian's words from our afternoon meeting came back to haunt me in a new and alarming context: "International business is no different from the criminal justice system, or war, or even the church, where getting rid of someone is sometimes, well, you could call it an unavoidable evil. But it's always an option, something indispensable and occasionally even necessary."

Every possible obstacle to finding Maximilian lunged at me as I passed from room to room. Unfamiliar figures in masks grabbed my arms from right and left in gestures of friendship and merrymaking. But in my frantic mood, I could only interpret them as bizarre caricatures, sardonically grinning and laughing at me and, in the confusion of the scene, with the noise level increasing as guests tried to talk above the orchestra, I felt my stomach in my throat and my head spinning out of control. Finally I realized the mask was causing me to hyperventilate and yanked it off, standing with my back up against a wall to catch my breath. As the tall walls of the ballroom began moving in and out in a pulsating, throbbing ebb and flow, I stared at the ceiling in an attempt to focus my eyes.

The answer was clear: finding Max in the middle of this accelerating party madness was an exercise in futility. Talking myself down, I tried to reason as best I could: *You'll run into him later this evening if you just continue to circulate.*

But the ominous, unmistakable figure of Maximilian never reappeared, and I began to drown my fears in an endless river of champagne and worse, in an indiscriminate mix of whatever came around—manhattans, aged Scotch whisky, and finally sweet but potent cordials in strong espresso—without thinking for a second what I was doing. When I staggered toward my apartment, I was unaware of the time or even where my room was located. The deserted walls of each corridor began to look the same, and in one door after another, I found myself trying my key, barely able to stand up straight. Reaching the end of my patience, I thrust my key into what felt like a familiar door and after a slight push, found myself standing in the middle of my quarters.

The room still spinning, I stretched out fully dressed on top of the damask bedspread and said to myself, "A good night's sleep and tomorrow this will all seem like a bad dream." And as my mind drifted off, my body began to melt into the comforting softness of the mattress, yielding slowly to the irresistible draw of darkness and the immutable timbre of the night.

Stretched out on the bed, I continued to let my mind drift aimlessly, fighting the beginnings of a fierce headache. As I waited patiently for sleep to overtake me, my thoughts roamed over vaguely connected images from unexplored recesses of my mind, floating through blurred aerial images of abundant bustlines bursting like overripe peaches and pastel taffeta over lace petticoats gliding across polished parquet. Snippets of conversations from the day flew by in a disjointed torrent: ". . . whenever a sale takes place, the diaries disappear from circulation . . ." "You Americans have no sense of shame whatsoever." ". . . a masked ball can bring out all kinds of feelings . . ." "You're a man who likes to do business, I like that . . ."

Sleep was eluding me; the strong espresso disguised with sweet liqueurs was keeping my mind racing even though my body ached for rest. *Better get under the covers,* I thought, remembering the old butler's comments about the drafty windows. But it was impossible to pull myself up from my restful, inert position, and my mind continued to meander in a serpentine stream of consciousness. For some inexplicable reason, the line "Drink and dance and laugh and lie" reverberated in my mind and I struggled to remember the rest of Dorothy Parker's poem.

> Drink and dance and laugh and lie
> Love the reeling midnight through,
> For tomorrow we shall die!
> (But, alas, we never do.)

For a moment I lay completely still. Then it occurred to me that there was absolutely no hint of a draft anywhere. As I dragged myself to my feet, staggering, and tugged at the draperies covering the window, something curious caught my eye—the space between the window frame and the molding had been sealed tightly with broad bands of fresh white duct tape.

Examining the casements, I decided someone had been in to repair the windows as I ran my hand up, down, and around the sides with curiosity. Outside, the lucent beauty of the shimmering August moon surrounded by limitless expanses of illuminated clouds distracted me, but I pulled my attention back and proceeded to the bathroom, where I discovered the same temporary repair had been made.

Vaguely, I recalled an accident in ski country in Italy where an incorrectly installed heater had caused an entire family to die, asphyxiated by the colorless, odorless fumes of carbon monoxide while they slept. Still drunk, but struggling to be clear-headed, I peered through the windowpane to see the opening of the vent from the hot water unit. It was impossible to detect in the dark.

My heart began to race as I asked myself whether it was a coincidence. When I began to contemplate the worst of all possible scenarios, I imagined Max had the windows sealed and the heater sabotaged. A decision had to be made and fast: stay and sort out the situation or get out immediately. Surprising myself, I heard the sound of my own voice whispering, "God help me," while the ferocious pounding in my temples mounted. When I remembered Max's praise of homicide, thinly disguised as business philosophy, a violent surge of anger came over me and my survival instincts exploded. Furiously pulling open the drawers of my dresser, I stripped off my costume, and my prayer changed to "God, you've *got* to help me. For once, I'm not giving you any choice."

A burst of energy and determination swept over me and in moments I was ready to head out the door, wearing only jeans, a T-shirt, and a thick sweater. My sluggishness turned to lightning-quick decision making as I jettisoned my laptop with the total conviction of a sailor leaving a sinking ship. As an afterthought, I scribbled a few lines to Philippe to check the hot water heater. With the pounding rush of blood in my temples, I cracked open my door and glanced into the corridor. All was hushed and deserted except for drunken laughter echoing in some distant corner of the residence. With my sneakers silencing my footsteps, I moved quickly through the corridors to a side exit, where I soon found myself standing in total silence outside at the rear of Lord Williamson's residence.

In the cool night air, I murmured, "Now what?" as I filled my lungs deeply, experiencing the fragile stillness of the night with new awareness and clarity. Around me stretched a moon-drenched landscape of radiant and disturbing beauty: a secluded garden with a fountain and benches reminiscent of an abandoned park, the air saturated with the oily fragrance of old-fashioned hybrid tea roses. From the shadowy recesses, a worn statue of Roman antiquity, eroded by centuries of night air and dew, stared languidly over mounds of pale impatiens and sweet alyssum tinted with uncanny moonlight hues of midnight violet and blackberry blue. A meandering path carried my eye further into the shadows, where four moss-covered Renaissance cherubs offered the fruits of their harvest, symbolic sheaves of wheat and clusters of grapes, then deeper into the deepest limits of the darkness, where the faintest glimmer of an object caught my eye—a reflection from the broken mirror of a dilapidated bicycle, nestled against the ivy-covered walls of a latticework shed.

Fascinated by this gift from heaven that peered out, half-buried beneath the vines, I knew that the likelihood of hailing a taxi at this hour was practically nil and began rationalizing the possibility of taking it. At the same time, I noticed the shabby wicker basket on the handlebars, the semirusted chain, and the threadbare tires. But considering the alternative—walking hours to the nearest train station—I finally grumbled, "So sue me," and maneuvered the creaking heap of metal down the driveway.

The moon now floated serene and solitary in the sky, no cloud in sight. With effort, I pedaled down deserted side streets, the moon strewing what appeared to be handfuls of glistening silver-blue ashes over tile roofs, turning cobblestone streets into riverbeds of phosphorescent quartz. And as I struggled with the old bicycle, I tried to avoid the inevitable conclusion that returned again and again to haunt me: someone had tried to kill me. As the tired frame creaked, the relentless clicking of the pedals in the night air began to evoke faint echoes of the orchestra, now an evensong waning into the obscure recesses behind me, a note at a time.

# PART FIVE

# Geneva, Prague

*Thou hast the keys of Paradise, oh just, subtle,
and mighty opium!*
—THOMAS DE QUINCEY

Handing me several pills and a paper cup of water, Dr. Král said, "We'll begin fifteen minutes after this takes effect."

"What is it?" I asked as I swallowed them.

"Something to reduce your anxiety," he replied. "Inderal, a beta-blocker to prevent symptoms like heart palpitation and tremors. And today I'm giving you an additional milligram of Ativan: it's like Valium, but faster acting."

We sat in my darkened hospital room without speaking until he finally interrupted the silence. "Are you ready to begin?"

When I nodded, he said, "Close your eyes." And, in a deep, dronelike voice, he began to guide me. "You're going to move into a place removed from time. With each breath, you will find yourself drawn deeper and deeper into a state of relaxation."

As I let my mind succumb to his slow, deliberate monotone, I felt convinced for the first time that we were finally going to get somewhere. Remembering had become an obsession for me. Not knowing left me in a kind of prison, a limbo of virtual helplessness—regardless of the risks, I had to find out what had caused my accident.

His rich baritone voice began to calm me; the barriers in my mind were receding. "You will continue moving into a state of greater relaxation," he said. My eyes closed. I began to float on placid waves, over serene pastures and past tranquil lakes, soaring effortlessly, as if on wings. "With each breath, you will find yourself becoming more and more relaxed, going deeper and deeper."

And for the first time, I could feel the veil lifting.

# CHAPTER 24

*Separate thyself from thine enemies and
take heed of thy friends.*

—BOOK OF ECCLESIASTICUS 6:13

Conditions on the ancient commuter relic leaving London for
Dover contrasted sharply with the luxurious accommodations of
the previous weeks. The old train was furnished with hard vinyl
seats and decorated with faded reproductions of Victorian lith-
ographs, and the curtains were threadbare, the windows un-
washed. But I felt a sense of unbridled exhilaration—it was a
wonderful train, a safe train, and when it had pulled into the station at 4:00 A.M., I felt it was the most beautiful train I had ever
seen. With each mile it traveled, creaking from top to bottom as
it moved along the curves in the track, my unsettling experiences
in Chelsea receded into the distant mists. Sitting alone amid a
few half-asleep passengers with a total lack of creature comforts,
I was content, because no one had any idea where I was. Or so I
thought.

When the train arrived in Dover, I was fortunate, catching
a ferry without waiting and crossing the Channel, ending this
latest peculiar chapter in my life with the finality of a trip over
dark and turbulent waters. Once on the continent, my train continued on toward Paris, arriving in what felt like no time at all.
In the Gare d'Austerlitz, a new train—a splendid vision of sleek
steel and brushed aluminum—stood waiting, and I was able to
take my seat in a comfortable first-class compartment.

Plush tufted velour seats, climate control, and tinted glass
windows with tiny electronically controlled blinds provided a
welcome contrast to the London commuter train. The announcement that breakfast was being served drew me into the

splendid dining car, where the air was permeated with the pungent aroma of freshly ground coffee beans and croissants warming in the oven. Seeing the dining car full of cosmopolitan businessmen at breakfast made my ride on a rusty bicycle through the abandoned streets of Chelsea at night seem like a faint glimmer from a distant past.

As we left France and entered Switzerland, the passport officials boarded the train, so I headed back and took my seat in an empty compartment. Almost immediately another passenger arrived, a tall, solidly built, clean-cut man with medium blond hair, in his thirties, holding a Swiss newspaper. Dressed in an impeccably tailored suit and wearing designer glasses, he appeared to be just another businessman like the many I had seen on the train. Upon entering, he nodded politely to me as I reached for the printed itinerary on the seat across from me. After Switzerland, I read, the EuroCity would pass through Germany, then on to Vienna, where I would have to change trains for Prague. When the officials arrived, I handed them my passport and glanced at my watch, calculating that our next stop would be Geneva in approximately twenty-five minutes.

Geneva. The name suddenly triggered a flood of gruesome associations, and I found myself thinking intensely about Arnold Schott, the scholar-thief whose grotesquely disfigured body had been found at the bottom of Lake Geneva. I remembered the surprising revelation the viscount had made to me, namely, that Schott had been trying to sell a Mozart diary he found in Geneva, and my thoughts wandered briefly, wondering where he might have found it. The possibilities were reasonably clear—in an auction or a rare books shop that also sold manuscripts. But a more likely hypothesis occurred to me: could Schott have stolen it from a museum or archive? I wondered how I would go about retracing his steps if I had the time.

The answer arrived with surprising swiftness: the Geneva State Archives were the city's largest depository of handwritten documents from previous centuries. I also remembered that archives require a passport from anyone who requests material, so if Schott had scoured the archives in Geneva, his name would have been recorded, along with every file he examined. Watching the scenery passively, I was intrigued by the idea of exploring Schott's trail in Geneva. Yet if he had stolen something, it would be impossible to know what it was unless a microfilm had been made of it. But microfilm copies are common in many archives.

First, I had a job to do in Prague, which was probably no small task. And it was likely that the police or someone else had already thought of Schott and the archives. *Forget Geneva*, I said to myself.

My train of thought was abruptly interrupted by the voice of the businessman in my compartment. "Do you mind if I smoke?" he asked.

Glancing quickly at the sticker on the door, I replied, "It's a smoking compartment."

But he insisted, "No, but really, do you mind?" When I shook my head, he pulled out a silver case and lit a small, black Russian cigarette, reminding me of the affluent and elegant tastes at La Favorite. For the first time I noticed the unusually solid, squarish leather briefcase on the seat next to him, with brilliant lacquered brass trim and fittings that contrasted with the muted sheen of the buffed sienna leather.

When he offered me a cigarette, I replied, "No, thanks," and began examining the itinerary in my hands more intently, indicating that I didn't want to talk.

"You don't smoke," he continued. "You're much better off."

Not interested in revealing anything about myself, I didn't reply. As I continued looking at the itinerary, occasionally glancing out the window at the scenery, I caught a glimpse of the businessman looking at me. A snippet of conversation entered my mind intrusively, a comment made by Andrei: "On the street, I'd bet it would be hard to tell a crime syndicate kingpin, or even a paid assassin, from your typical Wall Street banker wearing a double-breasted suit and carrying a briefcase." And although I smiled to myself at my own paranoia, the sudden sound of the man's voice made me jump.

"You're American, aren't you?"

For a moment I couldn't decide whether or not to respond. "What makes you say that?" I asked.

"Jeans and sneakers," he said. "But," he added, flashing a sardonic grin, "without the traditional knapsack. And I saw your passport when you handed it to the border officials."

"How about yourself?" I asked, noticing for the first time that his briefcase was equipped with an electronic anti-theft device similar to the one I had seen in Maximilian's apartment.

"I'm, uh, German," he said. The split-second hesitation in his answer sent up red flags. He was trying to conceal something. And the conversation with Nadine at La Favorite—about organized crime running some kind of well-oiled machine to get rid of people for the right price—reverberated in my mind. The businessman continued, "I guess I should say that my nationality is German. But I've lived my whole life in Zurich, so culturally I feel Swiss."

Neither convinced nor reassured, I decided not to divulge any more information and took the lead in the conversation so as to keep it away from me. "Interesting piece of luggage."

He looked over at it and shrugged. "Not particularly unusual," he said with a shrewd smile, and I began to imagine he was playing a game with me. Hoping he would finally take the hint, I picked up a magazine and began reading. But the vivid image of the high-tech briefcase couldn't be erased. Could this be a hit man, carrying the tools of his trade in that leather case, with a commission to confirm my identity and then bump me off in the train?

As I tried to overcome the thoughts, my temples began pounding and I realized I was experiencing the beginning of a full-fledged anxiety attack. With great effort, I attempted to focus on the issue of Schott in Geneva, debating whether the police had checked out the archives. I reasoned that issue would be relatively easy to determine, simply by consulting with the director of the archives. I found myself tapping my knee nervously with my fingers and rocking my leg back and forth, and realized the stranger in my compartment was noting my fidgety behavior.

Overcome by a mounting sense of panic, I felt the need to stand up and walk, the urge to get away. Although I tried to talk myself down, my responses—dry mouth, fluttering heart, loss of breath, and a torrent of adrenaline pumping throughout my veins—were becoming too powerful to resist. Excusing myself clumsily, I leaped to my feet and feigned a trip to the men's room. Walking rapidly through the corridors from wagon to wagon, I told myself I was not in danger. A sudden loud, crackling voice on the loudspeaker jolted me: "Ladies and gentlemen, we are arriving in Geneva." With no luggage to retrieve, I made a split-second decision—to leave the train as quickly and inconspicuously as possible.

Brakes squealed as the Intercity slowed, but I couldn't control my mounting anxiety, continuing to press the OPEN button on the door as annoyed travelers with luggage looked on. "It won't open until the train stops," snapped a Swiss woman in a crisp cotton dress. "You'll break the door."

Suppressing the urge to tell her to go to hell, I waited impatiently for the train to come to a halt, then released the door mechanism and hurried down the stairs. By now, I was too caught up in panic to control myself and raced along the platform, mumbling, "Jesus Christ, you're really losing it, running away from imaginary assailants."

By the time I reached the station's large central hall, I stood behind a huge modern pillar, carefully observing whether anyone was watching. As I scanned the automated list of departures for the next train for Vienna, the name and description of the train I had just exited disappeared slowly from the board. "Great," I snapped when the full impact of what I had done hit me; with the train connection in Vienna, I had set myself back an entire day. But I remembered Arnold Schott and realized that, in a strange way, I had done exactly what I wanted to do: get off in Geneva and find out about his possible links with the archives.

Out of danger—real or imagined—I headed for the information desk, then into the city toward the archives, past a disorienting selection of sleek shop windows with dazzling displays of wristwatches of every conceivable shape, size, and price range. As I looked toward the hill leading to the old city, it occurred to me that the Swiss police might not have even been aware of my unexplored lead—that Schott was trying to sell a Mozart diary he found in Geneva. It was a long shot, but if I was ever going to learn anything about the grisly murder, it was here.

Walking across the bridge from modern, cosmopolitan Geneva toward the cluttered hill of the Old Town, I tried to convince myself it was absurd to think that the businessman on the train was a hit man; he had just felt like talking, and I ran out as if he was about to kill me. But an inner voice continued gnawing away at me: *What if?*

As I began the long ascent, my attention was turned to the Old Town, its stone and stucco facades in a meticulous and remarkable state of preservation. *If I'm in Geneva,* I thought, *I'm going to try to enjoy myself.* It occurred to me that Mozart and his family must have been captivated by Geneva, as it took little imagination to visualize what the city had been like during their stay. Refined and proudly Protestant, without the pomp and grandiosity of Catholic architecture, Geneva was a city of great wealth, yet at the same time a place that eschewed ostentation, a subtle city, defined by shades of gray, reminding me of a precisely etched black-and-white engraving.

Mozart's entire family—his mother, father, and sister— had arrived in Geneva at the end of their three-and-a-half-year concert tour of the greatest courts in Europe, and Leopold used the occasion of their stop to present the children in concert as a way of financing their travels. There was no court in Geneva, such as those of Louis XV in Paris and George III in London. Instead, Geneva boasted an affluent middle-class public in addition to an enthusiastic aristocracy, who greeted the arrival of "the young miracle" with breathless anticipation.

On the way up to the archives, I followed the serpentine Grand-Rue, the finest and best preserved street in the Old Town, passing rows of facades in a restrained classical style. A commemorative plaque caught my eye, citing the home of André Grétry, once a resident of Geneva, who became one of the most renowned composers of comic opera in Europe. He had been in the audience of Mozart's first concert in Geneva, when Leopold suggested that he write a new composition, the most difficult possible, which Mozart would play on sight at his next concert as a test to prove that the young prodigy had never seen the music. Grétry wrote a piece in E-flat minor, which Mozart performed fluently at the next concert before a wildly enthusiastic public, with the exception of one person: Grétry. Mozart had substituted occasional passages of his own while he played. But I wondered, as I walked up the winding path, whether the ten-year-old Mozart had found Grétry's music too difficult to read at first sight, or if he had simply decided it was too academic and mannered, changing it as he played to make it conform to his own "modern" lyrical style, and thus giving the older composer a subtle lesson in composition.

At the top of the hill, I arrived at the entrance of the solemn Town Hall. Inside, I found a spacious courtyard surrounded by a dozen Tuscan columns bearing the weight of a portico with vaulted ceilings, and my attention was captured by a hewn marble gate with delicately fluted columns. Beyond the arch, in the chambers above, Mozart had given his two Geneva concerts, improvising fugues and variations, playing in difficult keys and clefs, and performing his own works, as he had done in so many other cities. But a quick glance at my watch told me that I was wasting valuable time. I headed directly for the archives.

In no time, I was standing before somber gray walls with the name of the state archives incised in black letters on brass. As soon as I entered, a sense of calm came over me; the large panes of protective glass and the sleek elegance of modern security devices bestowed an atmosphere of refuge. And I found the Swiss efficiency and thoroughness reassuring as employees guided me through metal detectors and toward the administrative offices.

My casual attire raised some eyebrows, and I could detect

an unspoken censure as employees glanced at one another. Arriving at the secretary's desk, I asked politely to speak with the director. "He's in a meeting now, *Monsieur*," she replied, scrutinizing me from top to bottom, her critical gaze finally resting on my sneakers. "It could be an hour."

After reflecting a moment, I replied, "I'll wait."

With a hint of suspicion, she asked, "May I tell him who's calling?"

"Dr. Albert," I replied, offering my grandparents' name and surprising myself by coming up with a false name so easily.

"Please have a seat," she said coolly. Within a few minutes, she appeared to have a change of heart and added, "If you like, I can have someone show you around while you're waiting."

"That would be excellent," I replied.

The young archivist enlisted to give me a brief tour was typical in my experience—she was professional, educated, and modest, probably overqualified and underpaid as well. Wearing glasses with square black frames and no makeup whatsoever, she gave the impression she was serious, yet her youthful enthusiasm was refreshing. "What is your area of research?" she asked as she led me across polished marble floors.

I noticed an impressive display case with Bibles from different periods and replied, "New Testament studies."

"We have a great deal of archival material here, and I'm sure you know about our ninth-century copy of the four Gospels."

"Of course," I replied, lying, as we passed a large display room. "By the way, what's that? It looks like a museum."

"Yes," she said, leading me inside. "We have a number of Roman antiquities here, as well as a gallery of oil portraits of Calvin, Beza, Farel, Luther, and others." My eyes wandered over the remarkable exhibits, from a prominently displayed manuscript copy of Terence to folios from a huge Latin Bible, and past countless amphoras and vases to towering bronze figures from Greek and Roman times. Her tour was interrupted by the arrival of a staff member who informed us that the director's meeting had ended early.

The secretary led me into the director's office, where a man in a gray suit with round spectacles sat waiting. Greeting me with a smile and a cool, professional manner, he asked, "Did you like our collection?"

"Very much," I replied.

"It's been kept in this same building for centuries," he continued, still beaming. "So, how can we help you?"

"Well, it's a rather delicate issue," I replied. "I'd like to find out if there's any record of someone doing research here in the archives."

His hospitable expression disappeared and he responded in a bureaucratic tone, "We don't give out that kind of information." But his curiosity had been piqued and he asked, "Who were you interested in?"

"Arnold Schott," I answered.

An abrupt change took place in his expression and he snapped at me, "What are you exactly, a reporter?"

The hostile tone startled me and, grabbing the arms of the chair as a reflex, I replied, "No, I'm a musicologist, a researcher . . . trying to find out something that could be of interest to both of us."

Although he remained cold and immovable, after a long, painful pause I ventured to continue. "My work is in Mozart studies. I've heard some privileged information—that Arnold Schott was trying to sell a Mozart diary he found in Geneva before he was murdered."

The director broke his silence and replied with a hint of arrogance, "And what makes you think you can find out something the police don't already know?"

"I had an idea that might not have occurred to them," I answered. "Something that could be checked out very quickly. All I'm asking for is a minimum of your time."

"What did you have in mind?"

"To see if Schott ever did any research here . . . and to see if anything is missing."

"You're treading on sensitive territory," he replied. "If something were missing, our security procedures would be called into question. And people would want to know how it could disappear without our knowing about it."

"I promise you complete confidentiality," I said. "And if a document was missing, there might be ways to restore it to your collection, to establish a claim to whatever he took."

The rapidness of his response surprised me. Without a word, he reached for the phone and began whispering, "Yes, I want to know if someone named Schott was here doing research. That's right, Schott, Arnold Schott. Call me back as soon as you find out."

Within minutes the answer came back: "He was here." Almost immediately, he made another call and ordered several staff members to come into his office. "I will help you," he replied with an intimidating tone. "But if you come up with anything, I must know immediately." A knock on the door brought the young woman who had shown me the collection, and shortly thereafter an older man appeared. "How do you want to begin?" the director asked me.

"First I need to know the names of all the files he examined," I replied. "Then I can decide which ones we should look through."

The director reminded me again, "Don't forget, if word gets out about any of this . . ." With the help of his staff, I began examining lists of archival cartons ordered by Schott and we then proceeded to the consultation room. With limited time, I had to trust my intuition, selecting those dates roughly corresponding to Mozart's stay in Switzerland, namely summer and fall of 1766. When the stacks of cartons began arriving, the two staff members and I divided up the work to cover as much ground as possible.

Leafing through mountains of old documents reminded me of the tedious years I had spent doing archival research—hour after hour, week after week, always in search of the "big win." After an hour, the young woman interrupted my work to ask my opinion. "This carton has an empty file. It's marked Geneva; Diverse Letters; 16th–19th Century."

Examining the handwritten inventory of the contents, I

confirmed that a document was missing. "Miscellaneous folio; French; 1766," I said. "This could be what we're looking for."

After we returned to the director's office, I asked, "Were any microfilms or photocopies made of this material?"

"If they were," the director replied, "the order would have had to go through the Office of Copying Services and we would have a record of it." He reached for the phone once more.

The question was quickly answered. No copies of the carton had been made. Disappointed, we stood looking at each other, but I was not completely satisfied. "Could anyone have made a copy for themselves?" I asked. "Unofficially?"

"Impossible," he replied. "All copy requests go through the main office. There's not even a photocopy machine in the reading room."

"Then I guess we're out of luck," I said.

The young woman interrupted. "A few years back, this carton was examined by Suzanne Kienzle. Wasn't she the one doing her thesis on urban history in Geneva?"

Her male colleague replied, "Yes, I remember her. She's hard to forget." With that, he made a gesture that's universally understood: he pinched his nostrils, indicating that the student in question had a strong body odor.

"She was around here for years," the woman replied. "But I haven't seen her for some time. She might remember something about it."

The comic gesture about the student's bathing habits loosened the tension in the room and I felt comfortable enough to say, "I always had the impression the Swiss were meticulously clean."

The man replied, "Geneva may be a modern city but we're surrounded by farm country and there're still a lot of people who traditionally take a bath only once a week."

The young woman changed the subject. "Did she ever get her degree?"

"I heard she had problems with her department," the director replied enigmatically. "But perhaps she's in the phone book." In a few minutes he had found her number, and a lively conversation in the melodic dialect of Swiss German ensued.

"She was planning to go out, but she'll wait if you go right now," the director said, apparently pleased with his own efficiency and the optimistic turn of events. But he wasted no time insisting, "Give me a call to say how you've made out," as his secretary began drawing the route to Suzanne Kienzle's apartment on a map.

"It's not very far," the secretary said. "You can walk." And without excess formality, I said brief goodbyes to the staff members, curious as to what secrets this peculiar, shadowy woman might reveal.

# CHAPTER 25

*What is the student but a lover courting a fickle*
*mistress who ever eludes his grasp.*

—SIR WILLIAM OSLER

Suzanne Kienzle's apartment stood on the fourth floor of a relatively seedy building. Although the outside boasted a splendidly restored facade, the inside fit the stereotype of a run-down
student apartment, with lightbulbs missing and bicycles and
boxes cluttering the entranceway. After I rang, she came down
to let me in and I followed her up the stairs, noting immediately
that the man at the archives had been quite right about her
tremendous body odor. But I cheered myself with the thought
that smell is the first of the senses to tire.

Almost as soon as she spoke, I knew that Suzanne was
bright—her keen intelligence was tempered by her modest, understated manner. Although she looked somewhat overweight,
her face was attractive, with delicate features and large
chestnut-brown eyes that reflected a violet hue. As she led me
into her apartment, she described how she had been working
for eight years on a doctoral thesis about urban planning in
Geneva in the seventeenth and eighteenth centuries. Following
her into a room full of papers and photocopies, with labeled
boxes on all sides, I saw a huge computer and printer on a desk,
surrounded by several thousand handwritten cards stacked on
the floor. "I took so many notes," she said after I described the
missing file. "It's going to be like looking for a needle in a
haystack."

"You're writing your dissertation?" I asked.

"Well, I'm going through the motions," she replied. Seeing
the questioning expression on my face, she continued, "There's a

professor who's determined to see that I don't get my degree. He's as much as come out and said it."

"What does he give for a reason?" I asked.

"Probably better not to go into it," she said. "He actually told me once to my face, 'We don't want your kind around here.'"

She saw my shocked expression and I said, "That's awful. What's it supposed to mean?"

"Your guess is as good as mine," she replied stoically. "But, as you can see, I'm not going to let him discourage me. Now, what was the name of the carton with the missing file?"

"Geneva; Diverse Letters; 16th–19th Century. And the document inside was marked Miscellaneous folio; French; 1766."

"Give me a few seconds and I'll figure out where to start," she replied.

Suzanne's manner was businesslike and thorough, and it was apparent she took her work very seriously. But while she was deciding which pile of boxes to tackle first, I could not help noticing her athletic form. As she bent over cartons, she revealed an earthy, buxom figure with full and shapely hips, and a surprisingly slender waist. In a word, Suzanne was voluptuous, her body type out of style in the fashion industry, but one I had always found exciting. And the casual observations I was making about her figure soon changed the way I found myself looking at her. It appeared that, under her unassuming gray-brown sweater, she was wearing nothing else, and I suddenly found myself violently aroused, imagining her nipples being gently stroked and brushed by countless fingers of the softest worn wool. The erotic tension literally caused my hands to tremble.

"I think I know where it might be," Suzanne said, unaware of my reaction. As she bent over to unearth a corrugated carton from the wall of boxes, she said, "Give me a hand," and I imagined responding literally to what she said. I envisioned how she would feel, emerging from the bath, her skin glistening with warm droplets of water, her dark auburn hair soft and fragrant.

She handed me several boxes in rapid succession and I was abruptly awakened from my reverie. "Look through these for anything that says state archives," she ordered. As she continued searching, she added, "I have to admit, I'm really curious if I have any record of it in these boxes."

To break the monotony of sifting through mountains of notes, I said, "Certainly reflects a lot of work. I'm sorry to hear about your professor." Suzanne acknowledged my comment with a tired smile and continued sorting through large cards one at a time. "Academia seems to be the same all over the world," I continued. "So many professors are world experts in their fields, yet totally underdeveloped in terms of basic social skills and humanity."

"Not that it would make any difference," she replied with a bitterness and cynicism that ran far deeper than I had suspected. "Even if I were to get my degree, it's impossible to get a university position. All the professors are in their forties or fifties. There won't be any appointments for the next ten or twenty years."

"That's a shame," I replied. "A prosperous country like Switzerland, and no job prospects."

"To tell you the truth, I'm really not that enamored with Switzerland," she continued. "Here money means everything, and I'm not so impressed with things like status and prestige as everyone else is."

"Believe me," I said, "it's the same all over the world. In America—"

"No," she interrupted, firmly. "It's different here. The preoccupation of the Swiss with wealth is nothing less than an obsession. In Switzerland, money doesn't just talk, it shrieks, it bellows. People look down on me; they couldn't care less that I'm a historian, that I'm doing original research. All they care about is how much money a person makes, how they dress, what kind of car they drive."

I conceded, "I guess Switzerland always struck me as a strange country, surrounded by all the intense creativity of Italy, Germany, and France, yet unable to produce anything of its own in the way of artistic greatness."

"It's a scandal," she continued, getting a little agitated as she tossed papers. "We have to rely on foreigners for everything cultural: orchestra players, singers, even piano bars. It's almost as if all the complacency is contagious, as if it were anathema to artists." Putting down the pages she was sorting, she looked at me, exasperated. "How would you feel living in a country that produces nothing but bankers and hotel management trainees?"

Trying to concentrate while going through her notes, I replied, "If it makes you feel any better, money has never been much of an obsession for me because I never had any. Musicology isn't exactly lucrative." But as I spoke, I remembered my experiences with six figures and added, "And my only brief encounter with money wasn't terribly satisfying."

Suzanne stopped what she was doing and waited for me to go on. "Don't ask me to explain," I said. "But I can tell you one thing: money can't buy you friends, but it guarantees you a better class of enemies." She looked at me with a puzzled expression and we continued sorting through her notes and notebooks.

It was clear she was getting tired and I wasn't surprised when she finally sighed, "This is a much bigger job than I thought." As she spoke, a file caught her attention and she opened it. "I think I have it." Sorting out loose pages, she extracted several papers clipped together. "These are the ones," she said, with cautious excitement. "I remember this document because of a reference to cleaning the streets in Geneva in the eighteenth century."

As I examined her meticulous notes, I asked, dumbfounded, "You copied the whole thing?"

"It must have been at the beginning of my research," she replied. "Because today I wouldn't bother to write everything down. In those days I went overboard."

As I admired her transcription, I noted that she had used several colors of ink. "Why did you do that?" I asked.

"Because in the original, someone had made corrections and I tried to reproduce it in the exact way."

"Why do you think it was corrected?" I asked.

"It was written by a child," she replied. "And there are mistakes in the spelling and accents in French."

Under my breath, I said, "This is just short of miraculous," as we both turned our attention to the document.

> *September 2, 1766*
> *1. We are lodging with Mr. Huber, who is great fun. He*
> *tells stories of his travels as an adventurer and knows*
> *many things. He can name every bird, every animal,*
> *and every plant he sees. He has a great talent for making*
> *silhouettes and last evening made one of my sister and*
> *me. All the time he was cutting it, he was laughing and*
> *saying funny things.*

"You're right," I said. "It must have been a French exercise, because several accents have been corrected in a different color ink." But I had already decided not to tell Suzanne that the name Mr. Huber immediately struck a chord with me; when researching Mozart's travels through Switzerland, I had come across it. Leopold Mozart had entered *chez Huber*—meaning they had stayed with Mr. Huber—in those precious travel notebooks he compiled during their three-and-a-half-year trip through Europe, notes invaluable to posterity for retracing their travels. Vaguely I remembered what I had read about this Renaissance man, Huber, a knowledgeable naturalist who had traveled the world extensively. And the mention of silhouettes brought a vivid stream of visual associations to mind, as I recalled those detailed black paper cutouts that were so much a part of eighteenth-century culture.

"Here is the part about cleaning the streets," Suzanne said. "It's why I copied this document."

> *2. In Geneva, no one is hired to clean the streets as in*
> *other cities. Here, the privilege is sold to one man who*
> *removes the dirt and sells it to the farmers as manure.*

As I tried to understand what was so remarkable about the reference, Suzanne interjected, "I thought it was an interesting footnote about urban administration in the eighteenth century, a way that Geneva's organization was different from the rest of Europe. Where else could you find someone selling the dirt off the streets?" We continued examining her notes in silence.

> *3. The city has many large new buildings to store grain.*
> *4.* [Crossed out, but legible:] *Here, a marriage to a Catholic is regarded as invalid.*

"Why do you think the part about marriages between Catholics and Protestants was crossed out?" I asked.

"No idea," Suzanne responded. "It's a well-known fact."

Without wanting to divulge what I suspected, namely that the document had been written by the ten-year-old Mozart, I reflected on the highly charged atmosphere of religious conflict in Europe during the eighteenth century. Since the Mozarts were devout, practicing Catholics who were guests in a Protestant city, I concluded it would have been the kind of comment a child would pick up from adult conversations. "It might have been politically incorrect to comment on it in those days," I said. "Say, if the person who wrote it was a foreigner."

My comment caused her to raise her eyebrows, as if to ask why I thought it was written by a foreigner. But she didn't press the issue. Instead, Suzanne continued reading to herself and I caught up with her pace.

> *5. Lake Geneva is very clear. We saw a large stone that is called Niton's Rock. It was an altar used for human sacrifices to the Celtic gods.*

"What about this?" I asked her. "Is there really a Niton's Rock in Geneva where human sacrifices were made?"

Laughing, she replied, "Partly true, I guess. Archaeologists have found instruments indicating Niton's Rock—it's a large stone rising out of the port—was an altar used for sacrifices. But I never heard anything about human sacrifice." I reasoned to myself that it could have been the product of a ten-year-old's overactive imagination, or perhaps even a folk myth circulating at that time. We continued reading.

> 6. *Today we walked on the Treille, which has many tall linden trees.*

With each word, I began to ask myself if I had read this somewhere before. It was an eerie, gnawing sensation, and I became more and more sure. Trying to retrace where I had come across it, I focused on certain key names and words that looked familiar. Over and over, I repeated to myself, "Niton's Rock . . . Niton's Rock . . . Niton's Rock . . . Treille . . . Treille . . . Treille."

"Jesus," I said. And in that split second, I knew exactly where I had seen Mozart's "Geneva diary."

The revelation jumped out at me like a lightning flash. The same words were repeated over and over again on the practice sheet among the effects of the murdered forger, Peter Arneis, whose materials I had examined in the police station in Munich. Suzanne noticed my reaction immediately. But I was absolutely determined not to drag her into the whole sordid mess. Instead, I pointed to the word *Treille* and asked, "What does this mean?"

"Oh, that's a promenade up by City Hall, near the medieval Baudet Tower," she replied. "It has the longest park bench in Europe. But I don't get it, why would anyone have stolen this from the archives?"

Determined not to get Suzanne involved, I shrugged my shoulders. But by now I was sure the document was a French exercise written by Mozart as a little boy, describing his experiences in Geneva in his own words. The most unsettling question was why anyone would have been murdered for it. Someone apparently wanted to get their hands on the diaries at any cost, regardless of their historical or commercial value.

Suzanne was looking at me critically and finally insisted,

"So, what makes this document worth stealing?" She continued staring, demanding an explanation.

Trying my best to disguise what I knew, I replied, "Regardless of why it was stolen, the director of the archives is going to be very glad you made a copy. If the original ever turns up, the archives can make a claim to it." As I spoke, I realized that it was nearly evening and blurted out, "I haven't even looked for a hotel yet. Do you know of anyplace nearby?"

"It's pretty late," she replied. "And the city's packed because of the music festival this weekend—you're going to have trouble finding a place to stay." She reflected for a moment, and finally said, tentatively, "You could always sleep on my sofa. It's not very fancy, but at least it's a place to sleep."

Her narrow living room was furnished with eclectic remnants from secondhand shops, and I glanced over at an overstuffed chair with frayed arms, tasseled lampshades with burn marks, and bookshelves—bookshelves everywhere loaded with paperbacks. It all reminded me of summers spent traveling in Europe, when an invitation to spend the night sleeping on someone's floor was a great option, as money was always running short. And the prospect of sleeping a few feet away from Suzanne was particularly exciting. Trying not to sound too eager, I replied, "I'd just as soon do that, instead of wasting time hunting for a hotel."

Suzanne appeared satisfied with the decision. "The price of hotels here is outrageous during peak season. Plus," she continued, "that will give us time to talk about why someone decided to steal a child's French exercise."

"Since you're saving me the cost of a hotel, let me at least invite you out to dinner." She accepted willingly and I tried not to be too obvious as I found myself admiring her ample curves pressing out from underneath her loose-fitting sweater and jeans. "Unfortunately," I said, "the only clothes I have are the ones I'm wearing, so it will have to be someplace casual."

"Don't worry, I know a little Greek restaurant," she said. "You'll be fine the way you are. Do you feel like going now?"

"I do. But you know, I spent the whole night on a train. Would you mind if I took a quick shower before we leave?"

Apparently my question caught her off-guard, and she reflected for a second. "All right," she finally said, explaining her hesitation as she led me toward the bathroom. "My landlady is incredibly cheap. She doesn't like it when I use hot water." As she hunted for a towel, she added, "I hope she doesn't make trouble."

"Trouble?" I replied, wondering what I had gotten myself in for.

"She listens and even bangs on the pipes. But it's hard to find an apartment at this price, so, crazy as she is, I have to put up with her."

Amazed that a landlady could spy on how much hot water someone used, I replied, "I really don't want to inconvenience you."

"It's no inconvenience," she said as she motioned for me to join her on the side of the bathtub. "It's always the same with her . . . but nothing serious." She demonstrated how to entice hot water from the ancient faucets. "I was actually going to take a shower myself, but I'll do it another time."

"Look, I really don't want to impose."

"Don't be silly," she insisted. Continuing her explanation, she said, "Let it run for three or four minutes and it will start to come out hot. That's when you have to soap up quickly. Then shut it off or you'll use up all the hot water and have to rinse off with cold. If you hear banging on the pipes, it's my landlady—just ignore her. It's her way of saying she's listening."

Suzanne closed the door of the bathroom, leaving me alone to work out the mechanics of coaxing hot water out of the heater. After stripping, I climbed in and tried repeatedly to get it to work. Finally, my patience was at an end. I stuck my head out the door and called, "Hello, Suzanne?"

When she didn't respond, I walked through the apartment with a towel draped around my waist, looking for her. Finding her in the tiny kitchen, I startled her, saying, "I'm not having any luck with the hot water." She was accommodating, even pleasant, and absentmindedly threw a furtive glance over me. For a brief moment, I saw a glimmer in her eyes, as if she had seen me for the first time as a man and not as a scholar. As she led me back into the bathroom, I remembered a line from *Brideshead Revisited,* what Evelyn Waugh had termed "a thin bat's squeak of sexuality, inaudible to anyone but me." And I felt that something in the delicate chemistry had changed.

Inside the bathroom, I was overwhelmingly aroused by the situation, and the insistent, swelling bulge beneath my towel made it clear. As she adjusted the two handles, trying every combination of hot and cold and of water pressure, I stood nearby, aware of the rock-hard protrusion.

"That should do it," she announced as she stood up, satisfied with the flow of hot water. "Don't waste any time."

Just as she started to leave, a banal joke crossed my mind and I spoke almost before I had time to think. "Did you ever hear the expression . . ." She stopped and looked at me for a moment with sly curiosity. Smiling, I continued. "'Save water, shower with a friend?'"

During an excruciating moment of suspense, I wondered whether Suzanne would throw me out of her apartment. To my surprise, she walked back into the bathroom and began peeling off her sweater, revealing an astonishing figure—the kind that recalled all the fantasies of my adolescence—as I looked on in amazement. Staring directly into my eyes, she unzipped her jeans and began stripping them off. "Don't get the idea that I do this all the time," she said.

In disbelief, I watched her deliberate, sensual striptease, as she removed her woolen socks and proceeded to her panties, revealing a delicate nest of fawn-colored angora between her legs. Still unsure if I was dreaming, I stood mesmerized by her bountiful curves, with firm, shapely buttocks and mountainous breasts for exploring. Shutting off the water, she guided my trembling hands to a bar of soap and turned her back to me, her warm, shapely calves brushing uninhibitedly against my erection. Not knowing what to expect next, I found myself lathering her, down her shoulders to her back and around to the warmest, softest, and fullest of breasts I had ever touched, as she nestled casually into my crotch.

Massaging the lather over and around her ample nipples, I almost lost consciousness until I heard her voice, half-whisper, half-murmur, "They must be clean by now." Gradually I felt comfortable demonstrating more playfulness, exploring different types of touch: stroking her gently with my fingertips, then with the backs of my fingers, running my hands over the contoured line from her wrist, up the insides of her arms, and around her breasts. Lost in a delirious state of mind, I repeated the gesture over and over again before continuing on to more deliberate exploration of the fine line between pain and pleasure, pinching her huge, erect nipples, first gently, then with more force, until she moaned in soft bursts of ecstasy. With circular motions I moved down her tight, firm abdomen, around her waist, finally reaching the moist cleft between her legs, which was burning with the intensity of a furnace.

Slowly and with the delicacy of a massage, I began penetrating her with a gentle thrust until I felt her begin to open up to me. As I prepared to advance deeper, she stopped me. Instead she gently maneuvered the throbbing rod with her hand, sliding it between the cheeks of her ass and inside her, where the lather acted as a lubricant, creating waves of ecstatic pleasure for me. As she bent over, head almost to the floor, her fingers slipped inside her from the front, and she pulled my hips deeper and deeper into her in a delirious *pas de deux*, moaning with an intensity that echoed throughout every corner of the room.

Our gasps and unrestrained cries of rapture were deafening, and within seconds, other sounds thundered in the room, creating an incongruous counterpoint—a loud, furious banging on the pipes accompanied by a voice shouting from the distance. As our bodies exploded with the jetting, rhythmic explosions of an orgasm that never seemed to end, I immediately pulled out and collapsed over her, holding her tightly and massaging every part of her body I could reach, my heart pumping like a powerful engine, while the relentless clank of metal on the pipes continued unabated.

Suzanne gradually disengaged from our pose, and I was brought back to my senses by the pleasant sensation of a warm rinse. Her expression radiant, she climbed out of the bathtub and returned with a cotton towel that had been sitting on a radiator. But as we put on our clothes, she began to speak with the same analytical tone she used before our shower. "You're going to tell me what you know about this document, aren't you?"

My head still swimming in the aftermath of an earth-shattering experience, I had difficulty refocusing my thoughts. She repeated her question as we left the apartment for dinner. While we walked, I hunted for the nearest bank machine, where I entered the viscount's ATM card, withdrawing $250 in Swiss currency. But by the time we arrived at the restaurant, Suzanne had stopped asking and I had made up my mind that the risk of her knowing would far outweigh any benefits to her. Fortunately, in the noisy restaurant crowded with students, it was difficult to have any kind of serious discussion. In the festive party atmosphere with lively folk music, she appeared comfortably resigned to the fact that she would have to put off her curiosity and enjoy the meal.

As we walked back to her apartment, Suzanne again brought up the document. After unlocking the door, she stood waiting for my response, and I took her forefinger and placed it over her lips, as if to say no. Time was running out, and a sense of urgency began to overwhelm me. Like Aeneas toward Rome, I felt an irresistible need to get back on my way to Prague.

"I'm going to try to catch a late train," I finally said to Suzanne, who looked at me in total astonishment. When she recovered from my sudden change of plans, she sighed in weary resignation as if she had already begun to understand me, as if she knew it was pointless to try to change my mind. We said goodbye with genuine warmth but without any display of affection that would have provoked the wrath of her landlady. "I hope we'll see each other again," I said.

"So do I," she replied. "But only if circumstances are less pressing . . . less complicated."

As I headed down the hill of the Old Town toward the train station, I thought about the document that had been stolen. Suzanne was absolutely right in her conclusion that it did not tell us anything we didn't already know. Neither did it tell us anything new about Mozart's visit to Geneva. So why had Schott been kicked in the face until he was unrecognizable, then dumped in the lake with his penis sewn in his mouth?

Then the significance of the French exercise hit me like a sledgehammer: this modest little document, when placed with the other Mozart diaries, had the unique distinction of being the earliest of them all—the oldest "Mozart diary" in existence.

But that still wasn't enough. The diaries had to fit into some larger scheme. What happened to Arnold Schott was beyond imagination. As a scholar, I imagined how ecstatic he must have been when he realized what he had discovered. But ultimately, it led to his grisly death. *Finding the Milan diary could result in the same end for me,* I reflected, shuddering at the thought. And I remembered what Max had said about the unfortunate characters trying to double-cross their clients. He had also intimated that the forger in Munich had played with the wrong people. Perhaps Schott had done the same, and they decided to make an example of him.

"I just hope they killed him first," I mumbled absentmindedly. *Before they sliced off his body parts.* It occurred to me that now Max was likely feeling the same way toward me as the clients of the murdered forger felt toward him.

A sense of overwhelming weariness set in. After spending most of the night sitting up in a train, the excitement of the day had taken its toll. On the bridge over the Rhone, I stopped a minute to admire the canopy of night sky above me, a thousand sequined beads shimmering with crystalline clarity, mirrored on the waters of Lake Geneva. The subdued reflections of streetlamps, all glittering like luminescent sparks, created a sea of fireflies shrouded in a veil of amber-gray mist. And I looked back at the Old Town, rising up out of the lake in a languid spire of weathered stone. From atop the cluttered hill, it seemed to have the casual indifference of a purebred Himalayan cat, gazing down complacently upon a world that was clearly inferior in every way.

\* \* \*

On the way to the station, I realized I would need more cash to cover the cost of trains and hotels. When I reached in my wallet for the viscount's bank card, I discovered that it was missing—I must have dropped it at the machine or somewhere along the way.

"How could I be so stupid?" I heard myself saying. Heading directly back toward the bank machine I had used, I noticed something peculiar in the distance—a dark-haired man, about forty, with a flattened nose that vaguely reminded me of a professional boxer, emerging from a side street and racing in the same direction—merely a few hundred feet in front of me. Looking around the corner, I watched in disbelief as the man arrived at the bank machine and joined someone else in brutally kicking a man on the ground in the face. With astonishing violence, they pummeled him with kicks in the groin, in the neck, and in the back. My head began to swim.

Between gasps and moans, the man repeated in German, "But I just found the card . . . on the ground . . ." Both assailants stopped. They looked at each other in disbelief and examined the face of the man. When he began to vomit blood in a projectile arc, I inched my way backward into the shadows of the alley.

In the excruciating silence, I held my breath. As the two men were leaving, one spit at his victim—who was still writhing on the ground in agony—and mumbled, *"Che pezzo di merda"*— what a piece of shit.

After the two assailants left, I wrestled with the idea of taking a chance and helping the man on the ground. My mind raced in a jumbled stream of consciousness: *I'd better get out of here fast, it's far too risky to try and help. But how can I leave this guy on the street? If he isn't already dead, he's going to need an ambulance.*

Finally, I emerged from the dark street and reached cautiously for the derelict's pulse. *Still alive, thank God!* In his hand was my bankcard, which had caused his almost fatal beating. Around the corner, I found a phone and dialed emergency. After explaining the situation, I realized I was in danger of not having enough cash to get to Prague. Quickly I returned and inserted the ATM card, withdrawing the maximum allowed, an additional $250 in Swiss currency. The man on the ground was trying desperately to speak, so I knelt down to lift his head. "I called for help," I said in German. "They're on their way."

Then I heard the sound of rapid footsteps approaching and understood my worst fears were suddenly coming true: the two assailants were heading back at full speed.

# CHAPTER 26

*No mask like open truth to cover lies,*
*As to go naked is the best disguise.*

—WILLIAM CONGREVE

Without wasting a second, I took off in the opposite direction. Followed by the relentless sound of footsteps, I sprinted through the city, ducking into empty side streets and climbing over wrought-iron fences and huge trash recycling bins. How long I ran, I can't remember. When I thought I had lost them, I stopped and listened for footsteps. Instead there was a piercing silence. Nervous and out of breath, I looked around the dark quarter of Geneva and noticed flashing neon lights everywhere, and dark recessed glass windows advertising X-rated films and strip shows. Walking aimlessly, I continued to listen for sounds until a huge woman burst out of a door and said in English, "Hey, honey, come over here."

She took my arm slowly and drew me through a beaded curtain, where I found myself in a shop offering every kind of tattoo and body piercing, stocked with an endless selection of sex toys and leather goods. "You look like you need a drink," she said. "Or maybe something more."

Dazed, I looked around the shop: thousands of porno films lined the aisles and plastic blow-up dolls and dildos covered the walls. Weakly, I answered, "A drink."

"Anything you want, honey," she said. "Name your poison."

"Brandy," I replied and she bent over to rummage through an overstocked cabinet. Disoriented, I slowly realized that she was a transvestite. As she poured the brandy, I hoped that she might be willing to help me. Downing the entire glass in a single gulp, I said, "I'm tired of the way I look."

Rather brusquely, she replied, "You want a disguise."

When she saw my look of apprehension, she changed her tone. "I mean, a little makeover. How about a few tattoos in henna? They only last ten days."

Thinking of the man on the ground at the ATM machine vomiting blood, I said, "Something more. I've got to walk out of here unrecognizable."

She stared at me for over a minute. Finally she exclaimed, "The exact opposite of what you look like now: a skinhead. And I do piercing here—any body part you want."

Within minutes, she was stripping off my clothes and shaving my head, racing to find leather trousers my size. "Chaps are nice," she suggested. As an afterthought, she added, "I hope you can pay for all of this."

"I don't care how much it costs."

"We'll keep it on the cheap," she replied. "Where do you want your rings?"

A shudder went through me as I contemplated having my body pierced. "Just one in my left ear." But when I remembered the scene at the ATM, I added, "One in my nose. And a nipple ring."

"Oh, baby," she replied, immediately getting to work, rummaging through fake diamond earrings in a drawer. "You're getting me all hot."

Talking nonstop, she shaved my head and mustache with an electric razor, leaving only a two-inch Mohawk strip from the back of my head to my forehead, which she lacquered stiff and sprayed with highlights of neon pink and green. The henna tattoos were painless, but not the piercing. But when I thought of the man getting kicked in the face, I realized that anything else was preferable. Then she led me to a mirror, where I looked at myself in disbelief: head almost completely shaved and naked above the waist except for a leather vest.

"How much do I owe you?" I asked.

"Two hundred dollars. Cash."

After folding out two hundred dollars in Swiss currency, I peered out into the street. Unaccustomed to not wearing underwear, I felt myself strangely aroused by the peculiar costume. And as I walked for a half hour through dark, hidden side streets to the train station, I began to think more and more about Suzanne, even contemplating ringing her bell in the middle of the night. But I didn't want to get her involved; I just had to get out of Geneva immediately.

The train station was abandoned except for several teenage tourists in sleeping bags in the waiting room. Pulling out my cash, I quietly asked for a second-class ticket, one way to Prague. "What?" the man at the ticket counter barked, evaluating my appearance. Out of the corner of my eye as he spoke, I was dumbfounded to see the two assailants entering the station.

Almost whispering, I again asked for a ticket to Prague. "Are you on drugs or something?" the man shouted. "You can't go to Prague now. The best you can do is catch the local that leaves in twenty minutes in that direction."

"Jesus," I mumbled under my breath as I grabbed the ticket and my change. Trying to appear nonchalant, I walked slowly toward the exit, glancing over my shoulder as the man with the boxer face pulled a manila envelope from his pocket. For a second, the two men examined a photograph and then, in an explosive instant, started to run after me.

At full speed, I darted out of the train station, the metal plates on my heels clanking mercilessly on the cobblestone side streets. As the two men converged on me, I saw the lights of a bar in the distance, surrounded by two dozen motorcycles. In a flash, I decided to head inside and within seconds I was screaming at the top of my lungs in German, "*Hilfe*. They're going to kill me. Fascist pigs."

Almost immediately, I heard the sound of tables being kicked over and a dozen switchblades snapping out. Heading for the emergency exit, I looked over my shoulder and saw the glimmer of brass knuckles being raised in the light. When the two assailants burst into the bar, they were greeted by thirty angry bikers, who descended on them with a rage and ferocity that surpassed even what I had seen earlier. With the sound of the emergency exit alarm shrieking in my ears, I ran back to the train station and jumped on the local in the direction of Prague a few seconds before it departed, mumbling, "Now what?"

I spent the night on a park bench covered with newspapers, in a small town at the end of the local train line. The next day I took the early morning train for Vienna, anticipating difficulties because of how I looked. But when I reached the Vienna Süd-Bahnhof and boarded the train for Prague, the reaction was more immediate—and violent—than anything I imagined. The conductor took one look at me and began shouting at me in Czech, acting more like a prison guard than a train employee. Passengers left the compartment, and I sat alone until the train started filling up to capacity. People whispered, and although the Czech language remained a mystery to me, I understood certain things that are a universal language, like hostility and prejudice.

My mind wandered over the events of the previous twenty-four hours: the archives, finding the diary, Suzanne, the two assailants, the breathless race through Geneva. Trying to put together the complicated scenario, I focused on the limited pieces of the puzzle at my disposal. Maybe Max had learned about the ATM card and located me when I took money out of the viscount's account. But I was in a state of total isolation, grappling with problems that were too big to handle, without guidance or assistance. Like Plato's blind men with the elephant, I was trying to describe an unknown colossus, having access only to single parts like the tail or the trunk or the tusk.

Yet the single parts at my disposal were numerous, like the exaggerated values the diaries were drawing at auctions. On the way to Munich in the limo, Nadine mentioned in passing, "It wouldn't be the first time a large criminal operation sought out a money-laundering scheme that gave an impression of legitimacy."

"Money laundering!" I said aloud, surprising the other passengers in my compartment, who stopped their discussion in Czech for a few seconds. Money laundering would explain a lot, like the grossly inflated prices. As passengers resumed their conversations, I continued exploring the idea, perplexed that Nadine had not mentioned the possibility to the viscount, since he had no idea why the diaries were drawing exorbitant prices and then disappearing from circulation.

Yet everything was beginning to make sense. I remembered how interested Nadine was in Max and vice versa. So much appeared to revolve around him. As Nicoletta had said, Max was a great lover of culture and an avid connoisseur of art. And of course, he had made it clear during our discussion at the dinner table that he believed criminality could be raised to the level of an art form.

But how exactly was he involved? He knew about the forger in Munich and his clients, who he implied were like his own—"high stakes players who don't like it when someone fools around with them." Somewhere along the line, things had gone terribly wrong. If ruthless players had been brought into the picture, something was bound to happen.

But for now, I was out of touch with Nadine and the guests of the foundation. The viscount had given me explicit instructions not to call or write. Some pieces in the puzzle were beyond my grasp, like the forger's death and how he had obtained copies of the diaries Schott and I had found. Braun must have had something to do with it, because the copy of the diary I sent him ended up in the hands of the forger.

"Species of madness." That's what it was, I decided, unable to remember the rest of the quotation. The murders of Schott and Arneis over Mozart diaries. And what about Denise and von Horvach? And the near-fatal attempts on the lives of Teal and Ibsen, and on me?

The rest of the line from Spinoza came back to me: "Avarice, ambition, lust are nothing but species of madness." The philosopher had drawn what sounded like a fitting evaluation of Maximilian De Angelis. "It's a big shark pool out there," Max had said, "in the midst of a massive feeding frenzy."

Max's contention that crime could be raised to the level of an art form enraged me; to clothe criminal schemes with the name "art" and imagine himself an artist was perverse. Then I thought about the inevitable difficulties of the artist—even my own life, scraping together a living to support my art. I began to list all the things I had done without profit, without recognition, things that would perhaps someday, in some small way, benefit the world. Too little acknowledgment, too few financial rewards, too many obstacles created by professors and other scholars. And of course, researching and publishing articles for nothing. But it was all for a legitimate cause, wasn't it? Or was I deceiving myself? Max's cynical words reverberated in my mind: "Of all mistakes you can make, there's none more stupid than trying to improve the world."

My dedication felt like another kind of madness: the artist driven to make irrational choices. For a moment, I remembered what Henry James had said: "We work in the dark—we do what we can—we give what we have. Our doubt is our passion, and our passion is our task. The rest is the madness of art."

So, Max and I were both madmen. We were in the same boat. Yet we were at opposite ends, as far apart as two human beings could be. As far as I was concerned, Max was responsible for sabotaging the heater in my room in Chelsea and for sending the two men to kill me. I vowed if there was going to be a showdown, he was going to get a run for his money. Because I was now a madman, and no one can ever predict what a madman will do.

When I arrived in Prague, I immediately relaxed in the anonymity of a large metropolis, where there were enough young people dressed like me. After arranging hotel accommodations at the Prague Main Railway, I made my way on foot. This was not my first visit to Prague, but I had forgotten the overwhelming natural beauty of the setting, with the fortresslike Prague Castle looking down from a massive rock upon the patrician city. Like Rome, it was a city of layers, of peoples and of epochs, with distant voices of Celtic tribes still echoing across thousands of years. And although German culture and language had flourished in Prague during the time of Mozart, the city that now stretched before me was profoundly Slavic, nationalistic and proud.

But layers were also reflected in the architecture, and everywhere I looked medieval turrets sprang up next to Gothic landmarks and baroque facades arose from Romanesque foundations. The result was an exciting mélange with splendid views and vistas, calculated to create an unsurpassed theatricality. Stretching out above me was an expanse of piercing blue sky looking over a vast sea of verdigris domes and burnished rust roof tiles. *A city of color,* I thought, as I surveyed the countless facades washed in the softest tints from an artist's palette: light shades of celeste and salmon, side by side with delicate tones of milk white opal and the lightest amber gold.

My casual walk led me toward the Staré Město, the old town and historic heart of the city, and I strolled by the splendid pastel green, neoclassical Estates Theater, where Mozart's *Don Giovanni* had first been performed. In Old Town Square, a row of carriages with horses eagerly awaited clients and my eye was drawn to the impressive astronomical horologe, a marvel of chronometric complexity. Two huge circular clocks stood one above the other, each with decorative faces that disguised a world of intricacy beneath the surface: the upper in luminous shades of sapphire and russet, the lower in polished brass and gold with symbols of the zodiac circling a medieval coat of arms.

My watch said ten minutes to the hour and a small crowd had gathered, so I assumed we would soon be treated to some kind of mechanical pageantry. In the meantime, I entertained myself by observing the children around me, who were fascinated by my appearance, and whose good-natured antics were taking place under the vigilant eyes of their parents. Their short attention spans were comical, as they bounded from one spontaneous game to the next, their interest riveted for a moment with surprising intensity, then ricocheting tirelessly to another with hardly a moment's interruption.

But when the two doors above the clocks opened, the colorful figures of the horologe came to life, and the children's attention was held no less than that of the adults. After a solemn miniature procession of the apostles, two by two, a skeleton began to ring his bell over an hourglass, scrutinizing a colorful Turk nearby. As the figure of Greed weighed his substantial money purse, Vanity examined himself in the mirror, nodding contentedly.

"Greed and Vanity," I mumbled, thinking of Maximilian De Angelis and Nicoletta. And it occurred to me that I was beginning to sound a little like Leopold Mozart, unable to enjoy sightseeing without moralizing. After the brief spectacle, I headed toward the Malá Strana, the small town where my hotel was located.

When Miloš Forman was filming *Amadeus*, he chose the famed Golden Prague as a location because of the countless edifices that were intact and remarkably preserved. Now, decades after the film, I knew the city was even more beautiful—more multicolored, more vibrant, and in the midst of a renaissance of sensitive and imaginative restoration. It was unquestionably the city in the world most evocative and representative of the time of Mozart.

And Mozart had been welcomed here with open arms when he arrived in 1787, by a city that adored his opera *The Marriage of Figaro*. He was thirty-one and at the peak of his talent, with some of his most adventurous works about to be created here: *Don Giovanni*, where dark, Mephistophelian elements of the overture and last act alternate with shimmering moments of light and melody like *"Là ci darem la mano,"* sung by Don Giovanni as he attempts to seduce Zerlina during her own wedding. And his *Prague* Symphony was written here, in four days, as was his last serious opera, *La clemenza di Tito*.

For Mozart, Prague was also a city of frivolous and exuberant balls, and his artistic production of festive contredanses reflected those events. As my eyes wandered across the cityscape, I understood that the musical character of Prague was stamped on its buildings, lyricism reflected in architecture. Approaching the Charles Bridge across the expansive Moldau River, I could see that even the most practical of necessities, a bridge, had been transformed into the highest expression of aesthetic imagination: massive religious statues and sculptural groups made it feel as if I was immersed in a deeply devotional world, where pious mysticism had encompassed beauty, and where beauty had been woven into the fabric of worship.

At the end of the bridge, countless baroque spires, reaching upward in a symbolic gesture, awaited me. Prague had been called the city of a hundred spires, I remembered as I looked out over onion domes and imposing bell towers from every period, rising from churches of a unique richness, all surveyed silently from above by the expansive Strahov Abbey.

Yet at the same time the pedestrian streets were bustling with an irreverent, almost pagan joie de vivre. Finally arriving at my hotel, I left the sea of sightseers with a distinct sense of regret. I would soon have to leave Prague and figure out how to get to the Benedictine monastery Lesní Klášter. But after settling into my room, I continued to enjoy the view of the city from my window as a slow gray blanket of clouds reached in from the surrounding hills with long, languorous arms. One at a time, almost imperceptibly, the streetlights of the city began to appear—a chorus of faint flames flickering, slowly building in an implacable crescendo as I watched, temporarily suspended in the timelessness of Prague.

Tomorrow, another diary awaited me, and with it, perhaps another piece of the puzzle that would explain the mysterious and deadly events taking place each time a new diary was discovered.

CHAPTER 27

*I like a church; I like a cowl;*
*I love a prophet of the soul;*
*And on my heart monastic aisles*
*Fall like sweet strains or pensive smiles;*
*Yet not for all his faith can see*
*Would I that cowlèd churchman be.*

—RALPH WALDO EMERSON

Dismal plains and monotonous countryside stretched in limitless succession, interrupted only by an occasional small village, where herds of cows stood waiting with inquisitive faces at the railroad crossing, fascinated by the novelty of this odd and exceptional event. Gradually the train approached more rugged, hilly terrain, which became more mountainous and cool as we ascended thickly forested areas. The old woman sitting in my compartment apparently sensed that there was only one place a foreigner could be heading in this abandoned region, and as she flashed a toothless smile, she pointed in the distance, saying, "Lesní Klášter."

The view of the monastery took my breath away; it was a drama, a spectacle, a moment imprinted in time. The stern, impregnable fortress jutted out with grim severity above a massive outcropping of rock, with the tops of two imposing baroque onion-domed towers just barely visible. The juxtaposition of this architectural tour de force with the isolation of the setting was striking; for a moment, I imagined what someone in medieval times would have felt, looking up at the exclusive and closed world towering in the lofty distance.

When the rest of Europe was in political decay and turmoil, Lesní Klášter and similar monasteries had been the sole centers of learning and culture, preserving the underpinnings of Western culture. I made a comparison with other great monasteries I had seen and visited: the baroque sumptuousness of Melk, the aristocratic severity of Mont-Saint-Michel, and the stern, impenetrable Sacra di San Michaele. And there were countless others whose names I had forgotten, but whose breathtaking locations were fixed forever in my memory, such as the visionary mountaintop views from high above the Amalfi coast and the splendid isolation of Lago d'Orta. In contrast, Lesní Klášter was far more simple, more stark, more bleak and cold. But it seemed to me that the architects of monasteries all had one thing in common—they knew how to choose sites offering the most spectacular views, and how to shape their structures so that they rose up in ways that inspired admiration.

When the train came to a halt, I climbed out and waited for the bus. But after half an hour, the centuries-old path leading up the side of the mountain, disappearing into the trees and rocks like a romantic stage set for an opera, began to elicit a certain fascination. Increasingly impatient for the bus, I finally decided to head up the path, past somber green mountain laurel spread out under the sparse canopy of lanky pines jutting upward in vertiginous pillars that blocked the sky.

Tiny yellow-and-black spotted lizards scurried across my path, and small groups of local residents could be seen hunting mushrooms and carefully placing their finds in wicker baskets lined with cloth napkins. As the path grew more treacherous, I found myself climbing worn rocks and realized the walking trail was also the natural course of a small stream descending from the peak. Deciduous saplings sprouted everywhere on it, their brighter foliage in contrast to the drab, darker sheen of native shrubs lining the route. And an ample layer of leaves indicated that few people ever walked this way.

Out of breath, I arrived at the massive walls of the monastery and stared at the outer gate, an ornate wrought-iron construction revealing traces of rust and decay. Inside, I found a huge complex dominated by the two baroque church spires, and my attention was drawn to the spacious courtyard, and to the impressive wooden door that guarded the monastery.

After ringing the bell, I was greeted by a somber-faced brother in a dark brown habit, just how I imagined monks would look. When I tried to tell him who I was, he slammed the door in my face. It took several repeat attempts to get him to listen to me. When it became clear that he did not speak a word of English, I pointed to myself, "Matthew Pierce," and gestured, "looking for Brother Cyril," and he finally understood. Begrudgingly, he led me through pristine corridors surfaced in dark wood paneling, their floors glistening with a fresh coat of wax, eyeing me suspiciously all along the way. Within minutes the abbot arrived in his office.

Although he was taken aback by my appearance, Brother Cyril's demeanor immediately put me at ease. About five foot six and with a neatly cropped reddish brown beard flecked with gray, he struck me as an extrovert with a good sense of humor who was amused by the way I was dressed.

"Please excuse—" I began, but he interrupted me in midsentence with a gesture.

"English, no," he replied, and then, switching to German, he continued, "I'm sorry, I don't speak English."

In German, I replied, "Please excuse how I'm dressed, but if I hadn't changed my appearance I might not be alive. Two men followed me in Geneva."

My narrative caught him off-guard and he asked, "Do they know you're here?"

"No," I said. "And there's no way they can find me."

"Good," he responded. "You'll be safe here, Dr. Pierce. Lesní Klášter is a protected place, remote and detached from the world. We see barely ten tourists a month, and they're only permitted in the church and in the main courtyard outside. Food and supplies are delivered from the neighboring towns by local farmers and merchants who have lived here all their lives."

As he spoke, his face revealed a flash of inspiration. "If you want, I can even arrange to integrate you into the community."

"Absolutely," I replied.

"Perhaps I could allow the others to assume you are a visiting brother. Right now, only Brother Georg, our administrator who brought you here, and Brother Tomáš, our librarian, know who you are, and I will communicate to them your desire for anonymity."

"Thank you," I said.

"There's a younger brother who speaks a little English. I'll call him to get you a robe. He might also be of service during your stay."

"That will help," I said, "because I don't speak a word of Czech."

"The older brothers here all speak German. It was the second language everyone learned in school. But after the war, Russian was substituted by the Communists—the younger brothers here are part of that generation. But no one will speak Russian as a point of honor. Did Viscount René tell you that the monastery was dispersed by the Communists in 1950?"

"No," I said. "He didn't tell me much. But he was quite emphatic about preserving the integrity of the institution."

"Excellent," Cyril responded immediately. "Because it's a miracle we recovered from what the Communists did. All our books and documents were sent to the regional archives and the furnishings were removed. The monastery itself was left intact; it was never turned into a public building, only because of its remote location. After the Velvet Revolution in 1989, the order was reconstituted and many of us were able to return. If we are able to sell the manuscript, we can begin some much needed renovations."

"The manuscript," I repeated. "I'm very much looking forward to examining it," I said. "How did you find it if the Communists took everything?"

"A few years ago, Brother Tomáš came across a number of boxes that they left because the contents were unintelligible. Tomáš was reluctant to throw them out and suggested we try some new techniques to see if the texts could be restored. None of them revealed anything, except for one set of pages with some very pale writing that reemerged. And the signature alone was enough to indicate to me that I should call my friend Viscount René, who is the keenest devotee of Mozart's music I know."

"What was the signature?" I asked.

"Wolfgang Adam Mozart," he answered.

"Wolfgang Adam?" I replied, lost in thought. "That's quite

remarkable. Did you know that Mozart signed his marriage cer-
tificate that way in 1782?"

"At first I didn't know," he replied. "But the viscount explained that in 1916 a musicologist named Hajdecki noticed that
Mozart had not signed it Amadé, but Adam. It had taken over
a hundred years for someone to spot it."

As he spoke, I began thinking about the possibility of forgery, but reasoned that the middle name Adam was too specialized a piece of musicological information: if it were a forgery, it
would have to date from after 1916 when Hajdecki made his discovery, and the forger would have to have been very knowledgeable. Not eager to jump to conclusions, I merely said, "Very
interesting. When can we take a look at them?"

"Tomorrow," he said. "It is almost time for the evening
meal. And I'm sure you'll need a good night's sleep after your
trip. Let me ask Brother Michal to show you where you'll be
staying. Your first name is Matthew, isn't it? Let's see, the equivalent in Czech would be Matěj—I'll introduce you as Brother
Matěj."

The young monk who arrived to help stood about six foot
one and was eager to please, his clear blue eyes radiating goodwill and enthusiasm. In contrast to the rugged cleft in his chin,
his features were delicate. And his relaxed auburn eyebrows and
slight beard suggested he didn't have a care in the world. The
abbot said something to him in Czech, and the young man
smiled as he led me out the door. As we proceeded through the
corridors, Brother Michal asked me in English, "Where in
America are you from?"

"Boston," I replied.

"I'm a big fan of American and English music," he said enthusiastically. With that, he mimed playing an acoustic guitar
and sang a brief instrumental riff. "Eric Clapton," he informed
me, smiling from ear to ear. "Sunshine of Your Love."

The unexpected touch of worldliness made me laugh.
After handing me the huge key that was in the lock of my door,
he said, "We usually don't use keys for the cells, only for visitors." He led me into a room decorated with only a simple

carved crucifix over the bed and a faded Renaissance-style fresco of hell, complete with tortured sinners in flames, on the wall above a wooden kneeler.

"Cheerful," I said under my breath.

"You'll be alone up in this wing," he continued. "I hope you don't mind that."

"It's fine," I said. Brother Michal opened the huge wooden shutters, revealing an expansive panorama of untouched country-side and forest.

"I'll be right back after I find you a habit," he said. "Let's see, you're a little shorter than me." Under his breath, he said, "You should probably wash the color out of your hair. Or maybe you could shave your head completely—you'll fit in better that way. I'll bring you a razor." As soon as he left the room, I began to explore my new surroundings, fascinated by the surreal world in which I now found myself. The wide, rustic floorboards were warped and creaked with each step. Yet they had recently been polished; the bitter fragrance of butcher's wax still lingered in the room. Other exotic aromas caught my attention: aged cedar from inside the chest of drawers, the perfume of bunches of dried lavender placed in the wardrobe, and the pungent incense of beeswax candles.

Curious, I tried out the bed and found myself swallowed up in a mattress of the softest goose down, in textures of rough, worn woolen blankets and freshly laundered cotton sheets. From deep within the monastery, the strains of a muted choir res-onated, ethereal and serene. Vespers was being sung, and I lis-tened to the purest of melodies echoing in the distance.

After exploring the cell, I moved to the window to enjoy the spectacular view of a landscape in shades of faded green and umber. Lit by the earliest reddish rays of the setting sun, virgin forest stretched out in placid repose. But when I looked down, I was stunned, totally unprepared for the steep drop, a view of such uncompromising severity that I lost my breath. Instinc-tively, I grabbed the marble ledge. Trying again to look down gave me an uncharacteristic rush of vertigo as a fleeting sensa-tion of panic swept through me.

"Quite a view." The voice behind me startled me and I saw that Brother Michal had returned with a monk's habit under his arm, complete with a hooded cowl, a belt of braided rope, and other garments.

"I didn't realize it was such a drop," I answered. "It doesn't give you that impression from the other side of the monastery."

"It's deceptive," he said. "This entire rear section, where all the cells and the library are located, rises directly out of a cliff. It was designed this way to protect the monastery from marauding bandits and armies that crossed the area for centuries."

After Brother Michal left me alone to dress, I removed the rings from my nose and ear and shaved the rest of my head, listening blissfully to the music rising from the far recesses of the monastery. When the singing ended, he again knocked at my door and smiled in approval at my transformed appearance. As he led me down through the corridors, he whispered, "In the refectory, there is the rule of silence." Near the end of a table seating thirty-five or forty, he found two seats. After a brief prayer, we no longer spoke, but occasionally I caught him glancing over at me and smiling almost imperceptibly, curious about the new brother who had just arrived on the scene.

Not knowing what to expect for meals, I imagined some version of "bread and water," and was surprised when freshly baked pumpernickel loaves strewn with coriander seeds and dried rosemary were passed around, along with other remarkable breads made from chewy grains. With the arrival of each dish, I was increasingly astonished—large crockery terrines with potage of carrot and pumpkin, slightly sweet, yet pungent from coarsely ground nutmeg. Roast pork followed—extraordinarily tender in a savory cognac reduction sauce—complemented by paper-thin slices of dauphin potatoes in an aromatic blend of cheeses, accompanied by a medley of seasonal baby root vegetables.

As red wine similar to the finest Beaujolais-Villages was poured into rough-blown goblets, I marveled at the subtle refinements of the preparation and seasonings. The dessert arrived from the kitchen—individual fluted ramekins of mocha crème brûlée topped with toasted hazelnuts, the caramelized sugar still sizzling from under the flame, and I concluded that this was the best-kept secret of all time. The rustic setting—a sea of monks clad in rough brown cloth, sitting arm to arm in unyielding silence—was totally incongruous with the sumptuous cuisine, and I made up my mind to find out more about the chef responsible for the epicurean refinements.

After dinner, we entered the chapel for compline and, for the first time, I had doubts whether I could successfully pull off the ruse of being a monk. Intimidated, I began watching others from the corner of my eye and soon realized it was not difficult to blend in if I paid attention carefully. Only the Gregorian chant presented an obstacle, but within seconds I was able to give an impression of being well acquainted with it by merely following the other voices by a split second, mirroring the cadence of the melodies. And by the end of the service I had begun to feel the natural direction and flow of the chant without having to concentrate.

An unexpected aftereffect was that the waves of voices, the repetition of phrases in Latin in a centuries-old tradition, gradually entered my consciousness. Within a brief time, I found it was becoming a part of me, lulling me into an irresistible state of calm. Even when I returned to my cell, the waves of sound continued to swell and diminish in my mind, and I found myself ready for a sleep that descended with astonishing rapidness, comparable only to a drug-induced state.

A knock on my door woke me early the next morning. Disoriented, I looked at my watch and was stunned to realize it was only 5:20. Quickly I donned my vestments and headed to chapel. Although I was half-asleep, I soon found myself participating in the singing of vigils, a ritual reaching back for centuries that immersed me in a world removed from time.

Following chapel, the flow of the monks led me without thinking to the refectory, where the breakfast that followed was as extraordinary as the previous evening's dinner: huge artichoke hearts topped with poached eggs, on freshly baked and toasted shortcakes, served with points of fresh asparagus and hollandaise sauce. I watched the expressions of the monks as they began to eat, but no one appeared particularly impressed by the food.

By the time the abbot arrived to take me to the library, I was quite awake. Chatting quietly, he led me past courtyards with miniature gardens of flourishing herbs in pristine geometric beds, all still glistening from heavy dew. After climbing several carved staircases, we walked through an enormous baroque portal of variegated pink and green marble. "Brother Tomáš speaks Czech, Slovak, and German," he said as we entered an antechamber paneled entirely in wood, with faded trompe l'oeil scenes made from intricate wood inlay in subtle shades of cherry and mahogany. "And Russian and Latin, but no English."

Brother Tomáš soon arrived, a dark-haired, heavyset man with a broad, flat nose and bright ebony eyes that revealed a quick intelligence. After our introduction, Brother Tomáš led me through the immense library, lined from floor to ceiling with massive shelves, all of which were empty. "The Communists took everything," he said with disgust. "You can hardly call this a library anymore."

On a huge table of dark wood, a nondescript archival file folder had been strategically placed. As Brother Tomáš untied it, he asked in German, "Would you like a magnifying glass?"

"Perhaps," I answered.

"What will you do first?" he asked.

"I'll begin by making some general observations on the manuscript, and afterward do a vis-à-vis translation into English. And I'd like to see the transcription you made—it could save me some time."

"Of course."

My immediate and unspoken reaction to the folios he stacked on the desk before me was, *What a crumpled mess.* The sturdy eighteenth-century paper was familiar to me. But these pages were a gnarled, disheveled lot that had clearly been soaked and dried. While he stood waiting, I examined the first page and conceded, "I can barely make out a word."

As if waiting for my reaction, Brother Tomáš proceeded to mount an exotic-looking electrical lamp on the desk, plugging it into an extension cord outlet that had been prepared in advance. An eerie phosphorescence soon began to stretch across the surface like translucent fingers, revealing a phantom writing that glistened with an iridescent sheen. "These ultraviolet bulbs were ordered specially by the rare books library of the Klementinum," he said. "After I soaked the sheets in four different chemical baths, I treated them with a fixer solution. It's quite a science."

When Brother Tomáš realized I was able to proceed, he said, "I'll leave you." Painstakingly, I began recording my observations, beginning with a general, global survey, then proceeding to more specific detailed comments. Throughout the diary, I began noticing examples of a handwriting similar to the style of my Milan diary, but different enough, as it would have to be, coming from a later period in Mozart's life. As I finished examining the folios the first time, something bizarre caught my eye and I beckoned to Brother Tomáš, who was watching me discreetly from a distance.

"There are two different handwritings in this diary," I said. Brother Tomáš's normal reserved expression was replaced by astonishment. "Can you see this?" I continued, pointing out occasional slight differences in the ways the letters *d* and *f* were written. "And there are other orthographical discrepancies such as slant."

"What do you make of it?" he asked.

"I'm not an expert in handwriting, but even I can see it. Two different hands, I imagine. In other words, what initially appeared to be one diary is written by two people."

Motioning for me to continue, he sat down next to me, saying, "Please. I won't disturb you."

Using Brother Tomáš's meticulous transcription to decipher words that were difficult to read, I began examining the diary for content, under the constant glare of the ultraviolet light.

*3 November 1787*

*In the spirit of intrepid travelers, Constanze and I set
out on the long journey through Moravia and Bohemia
to Prague with miserable horses in a wretched wagon
that had been conscripted for use as a coach. Along the
way, the countryside was barren and flat, and the
weather extremely hot or extremely cold, often rainy as
well. But the Lord maketh the rain to fall on the just
and the unjust alike, and we resigned ourselves to it,
amusing each other by telling stories and inventing
games to break the monotony.*

*Alas, no provisions of any kind were offered during
this luxurious ride, so we were forced to subsist on stale
black bread and water and a single pint of sour milk
until we arrived at Kolín, where I was able to order us a
pigeon and a glass of pathetic wine for the king's ransom
of thirty kreuzer. But when I saw the people, attracted
from the fields to witness our arrival, many half-starved
and suffering from the previous conflicts with Prussia, I
remembered the lesson of the apostle Paul, "In whatever
state I am therewith to be content."*

*Alas, war is death's banquet, and I found myself
asking, "Are not death and misery soon enough upon us
without the diabolical machinations of warfare?" The
oft-repeated words of my father came to mind, "War
leaves the country with three armies: an army of cripples,
an army of mourners, and an army of thieves."*

When I looked up, Brother Tomáš was eager to hear my
opinion. "The last page," I said, "the one with the signature,
looks very much like Mozart's writing. But this first page makes
me a little suspicious—it might be an attempt to imitate
Mozart's hand. And the content is suspect. It's full of all kinds
of moral clichés that are not Mozart's style."

Brother Tomáš looked confused. "So you think some parts
are a forgery?" he asked.

"It's too soon to make any definitive conclusions," I replied. "I need to read one of the folios in the other handwriting, the one that looks like Mozart's." With that, I turned my full attention to it.

*We have been compensated for the problems we encountered arriving in Bohemia by the remarkable musicality of the people. It was the opera public in Prague that inspired me to surpass my most daring music, as the situation was ripe for a bold, controversial subject that might have raised eyebrows in Vienna (that supposedly cosmopolitan city). In reality, Vienna is haunted by the prudish specter of the empress, who even after her death governs from the other world. The subject of my opera* Don Giovanni *is the Don Juan legend, based on a man unable to stop himself from pursuing the delights of the fairer sex, and it was appropriate that da Ponte, my faithful librettist, and I were aided in every way by no less of a personage than Giacomo Casanova himself, who lives here and serves as librarian for Count Waldstein. Like Don Giovanni, Casanova made innumerable conquests in Italy, France, and Spain, and kept a list, which has taken shape as his memoirs, candid and full of legendary exploits. Casanova contributed delightful suggestions taken from his own colorful life and he even penned verses for Act II, Scene X, where his expert help surpassed our expectations entirely. This renowned sexagenarian also astonished da Ponte and me by showing us a device of his own invention that prevented him from impregnating the many women desirous of his reputed talents. Sewn from the bladder of a sheep, it is worn on that part of the male anatomy that women find most engaging, and it is even reusable! And judging from the impressive size of the device he showed us, women are never disappointed.*

*In addition to my musical involvement with the subject, namely my desire to paint a convincing musical portrait of Don Juan, I am surrounded each day by other womanizers like da Ponte, Casanova, and the Italian singers here, so I must admit I find myself in good company. If I were to join them and indulge myself more than mere looking, the object of my desire would of course be the ravishing Josepha Duschek, who insists on tormenting me daily by her irresistible beauty, charm, and desirability. Fortunately, my dearest Constanze understands that a man, by his very nature, must stray from the nest, even when he is deeply enamored with his wife, as Casanova has taken pains to articulate.*

*There are always those eager to condemn Don Giovanni and Casanova for the prodigious number of their sexual conquests. The issue for me is perhaps not the number, but the drive behind them. For when it becomes beyond control, when one is driven to repeat the act endlessly and always with new objects, it is often for reasons of the deepest, insatiable loneliness or worse, the lowest estimation of oneself.*

As I read silently, Brother Tomáš sat riveted at my side. "Now *this* is different," I finally said. "The opening gives me the impression it was written by Mozart." But pointing to the last paragraph, I said, "Look here, at the text beginning with the words *There are always those eager.* Subtleties in handwriting indicate it was written by a different person than the one who wrote the preceding passage. And the ideas are in sharp contrast to what goes before it, almost as if someone added it to tone down Mozart's admiration of Casanova."

Brother Tomáš said, "I don't understand. You think part of it was written by Mozart and part written by someone else?"

"Yes," I replied.

He looked relieved to believe that Mozart could have written at least part of the diary, and I sensed a wave of deference. The moment was right, so I interrupted my transcription and said, "That's all I can do for now. I didn't get much sleep last night."

Brother Tomáš nodded, amenable to anything I suggested. I continued, "I think I'll head up to my room and catch a nap before lunch. And if you don't see me here this afternoon, I'll be out taking a walk around the grounds."

"Oh," he said, "I forgot to tell you, Brother Georg, our administrator, wants to see you."

"Could it wait until after lunch?" I asked.

He hesitated. "It probably would be a good idea if you saw him as soon as possible," he answered.

Slightly confused, I said, "All right. But what's it about?"

Communicating with a universal gesture, he shrugged his shoulders and made a slight upward gesture of his chin, meaning, *Who knows?*

As I followed Brother Tomáš's directions to Brother Georg's office, I couldn't help feeling a flood of confidence. Satisfied with the way things were turning out, I headed optimistically through the silent, glistening corridors, unaware of what was waiting for me.

# CHAPTER 28

*Wherever a man goes, men will pursue him and paw him*
*with their dirty institutions, and, if they can, constrain*
*him to belong to their desperate oddfellow society.*

—HENRY DAVID THOREAU

"Everything about the monastic situation is working out well for me," I was planning to say, just in case Brother Georg asked me how I was adapting to Lesní Klášter. His somber office, unlike that of Brother Cyril, was an extreme model of austerity and frugality; the walls were bare, except for an unadorned crucifix on the wall directly above his desk. I found myself admiring his bureaucratic efficiency, as not a single paper or note of any kind cluttered his desk, even though he was responsible for the entire fiscal management of the monastery.

Heavyset, but not excessively so, Brother Georg had a ragged beard and mop of grayish brown hair that encircled his face. As he sat with his hands folded on the desk, my buoyant mood and good spirits were met with a wall of stern and sour scrutiny. Gesturing for me to sit down, he said, "We should begin by discussing your duties here during your stay with us," speaking German with a thick Slavic accent. "Each of our brothers performs chores every day and we must decide what work around the monastery will be suitable for you."

"Work?" I asked.

"There is always help needed in the garden and there are, of course, kitchen and general cleaning chores to do each day."

Speaking softly through a lump in my throat, I said, "My work is in the library. That's why I've been invited here."

Ignoring my reply, he continued, "In order to cover the costs of your stay here, we must ask you to share the responsibilities. But only for half a day, you understand, unlike all the other brothers, who must work a full day."

My visions of leisurely walks in the gardens and country-side rapidly evaporating, I tried to assert myself a little more. "I'm here to examine a manuscript in the library, and that will take most of my time."

Irritated at my response, Brother Georg continued, "You said *most* of your time. But what did you intend for the rest of the time on your hands? Every moment of our day here is carefully allotted to some specific activity."

Cautiously, I replied, "But the amount of time I participate in the activities of the community should be left to my discretion."

Speaking as if he were unaccustomed to having anyone disagree with him, the monk continued with a subtle smile of superiority and an unflinching tone. "Then let me humbly try to persuade you to understand the wisdom of our community. The philosophy is simple: it is the rule of self-denial. It strengthens a man's soul and body and even makes his life longer."

Tempted to snap back, "No, it only makes it seem longer," I realized it was essential to maintain my composure. "You're one of the few here who know I'm a musicologist and not a monk," I said. "And I'm a guest—you don't invite a scholar to travel all this way as a consultant and then ask him to scrub floors and pick string beans."

Brother Georg looked thunderstruck. Indignantly, he mumbled something under his breath in Czech.

Hoping to bring the issue to a close, I said, "In order to give the diary my full attention, I'm going to need some time to unwind, perhaps walking in the grounds around the monastery. I don't believe in burning myself out."

After a painful pause, Brother Georg said, "If that's how you feel, then at least have the decorum not to set a bad example to the other brothers. Spend whatever 'free time' you feel you require in a way that will suggest contemplation and prayer; for example, by always carrying a spiritual book in your hands when you're not working in the library."

Reaching into his desk, he pulled out a small, tattered volume and placed it on the desk in front of me. I remained silent, hoping the matter was resolved and finally stood up, saying, "If that's all . . ."

But before I reached the door, I again heard his imperative tone: "Brother Matěj . . ."

"Yes?"

"You forgot your prayer book."

As soon as I left his office, a wave of indignation swept over me. Annoyed, I fingered the book he had chosen for me and read the title—*The Lives of the Saints*—in old German script, no less.

Behind me, a voice interrupted my thoughts and I realized someone was speaking to me in Czech, a brother with curly, reddish hair, animated blue eyes, and a gold earring. When I gestured with my hand to indicate I couldn't speak Czech, he surprised me by switching to French. "You look like you could use a little cheering up," he said.

"How can you tell?" I asked.

"Well, it's to be assumed that anyone coming out of Brother Georg's office needs a little cheering up."

"Brother Cyril didn't mention that someone in the monastery spoke French," I said.

"He might have 'forgotten' to mention it because my presence at Lesní Klášter is a little, well, controversial. I'm Zachariáš, the cook."

"Aha," I said, almost inaudibly, when I realized I was face-to-face with the mystery chef responsible for the astonishing cuisine.

When I smiled, he said, "I saw you up in the library this morning. *Semper laborando nunquam ludendo Joannes uer fit insipidus.*" Thinking for a second, I realized he had quoted the Latin equivalent of "All work, no play makes Jack a dull boy." Pointing up to a window overlooking the courtyard, he continued, "If you ever find that the boredom around here gets too much, stop by my room after compline. We can have a drink and chat."

"I'll take you up on that," I replied, suspecting that he had more than his share of stories to tell.

"People around here could all use a good laugh," he said. And as he was leaving, he added, "I probably don't need to tell you, but don't let Brother Georg find out. He wouldn't approve."

"There's not much Brother Georg would approve of," I said, and he smiled knowingly, disappearing around the corner of the courtyard and leaving me with a surge of curiosity about the world-class chef who had described himself humbly as "the cook." To the animated accompaniment of church bells, I began following the other monks in the direction of the chapel for sext, throwing a glance upward toward the room where I would later get together with the mysterious, colorful Brother Zachariáš.

After a splendid lunch, I strolled around the interior courtyards of Lesní Klášter, the little volume given to me by Brother Georg strategically poised in my hands. The gardens of the monastery, each one open to light and rain, were a kaleidoscopic sweep of colors, textures, and shapes, fragrant with varying perfumes—honeyed myrtle, aromatic English lavender, and pungent, bitter marigold—and bursting with the subtle hues of blue thistle and bright crimson berries. And there was no lack of variety in the foliage, which ranged from the exotic leaves of castor bean and the soft, downy spikes of foxgloves to tiny prickly hedges of crimson barberry.

*It's almost an impressionist painting,* I thought as I surveyed the gardens stretching out in a canvas of shimmering light and vibrant pigments, bursting as if from an artist's brush. But it was a living, moving tableau, with espalier dwarf fruit trees full of tiny birds, chirping and twittering in a captivating, unfamiliar vocalise. The monks had managed to create a miniature world in their intricate garden work; crops were meticulously tended with an attention to detail that far surpassed practical requirements, and the landscape design revealed great sophistication. As I surveyed the flourishing horticultural marvel they had created upon the vast, barren rock ledge, I concluded it was a perfect merger of necessity and beauty.

The monastery, so bleak and forbidding from outside, was a treasure house of architectural objets d'art in every medium: sculptured bas-reliefs in terra cotta, carved pillars with richly detailed capitals, mosaic floors with tiles ranging from the rough-hewn to the finely polished, and wall frescoes whose muted, washed-out colors managed to enliven vast stretches of unadorned plaster walls.

Refreshed by my walk, I returned in the late afternoon to the oppressive confinement of the library. Promising myself just one more hour, I watched as the ghostly light of the ultraviolet lamps again illuminated the folios and shrouded my fingers in a phosphorescent glow. For once in my life, I was determined to fight the temptation to work countless hours on end and decided to try to create a balance between work and play, alternating long, peaceful walks with periods of intense concentration in the library.

High above me, the distant sounds of flying geese reminded me of the vibrant outdoor setting I was relinquishing for the tomblike chambers of the library. But I had experienced serene nature in all of its fullness and was now ready to tackle the barely legible sheets stretched out before me.

*Despite the disagreeable conditions of our journey, my lovely little wife managed to look splendidly beautiful and desirable. As we approached Prague, the surrounding countryside became suddenly verdant and I again fell in love with this beautiful city, stretched out over several hills with the wide river Moldau running through it. So much more than Vienna, this city has welcomed me. But we know all too well that a prophet is never accepted in his own country, and there is little to be gained by fighting it.*

*After we entered the city through a gauntlet of gates and barriers, another obstacle almost defeated us. A particular customs official ransacked our baggage, and*

> *Constanze cautioned me not to protest, as she was*
> *convinced he had an eye on her and that his actions*
> *stemmed from this unofficial interest. When all seemed*
> *lost (for these bureaucrats wield inordinate power), a*
> *young official whispered something to him. The older*
> *customs official asked if I was the same Mozart who had*
> *written the music to* Figaro, *and when I nodded this*
> *loathsome barbarian fell into a frenzy of praise and*
> *admiration, telling me he himself had played most of the*
> *arias and pieces, arranged for wind band, with his family*
> *playing the other instruments. The transformation in his*
> *person was incomprehensible, and I again realized the*
> *ability of music to ennoble the human spirit. And the*
> *deep musicality of the Bohemians, legendary throughout*
> *Europe, was once more brought home to me.*

With the sound of the bells, I closed up for the day and left the library to follow the monks' established routine: vespers, dinner, compline, and a return to the monastic cells in preparation for bed. When I finally settled in under the covers, I casually opened *The Lives of the Saints.*

The text was not like anything I expected. The first I read described Saint Rhipsime, a Roman virgin who settled in Armenia and was martyred by being roasted alive, then torn limb from limb. Saint Maximus had been scourged, then his tongue and his right hand cut off, followed by more gruesome mutilation. One after another, the accounts were detailed and grisly, each competing for graphic shock value: Saint James stoned, Saint Philip's flesh beaten to a pulp, then his legs and feet buried in the earth up to the knees before he was burned alive, Saint Ischyrion impaled, Saint Cuthbert disemboweled.

A little too late, I realized it had hardly been the best choice for bedtime reading, given my recent experiences. There were even stories of martyrs who asked for a worse death: Saint Laurence, stripped, bound upon a gridiron, and roasted over a slow fire, telling his executioner with a cheerful smile, "Turn my body, as one side is broiled enough."

Unnerved, I turned off the light and wished I had never seen the grisly catalogue of torture that rhapsodized saintly agonies with lurid fascination. But each time I tried to doze off, a disturbing stream of savage visual images haunted me. Unable to sleep, I floated restlessly in a foggy, nebulous world, suspended somewhere between semiconsciousness and dreams.

Despite Brother Georg's suggested reading, my daily experience with monastic life was characterized by a stillness, a pervasive calm that began to profoundly alter my state of mind. Never in my life did I feel so well, so safe, so comfortable, as I knew every day would be like the previous one, each aspect of life planned according to an ancient rule, an ancient time clock that had been tried and perfected over the centuries. And I began to experience the basic rhythm of life as vast and unchangeable, freeing me from distractions, so that I was able to work in an untroubled frame of mind, almost a state of heightened consciousness. Although the monks rose punctually at 4:00 A.M. and retired at 9:00 P.M., I was awakened at 5:20 A.M. and allowed to turn in whenever I wanted, usually about 10:00 P.M. In so doing, my energy had somehow been directed into a rhythm that opened a world free from time pressures, a world of predictability. And the result was a peacefulness and freedom that stimulated creativity.

Lesní Klášter as an environment made me more alive and able to taste the flavors of life. The pure beauty of the plainsong was itself a revelation—pulsing waves of controlled, passionate song, sometimes subdued, sometimes ecstatic. The simplicity of the lifestyle and the lack of practical decisions like choice of clothing freed my mind for higher pursuits.

Before arriving in the monastery, my usual work pace had been feverish—hours on end, weeks and months at a time, followed by periods of overwhelming physical and emotional exhaustion. In Lesní Klášter, my sessions with the diary were strictly proscribed, initiated by punctual reminders from the bell tower and terminated by the same. And it was impossible to refuse the summons; everyone ended work without protest and headed to the chapel—that was that.

The simplicity of the religious ritual was surprisingly moving, from the elegant formality of the Mass recited in Latin in monodic waves, to the ritual prayer recitation during the day. Everyone stopped—the monks in the fields tending crops, the cooking staff preparing vegetables, and even those walking through the corridors—and turned their attention to a higher call.

The only drawback was my limited personal contact with people. The monks spoke to each other only when necessary and, on top of that, there was greater silence from nine P.M. until after Mass each day at ten A.M., when absolutely no one spoke. In addition, the language barrier for me was impenetrable, making meaningful dialogue impossible. The result was that brief encounters—few and far between—had a far greater impact.

For example, whenever Brother Michal came over to chat, I savored the contact, as he was someone who spoke my own language. One morning, as I sat looking out from a sheltered portico into a small courtyard, where a light rain had transformed the foliage into a patchwork quilt of olive gray and green, Brother Michal stopped to say, "The life of a monk doesn't appear to be at odds with you."

His comment caught me off-guard, and I replied, a little defensively, "Only a few people here know I'm not a monk. And I'd like to keep it that way."

"I respect that," he said, with his usual rascal smile. "But I'm convinced you were a monk in a previous life."

Chuckling at the idea, I replied, "I have an idea about you as well, but it's just the opposite: even in this life, you weren't always a monk."

Instead of taking it as a joke, he looked away. For a moment he sat lost in thought as I scrutinized him. Brother Michal reminded me of a rugged, virile peasant, but with infinitely more sensitivity and refinement. With the stubble of fine light brown down around his cheeks and with his boyish good looks, he seemed like a young Saint Francis. To my surprise, Brother Michal began to talk openly about his life before the monastery, how he had worked as a bartender in a restaurant in Prague that was famous with tourists, where he earned a phenomenal living exchanging foreign currency on the black market. With his newly acquired wealth, he had bought and restored a classic Harley-Davidson and devoted his free time to repairing and showing classic American cars.

"You know," he said, "I owned a '59 Cadillac Eldorado—the one with the big fins and the bullet taillights. And I had plenty of time to indulge my passion—playing rock music on my guitar."

Feeling a bit playful, I commented, "I'm sure there were many women in the picture too."

"Plenty of women," he replied candidly. "They were always around, always interested, always available. But somehow I was dissatisfied, always feeling that something was not quite right. Like Saint Augustine, part of me kept praying, Dear God, give me chastity—just not now."

"When you decided to enter the monastery," I said, "I bet there were a lot of broken hearts."

He laughed, but for the first time, I heard a distinct note of bitterness. "'I had not yet loved, yet I loved to love.' Again, that's Saint Augustine—he's been the greatest inspiration to me. 'I sought what I might love, loving to love,'" he continued. To my amazement, I watched his eyes well up, and a tear began to make its way down his cheek.

"It finally happened," he continued, a little embarrassed as he wiped his cheek. Sitting up straight, he continued, "I met the woman I wanted to spend the rest of my life with. But it ended. A long story. I didn't think I could go on living; my heart was shattered."

"How long ago was that?" I asked.

"Five years," he replied. "That's when I entered the religious life. And it was what saved me—I really mean that."

Trying my best to be tactful, I asked, "And you were comfortable giving up all your interests?"

His steel blue eyes flashed as he said, "It was the right decision. Some of my friends said I was hiding. But when I read *The*

*Seven Storey Mountain* by Thomas Merton I understood that by becoming a monk, by hiding in a sense from the world, you become not less of yourself, not less of a person, but more."

"But what about your music?" I asked as I imitated plucking a guitar with a fingerpick. "Eric Clapton?"

He flashed a wide grin. "Eric Clapton has also been an inspiration to me. Some of his lyrics have a deeply spiritual side." Brother Michal started singing softly about how he would soon open every door, how he had finally found a place to live, in the "Presence of the Lord."

The sounds of bells from the distant tower, usually pleasant to my ears, were now intrusive and ill-timed because it meant I would have to end my conversation with Brother Michal. As we walked in silence to the chapel, his comments continued to play out in my mind: his poetic allusions to Saint Augustine, Thomas Merton, and Eric Clapton had merged into an upbeat, spiritual approach to life.

Even in the chapel, I had difficulty concentrating on the singing and instead continued thinking about what he said. His articulate, non-invasive spirituality was making me look at my surroundings and my task through a different lens.


Dinner after vespers was again both notable and mystifying: a delicate bisque of crab, sweetbreads rolled in chestnut flour, and a dessert of fresh blackberries topped with warm *zabaglione*. Ironically, I told myself, *The usual fare.* The discussion with Brother Michal had whet my appetite for more conversation, and, as I followed the other monks into the chapel for compline, I looked forward to my visit with the "mystery chef," whose monastic cell promised good conversation.

After the monks had retired, I peered out into the hallway, waiting for the right moment to begin making my way to Brother Zachariáš's room. Feeling somewhat like a criminal, I crept on little cat's feet through dimly lit corridors, finally arriving at his quarters. After a quiet knock on his door, a tiny crack of light appeared and he invited me inside, smiling.

The muted sound of an old LP record player caught my attention and I recognized the sultry voice of Marlene Dietrich singing "Falling in Love Again." Looking around, I was astounded by the decoration of his cell: the walls were cluttered with playbills, photographs, and posters of famous cabaret singers and actors, and chairs and tables were covered with colorful, tasseled fabrics. On the floor and bed, tabloids and crime magazines in French and Czech were scattered about, as I had apparently interrupted his reading.

"Wow," I said as I sat down. In the midst of an austere religious bastion, Brother Zachariáš had created a warm living space with a bohemian flair. "A very comfortable place you have here," I said in French. Brother Zachariáš, dressed in a long, flowing black silk Japanese robe with an impressive embroidered landscape on the back, was delighted with my compliment and draped himself on the chair across from me.

"So, you like my little hideaway," he said, reaching for a bottle of clear liqueur with a whole pear preserved inside. As he poured, he said, "Let's face it, there's a limit to how much saintliness a human being can tolerate. By the way, I didn't even ask you if you drink."

When I smiled, he continued pouring and said, "My father used to repeat an old Russian proverb: 'If you drink you die. If you don't drink you die. So it's better to drink.'"

"I'll definitely toast that," I said as we raised our glasses. Almost immediately, he offered me a dish of almonds and large irregular pieces of dark chocolate broken from a block.

"We shouldn't forget to drink a toast to self-denial and abstinence," he continued. "Here's to Brother Georg—please, try a piece of chocolate."

Feeling immediately at ease with Brother Zachariáš's unconventional style, I asked, "So what brought an extraordinary chef like you to this place in the middle of nowhere?"

"When the monastery was reinstated in 1990, I applied for a job in the kitchen, and after many years of getting to know the tastes of the monks, I became quite indispensable. It was almost natural for me to become a monk. Then, about four years ago, I had a crisis and told Brother Cyril I couldn't take monastic life any longer; I decided to leave Lesní Klášter and go to culinary school in Paris. He was kind enough to offer to pay for the school if I would agree to come back. And for the six months I was gone, it turned into a genuine disaster here—several people who tried to fill in for me had to leave, because no one else knew the monks as well as I did: forty-seven spoiled bachelors, all picky eaters and set in their fussy ways. The older monks got depressed and all kinds of arguments broke out. Regardless of what you've heard about their otherworldliness, monks really love their food—it's one of the few pleasures left them."

"So what was it like to come back here after Paris?" I asked.

"Not easy," he said, grimacing theatrically. "Especially at first. In fact, a couple of times I tried to escape and Brother Cyril offered me anything I wanted if I would just stay on. So I said I would try, but that I absolutely needed freedom and space. And I'm still here, basically writing my own ticket. But what's your story? I saw you in the library looking at papers under ultraviolet lamps."

"Brother Cyril invited me here," I said. "For research."

"What kind of research?" he asked.

"To be honest," I said, "I'm really not at liberty to say. I'm sorry . . . and I hope you're not offended."

"No, not at all," he replied. "I also saw you sitting in the courtyard, always carrying the same prayer book."

"Something Brother Georg suggested when I'm not working in the library," I said. "So that I don't set a bad example to the other brothers."

"Since you're new," he said somberly, "I should probably warn you to tread lightly when it comes to Brother Georg. He and a few other monks can ruin a person's life. They're into power and politics. The scenario is always the same: Some new brother who's a bit unconventional irritates one of them. Or his talent or enthusiasm makes someone jealous. Then, little by little, they begin sending out signals—to the other small minds, who suddenly find they have been invested power by the group if they go along with the agenda. Gradually, they isolate their victim, sabotaging anything he tries to do while chipping away at his self-esteem. Eventually they ostracize him completely— it's a very effective way to drive a person insane, especially someone sensitive or a little naive."

"Whew," I said, taking a breath. "That's heavy." In the back of my mind, I reflected on the identical scenario in the world of university politics: A young professor incurs the wrath of the power structure—those individuals who shape and broker events. But because of the lack of jobs, the situation in academia was perhaps even more desperate than the monastery—and the bleak reality was that the idealistic world of scholarship was now a battlefield of savage politics, with professors in secure, tenured positions cherishing their ability to destroy others more than their own art and expertise.

Seeing me lost in thought, Brother Zachariáš threw me a wry smile and replied, "Suffice it to say, I'm not afraid of Brother Georg anymore and he knows it. Like this morning, he made a comment to me, 'There's no hope for those who refuse to renounce the flesh.' I looked him right in the eye and said, 'Thank you, Brother Georg. Now that I've given up all hope, I feel so much better.'"

"How does the abbot allow Georg to have so much control in the monastery?"

"Georg has invested his entire life in his pathetic little power struggle; it's all he has. Up to a point, Cyril allows Georg to get his way because, let's face it, someone has to keep this place running." Pouring pear liqueur, he said, "Have another drop."

"You remind me of a person living in exile," I said. "So many great thinkers and artists have lived in a kind of cultural exile, sometimes imposed by others, sometimes self-imposed. It's a huge list: Dante, Montaigne, Lord Byron. In fact, quite staggering when you think about it—Voltaire, Wagner . . . Sappho banished to Sicily, Ovid writing bitter poems from the Black Sea."

"It's a coincidence you would bring that up," he said. "I just finished reading *Freedom in Exile* by the Dalai Lama. Although he was happiest in his own country, he writes that a person can be at complete peace, regardless of where he is—if he chooses to be."

"Did you know there's someone here who's also exploring spirituality outside the traditional paths: Brother Michal just opened my eyes to the spiritual dimensions of Eric Clapton, no less."

"Brother Michal," he replied with a wistful smile. "He's one of a kind."

The shots of liqueur and the late hour were starting to have an effect on me and I could hardly suppress a yawn. "I probably should call it a night." Brother Zachariáš stood up to accompany me to the door. As we shook hands, the headline of a tabloid on the floor caught my eye: SEXUAL MANIAC ROAMS A 250-YEAR-OLD FRENCH CHATEAU, and for a split second my eyes were involuntarily riveted on it, as I realized it was describing La Favorite.

"Take it along with you," Brother Zachariáš said. "But for your own sake, make sure no one catches you with it."

"I'll be careful," I said, hoping to disguise my eagerness as I slipped it into my ample sleeve. After saying good night, I returned to my cell through corridors that were illuminated by tiny, piercing slivers of light from underneath the doors. Barely able to see, I walked quietly, occasionally accompanied by phantom shadows that darted in all directions, catching me off-guard and setting my pulse racing.

Within seconds of arriving in my cell, I was immersed in the article about the investigation into the murders of Denise and von Horvach, hoping to find out if there was any news. The pear liqueur was astonishingly potent and I felt light-headed as I feverishly read the lurid account. There were graphic details I had been spared, along with artists' renditions that filled in gaps my imagination had left out. The text repeated what I knew about Denise, that she had been sodomized, then savagely beaten before her neck was snapped by someone's bare hands: a maniac with supernatural strength.

"Poor Denise," I mumbled. The tabloid called it an unsolved murder and noted that a certain French newspaper reporter had brought documents to light, revealing von Horvach's extensive history with the police. I learned that the French, Italian, and Austrian police were requesting blood samples from every person connected with the foundation to match DNA found at the crime scene.

One last item caught my eye: there was an ongoing search for a "mystery boyfriend," but there had been few leads. I wondered if Nadine ever followed up on my idea about the man who jumped from the Frauenkirche in Munich, Bruno Abruzzese, and if she had tried to retrieve DNA samples from him. But it all seemed so remote, worlds away. And I was in absolutely no position to do anything about it.

My head spinning, I climbed into bed, the explicit details of the tabloid coloring my drifting thoughts as I dozed off. Tossing and turning, I realized that the isolation of my retreat was deceptive and fragile, and I was still very much a part of the complicated and tragic events that were unfolding inevitably.

# CHAPTER 29

*Doubt, it seems to me, is the central condition of
a human being in the twentieth century.*

—SALMAN RUSHDIE

Hour after hour under the unearthly luminescence of the ultraviolet light was having a strange effect on me, one that crept up slowly without my being aware of it. Experiencing a kind of irritable restlessness, I found myself blinking nervously and jumping whenever Brother Tomáš approached my table or if I heard a sound. As the days passed, I began to attribute some personality changes to the lamp and I felt my symptoms of clinical paranoia returning full-force. Although the monastery was as protected as any place on earth could be, I found myself dealing with far-fetched interpretations of trivial events and conspiracy theories.

Finally I mentioned it to Brother Tomáš. "This light is making me crazy," I said. "But I don't mean figuratively . . . it's literally making me crazy."

He laughed and said, "Now that you mention it, I remember I was a little on edge toward the end of my transcription. But I didn't realize it was caused by the ultraviolet light."

"This morning," I continued, "a brother touched my arm to pass the butter, and I almost jumped a foot out of my chair."

"I wouldn't worry about it," he said. "It will all pass very quickly after you're finished."

I knew he was right. But as I continued my examination of the diary, I found myself struggling with increasingly erratic thoughts that I had to systematically push out of my mind: *The people buying up the diaries have known all along that you're here. This is all a transparent charade and you're the only one being fooled.*

As I continued working, a voice in the back of my mind insinuated, *After you finish, the monks are planning to poison you so you won't tell the world about their diary.*

"Wow," I whispered, flabbergasted at the bizarre direction my thoughts were taking. With ever greater effort to put aside the torrent of paranoia, I focused on translating the text of the Prague diary.

> *But Constanze knows she is and will always be the real anchor and object of my heart. This adorable creature gives me the greatest gift a man can receive, the gift of laughter. Two days before the premiere of my opera, I had composed several different overtures in my head, but had not yet succeeded in putting a single note on paper. She kept me in the mood all night by serving me punch and telling me funny stories as I wrote, finally allowing me to sleep two hours before the copyist arrived.*
>
> *My dearest Constanze knows exactly how to soothe the heart of the artist within, especially when I am most troubled with the serious financial issues of maintaining and nurturing my family. Sometimes I am so overwhelmed, I say, like Figaro, "I hasten to laugh at everything for fear of being obliged to weep at it."*

In contrast to his usual habit of not disturbing me, Brother Tomáš suddenly interrupted me to say that the abbot and Brother Georg wanted to see us. "The abbot is interested in the progress you're making and Brother Georg would like to sit in and listen." In the middle of my transcribing and translating, the timing of this impromptu meeting with Brother Cyril and Brother Georg was atrocious. But they had every right to ask, and it was probably a good thing that they were keenly interested in the diary. I wrapped up my work and left the folios in the hands of Brother Tomáš, who promised he would join us shortly.

On the way to the office, I washed my hands, but they still felt gritty from the dirt of centuries lodged in every crevice.

After entering the spacious office of Brother Cyril, I sat down facing the two monks, and shortly thereafter Brother Tomáš joined us, as it were, on the sidelines. Calmly, Brother Cyril asked, "How is the work proceeding?"

"Rather well," I replied. "I'm more than half finished."

"Is it too soon to make any conclusions as to whether it's by Mozart?"

"It's too soon for anything definite," I said. "But I have some preliminary ideas." No one spoke, so I continued. "There appear to be two different handwritings in the diary. And two differing viewpoints. One of them I would call 'moralizing.'"

Brother Georg interrupted, "Which means?"

"There are numerous references to the Bible," I explained. "For example, 'In whatever state I am therewith to be content.' And expressions like 'The Lord maketh the rain to fall on the just and the unjust alike' and 'War is death's banquet.'"

Turning to the abbot, Georg said, "Well . . . I rather like that." Smiling, he asked me, "And the other point of view?"

"The other," I continued, "is more—how can I say it?—more audacious. It strikes me as more the style of Mozart."

Georg looked momentarily confused. "You don't think the moral parts are by Mozart?"

"To tell you the truth . . ." I replied, a little guardedly. Then, after a pause, I continued, "No, I don't."

By now, Brother Georg had taken over the questioning and asked, "What does the other one say—the one you think is Mozart?"

For a moment, I wondered how much I should reveal, but I concluded the content of the diary was a matter of pure scholarship and decided to plunge ahead. "There's an interesting passage about Casanova."

"And how is that 'interesting'?" Georg asked, with a tight, frozen smile on his face.

"Well, to cite just one example, the diary mentions that Casanova invented a device sewn from a sheep's bladder that prevented women from becoming pregnant. It's a reference to a prophylactic device, in other words, a condom."

Brother Georg flushed and his expression changed. "A condom?" he asked incredulously, looking at the abbot and Brother Tomáš. "And this Casanova—wasn't he some kind of unrepentant adulterer?"

"But he was also an ecclesiastic," Brother Tomáš said quietly. "A priest—and a great man of letters. He translated Homer's *Iliad* into Italian among other things."

Brother Georg, visibly ruffled, turned his attention again to me. "Does Mozart voice his disapproval of such licentious behavior?"

All eyes were focused on me, and I winced in amazement that anyone could ask such a question in this day and age. "Well," I replied, "not really. In fact, I get the impression that Mozart rather admired Casanova."

Georg became dead serious. "You don't mean to tell me Mozart admired an adulterer? He himself was happily married, wasn't he?"

"Yes," I said, emphatically. "Absolutely."

Brother Georg looked relieved. "So, Mozart would have nothing to do with adultery?"

It became patently clear to me that it would be impossible to hide the content of the diary forever. So, instead of beating around the bush, I said simply, "Actually, the diary suggests that Mozart may have occasionally strayed from the nest."

"Mozart confesses to straying from his wife?" he asked.

Realizing I was skating on thinner and thinner ice, I hesitated. "Confesses is too strong a word . . . it's only implied, not stated."

With the icy tone of an inquisitor, Georg continued, "Mozart implies that he's an adulterer?" Before I could answer, Georg exploded, "A private sin in this world is not so harmful, but this is far worse. This is a public indecency." Venting his rage with a fury that took my breath away, he shouted at Brothers Cyril and Tomáš, "I knew it was ill-advised to bring in outsiders. I was against it from the beginning and now I know I was right. This is tantamount to revealing Mozart's indecency to the world. It must be stopped at once before greater damage is done."

As I sat stunned, the abbot remained silent, his expression passive. Gently trying to dissuade Brother Georg, Brother Tomáš said, "Things like this are not so shocking to people in this day and age."

Ignoring Brother Tomáš, Georg continued his flood of outrage. "He that falleth into sin is a man, but he that boasteth of it is a devil. This diary must never leave these walls." Sitting passively, Brother Cyril and Brother Tomáš let Georg talk himself out. "All this idle, loose talk about prophylactic devices from sheep's bladders and adulterous behavior and unrepentant fornicators. We are here for the edification of sinners and everything we do must be for that purpose. If something is not edifying, we must reconsider why we are doing it." No one dared interrupt as Georg's rage continued unabated. Pounding his fist on the desk, he screamed, "One leak will sink a ship. We must guard ourselves lest this monastery itself be brought down."

Quietly, the abbot turned toward me and said gently, "Dr. Pierce, perhaps it would be best if the three of us were to continue discussing this among ourselves." It took a split second for me to realize I was being asked to leave, and with an involuntary sigh, I stood up and walked out. "I'll come and find you later," he said as I left.

In one of the courtyards, I sat alone, making sure to follow Brother Georg's "order" by opening my copy of the *The Lives of the Saints*. Unfortunately, I opened to Saint Irenaeus, who was sentenced to be drowned but instead, upon his own request for a worse death, was beheaded and his body cast into the river. The wait for Brother Cyril was interminable. Trying to cope with the madness of the whole situation, I asked myself how intelligent, educated men like Brothers Cyril and Tomáš could allow themselves to be bullied by someone so hopelessly anachronistic and bigoted. In the middle of my thoughts, I looked up to see the abbot standing next to me. With a gentle voice, almost a murmur, he said, "We've decided to put everything on hold . . . for now."

Speechless, I looked away and shook my head in disgust. With my last ounce of energy, I said, "I've come all this way . . ."

Holding the palm of his hand toward me with the quietest, most gentle of gestures, Brother Cyril said, "The final word rests with me. *Patientia.*"

The Latin word for patience rang in my ears and, inexplicably, the urge to protest seemed to dissipate. When he sensed I could listen, Brother Cyril continued, "I promise to let you know soon of my decision." After he left, I continued to replay our meeting in my head, and each time a surge of outrage rose up inside me. But it was soon quelled by the visual image of Cyril's gesture and the memory of his baritone voice saying, "*Patientia,*" which lulled me with the effect of a muted, hypnotic drone.

Cyril's promise kept me going for a while, but ten days after the cataclysm with Georg, the aftereffects still reverberated in my mind like shock waves. Georg's violent, caustic scene had been devastating, as was the subsequent decision of the abbot to put a hold on my research. Gradually, I succumbed to a numbing depression and found myself staring off into space like a catatonic schizophrenic. A quiet, secluded courtyard with rough-hewn benches of stone was the logical place for me to pass the time, as it was the only spot where I could avoid contact with everyone and everything.

From time to time, I found myself looking up toward the library with bitterness, imagining what I could be discovering in the diary. And the time on my hands became unbearable, like poison dripping in my veins. Although I was still the same driven person, I was now a driven person with nothing to do, and my usual restlessness was heightened. Again and again I found myself returning to the question, *What am I doing here?* and worse, *What am I doing, period?*

Fighting a losing battle, I found myself dealing with major issues in my life that I had never been able to resolve, such as my never-ending war with the power structure. The meeting with the monks stirred up memories of all the university committee decisions that had adversely affected my life. To make it worse, a nagging voice insinuated that my lack of success with Brother

Georg had been my own fault, precipitated by my own lack of tact. Although I struggled to resist the ominous black dogs of self-pity, I could feel them yapping at my heels. I found myself thinking, *Here I go again, pursuing one hopeless project after another.*

When I finally concluded that the Prague diary would never make it to the light of day, more distant and dangerous doubts invaded my thoughts: Landry must have been livid when he found out I didn't follow through with his agenda with Braun. And after "double-crossing" Max and his clients, there was a real possibility that, like Nadine, I was going to need a bodyguard for the rest of my life. At one time, such thoughts seemed far-fetched, but now they were all too real. The outside world was hostile, and now this protected, secluded place was inhospitable. At that moment, I heard someone directly behind me and looked up. "Are you all right?" It was the voice of Brother Michal. "You don't look too well."

"I'm fine," I replied, turning my head away.

"What's wrong?" he asked. "Really."

"It's nothing," I replied, indicating that I didn't want to discuss it.

With slow tact, Brother Michal continued, "Have you ever been outside the walls of the monastery? It's pretty spectacular. This might be a good time to take a short walk."

Although I had no intention of talking about what was bothering me, I let him lead me to the limits of the huge stone walls. And he was right: the countryside was breathtaking. As we descended the massive rocky ledge from which Lesní Klášter rose, the steep hills behind the monastery became increasingly fertile and lush. Nestled among undulating waves of wildflowers in shades of strawflower blue and campanile pink were hills of fruit trees bursting with pears and apples. On the sides of a small brook, purple loosestrife stretched their spires toward the heavens and thick, flourishing grapevines crowded the valley.

"Lesní Klášter is Czech for 'monastery in the woods,'" he said quietly. "There were several previous abbeys on the site, going back over five hundred years." When I looked back, I realized we had covered a great deal of distance and the fortress of

Lesní Klášter now appeared to look down on us with an attitude of arrogance and superiority. Carefully, Brother Michal tested the waters. "You're sure nothing's bothering you?"

"I don't want to talk about it," I replied.

"Not to pry," he said, "but if there's anything you want to say, I promise I won't repeat it."

Thinking for a second, I stopped in my tracks. "Brother Georg is standing in the way of my accomplishing the work I came here to do."

Smiling, he said, "I should have guessed. That dude needs to chill out, major."

With his unexpected use of American slang, the tension in the air evaporated and, for the first time, I was able to say what was on my mind. "I'm beginning to wonder what I'm doing here."

With firm, quiet conviction, Michal finally said, "God led you to us for a reason."

My skepticism surged and I retorted, "Spare me the sermon."

"No," he said quietly, "I really mean it. I feel it. There are important lessons for us to learn from you." After we had covered a long distance in silence, Michal continued, "It might be a little painful for you to hear it right now, but there are also lessons for you to learn from being here. Unfortunately, if we don't listen to what the universe is trying to teach us, we'll have to experience it over and over again until we get it."

Frustrated, I said, "Just tell me one thing. What is a negative person like Georg doing in the religious life?"

Taking his time, Brother Michal responded, "Like every community, there are good and bad here. To be honest, when I first entered Lesní Klášter, I came to the conclusion that most of the men here had given themselves to God only because the devil wouldn't have them. Gradually I began to feel compassion toward weaknesses that are even more evident here than outside the walls. Now, when I look at Georg, I feel compassion toward him and his obsession with sin. In reality, there are only two kinds of people in this world: decent, good people who think they're sinners and sinners who think they are good, decent people."

"There are Brother Georgs all over," I said. "If this were some kind of isolated incident, it would be one thing. But I'm afraid things like the blowup with Georg happen to me all the time. I'm beginning to think I'm responsible."

"Don't blame yourself for Brother Georg. If you had never come here, he'd still be doing exactly what he's doing. And I don't want to excuse him or what he represents. But a great man of God once told me, 'Even the most dreadful, unpleasant people we meet have been given to us for a reason—as a gift, to teach us something we need to learn.' Focus on the bigger picture," he said quietly. "The issue, it seems to me, is not Brother Georg, but, 'Why were you sent here?'"

At a loss to understand what he was saying, I kept silent. He continued, "Because you were brought here for a reason and it's just a matter of figuring out what the reason is."

Rubbing my temples, I sat down in the tall grass. Brother Michal joined me and, after a long pause, spoke softly. "Let me tell you what I sense about you," he said. "I see in you the urge to create, to express beauty, to contribute—you are part of the song of creation." He looked at me intently. "You've had a glimpse of a higher spirit but you're tormented by doubts," he said. "Accept the vision and continue to allow it to express itself through you. You must bow to the god of creation within you."

It was all too abstract and I was in the worst of moods. We continued our walk through the natural paradise that stretched out beyond us. Finally, I said, "To tell you the truth, I've just made up my mind. If I can't do the work I came here to do, I'm leaving."

Michal listened with a serious expression and paused. "Right now, things aren't going the way you want. But true contentment is not a short-term issue. It's far-reaching—it's the power of getting everything you can out of any situation. Unfortunately, it's hard work and not too many people succeed."

"No," I said. "I'm not used to having time on my hands."

"Then take the opportunity to better appreciate your setting and the people here," he said. "We're surrounded every-where by beauty and kindness but we must try to stay in the present to enjoy it."

The more he spoke, the more I realized how difficult it was to see beyond the crossroads where I was standing. Seeing my frustration, he said softly, *"Patientia."* The quiet, hypnotic reso-nance of this simple word brought back the image of the abbot's gesture and I realized that everyone was telling me the same thing. Perhaps it was time to listen.

As we headed back to the monastery, my steps were lighter. Although I had not yet settled on a course of action, I felt more resigned, more at ease with being kept on hold. Finally I de-cided—regardless of the apparent futility of the situation, I was going to try to make the best of it. Turning a bend before we en-tered the steep, rocky path to the monastery, I began thinking that it could be interesting, for once in my life, to keep my eyes open and try to appreciate what I saw, instead of what I was ex-pecting to see.

As we reached the rock ledge and began our ascent, a flash of faded blue in the woods below caught my attention. Absent-mindedly, I stopped and said, "What's that over there?"

Without much thought, Michal replied, "Let's go take a look." Together, we headed down toward the edge of the forest and within seconds we were standing in front of a dilapidated car—a blue older model Fiat—parked barely off the path and almost completely hidden from view.

"Whose car is it?" I asked.

"Haven't the slightest idea," Michal responded. "And I can't imagine why anyone would park it out here."

"It has Italian plates," I continued. "M-A. That means it's from Messina, in Sicily."

"Probably some teenagers who came up here to drink beer and couldn't get it started," he said.

"Then why would it have foreign plates?" I asked.

"You're right," he replied. "Maybe it's some adventurous tourists. If it isn't gone by tomorrow, I'll call the village and they'll send someone up to take a look." Again we started our ascent, the most difficult climb toward the monastery, just as the chapel bells began to ring, summoning us back into a quiet world of meditation, prayer, and song, and drawing us as individuals into a larger, more timeless tapestry.

Early the next day, I passed Brother Tomáš in the corridors and he looked approachable. "I'm feeling as if much of this situation could have been avoided," I told him. "If I had only been more careful about what I said."

"Don't blame yourself," he said calmly. "No one can predict how Brother Georg will react—he's a master of surprise, you know."

"I think the part about the prophylactic device set him off. I shouldn't have said it."

Kindly, he replied, "That shouldn't have had anything to do with it. Herbal medicines to prevent pregnancy and advanced methods of birth control were collected by nuns and monks for centuries. They were the physicians of their time."

"But I'm afraid it's not the first time I've gotten myself in trouble by saying too much," I said.

Inviting me to walk with him, Tomáš continued, "Well, your openness is a remarkable quality, but the first thing we have to learn in life is how to protect ourselves. It's a virtue to be innocent, but not to be naïve. Am I right?" His words struck home and I nodded. "So, how are you doing in the meantime?" he asked.

"I'm getting by," I replied. "But I've come thousands of miles and I'm being asked to sit around indefinitely."

Stopping for a moment, he reflected. "The abbot decided to suspend work on the manuscript," he said. "But I don't remember him saying anything about the transcription I made."

Incredulously, I asked, "You'd let me look at it?"

"If it were done in a way that created no appearance of evil—in other words, if no one found out about it—I can't see any reason why you couldn't take it up to your room and work on it."

Brother Tomáš saw that I had no ambivalence whatsoever. Within minutes, he returned with his carefully handwritten pages beneath his sleeve. "Please," he reminded me again, "just make sure . . ." Not even allowing him to finish his sentence, I eagerly buried the rolled-up pages in my sleeve and headed back to my room. In no time, I was again immersed in translating the text of the diary into English.

*At Strahov Abbey, a remarkable institution of art and learning, I played the organ for the canon, Brother Lehmann, a monk of exemplary character and musicality. All four reed stops seemed to me to be too loud, so I chose the eight-foot trumpet bass and the usual pedal without mixtures, and played a four-part fugue with a great number of mordents, executed mostly with the fourth and fifth fingers of each hand. The difficulty of my improvisation was not wasted on Brother Lehmann, as he immediately understood what I had set out to do and the many difficulties that had to be overcome. Beginning in G minor, I modulated through B minor to D-sharp major, then to B major over a B-flat pedal before the end. The monk could not stop praising it, declaring it to be the greatest improvisation he had ever heard. The musicality and intelligence of this man proved to me again that monastic life was a calling that cultivated the noblest of character.*

The new, unfamiliar element of secrecy made my work on the transcription even more intense. But unresolved issues about the diary were becoming more evident: the question of forgery was casting doubt on the whole project. Pausing for a moment, I reflected on what I knew about the diary to date.

The pages were clearly out of order. The only indicators of sequence were the date on the first page and the signature on the last. And I reflected on what appeared to be a case of multiple personalities in the diary—two people were involved in writing it, but how could that happen? The parts expressing sexual openness struck me as Mozart's style, but the other parts, quoting scripture and praising monks, were clearly by someone else.

Perhaps the original part of the diary had been written by Mozart, then circulated like the gospels of the New Testament. A layer or layers with a different editorial slant could have been added later. Suddenly Dennis Landry's argument came to mind, that editors have the ultimate power to create history. And I began to formulate a hypothesis: someone who wanted to shape history—an editor of sorts—forged parts of the diary.

The part about Mozart playing the organ for Brother Lehmann had the ring of truth, almost like an eyewitness account. But the fact that he was described with such glowing praise made me think for a moment that he might even have been the person to write it. With the meeting with Brother Georg so recent in my mind, I began contemplating how unbending a monk's point of view could be and the answer was obvious: the forged portions had been written by a monk who added his own moralistic slant to what was an otherwise candid text. Perhaps Brother Lehmann or some other monk found the diary written by Mozart a bit too scabrous for his taste, and superimposed another layer to soften the tone.

For a second, I found myself wondering if Dennis Landry had not been right on the mark. As the sound of bells from the tower in the courtyard filled the air, I buried Brother Tomáš's transcription under my mattress and hoped that no one had become suspicious about my being up in my room for such a long period. With eyes everywhere, I suspected that there were few secrets in a monastery.

## CHAPTER 30

*Men never do evil so completely and cheerfully as when they do it from religious conviction.*

—BLAISE PASCAL

After chapel the next day, one of the brothers intercepted me on my way to my cell and pointed to the office of the abbot, saying, "Cyril," indicating that I was being summoned. As I headed through the corridors, I wondered if anyone knew I had been working on the diary.

With great dignity, the abbot began to speak about the difficulty of making his decision on the diary and I surmised he was setting me up for bad news. Describing the contributions of Brother Georg to the monastery in glowing terms, he said, "He has admirable talents for keeping this old place running against all odds. He's following his own conscience, trying to be conscientious as a good steward of the Lord should." After many words of praise, the abbot finally said, "Of course, his views reflect those of another generation. I ultimately decided the issue on reasons of greater conscience. Work on the diary must proceed."

I couldn't believe what I was hearing. "As for now," he continued, "the less said to Brother Georg about it, the better. I'll handle him in my own way."

With renewed confidence in the abbot's wisdom and his appreciation of scholarship, I headed back to the library full-steam, running into Brother Michal in the corridors as I sped by. "You look a little different than yesterday," he said.

"Thanks," I said. "There have been some positive new developments."

He waited for me to tell him but I resisted saying too

much. "All right," he said, smiling, "I can see you're in a hurry and I don't want to keep you. Just wanted to tell you about the car."

"The car?"

"The car parked in the woods, with the Italian license plates." When I remembered what he was talking about, he went on, "It's not there anymore. I went down this morning and checked."

Eager to get back to the diary, I thanked him for following up on it and headed directly up the stairs to the library. Brother Tomáš, always the cool professional, sounded friendlier than usual. "The abbot's decision is a victory," he said.

Thanking him profusely for allowing me to work on his transcription, I said, "You know, it really saved me from going over the edge."

"Such a little thing I could do," he replied with a hint of irony.

"You broke the rules for the greater good," I said.

"I never was much of a believer in Kant," he said. "You know, the moral imperative. In my opinion, rules are only of value when they make sense. After that, there's always a way to break them. Even in the most extreme of cases, which is the vow of secrecy about things said to a priest in confession."

The discussion had taken unexpected directions and I replied, "There are times when the covenant of silence for confession can be broken?"

"Technically, no," he replied. "Canon 1388 from the Code of Canon Law says, 'A confessor who directly violates the seal of confession incurs immediate excommunication.' But even for that rule, there are ways."

Thinking a moment about Bruno Abruzzese, I said, "There was a paid killer in Munich who gave his confession to an old priest just before dying. If we knew what he said, it might clear up a lot about who's responsible for some of the illegal activity surrounding the Mozart diaries."

Brother Tomáš continued, "There have been times when priests have broken the rule of the confessional—for reasons of conscience. In my opinion, there are valid reasons, such as when the confession will exonerate someone sentenced to death for a crime they didn't commit."

"And what if revealing the confession could prevent other people from losing their lives?" I asked.

Tomáš nodded. He began to cite specific cases in church history when the rule of secrecy of the confessional was broken, some that were ancient. "But the elderly priest from Munich adamantly insisted that the privacy of the confessional can never be broken under any circumstances."

"Perhaps I shouldn't say this," Brother Tomáš replied, with an enigmatic smile. "But ultimately a prince should never lack legitimate reasons to break his promise—and that includes a prince of the church."

"Is that from the Bible?" I asked.

"No," he smiled. "Machiavelli."

Not sure if he was pulling my leg, I listened carefully. His voice now authoritative and serious, he continued, "If other people are in danger of losing their lives, as you say, then that priest should notify the authorities. If his conscience does not permit him to do so . . . well, there are always ways to persuade someone. After all, priests are only people, and everyone has skeletons in their closet." Making a mental note, I decided to have Nadine follow up on Tomáš's arguments to try to convince the old priest to change his mind.

As I returned to my work on the diary, I felt Brother Tomáš and I were on the same wavelength; each of us believed in following the rules, but we were also willing to sidestep them for the greater good. And this had somehow created a bond between us.

Tomáš retrieved the familiar archival folder for me, and I took out the folios and hunted for the exact place I had reached in his transcription.

*When we arrived, Constanze and I stayed at the Three Lions Inn where, during our dinner, three musicians came to play: a peculiar combination, harp,* violin, and horn. *But they knew the music to my opera* Figaro, *and the violinist then set aside his instrument and took up the clarino trumpet, which he was equally adept at playing, to perform the military march for Cherubino in* Figaro. *This he did admirably, in fact on a par with some of the finest court musicians in Vienna. And it was not the last time we were to hear* Figaro: *everywhere we went, praises for* Figaro *were in people's mouths and the music was in the air, arranged for wind band, as minuets and contredanses at balls, performed by street musicians—even by the organ grinder outside our window!*

*My librettist, da Ponte, was staying across from our window in the hotel Zum Platteis. It was a congenial arrangement, as we were able to call to one another from our respective rooms as we worked on last-minute changes to* Don Giovanni.

*Josepha Duschek—the mere mention of her name, like the faintest whiff of her perfume—drives me wild: her lips are an invitation to graze on verdant pastures, her eyes deep, lucent pools of cool water, her skin luminous, soft velvet. When I visited her at her villa, a servant had me shown into a garden pavilion, where I sat and eagerly awaited her arrival, hoping we might be alone. Looking around the room, I noticed music paper and fresh quills and ink, a pianoforte and all kinds of amenities. A few minutes later, I heard the sound of the key in the door and found a note from Josepha under the door that she would release me from my captivity only after I had written down the aria I had promised her. Feeling myself bound and at her service, I composed "Bella mia fiamma." It is not music for the weakhearted or for dilettantes and is perfectly suited to her unique expressive style and temperament. But I had to punish her for my imprisonment, so I made the aria wretchedly difficult with unusual chromatic modulations that will require serious study before she can sing it. She is in love*

*with it, but scolded me for making it so complex and
intricate.*

*And, of course, just as a servant is entitled to be
rewarded for his efforts, I exacted from her what is due a
humble slave to love.*

Before the sound of bells announced it was time to finish,
I glanced at the remaining text and realized that my work on the
manuscript was rapidly coming to an end—there was a single
page left. Taking a deep breath, I began to think about what I
would do when I finished: head back to Prague, stay a few days
in a hotel, then continue on by train toward Nancy, making contact with the viscount at some point when I was far from the
monastery. I had followed all his precautions to the letter, but
now it was time to tell Brother Tomáš the full extent of the
events surrounding the diaries. As he took the archival folder
from my hands, I said, "My work here is almost done, so I'll be
leaving Lesní Klášter." He remained silent and I continued,
"There's something I have to ask you. Is the manuscript going to
be safe here?"

Surprised, he sat down next to me and I continued, "In case
people interested in the diaries were to find out about it?" As I
voiced my concerns, Brother Tomáš listened intently. When I
heard the bells ringing in the distance, I stopped to ask, "Aren't
we going to be late for chapel?"

"Just for once," he said, "it won't hurt us. Tell me more."

Beginning with the newspaper clippings of murders and
disappearances, and the exorbitant prices the diaries were getting at auction, I told Tomáš everything I knew about the diaries—and what pieces of the puzzle I didn't understand.
Concluding, I said, "Something worth considering is that the
person or organization interested in the diaries wants them regardless of whether or not they're authentic."

When I finished, Tomáš stood up and said confidently, "I'd
like to show you some things that will put your mind at rest.
First of all, I always keep the library locked. Second, we have so
many places in this monastery to conceal things, anyone trying

to steal it would never be able to find it, even if they tried. And if someone from the outside ever got in, we have ingenious ways to get out with it."

What Brother Tomáš proceeded to show me was astonishing, beginning with a shelf of books that opened to reveal a doorway behind it, concealing an entire room enclosed in the library. Taking me downstairs, he showed me cabinets in the wine cellar specifically designed to hide a man, yet displaying only bottles of wine on shelves. Afterward, he demonstrated a staircase exit carved into the walls of the monastery itself, and a crawl space that led over the roof, opening the way from one part of the monastery to the other. And he led me through a tunnel behind the wine cellar that opened into an unlit cistern where someone could hide if necessary.

When we emerged from the wine cellar, a detail caught my eye. "The glass on that outside window is smashed," I said.

"There's always something to be repaired around here," he replied. "I'll tell Brother Georg." Continuing his tour of surprises, he said, "So, that's just the beginning. There are so many more hiding places and escape routes in this monastery, I couldn't begin to tell you them all. There's even one in your cell."

My curiosity aroused, I asked, "In my cell?"

"All those old cells on the back wall of the monastery," he continued, "have a means for escape—it hasn't been used for centuries, but it's still there." Leading me to the back of the library, Brother Tomáš pointed outside the window to a series of wrought-iron bars, bent to form narrow steps protruding from the wall.

"The color of the finish matches the walls and creates a kind of optical illusion. So you have to look very closely to see them," he said. "And they're not visible from the ground, in fact they're almost impossible to see from inside the rooms. It's a shame they weren't maintained throughout the centuries. They're a remarkable feature."

The unusual piece of history captured my interest completely, and when I returned to my cell for bed, I wasted no time in opening the huge wooden shutters, peering down in the dark to see if I could catch a glimpse of the iron bars. Sure enough, they were there, barely visible, just as Tomáš had said.

Before retiring, I paused to look out into the night sky, and was momentarily spellbound by the view. My open window created a frame for the limitless sky and countryside beneath, bathed by the full moon with a bluish, frozen luster. Without a solitary cloud or star in the sky, the moon looked bleak, stark, bathing the monastery and its surroundings in a glacial palette.

More and more, Lesní Klášter had become a marvel, and the beauty of the monastery and the richness of the people played a major role—like Brother Tomáš, whose morality focused on the greater good. Knowing I would soon be leaving left me with a sense of dismay, a kind of separation anxiety. But departure was imminent and it was clearly time to begin preparing myself and others.

As I continued surveying the tableau, a tiny yellow-green flash from one of the hills caught my attention. Neither a reflection of any kind, nor a play of light, it had been a clear, discrete bolt of light, reminding me of some kind of electronic device or signal. For a second, I thought of a night sight. Holding my breath, I waited for it to reappear.

When the flash did not recur, I stood a few more minutes before reluctantly closing the shutters, saying to myself that someone was out there. Immediately, I realized the risk of embarking upon another onslaught of paranoid thoughts. But as I turned down the bed, I knew that I had absolutely seen something. It was disturbing: first the car in the woods, then this.

The only thing to do was wait until morning and ask Brother Michal about it. And as I fell asleep, my thoughts were replaced by the striking visual images of the remarkable, bleak lunar diorama that had been indelibly stamped in my memory.

Almost everyone, from the abbot to Brother Zachariáš, now knew that my work with the manuscript was ending and that I would soon be leaving. As I sat in the library for the last time under the bluish purple glare of the lamp, I picked up the last

sheet—with the famous signature of Wolfgang Adam Mozart—
and began the process of examining and translating it.

*Even as I write this, we are immersed in preparations
to leave this beautiful and welcoming city. In addition to
the remunerative benefits, I reaped the pleasure of
meeting kindred souls touched by my music in a profound
and genuine manner. My talents have received
recognition here, and I was barraged with requests to
stay several months longer. But it is impossible.*

*Having received so many offers to persuade me to
move permanently to Prague, where my music is
understood, I find myself again returning to Vienna,
where there is more and more resistance to the directions
my talent is leading me. My destiny seems to have only
one face: contradiction, sometimes gentle, but most often
violent. As I leave this beautiful city where I am well
treated, admired, and compensated, I ask myself, "Why
not embrace Prague and settle here?"*

*Yet there is ultimately no doubt in my mind that my
life is inextricably tied with Vienna. It is simple, I must
return. I am irresistibly, irrationally drawn to that city
that confounds me, that tries me, that resists my talents
and that takes my offerings without gratitude or
acknowledgment. At least for now, there is no change
looming on the horizon. But as to the future, who can say?*

*Wolfgang Adam Mozart*

My translation finished, I stared at the extraordinary signature. And I reflected on the text of the diary, with so much detailed information about Mozart's trip to Prague, probably
eyewitness testimony. Perhaps I was fooling myself, perhaps I
merely wanted to believe it was authentic, but it had the ring of
truth. As I jotted down my thoughts, I realized Brother Tomáš
was standing next to me.

"I see you've reached the end," he said. "Where do we go
from here?"

"Unfortunately," I replied, "the last word about authenticity will have to come from specialists who can date ink and paper. When you're ready, you'll have to undertake that next stage."

"That might not be for a while," Tomáš replied. "Decisions around here take a long time." As we spoke, I realized the advice I was giving him was the same for me: I would soon have to pursue the identical course of action for my own diary, which was buried in the viscount's safe. Handing Tomáš the ancient pages for the last time, I thanked him and left the library, heading toward the abbot's office as the other monks moved in the direction of the chapel.

After being seated in his office, I said, "Brother Cyril, now that my work here is finished, I have to deal with practical matters of leaving." Sitting down next to me, Cyril began thanking me in glowing terms and we used the time to reminisce about my visit at Lesní Klášter. After a prolonged exchange, with the sound of monks singing in the distance, I asked him about finding a hotel in Prague.

"Of course," he said, "we'll call them to make a reservation." For a second, he hesitated. "As soon as the phone service is restored."

"The phone service?" I asked.

"For about two days now, we haven't had any. But it's nothing to be alarmed about—this has happened many times before. Usually it takes a day or two to restore it."

"If the lines are still down the day after tomorrow," I said, "I'll just head back on the train to Prague and take my chances."

As we left his office, Brother Cyril invited me to walk with him to dinner and asked, "Does Brother Zachariáš know yet that you're leaving?"

"Yes," I said. "Why?"

"Because," he continued, "I'm sure he'll do something special on your last day with us." Vaguely I knew what that meant, but I suspected that any event created by Zachariáš would radically surpass all expectations.

\*    \*    \*

It would be my last day in Lesní Klášter, so I made the rounds saying goodbye to those I knew, and smiling and shaking hands with the amiable, elderly monks I didn't. The rich aroma of slow-roasted Moravian ham permeated the walls of the monastery and I sensed a festivity and anticipation reminiscent of Thanksgiving dinner.

Brother Zachariáš had asked to see me, so I knocked on the door of the kitchen. When Zachariáš emerged, smiling, he explained, "There's still the rule of silence during dinner, so I wanted to say goodbye now . . . and give you something." In one hand, he had a tiny wrapped box. "Some chocolate truffles I rolled for you myself this morning." In the other hand was an intriguing binder of some kind and when he presented it to me, I realized it was a book cover—a collage composed of pictures of Marlene Dietrich in all different sizes.

Thanking him, I started to look inside and Zachariáš stopped me. "Don't open it now. It's something to read on the train to Prague, a copy of *Architectural Digest*." With an embrace, Zachariáš pushed it under my arm and said, "You've been a gift to us."

Brother Michal was next on my list, and I searched for him through what felt like an endless succession of monks wishing me well. When I finally found him, Michal was more charming than ever and presented me, with great formality, a handmade lacquered bookmark composed of dried, pressed wildflowers. "When things are getting stressful," he said, "this is to remind you of our walk outside the walls."

It was clear we were both making an attempt not to be overly emotional, and as we stood, our arms firmly locked, he surprised me by asking, "You wouldn't be planning to take a habit with you as a souvenir?"

"A habit?" I asked. "No, why?"

"It's just part of my job to ask," he replied. "I noticed there's a robe missing . . . it's your size."

"Lost things like that turn up eventually," I said.

"Not around here," he replied. "Everything in Lesní Klášter is accounted for, nothing ever gets lost."

"Sorry I can't help you on that one," I said.

"Strange," he continued, lost in thought. Then with a shrug of the shoulders, he gave me a firm handshake and said, "Keep in touch."

Struck by how inadequate words were in such occasions, I replied, "I'll miss you," and he smiled.

My last visit was to the library, and when I arrived, Brother Tomáš was sitting alone, uncharacteristically idle. He gave me a half-smile as I entered on an ebullient wave. "Lesní Klášter has been an amazing experience for me—thanks to you," I said.

Brother Tomáš, a master of unemotional, correct small talk, returned the compliment and we chatted for a few minutes. But I found myself doing most of the talking and began to wonder at his lack of enthusiasm. "Promise me you'll put the diary in a safe place," I finally said.

"Of course," he said, as if he were going through the motions, and I began to realize just how strangely he was acting. Before I stood up to leave, I asked, "Is it my imagination or is something wrong?"

His expression guarded, Tomáš paused, then went to shut the door of the library. "I promised not to say anything," he said somberly. "But I'm going to tell you anyway. It's bad."

"What?" I asked, almost afraid to hear.

"There's no diary anymore. It's been destroyed."

"Jesus!" I exclaimed. "How could that happen?"

Picking up a large marble dish from the corner, he carried it over and placed it in front of me. "It's a mortar used for grinding herbs. Someone came in here last night and burned the diary, leaving the ashes for everyone to see."

"Brother Georg," I blurted aloud.

Visibly shaken, he replied, "It makes sense . . . he's the only one besides the abbot and me with a key to the library."

After a long and stunned silence, I replied, "Well, he got the last word, didn't he? He said the diary must never leave these walls."

"Don't remind me," Tomáš said morosely.

"What's going to happen to him?" I asked, trying to control my feelings of shock and outrage.

"Within the community," Tomáš replied, "we have our own system of justice and punishment. No police are ever brought in."

"He burned a priceless document," I said somberly.

"What's the abbot supposed to do?" he asked, trying to control himself. "Put him out on the street at his age, after what the Communists did to him? I don't think so."

There was little I could say, and we sat in silence until I realized, "Wait. What about your transcription?"

"I still have that safely away," he said. "Why?"

"Well, it's at least something. Between that and my translation, we have the text."

"That's true," he admitted without enthusiasm. "But didn't you say that the only way to evaluate authenticity is to have experts look at paper and ink?"

"Yes, I did. But at least the text will be of interest to the world. It's the kind of thing that will stimulate discussion for centuries."

"I'm afraid I'll have to leave that part to you," he said sadly. "After all the trouble I've gone to, I don't want to be involved with it anymore."

Brother Tomáš was a crushed and defeated man, and I knew nothing I could say would help. Before I left, he insisted, "The others know nothing about this. Don't even let the abbot know I told you. We don't believe in hanging our dirty laundry out for others to see."

And that evening, despite the fact that Zachariáš prepared a meal fit for a king, I was devastated by the news. Yet I was obliged to put on a convivial face, so as not to divulge what I knew. It was a painful duty.

As entire hams were ceremoniously carried through the dining room, then returned to the kitchen to be sliced and presented on individual plates like artwork, I reflected on what a bitter sendoff it was. Seeing Brother Georg sitting across the room, in a distant corner of the refectory, I looked over at him repeatedly, but our eyes met only once. Behind that immutable expression, I could only guess what he was thinking: there was no ambivalence, no remorse, and he was saying, "I won." To me it was proof once again that narrow little minds prevail. Painfully, I realized that this festive meal, meant to celebrate my last night at the monastery, was instead a perverse celebration of Brother Georg's greatest triumph. It was his victory feast.


Looking at my alarm clock, I realized it was shortly after one. There was no way for me to sleep, so I reached over and turned on the light. The copy of *Architectural Digest* that Brother Zachariáš gave me was sitting on my nightstand. But I didn't feel like reading and climbed out of bed, opening the shutters to enjoy the view for the last time. The moon-drenched valley, shrouded in somber shadows, appeared aloof, remote, and unfathomable. After a half hour, I decided to try again to sleep. Just as I was dozing off, there was a noise, very muffled, and I glanced at the clock. It was past two.

Sitting up in bed to listen, I heard it again. Someone was knocking on my door. For a moment, I waited; then I heard it a third time, a little louder. Up close to the door, I whispered, "Who is it?"

The voice I heard astounded me. "It's me, Doc. Open up."

It was the voice of Enrique.

## CHAPTER 31

*In the whole vast dome of living nature there reigns an
open violence, a kind of prescriptive fury which arms all
the creatures to their common doom . . .*

—JOSEPH DE MAISTRE

The barely audible voice of Nadine's bodyguard, Enrique, from
outside the door of my cell was so incongruous with my life behind the walls of the monastery that I had difficulty believing
my ears. Stunned, I was unable to reply. Again I heard the muffled knock. As I hesitated at the door, the light next to my bed
suddenly went out and I found myself, in addition to everything else, in darkness. The voice of Enrique, now louder and
more insistent, startled me again. "Doc, please. We ain't got
much time."

As I unlocked the door, I whispered incredulously, "What
are you doing here?"

"Get dressed," he said, pushing the door back and striding
past me. "I'll explain later." With his broad shoulders, Enrique's
massive height seemed to dwarf the room. Dressed in a monk's
habit with a cowl over his head that concealed a heavy knit ski
cap, he looked ridiculous.

"So that's what happened to the monk's habit that disappeared," I said as I locked the door behind him.

"Don't know what you're talking about, Doc," he said. "I
brought this along with me . . . just a little planning ahead, if you
know what I mean."

"How did you know which room I was in?" I asked.

"Easy. From down below I could see you standing in the
window."

"What's so urgent that you had to come here in the middle of the night?"

"First get your shoes on," he urged. "I'll tell you later. We gonna get you outta here."

"No," I insisted as I hunted for my shoes in the dark. "Tell me first."

Enrique whispered impatiently, "It's a little complicated. But to make a long story short, I decoded an encrypted message from Max's cell phone to a company that specializes in . . . well, commissions."

"Commissions?" I asked, fumbling with my shoestrings, unable to follow what Enrique was trying to say.

"Yeah, but we don't know what kind exactly. Someone was sent here, maybe just to do a little breaking and entering to get the diary in the library. But maybe—and look man, I don't want to alarm you or anything—he might be here for another reason."

Listening as I finished tying my shoes, I was at a loss to follow what he was saying. "But he's definitely in the building right now," Enrique said. "And we ain't sticking around to meet him. I followed the same route he used to break in, through the window in the basement. Let's go, Doc, we're outta here."

Through a crack, Enrique peered into the blackened corridor, then immediately closed the door, jerking his head back in. "What is it?" I asked.

Putting his finger to his lips, Enrique said, "I thought I heard someone coming up the stairs." Without a sound, he locked the door, whispering, "We'll wait a minute to make sure the coast is clear."

Whispering almost inaudibly, I asked, "Why didn't you just call and tell me?"

"I only found out the day before yesterday," he said. "The monastery phone's been out. Somebody probably cut it, and now the power's out too."

"Then why didn't you call the police?"

"The Czech police?" he asked incredulously. "Yeah, right."

"When the hall's clear, what are we going to do?" I asked.

"We gonna get you the hell out of here just as fast as our butts can take us. And hope he's here for the diary, not for you. These guys can be real mean, sort of like killing machines."

"Killing machines?" I asked. The impact of what Enrique was saying finally hit me.

"Don't want to alarm you 'cause we don't know for sure. But we definitely don't wanna tangle with this guy if we don't have to."

Periodically placing his ear on the door, Enrique continued explaining: "If he's a hit man, he may not even get the money for the job. Sometimes they're blackmailed—somebody in their family's got a drug habit or a big gambling debt and is about to get iced. But once they agree to take on a commission, they'd better not slip up—"

In midsentence, Enrique was startled by a knock on the door. He jerked away and pulled me with him. "Shit," he whispered. His face contorted in a grimace, he continued mouthing the words, "Shit . . . shit." Immediately he became still and put up his hand to tell me not to move or speak.

A second, louder knock started my heart pounding. "Who's that?" Enrique whispered to me.

When I gestured that I didn't have the slightest idea, he signaled me to wait. With the third knock, he motioned for me to find out who it was.

"Who is it?" I asked softly.

"Brother Tomáš," was the reply. But his voice had a strange, unemotional tone.

"Ask him what he wants," Enrique whispered. "And don't keep him too long."

My temples throbbing, I asked, "What do you want?"

"I have to talk to you," he said, speaking each word in an unnatural monotone.

Enrique gestured emphatically, *No!* and I immediately said, "It'll have to wait until tomorrow."

To my amazement, the key to my door popped out of the lock and fell to the floor with a dull thud, setting my heart racing. One by one, I could hear the sound of keys slowly being inserted and removed; he was trying to find the right one to open the door.

"Jesus," Enrique whispered. "This looks bad, real bad."

Looking around the room, he whispered, "I'll handle it—you just get outta my way. Got that?"

Events were taking place too fast, and a sense of panic swept over me. When I hesitated, he pushed me and insisted, "Move! Now!" Removing a revolver from under his habit, Enrique propped himself behind the door as I looked for a place out of the way. Pointing to the large wardrobe, Enrique was suggesting I climb in, but when I looked inside, it felt too claustrophobic.

As Enrique double-checked his gun, the sound of keys being inserted one by one continued. My head pounding fiercely, I surveyed the space under the bed as Enrique gestured impatiently with his finger for me to get under. At that point I froze for a second and realized that I was right in the middle of my recurring nightmare. *But this time it was really happening.* Some event of unthinkable violence was about to take place. Something was lurking outside the door and time was running out. Again I was frantically trying to find a place to hide. And there was none.


As Enrique gestured impatiently for me to get out of sight, another solution came to mind. Quietly, I unlatched the huge wooden shutters and opened them out into the night air. But when I looked down the sheer face of wall plunging below, a cold shudder swept through me.

This new, risky possibility was my only option. Not waiting for Enrique's approval, I climbed out on the marble window ledge. With the sound of my heartbeat pounding in my temples, I tested the top two rungs with my foot and began descending the ancient steps one at a time.

With each step, a rough, gritty dust came off on my hands and face, and as I reached the fifth rung, I felt it sagging precariously under my weight. The sixth felt solid enough, but the one below it was loose, sending the plaster cascading down the side of the wall. Although my forehead still protruded above the windowsill, I had gone as far as I could go. Looking back into the cell, I could see Enrique, still standing alert at the side of the door, gesturing, *Get down.*

Transferring my grip to the marble threshold of the windowsill, I understood the risk. It was surprising how clearly I could see Enrique, his figure bathed in the bluish light of the full moon that poured in through the window. The violent rhythm of my pulse pounding in my ears, I crouched down, my head just barely hidden under the marble ledge. Within seconds, I heard the sound of the lock opening: a soft, brittle snap that resonated in the tomblike silence.

Almost involuntarily, I tried to see what was happening. As the door opened in a slow, agonizing arc, I watched breathlessly. No figure emerged, no one came in. In the interminable silence, Enrique became impatient. Poising his revolver, he slowly moved his head to peer around the door.

In a shattering instant, Brother Tomáš flew through the air with what seemed a supernatural burst of energy, hitting Enrique frontally with startling force: his hands tied behind his back, Brother Tomáš had been thrust into the room like a battering ram. Enrique was lying on the floor under Tomáš, whose face was beaten and bloodied almost beyond recognition. From behind the door, a short, stocky figure in monk's garb leaped in like a wild cougar. Descending on Enrique with a savage violence, he delivered three rapid, powerful blows from a long, narrow knife into Enrique's body.

The speed and strength of the attack sent a sudden rush of adrenaline to my brain and I was unable to look away. With a single, broad sweep, the assailant grabbed Enrique's thick mane of hair and slashed his throat from one side to the other, practically decapitating him in front of my eyes. The sight of gushing blood, splattering like a geyser over Brother Tomáš, was so surreal, my vision began to go in and out of focus. Like a rag doll, Enrique's body was twitching and jerking in a widening pool of blood, with Brother Tomáš, crouched on his knees, his head down to the floor, being bathed in a shower of thick, mahogany-black blood.

My temples pounding ferociously, I crouched down and

buried my face against my knuckles, clenching the rusty wrought-iron bars with a grip that practically cut off my circulation. Gasping for breath, I remained immobile. *He didn't see me. He doesn't know I'm here.*

Balancing my support between the braces in my hand and the ones under my feet, I reached down with my toe, stretching for where the eighth rung should be. Still holding tightly with one hand, I lowered myself and landed. It felt like the rung would hold my weight but, within seconds, it started to give, and I heard the sound of rocks and dust ricocheting down the side of the monastery.

My heart pumping violently, I scrambled to grab the upper rung and reached my original spot, just beneath the window ledge. In the distance, the voice of Brother Tomáš resonated over and over again in a ghastly moan, "Oh God, oh God." Above the sounds, the voice of Enrique's attacker rang out in a coarse, guttural Italian dialect. "*Zitta!* Shut up or I'll kill you too."

Suspended in the tortured stillness of the night, I waited, praying that the assailant would leave. But soon a new sound arose from within the cell: in a thick Sicilian accent, my name was being repeated. The only response from Brother Tomáš was the agonizing ostinato, "Oh God." But the assailant continued questioning furiously, until the air was filled with the sounds of kicking and pounding, followed by Brother Tomáš, gurgling and choking through a throat full of blood, "No Pierce. Pierce no."

Inching down into my crouched position like a hunted animal, I prayed frantically that I wouldn't be noticed, prayed that the night would somehow shield me. But within seconds, I looked up to see what I dreaded most: the assailant was peering out directly over me from the window ledge.

"*Porca Madonna!*" I heard him swear. Within seconds, I had to move. Stretching my foot to where the ninth rung should have been, I grabbed for any steps that would hold my weight. In a shower of tiny rocks and plaster, the rung in my right hand pulled free from the wall, choking me with a cascade of debris.

Less than four feet above me, covered by a monk's cowl, the

killer's head reemerged through the window. The long blade he had used to slice Enrique's throat was in his hand and, within seconds, his arm swept by my face in a rapid arc. But I was just beyond his reach, and he disappeared from the window.

Again I tried to proceed with my descent but the next metal rung gave way beneath my feet, plummeting down the side of the monastery to the rock below with a hollow echo. And now I looked up to see the killer, his thick head of jet-black hair exposed and his monk's habit stripped off to reveal a set of guerrilla fatigues. Frozen, I watched as he climbed over the ledge to test the precarious steps, the gleaming stiletto still in his hand.

The danger to him apparent, the assailant gripped the marble ledge with his arm, rested his blade on the ledge, and began swinging his foot violently to kick me off the steps. With the blood rushing feverishly through my temples, I contemplated my only alternative: to jump off into the dark to certain death. When he reached for his knife, I began to hear a relentless humming in my brain. I heard myself saying, *Jump now or it's all over.*

Twisting his body away from the window, the killer lowered himself slowly, holding on to the ledge. As I looked down into the black abyss, a feverish pulse throbbed in my chest like wild pounding on an anvil. Holding on to the ledge with a few fingers, the assassin stretched himself downward, adjusting his hold so as not to lose his balance. The more I struggled to breathe, the louder my frantic gasps for air rang out. As the killer stretched out his arm, his knife poised just above my face, his fingers, gripping the ledge for balance, suddenly flew up in the air and his knife went plummeting directly past my face. With an outraged grunt of surprise, he struggled with both hands to hold on to the ledge. Above the window, the ghoulish figure of Brother Tomáš emerged, his face bloodied, one eye a sunken hole. Ripping the killer's grip from the ledge, Tomáš sent him flying with a single, deliberate thrust—through the air, plunging past me into the darkness with a brutal finality.

When I understood what had happened, I heard myself saying, "Jesus!" Looking up, I saw the outlined silhouette of

Brother Tomáš, his arm outstretched to pull me up. With a deep sigh of relief, I began to climb back up, but immediately froze—the bottom rung that had been supporting my weight was now giving way under the movement.

Trying to remain still, I heard his voice, speaking softly, "Give me your hand."

Afraid to move a muscle, I whispered, "I can't, the step is giving way."

Alarmed, Tomáš reached as far as he could out the window, saying, "Quickly then, grab my arm."

With all my strength, I lunged upward and aimed for his outstretched arm. With a violent snap, the rung under my feet burst from the wall. Our fingers had barely touched and now, with both feet dangling in midair, I was frantically hanging on to a single rung with both hands.

With a glazed look of terror, Tomáš shouted, "Quickly, pull yourself up." But as I struggled, the weight of my body began to loosen the rung. As a trickle of gritty plaster poured into my eyes and nostrils, I heard myself screaming, "It's coming off."

For an endless moment, I was sailing downward in a free fall.

It happened so quickly—it lasted an eternity. For a brief moment, I remembered Bruno Abruzzese, plummeting from the dizzying heights of the Frauenkirche in Munich. But all the fragments of impressions—the visual and tactile memories of my fall—are subsumed by what happened next: the impact.

The pain must not have begun immediately because I was unconscious for some time. When I finally came to, the agony was beyond imagination. In my left hand, I was still clutching the iron rung, as if my grip had been locked in a dress rehearsal for rigor mortis. Lying in the dark, unable to move, every pain I had experienced in my life until then was meaningless.

Delirious, I heard words coming from my mouth, a ghastly moan: *"De profundis clamavi ad te, Domine, Domine, exaudi vocem meam."* For a moment, I didn't even know what it meant—something my mind had gleaned from hours of chanting in the chapel. Eventually I realized that the Latin words were a prayer rising from the core of my being: "Out of the depths I have cried to thee, Lord, Lord, hear my prayer."

The excruciating surges of pain made me scream out in the dark. Every time I tried to move, the agony was magnified. For now, I was forced to stay put, immobile, a virtual prisoner. Gradually my prayers became a desperate plea to take me out of my misery.

In the distance, I could hear the faint sounds of brothers calling my name. And I knew it would all soon be over. That's when I realized where I was—on a bare, rock-strewn hill. To my astonishment, about twelve feet away from me was the body of Enrique's killer, crumpled like a pathetic heap of soldier's fatigues. Staring at my surroundings, I saw the monastery rising high above me and realized that my body was covered by gritty dust and plaster.

For one gruesome moment, I imagined I saw my assailant twitching. Straining harder to see, I watched intently for any sign of motion. Before long, I realized he was breathing—he was still alive.

My heart pounding, I heard voices approaching from the distance and struggled to shout, "Over here." For a second, there was quiet and I was sure they had heard me. But the sound of my voice had an effect on the assailant. To my horror, he began to move again, first almost imperceptibly, then more; he was trying to stand up.

Within seconds, he had again collapsed into a heap. Once again, he managed to stand, only to fall. With a terrifying determination, he tried over and over, collapsing each time. Watching his efforts, I saw his stiletto reflecting the moonlight with a grisly, piercing brilliance, the sight of it sending a shudder throughout my body.

As I lay stretched out on my back, he began dragging himself on his belly toward the knife. The situation was bizarre and incongruous: in the peaceful stillness of the night, with the sound of rescue voices approaching, the assailant had succeeded in clutching the knife and was dragging himself toward me. Another sound, more terrifying than anything I had ever heard, began to reverberate on the ground near my ears: the rhythmic crunch of a knife, plunging in and out of the earth as the killer— more animal than human—pulled himself, straining, closer and closer. As the sound grew nearer, waves of panic raced through my body. Frantically, I prepared the only weapon available to me, the iron bar still clenched in my hand.

Gasping for air, I waited as the sounds stopped, straining to hear in the frozen silence. All at once, his crazed face appeared directly above me, so close that his breath rebounded off my face. With every remaining drop of energy in my body, I swung the bar. But within seconds, the full weight of my arm was pinned down at my side. A rush of horror surged through me as I looked up to see his jet-black eyes. For a ghastly second, we stared directly into each other's eyes. Then he raised the blade high above me and, with a violent burst, plunged the knife into my chest.

He collapsed on top of me . . . that's where it stops. I can't remember any more.

# PART SIX

# Nancy

# INTERLUDE

*I that in heill wes and gladnes*
*Am trublit now with gret seiknes*
*And feblit with infermite:*
*Timor Mortis conturbat me.*

*I that was in health and gladness,*
*Am troubled now with great sickness*
*And feebled with infirmities:*
*Fear of death troubles me.*

—WILLIAM DUNBAR

The intricate operations on my spinal cord were a pale
shadow of a dream. Endless months of recuperation were
followed by grueling weeks of physical therapy. My attempts to move my legs proved futile and I began to accept
the worst—that my lower body was permanently paralyzed. Normal activities were excruciatingly difficult and
my life was a struggle of pain, made tolerable only by massive doses of highly potent, addictive painkillers.

The eight months in bed had sapped my upper body
strength, as I lay immobile, in metal braces and plaster
casts. But I was resolved to at least regain that part of my
body. Gradually, the muscles in my arms became more re-
silient, and I soon found that I could maneuver myself on
the parallel bars, dragging my legs and my feet.

Then the faint, barely discernible moment when the tiniest feeling returned to my toes . . . at first I thought I
dreamed it. The next morning, I discovered I could move
my toes. My optimism soared, as did my expectations.
From then on, even the slightest progress I made raced
through the hospital like brushfire: every time something

came out or off—a pin or a brace—the staff was eager to see the new developments. And I knew everyone was cheering me on from the sidelines.

Physical rehab kept me busy, and the most important relationship in my life was with my physical therapist, Štĕpán, a young, articulate Czech from Brno. The day of my first step was memorable; Štĕpán's encouragement—"You're doing it, keep going"—continued to ring in my ears long after our session had ended.

Štĕpán knew intuitively how to push me to my limit without allowing me time to feel disillusioned or frustrated. The sessions were ingenious: passive exercise machines to promote mobility, stretching of every imaginable kind, and massage—some gentle, some astonishingly vigorous. In addition, there were experimental salves and unusual baths with salts, algae, and chemicals.

The operations on my spine generated enormous interest in and outside the hospital, as the procedure involved tissue, fluids, and stem cells from aborted fetuses, illegal in most of the world. I began to feel like a circus sideshow; week after week, teams of Czech doctors and foreign physicians arrived, along with a steady stream of medical students. When the head surgeon from the operating team arrived, I asked him what his prognosis was. "We're watching your progress with just as much interest as you are," he replied. "The very nature of your operation and postoperational treatment is experimental. Frankly, what we did could not have been performed anywhere else—especially not in the United States."

After the surgeon left, Štĕpán carried in a device that he left in the corner of the room—just in case. It was a solid, shiny chrome and aluminum walker, more thrilling than my first bicycle. Although at first I was doing little more than lifting and dragging my feet, barely perceptible improvements followed day after day, until I finally felt comfortable standing upright, then slowly alternating lifting each foot.

During my physical rehab, uniformed, armed guards

peered inside continuously with glazed, intimidating expressions. When I asked, Štěpán replied, "There's been round-the-clock police protection, in case another attempt is made on your life." Even in the protected confines of the Zaradník Clinic, there was the very real possibility that someone would again try to kill me.

My therapy sessions alternated with tedious interviews with the police: local police from Prague, inspectors from France, Italy, and Austria, and two officers from Interpol, who were always asking the same questions. Although I repeated ad infinitum what Enrique had said—that he had intercepted Max's encrypted mobile phone message—the usual response was that they would be sure to question him. When I asked an inspector from Interpol if he was planning to arrest Max, he told me frankly, "What you've told us is only hearsay; we have no proof. We could arrest him, but there's no way we could hold him. And, of course, he has top-notch lawyers."

Enrique, the only witness to the phone call, was dead. It would have been easy for me to linger on the past and wallow in depression and regret, if Štěpán had not made me realize that the present demanded my full attention—it was a choice that would determine my future.

Spurred on by the possibility that I might one day be able to walk using only crutches, I answered the many cards and letters I received with optimism about my recovery. News of my narrow escape had spread, and the notes were numerous: letters from Nadine, the viscount, and Lord Williamson; splendid handmade cards from the brothers at Lesní Klášter; get-well wishes with musical subjects from Elisabetta, Hélène, Suzanne, and Alison; and humorous, semipornographic postcards from Andreas Wolff.

My brother, the army officer, and his children wrote, as did my sister, the flight attendant, who sent newspaper clippings from America about the attempt on my life and my operations. They also wrote that the Zaradník Clinic had categorically prohibited any visitors.

Reading through the accumulated stacks of cards from my oldest and best friends in Boston, I caught up on a great deal of news. After all, I had been removed from the world for a considerable period of time—first for two months in the monastery, then for over nine months in the hospital. And people's lives did not stop in the meantime. Guests of the Fondation de l'Art éternel wrote cards, sometimes enclosing photos. Andrei Weidener and his wife, Caroline, had a baby boy. Hélène Benoit divorced her husband and had decided to stay single for a while; she sent her latest CD set of the five Mozart violin concertos. Even Jano, the young Slovak waiter, wrote, with astounding spelling mistakes and grammatical errors that kept me entertained as I struggled to decipher them.

In the few moments he could be serious, Andreas Wolff announced he was trying to reform his life and had begun reading great philosophers: Marcus Aurelius and Montaigne. Also, Alison Teal had begun visiting European spas again, taking time out from singing to restore her body and her spirit. And Véronique Ibsen was making arrangements to marry the young Roman doctor who saved her life.

Suzanne Kienzle in Geneva had done the impossible: by keeping careful records of procedural errors her professor had made—in her opinion, to deliberately sabotage her dissertation—she was able to appeal to the university administration, which had just implemented a procedure to handle student complaints. It was an unprecedented triumph—she was awarded her Ph.D., which she probably deserved more than anyone. Her next step was to find a job, and she was actively pursuing it.

Štěpán interrupted my reading to say, "Did anyone ever show you this?" Holding up a Czech newspaper, he read, "'American Musicologist Survives Murder Attempt at Lesní Klášter.' It's on the front page."

"Well, I guess that's my fifteen minutes of fame," I said. From the look on his face, I realized he didn't understand. "Andy Warhol," I said. "Haven't you heard of him?"

After thinking a moment, he replied, "Of course I have. In fact, his father was a Slovak." He continued, "By the way, you're going to have a visitor tomorrow . . . someone who's been waiting a long time to see you."

# CHAPTER 32

*As we grow older,*
*The world becomes stranger, more complicated*
*Of dead and living. Not the intense moment*
*Isolated, with no before or after*
*And not the lifetime of one man only*
*But of old stones that cannot be deciphered.*

—T. S. ELIOT

I could hardly believe my ears. *Nadine!* I wondered how I'd seem to her; in eleven months, I'd changed considerably. And I had plenty of opportunity to reflect on what had happened at La Favorite. But there were so many things I didn't understand. Nadine's arrival could not have come at a better time.

The next day she arrived, wearing a wide-brimmed black hat with white dots and trim, and a simply cut black dress. More than ever, Nadine evoked the elusive mystique of a mature Ingrid Bergman. As always, her eyes sparkled with the warm intelligence I had come to admire during the brief time we spent together. Within minutes of her arrival, we were reminiscing like old schoolmates. Yet her restrained beauty and seductive charm had a new impact on me: I found myself experiencing an adolescent crush on Nadine. Her every move, gesture, sent quivers through my body.

As always, Nadine was cool, clear, and focused. The events surrounding the Fondation de l'Art éternel were foremost in her mind. "The police have been running into a conspiracy of silence about the murders of Denise and von Horvach."

"Did you look into the possibility that they were committed by the satanic cult that's been celebrating Black Mass in Nancy since the French Revolution?" I asked.

"The police did," Nadine replied. "And the cult members were very indignant. In fact, they're suing a French tabloid for pointing the finger at them. Human sacrifice has never played a part in their beliefs, nor in any of their rituals."

She went on to explain that the events surrounding the diaries were still unresolved; when money-laundering schemes extend to several different countries, the complications multiply. "And," she continued, "anyone who knows anything has been silenced, or has disappeared."

"It's a shame the viscount can't bring everyone back together to La Favorite and have all the guests pool their information. Almost everything that happened could probably be explained."

She smiled as if she had long been considering the idea. "That could be arranged. But could you be there?"

"Yesterday someone mentioned the word *discharge*," I answered. "So maybe I'll get out of here one day. And bringing everyone back to La Favorite is probably the only hope of ever sorting out the whole mess."

"The viscount has considered it," she said slowly, "but it would only make sense if you were able to take part. If you feel you can, he has ways of making sure everyone else will come."

"Including Max?" I asked.

"Max?" she asked.

"He's responsible for what happened to me," I said. "Enrique told me that Max sent the man who tried to kill me to the monastery."

Nadine remained silent. "I feel just as strongly as you do about Max. But I've known him for so many years. I'd hate to think he went from an unscrupulous businessman to a killer."

"So you think Max isn't involved in all the things that have happened with the diaries?" I asked incredulously. "You were the one who set me on the track of money laundering. The whole thing is clearly a massive money-laundering scheme. And it's tied in with organized crime."

Nadine waited. "There are still so many things we don't know. Like who Max is working for."

"Then let's ask him directly," I replied. "It's probably the only way."

"How would you feel about seeing him again after all that's happened?"

I stopped short. From the day I regained my memory of the attack on me and the murder of Enrique, I had imagined this moment. Angry and determined, I replied, "I'm looking forward to finally confronting him face-to-face."

"The viscount could make sure Max was there," she said. "Because if he declined the invitation, it would be a tacit admission of guilt. But would you feel safe?"

A thought came to mind. "Could you arrange for Štěpán, my physical therapist, to come with me?" I asked.

"I'll speak with the hospital administration," Nadine said. "That's probably the least of our problems."


During her three-day visit, Nadine answered all my questions about what the investigations had turned up during my absence.

As to Denise's death, everything pointed to von Horvach: hair samples, clothing fibers, semen in her rectum. But the police didn't believe that he killed her; Jano was his alibi. Whoever did it had to be an extraordinarily strong man, as her fractured neck, with tearing of the spinal cord, indicated.

"The mystery boyfriend of Denise?" I asked. "Did you ever find out if he could have been Bruno Abruzzese, the hit man who jumped to his death in Munich?" Nadine had followed up my suggestion and taken steps to have his body exhumed in Sicily, with samples sent to Munich. But it was no simple matter and would take more time.

"What about the person who killed von Horvach?" I continued.

"Still no definitive leads," she replied. "We certainly turned up enough political enemies who were happy he was dead. Whatever organization, or person responsible, the police are sure the killer entered through the apartment of Baroness Paumgarten—all the other doors and windows were locked. No fingerprints or DNA of any kind were found, except for a few gray fibers, apparently from an Adidas jogging suit made in Chile."

I vented my rage. "In all this time, that's all the police have come up with?"

Nadine replied defensively that she had followed the money trail of the murdered forger found in Lake Geneva and some interesting information had surfaced. "We already know who paid Peter Arneis, the forger," she said. "A check from GRD—Girard Resource Development—was deposited in his account. And some new evidence has surfaced to suggest they're linked to SIN—Syndicat International—one of the largest crime organizations in the world. I've been documenting the extensive ties that Max has with GRD, but there's still nothing conclusive linking him with SIN."

Angry and discouraged by how little the investigation had turned up in eleven months, I was even more determined to proceed with the reunion at La Favorite.

"My uncle wants me to ask you what you want done about your diary," Nadine continued. "It's still in his safe."

"It's time for me to sell it," I replied.

Nadine said, "The viscount can arrange for it to be auctioned at Christie's in London, if that's what you want. But they'll need a statement of your conclusions regarding its authenticity."

"I'll send them everything I was able to determine," I replied. "My watermark studies of the paper and my comparisons of the handwriting with examples of Mozart's from the same period, all support the conclusion that the diary is authentic. As do content and style."

"Good," Nadine said. "My uncle will handle it from there."

"Did you ever follow up on the priest in Munich?" I asked. "The one who heard the confession of the hit man, Abruzzese?"

Nadine smiled. "I took your lead and sent a remarkable priest to Munich—he's a lawyer in addition to being an expert in canon law—to convince the old Bavarian priest to break the rule of the confessional. The lawyer argued that a priest may break his vow if other people are at risk of being killed, particularly in this case, since Abruzzese is dead and can't be brought to trial. But the old priest is still holding out, refusing to tell what Abruzzese said in confession. And his archbishop supports him."

"Can't you investigate him?" I asked.

"Investigate?" Nadine asked. "That's what I do for a living."

Repeating what Brother Tomáš had told me, I said, "After all, priests are just people. They have the same flaws we all have, the same skeletons in the closet." Firmly, I continued, "Find out more about him."

"I will," Nadine replied. "I promise. Speaking of skeletons in the closet, I do remember an unusual piece of background information about the priest: as a young man, he was involved in a Hitler Youth organization. Don't you think that's a strange thing for a priest?"

"I certainly do," I said. "Now, what about the person who was sending out all the threatening anonymous notes?"

Nadine was again silent, indicating that nothing new had materialized. "I have an idea," I said. "Something I've been thinking about the whole time I've been in the hospital. We need to set a trap."

After Nadine left, I thought about what had happened to me, and how I had managed to survive. Living in fear had only left me immobilized. Remembering Munich, I could hear Nadine saying, "There are never really any guarantees of safety in this world."

I continued to think about her last words to me: "Then we'll see each other back at La Favorite." La Favorite. The name evoked another world. And now an impending battle. As Nadine had said to me that night at La Favorite, she was waiting patiently for "one unexpected little slipup." And I knew I was the slipup that could bring Max and his whole house of cards crashing down.

But it was another month before the hospital decided I was well enough to be discharged. The viscount had agreed to the reunion, and the date he had arranged was rapidly approaching, which created an enormous amount of pressure. And although Štěpán and I both felt certain that I was well enough to travel, what we had not counted on was the massive wall of Czech bureaucracy. If I made it to La Favorite in time, it would be down to the wire.

When the day of my discharge finally came, it was clear that the only way to arrive in time for the viscount's meeting was by air. Nadine managed to arrange for use of a privately chartered helicopter to fly me directly to Nancy. Surrounded by my elaborate, streamlined wheelchair, my walker, and my shining chrome crutches, I waited in the central hall of the clinic for notification that the helicopter was ready. When we received word, Štěpán pushed my wheelchair, inching our way along the rooftop of the Zaradník Clinic, followed by two hospital employees who loaded what little luggage I had.

With the ear-shattering noise and powerful wind tunnel effect created by the helicopter, we climbed aboard. *Talk about an entrance,* I thought as the helicopter sped above the treetops of the Prague suburbs in the direction of Nancy. Closing my eyes, I prepared myself to return to La Favorite, once again to be in the eye of the cyclone. And I imagined what it would be like to see the guests of the foundation after such a long time. I had changed dramatically, both physically and emotionally. And my view of life was radically altered.

At that moment I realized just how much the experience in the monastery had transformed me. Having looked death directly in the face and survived, I had learned a lesson. Things were going to be different when I returned to La Favorite: I would never again allow myself to be manipulated by others. Or to live in fear.


In early afternoon, the helicopter touched down in the main courtyard of La Favorite. Shrouded with charcoal-edged clouds in an ashen sky, La Favorite was no longer the splendid, luminous estate I remembered, but rather a vast complex eerily reminiscent of a ghost town. The attempt at an extravagant welcome, with flags and banners of gold and white pouring into the courtyard, was overshadowed by a bizarre change. The beautiful baroque sculptures in niches on the facade and on pedestals in the park were without heads; they had been decapitated. I stared in disbelief at the mutilated forms that had once depicted casual frivolity.

Philippe, the majordomo, arrived to greet us, elegantly cool and distant as I remembered him, but this time with something darker and more evasive in his demeanor. He apologized that Nadine and the viscount had not been able to welcome me.

"What happened to the sculptures?" I asked.

"Vandalism," he replied icily.

His explanation did not convince me, as the damage was too calculated, too well executed. Stunned by the development, I asked, "Where is everyone?"

"The guests are staying in their rooms for the most part," he replied. "To rest before the evening, which may be quite taxing."

As the majordomo showed us through the nineteenth-century wing of the chateau on the way to our apartment, he added, "Thank you for the note you left me at Lord Williamson's residence—we had the hot water heater repaired after you left."

"With the windows taped," I said, "I could have been asphyxiated."

Philippe thought for a second, then replied, "I don't know what you're talking about. There was no tape on the windows."

Trying to get a handle on the situation, I said, "I'd like to speak with Nadine."

Philippe had Nadine paged and she arrived breathlessly. And beautiful. But clearly pressed for time. "You certainly like to cut it close, don't you?" she said, with an ironic expression.

"First tell me one thing," I said. "The statues."

Nadine looked at me somberly. "It's a clear message that the meeting tonight is making some people very unhappy. And to tell the guests to watch what they say. My uncle is devastated to see his home vandalized. But he's more determined than ever to go ahead with the meeting."

"And so am I," I replied.

In the distance, I could see Andrei and Caroline Weidener emerging from the viscount's park with a child in Andrei's arms—an energetic baby boy. After I said goodbye to Nadine, I was relieved to see them and to talk about anything besides the grotesque mutilation of La Favorite. "Just look at you," Caroline said as they approached. "We heard so many good things about your recovery, but I didn't expect this."

"Isn't he beautiful," I said of their little boy, watching his animated face and huge hazel eyes. "What's his name?"

"We decided to call him Adam," Andrei replied.

"Did Caroline come up with that name?" I asked.

"Actually, I was the one who thought of it," Andrei replied. "I don't know why. It felt like a fresh start, a clean slate, I guess. The new man."

As Philippe directed us through the residence, I spoke softly with Andrei. "What do you make of the headless sculptures?"

"If that's a shock, you won't believe what we just saw in the park: a white doe with its throat slit, lying across our path. A sight I'll never forget."

I remained speechless. Philippe appeared to be aware of what we were saying and Andrei changed the subject. "Have you made progress on your Mozart diary?"

Taking my time to climb the stairs, I said, "The viscount made arrangements to have it auctioned at Christie's in London. There are several advance bids by university libraries and private institutions ranging from forty to sixty thousand dollars."

"That's good to know," Andrei replied. "Because my aunt decided to have her letters by Constanze Mozart and Magdalena Hofdemel auctioned at Sotheby's. But first they're undergoing tests on the paper and ink at an institute devoted to authenticating manuscripts. We also sent photocopies to Mozart specialists."

"Who?" I asked.

Andrei smiled broadly. "Not Landry or Braun. The world expert on the handwriting of Mozart and his circle is comparing the letters with samples written by Constanze, and Mozart's piano student, Magdalena Hofdemel."

"Interesting," I said.

Passing the infant to his wife, Andrei replied with a wry smile, "There's something different about you. You're not the same person who left Chelsea that night."

"You're right," I replied, and I sensed he understood. As Caroline struggled to keep the child still, I asked, "So when does little Adam start piano lessons?"

"Just in case he turns out to have musical talent," Andrei replied, "I'm prepared to devote my life to his musical training, just as Leopold Mozart did."

"But we're going to let him be a little boy first," Caroline said. "That's something we both agree on, isn't it, Andrei?"

Jano, the blond Slovak waiter, arrived on the scene in a burst of energy, offering to help Štěpán get us settled in our apartment. As I waved goodbye to the child in Caroline's arms, I saw an expression that reflected the boundless curiosity of a typical baby. But there was something else in his eyes—a certain glimmer, an intelligence that captured my attention. And I imagined he liked me.


While Štěpán arranged our luggage in the apartment, I discussed the state of affairs at La Favorite with Jano. "Are all the guests here?"

Jano spoke quietly. "Just between us, I heard some resisted. But as you know, the viscount can be very persuasive."

"I know how he operates," I replied.

"And believe me," Jano said, "everyone felt it."

As Štěpán and I began to get settled into the apartment, I asked Jano, "Don't you find it a bit strange that all the guests are barricaded in their rooms?"

"They're apprehensive," he replied. "Maybe they have good reason to be. By the way, you probably should have something to eat sent to your room now. There's going to be a buffet tonight, but not until the meeting ends, whenever that is."

After a brief telephone call, our "last supper" arrived. We sat without speaking. Leaving the lights off, we watched sunlight bathe the room with a searing reddish glow as the smoldering embers of the sunset disappeared.

My doubts about seeing Max again brought an old saying to mind: "For the man who distrusts himself, silence is the best tactic." But after almost a year spent in the monastery and the hospital, my days of silence were over.

# CHAPTER 33

*Death is in my sight today*
*Like a man who desires to see home*
*After he has spent many years in captivity.*
—*The Man Who Was Tired of Life*, C. 1990 B.C.

A few minutes before the event, guests began to pour through the ponderous carved oak doorway of the library. Promptly at eight, with a harsh solemnity, the massive doors were shut, creating a hollow thud that resonated throughout the room. I looked around to see who was in attendance and realized that all the major players were in place.

Philippe spoke with cold efficiency. "Everyone is asked to remain for the entire meeting, regardless of how long it takes."

With that, the viscount began. "Normally, the foundation celebrates the greatest contributions to society. But tonight we're at La Favorite for another reason: to understand what happened here, then in Rome, where our stays were ruined by a series of terrible incidents.

"A few years ago," he continued, "I became enthusiastic about the possibility of finding Mozart's lost diaries, then actively involved in trying to bring them to light. Therefore I feel partly responsible for what has happened. I've decided it's time to find out for once and for all what's behind the complex and disturbing set of events."

The viscount continued, "Almost from the beginning, I suspected that something was seriously wrong. Recently discovered Mozart diaries, part of the cultural heritage of the world, were selling for extraordinarily inflated prices, prices too exaggerated for scholarly institutions. And after being sold to anonymous buyers, they immediately disappeared from circulation, one after another, with some of the people connected with them dying under suspicious circumstances. So this meeting is perhaps our last hope to confront the situation directly and bring it into focus. But it will take an enormous amount of goodwill on the part of everyone here, otherwise there's no way we're going to succeed."

Nadine interrupted. "Let me just stop for a moment to ask your reactions to what's been said."

Glances were exchanged but no one spoke. After a long pause, Elisabetta von Stahl replied, "How do you expect us to feel? We were asked to come to Nancy, but the invitation was more like a threat. And we've been treated like criminals, like suspects."

To my surprise, I saw many guests nodding. "I understand what you're saying, Elisabetta," Nadine replied. "And I apologize. But people have been murdered and we're no closer to knowing why these murders took place or who committed them. We all want an explanation."

Hélène Benoit cleared her throat quietly and stood up. "What you're doing is right, Nadine. No one who's innocent has anything to lose. I'll be happy to say anything I know and I hope everyone else here will do the same."

It appeared that there were two distinct camps: those hostile to having been obliged to come and those in agreement with the plan. Véronique Ibsen, apparently part of the antagonistic group, spoke up immediately. "I had to give up a very important premiere to be here. So I'm not happy about it at all. If anyone knows anything, I wish they'd just say it and get this thing over with so we can all go home."

Hélène continued, a little defensively. "I said I'd be happy to say what I know. But I simply don't know anything that could be of help. I assume that Denise was killed by her boyfriend; maybe he was part of a satanic cult. The police haven't told us anything so all I know is what I've read in the tabloids. But as far as the person who murdered Rudi von Horvach—and poisoned Alison Teal and Véronique Ibsen—I'm just as much in the dark as anyone."

Max, sitting holding Nicoletta's hand, interrupted. "Why

don't you tell us first what *you* know, Nadine?" he asked with his usual charm. "Instead of making us play guessing games."

Nadine looked very somber. "I really wasn't planning to begin, but perhaps I should try to summarize what we know. It's pretty clear who killed Denise."

The room became dead still. "The DNA evidence," she continued, "indicates Denise was murdered by her boyfriend, Bruno Abruzzese, who was a professional killer."

A wave of murmured comments filled the room until Andrei spoke up. "Hold on, Nadine," he said. "You've known this all the time and left us completely in the dark?"

"No," she replied calmly. "I just received the results today. The idea came from Matthew Pierce; he suggested I have DNA samples taken from Abruzzese. From his corpse, that is, because Abruzzese jumped to his death in Munich. It took months of bureaucracy to exhume the body, but eventually it paid off."

Clearing my voice, I asked, "Did you ever find out what Abruzzese said to the old priest before he died?"

All eyes were on Nadine. "Yes, I did in fact," she replied. "That was another idea of Matthew's, to convince an elderly priest to break the rule of the confessional. We sent a priest who is also a lawyer to Munich. He argued that a priest may break his vow if other people are at risk of being killed. The old priest held out. But we were able to come up with some extraordinarily damaging information about him: during the war, he had used information obtained in the confessional to help the Nazis hunt out Jewish families and the people who sheltered them. We were prepared to prosecute if he didn't agree to tell us what Abruzzese had said. The priest finally relented. Bruno Abruzzese confessed he had been hired to find his way in and out of La Favorite."

The news caught everyone off-guard and Ilsa raised her voice above the whispering to say, "But there are so many things I don't understand. What was Abruzzese doing with Denise? And how did he end up in Munich?"

Nadine continued, "Abruzzese met Denise at La Favorite and started dating her secretly as a means of getting inside. But something unexpected happened: he fell passionately in love with her. And he was a jealous, violent man. He killed her the night he found out she had slept with another man—Rudi von Horvach."

Philippe interrupted angrily. "Jano told me everything he saw that night between von Horvach and Denise. But it doesn't make any sense—Denise worked for me for years. Occasionally in the past, staff members have had relationships with guests . . . I mean, sexual liaisons. But she wasn't at all like that. She was completely professional; in fact, I would venture to say she was incapable of doing that kind of thing."

With a tone of superiority, Dennis Landry spoke up. "Well, you obviously didn't know her *that* well—she was part of a plan to infiltrate La Favorite, if I'm following this correctly."

"Perhaps I have no right to speak." Surprised, everyone turned to Jano, the waiter, who looked painfully shy and embarrassed.

"If I am not mistaken," Philippe interjected firmly, "everyone in this room *must* speak if they know something."

There were many nods. Jano continued, "A few years ago, Denise told me she was afraid she would end up unmarried and never raise a family of her own. When this mysterious man, the Sicilian, showed up and started paying so much attention to her, she must have felt like it was her last chance. But what I just don't understand is why . . . how can I say this? Why Denise went to bed with von Horvach if she had a violent, jealous boyfriend. And why von Horvach of all people?"

In the hush that followed, no one moved. Unable to remain silent, I said, "Sticking our heads in the sand isn't going to help." Looking around the room, my eyes stopped on Andreas Wolff. "Andreas, you know I value your friendship. But you apparently know more about this than you're saying. It's time to tell us what happened between von Horvach and Denise."

With an embarrassed smile, he looked around the room but remained silent. I continued, "I was in the library when you and von Horvach walked by, the day before Denise was murdered. You were asking him for money and he refused. But he said something to you, about 'the housekeeper, Denise.'"

Wolff continued his silence and Nadine intervened. "Andreas, if you don't speak up now, we'll never get to the bottom of this."

He hesitated, then sighed. "All right. I believe in loyalty, but honestly I can't think of a single reason why I should be loyal to Rudi von Horvach." Bitterly, he continued, "It's not exactly a national secret. I accumulated large gambling debts. And to pay them, I embezzled so much money from my own publishing house that it was on the verge of collapse. I even exhausted all possibilities for loans, so Rudi von Horvach was my last hope. For over thirty years I thought he was my friend. When I asked him for a loan, which I offered to repay with interest, his response was, 'I won't give you a cent. I don't owe you anything.' That's the conversation you overheard—or eavesdropped on."

Wolff stopped, apparently finished with his explanation. Hélène Benoit broke the silence, responding nervously to the mounting tension in the room. "But you haven't told us anything yet. We've been waiting for almost a year to find out what happened between Denise and von Horvach. So please just say it and get it over with."

Wolff breathed a deep sigh, then continued, "When von Horvach refused me the loan, a thought entered his mind. He said he was attracted to Denise, his housekeeper. He wanted her at any cost. So he made me an offer. 'That girl I'm interested in . . . the housekeeper, Denise. If you can persuade her to come up and spend the night with me, even if you have to pay her, I'll give you all the money you need.' Those were his terms for the loan to keep me from going to jail. I was to procure Denise as a bed partner for him. It was the most humiliating experience of my life. At that moment I hated him more than I dreamed I could ever hate anyone."

For a second, Wolff put his head down. Véronique, astonished, looked around the room and asked, "What does this mean? That Andreas killed Rudi von Horvach?"

"What?" Wolff asked, looking up, somewhat dazed. Ignoring her question, he continued, "Never in my life was I forced to do anything so low—I was no more than a pimp. But I was desperate. I went looking for her; I needed to try everything I could to persuade her. I was thinking of all kinds of arguments to convince her as I looked for her. Then an inexplicable thing happened: I found her in Matthew Pierce's room with a screwdriver right in her hand, in the act of stealing his Mozart diary. She immediately put the diary back in his briefcase, but it was too late—I had seen her. We went to my apartment and I bargained with her: if she would go up to von Horvach's room, I would get my loan and would not have to face a terrible, publicized trial and spend time in prison. But if she didn't, I would call the police, and she would have to tell them everything she knew. She cried, she said she couldn't talk to the police, that her boyfriend insisted she steal the diary. And she was terrified of what her boyfriend might do. Finally she gave in and agreed to spend the night with von Horvach. It seemed that everything would work out."

Grimacing, Wolff continued, "The next day I heard she'd been murdered. I felt responsible. Even though von Horvach made arrangements for my loan and I wasn't going to go to jail, I couldn't live with myself. By the time we arrived in Venice, I had decided to take my life. But Ilsa opened my suicide note ahead of time and Matthew found me alive. The rest we all know."

Everyone looked satisfied with Wolff's explanation. But immediately, a voice broke in: it was Hélène. Angrily, she shouted, "So you sent that innocent, unsuspecting woman up to von Horvach's room, knowing what he liked to do to women? Tie them up . . . sodomize them . . . and practically strangle them!"

"Please, Hélène," Ilsa interrupted, softly. "He knows it already. He's suffered enough."

Another voice rang out, that of Andrei's wife, Caroline. With slow, precise logic she said, "I'm sorry, Andreas. I believe you really have suffered. Except that there's one thing I know for sure: You're lying."

\*  \*  \*

The accusation was totally out of character for Caroline. Stunned, I listened as she continued, weighing her words carefully. "You said you found Denise stealing Matthew's diary. But the way you hesitated as you said it . . . and your eyes moved oddly when you spoke. It made me ask how such a coincidence could happen, that you were so lucky to catch her in Matthew's room, right in the act of stealing his diary. What are we supposed to think? That she left the door open? How did you know to look for her there? It's all too pat, too perfect. And frankly I don't believe you."

Wolff started to stammer. Unlike his previous, smooth presentation, he now couldn't speak and looked to Dr. Braun for help.

Nadine intervened. "Andreas, we need you to help us. It's now or never." She gestured to a waiter, who poured him a glass of water.

After a painful pause, Andreas began to speak. "I heard about the diary . . ."

"Oh, shut up," Manfred Braun barked, his face flushed. "Just shut up! I'll say what happened. It's not as if I committed a crime or anything." He continued his outburst. "I was the one who told him about the diary. I knew Pierce had it up in his room—after all, he told me about it. That morning, when Andreas informed me that his firm—the publishing house for my edition of the Mozart letters—was going belly up, *that* was the last straw. After all the problems I had putting together my *Mozart Millennium Edition,* his damn publishing company was going bankrupt because he had stolen all the funds. He needed some advice and I tried to help him. I told him the diary might bring a good price. And that's all."

Dennis Landry smiled. "So you suggested that Wolff steal the diary? You like to put ideas in people's heads . . . in fact, it wouldn't surprise me at all to learn that you're the one who's been slipping those malicious little notes under people's doors."

Alison Teal, who had been carefully following the discussion, suddenly began mumbling, "I'll never forget finding that ugly note under my door. It upset me so much, I couldn't sing my concert."

All eyes returned to Braun, as if demanding he admit or deny it, but he refused to speak. "So then, it's pretty clear," Landry continued with an expression of delight. "Wolff was heading—on Braun's suggestion—to Pierce's room to steal his diary, when he ran into Denise, who was doing exactly the same thing."

Alison Teal was acting bizarre, and Nadine moved next to her. The viscount asked, "Is Miss Teal going to be all right?"

Nadine asked her quietly, "Are you all right?"

Between sporadic bursts of tears and strange facial tics, Alison was losing control. All at once, she grabbed a pillbox from her handbag and swallowed several pills.

"Bring some water over here, please," Nadine said, beckoning to the waiter. Alison was now rambling incoherently. "The note was the last straw. How could Rudi do it? Why was he always so cruel to me?"

With quiet compassion, Nadine asked, "Alison, you think Rudi von Horvach sent you the note?"

"Of course he did!" she snapped.

Landry broke in abruptly. "But von Horvach couldn't have been sending the notes. They were still being slipped under people's doors long after his death."

Almost inaudibly, Alison spoke again. "What's he talking about?"

For the first time, Nicoletta Chigi spoke and the room was quiet. "Yes. I received another one last night. I have it here: 'Woe to her that is filthy and polluted.'"

"My!" Landry interjected, looking at Braun with a wicked smile. "Charming."

Nicoletta continued, "And I received this one yesterday: 'A good name is rather to be chosen than great riches.' There were also newspaper clippings about what happened to Matthew and Enrique in the monastery and about the forger murdered in Munich. But why would anyone send them to me? I can only guess it's to put ideas in my head about Maximilian. Slander—

like so many people have been doing for years. Our wedding is in three weeks and someone is determined to sabotage it. But I'm not going to let that happen. If anyone is that much of a coward, I don't want to hear what they have to say." With that, she began to rip up the pages, letting the pieces fall to the ground.

Max was beaming and gestured to her gently to say, *Sit down.*

But Landry, more and more agitated, began waving his finger at Braun. "We've already seen how Braun works—putting criminal ideas in people's heads. And now he's been caught redhanded. It must be apparent to everyone that he's the one sending the notes." Raising his voice, he asked, "Why don't you just admit it?"

Braun looked at him with total contempt and shouted, "This is just another one of your dirty tricks—to throw people off the track, because *you're* the one who's been sending them."

Nadine hastily intervened. "There's a way to find out," she said. "Did you both receive anonymous notes? Dr. Landry?"

"Yes, I did," he protested. "But I didn't keep them . . . I threw them away. I don't have time for that kind of nonsense."

Reluctantly, I said, "He's telling the truth. I saw one in his wastebasket."

Braun was livid and defensive. "But I've also been getting them," he shouted. "In fact, I just received one this morning." Reaching into his pocket, he snatched out a newspaper clipping, along with a piece of paper with the familiar pasted-on letters and read aloud, "'Be sober, be vigilant because your adversary the devil is a roaring lion, walking about and seeking whom he may devour.'"

"How interesting," Landry said sarcastically. "Everyone else gets threatening notes and you get the only encouraging one."

Ignoring Landry's comment, Nadine said simply, "Let me see that." Taking the newspaper clipping from Braun's hand, she opened her clipboard and began comparing it to a list. Finally, she looked up and directed her attention at Braun. "No one slipped this under your door."

Her comment was met with stunned silence. Nadine continued, "Dr. Pierce—Matthew—devised a means of finding out who was sending these notes and clippings. Do you want to say something about it, Matthew?"

With all eyes on me, I explained, "This morning, early, I had twenty-five newspapers delivered from all over Europe and the United States, each one different, and we kept a record of which guest received what. That clipping comes from the *Süddeutsche Zeitung*, Dr. Braun. And you were the only person to receive it."

Landry was almost delirious with excitement. "I knew it!" he said triumphantly, "I suspected all along that he was sending the notes."

Alison Teal had an immediate, violent reaction. "I don't understand. Rudi sent me that note. Were they both sending notes?"

Gently, I replied, "No, Miss Teal, Rudi didn't send you that note."

"He did, I know he did!" she said angrily.

Nadine turned her attention to Braun and all eyes followed hers. "Why did you send them?" she asked, as serious as I had ever seen her. Braun refused to say a word.

Looking directly at Braun, I said, "The anonymous notes caused a great deal of damage. You see what it did to Miss Teal. Did you deliberately want to upset her?"

Braun initially refused to speak, but suddenly he bellowed, "No, it was meant for *you*, Pierce. So that you would understand that something strange was happening with those diaries. But she changed rooms at the last moment. How could I have known she would take the room that had been prepared for you?"

For everyone else in the room, the reaction was speechless astonishment. Nadine remembered something and interrupted. "Speaking of rooms, whoever killed Rudi von Horvach had to have gone through Baroness Paumgarten's apartment to place the poisoned bath oil in his room."

Ilsa, with a shocked expression, asked, "You mean, the killer was in *our* apartment?"

"Yes," Nadine said quietly. "Because von Horvach's doors and windows were all bolted from inside, except for the one door leading from your room, since your grandmother has a fear of being trapped inside during a fire."

A voice rang out from the crowd: Baroness Paumgarten, now sitting up straight in her wheelchair as if she had just been woken from a deep sleep. "What did she say?"

"Shhhh, Grandmother," Ilsa replied.

"No," the baroness insisted. "I want to know what Nadine said about our apartment."

A hush fell over the room and everyone could hear Ilsa whisper, "Whoever killed Rudi von Horvach came through our room."

*"Ach, ja,"* she said. "Why didn't anyone ever ask me? I know who came through our room."

# CHAPTER 34

*Murder, though it have no tongue, will speak*
*With most miraculous organ*

—SHAKESPEARE, *Hamlet*

With every eye in the room riveted on the old baroness, she continued, "It was 12:47 A.M. Ilsa was out." Baroness Paumgarten spoke clearly. "I remember it perfectly. Miss Teal—Alison—came through our room wearing a gray jogging suit. Something I never saw her wear because she likes long white gowns. She walked right past me and didn't even say hello—maybe she thought I was sleeping. Afterward she came back through the room, looked outside the door for a while, and left. That's when I listened to my watch."

Instead of responding to the accusation, Alison screamed, "Rudi sent that goddamn note, I'm sure of it!"

Softly and firmly, Nadine said, "Miss Teal, the note you received was sent by Dr. Braun."

Quietly, I added, "It was meant for me. You received it by accident when you changed rooms."

Alison Teal's complexion lost all color. Seeing her rapidly deteriorating state, Caroline intervened. "Regardless of what's happened, I don't think Miss Teal can stay here any longer. She's not well."

Alison stood up and insisted, "He sent me that note!" She was becoming more unglued by the second.

"We've got to get her out of here," Caroline insisted, and Philippe joined her.

As they escorted her out, Alison mumbled, "I really loved him. Despite everything. But when he sent me that terrible note, that's when I decided I had to do it." An uncomfortable hush swept the library as people began to understand what she was saying. Within seconds, Miss Teal burst into tears. "And now he's dead. But I still loved him, even after everything he did."

As we sat in stunned silence, Caroline and Philippe led a sobbing Alison Teal to the door. I remembered my conversation with Hélène Benoit about women and children returning to the person who abused them. But when Alison thought von Horvach had turned stalker, she defended herself. All I could feel was a profound, painful sadness for her.

After she and Caroline left the room, Roberto, the young Roman architect, spoke up for the first time. "I thought von Horvach was killed by a chemist, because of all those rare poisons. How did she manage to get them all?"

Speaking tentatively, almost in a whisper, Andreas Wolff replied, "I think I know." Every eye on him, he continued, "When I was planning my suicide, I made a bizarre joke to Alison and she said that she knew everything there was to know about suicide. She gave me her worn copy of *Final Exit*—she said she practically knew it by heart—and she even mentioned the means I ultimately used, barbiturates and alcohol; that's what Alison had tried. But she also told me she spent years going to spas, picking up advice from specialists in herbal medicine. And then she confided something very odd—I'm surprised I didn't remember it until now. For years, she was secretly researching ways to commit suicide that were guaranteed to work. She must have collected an arsenal of poisons, and then decided to use them all on Rudi von Horvach when she thought she was in danger."

Véronique stood up and looked accusingly at the group. "So, Alison Teal staged the whole thing with the lozenges and losing her voice so no one would suspect her. But just in case no one noticed, she almost poisoned me." Indignantly, she continued, "I just hope no one feels sorry for her—it was cold-blooded and premeditated. If my fiancé hadn't recognized my symptoms, I'd be dead now."

As Véronique waited for some kind of demonstration of solidarity, everyone remained quiet. Impatiently, she looked around the room, then shouted, "I get it now. Everyone here feels sorry for Alison Teal and no one even cares that I almost died." She continued to wait for any trace of sympathy or support, but her gaze was met with silence.

"I look around this room and I understand the reason you don't give a damn about me: to all of you I'm nothing more than a poor black girl from Philadelphia. But you know what you all are? A bunch of racists."

Standing up, Elisabetta von Stahl said, "That's the last straw. I'm leaving." As she turned to walk toward the door, Roberto raced to block the exit.

"Please," he said, "don't leave now. I beg you to stay."

Visibly caught off guard, Elisabetta hesitated. Then, with an icy tone, she said, "All right." Returning to her seat, she beckoned to Roberto and commanded, "Sit here." After he joined her, she sat, glacial and aloof. "We've been here all this time," she said. "Couldn't we at least have something to drink?"

The viscount nodded to Philippe, who immediately unleashed an army of waiters with champagne and other beverages. "Perhaps," the viscount said dryly, "a drink will loosen up a few tongues."

After the atmosphere relaxed with the passing of champagne, I spoke softly to Véronique. "I don't think Alison Teal is going to be singing again for a long, long time."

Nadine added, "Véronique, I'm not taking her side, I'm not saying what she did to you wasn't terrible. But perhaps it's best, given the circumstances, that we try to start the process of healing."

The viscount had been staring at Braun, who refused to look at him. Finally, the viscount spoke. "For all the years I've known you, Manfred, I would *never* have believed you could do such a thing, in my own home where I welcomed you. And even now, you deny any responsibility for the results of your actions."

Braun shook his head. "Just like you, Viscount, I've known for a long time that something is very wrong with these Mozart diaries. What I've been doing is warning people. And if it had not been for my clippings, no one would have associated the murders with the diaries. Even you wouldn't have made the connection."

The viscount looked unconvinced, and Nadine broke in. "Then why didn't you just tell people your suspicions? An honest person doesn't have to send ugly, intimidating notes."

"All right," Braun finally said. "But I was scared. I had received offers to publish newly discovered diaries of Mozart. And time after time, the offer was retracted. Someone would send me a diary, like Pierce did, and Arnold Schott in Geneva, and after a while, they asked for it back. Then the diaries started disappearing without a trace! Those diaries would have made my edition of the Mozart letters the most widely read scholarly work of the century. Then, when I started to realize that people were being eliminated—like Schott, whose face was kicked in, and his . . . his . . ." He stopped short of conveying all the details. ". . . his body dumped in Lake Geneva, I got scared. And the same thing could easily happen to me. What was I supposed to do? One by one, right before my eyes, the diaries were disappearing. So I did what I could—I sent out notes and clippings to see what kind of reaction they would provoke."

Sensing that Braun was not coming completely clean, I interrupted. "You mentioned Arnold Schott and me contacting you about the diaries. But you haven't told us everything. When I was in Salzburg, I visited the mother of Georg Pahlmann. And there was a letter from you in his files."

Andrei spoke up next. "And there's something else you're not telling us. The day you read about the murder of the forger, Peter Arneis, you almost passed out."

Braun sat motionless, his lips sealed, and Nadine spoke. "Tell us."

When he remained silent, I repeated soberly, "Please, tell us, now."

But Braun had made up his mind not to speak. Andreas Wolff finally broke the silence. "Manfred," he said, "I realize there's much more going on than what you've told me. The day after Peter Arneis was murdered, you broke down and confided in me that you had been involved with him."

Immediately, I asked Dr. Braun, "Did Arneis contact you, or did you contact him first?"

Nadine followed my lead. "How did it happen? We have to know."

Braun cleared his voice. "It's very dangerous to talk about these things." Landry, rolling his eyes and making derisive laughs under his breath, was apparently unnerving him, preventing him from speaking. Looking blankly around the room, Braun said, "I've seen too many people killed . . . in horrible ways. And, frankly, I don't want to end up like that myself."

With cool logic, the viscount spoke. "Manfred, you're the one person who appears to have the answers. You can redeem yourself in some part for the harm you've caused. The decision is yours. Tell us now what you know."

Braun, with all the color drained from his face, sat frozen in silence. The entire room sat riveted as he tried to decide. He made an attempt to speak, but the words remained lodged in his throat. Then, as if finally getting a burden off his chest, he spoke. Bitterly he said, "I know all about Peter Arneis and the forgeries. After all, I commissioned him to make them."

The guests sat in stunned silence and I felt a sense of bewildered disbelief. Coolly, Braun continued, "The forger, Arneis, contacted me. He wanted to sell me something: a Mozart diary, the one that later sold for eight hundred thousand dollars in Zurich. I took one look at it and laughed in his face. It had obviously been written by some amateur who knew nothing about Mozart except what they had seen in the film *Amadeus*. But it had a few lines that astonished me, describing a lawsuit against Mozart by Prince Lichnowsky, something we've only known about recently. And when I examined it more carefully, I realized the lines were identical to a fragment I had been sent by Georg Pahlmann, who owns a rare books shop in Salzburg. So I confronted Arneis, not knowing he was a forger. I told him he owned a pastiche, a forgery that incorporates an authentic element—in this case, the tiny fragment from Pahlmann in Salzburg."

No one moved as Braun spoke. "Then," Braun said, "since I wouldn't buy Arneis's diary, he offered to sell me information about other diaries. When I told him I already knew about other diaries, that I had photocopies of several, he astounded me: he offered to make exact eighteenth-century copies from the photocopies I had in my possession."

Braun continued, "I thought seriously about his offer—I couldn't publish the photocopies of the diaries that were disappearing, but Arneis said he could make me copies so exact, no one would ever know which were the originals. I borrowed every cent I could and paid him. And for every photocopy I gave him—of diaries sent by scholars who suddenly decided to ask for them back—Arneis returned perfect copies on eighteenth-century paper, written with the original quill technique."

Braun's face began trembling. "And he paid for it with his life. I've already said too much. The way they tortured him for hours—with the rope tightening around his neck each time he moved—it sickens me."

Quietly, I interrupted. "Dr. Braun, they weren't planning to kill Arneis. The two men hired to do the job—the ones who tied him up—only wanted to scare him, to get him to tell them what he knew about the other diaries. It was the arrival of the police that chased them away, and when his door was broken down, Arneis strangled."

Braun looked confused, and Nadine continued, "We know this because the police in Munich got an anonymous tip from Bruno Abruzzese, who was hired for the job in Munich to scare Arneis into telling what he knew about the diaries. But after Abruzzese killed Denise, he was taken off the job and brutally beaten up. As revenge, he made the anonymous call to the police about Arneis. Then, alone in Munich, Abruzzese was guilt-stricken for having killed Denise and spent days trying to make a last confession before jumping from the Frauenkirche."

Andrei cleared his voice. "There's a question no one's addressing. Who is behind all of this? Who hired Abruzzese and the men who tied up the forger?"

All eyes returned to Braun. Quietly but firmly, Nadine asked, "Who are they?"

In a surprising outburst, he said, "How should I know? I've done everything I can to figure it out."

"Just tell us who you think is behind it," I said softly.

Braun looked around the room. "I only have suspicions."

"Then say what they are," Nadine insisted.

Involuntarily, Braun's eyes darted to Landry, but he repeated, "I have no proof whatsoever."

Landry interrupted. "It's clear to me, he's caught in his own trap. He's admitted he's been sending out ugly anonymous notes and that he's had documents forged. It's pretty clear to me that he's finished in the academic world . . . and good riddance."

Nadine tried to interrupt, but Landry could not be restrained. "Anyone who has so flagrantly betrayed the ethics and ideals of his profession should be prosecuted."

Braun remained quiet until the viscount turned to him. "Manfred, it sounds to me like you used the anonymous notes to alert us—like a 'warning angel.' And you apparently have access to information that no one else has. So tell us your suspicions now. Warn us, not by slipping pasted-up notes under people's doors, but by saying it out in the open."

Thinking intensely, Braun debated whether or not to speak. Again I intervened. "If we don't find out what's been happening, the killing's going to continue. How many people have to die?"

Braun was uncomfortable. Speaking in terse, clipped phrases, he said, "I don't know . . . for sure . . . who's responsible." Looking directly at Landry, he said, "But there are some things that just don't fit."

All eyes were fixed on Braun. "Like this English edition of the Mozart letters that Landry has scheduled for 2006, the same year my edition is coming out. Andreas Wolff and I sat down and calculated how much an edition like his would cost, just for the printing alone, and it came to far more than the selling price. Where is all the money coming from?"

All eyes went immediately to Dr. Landry. Indignantly, he replied, "That has nothing to do with what we're talking about. We're talking about criminal activity . . . commissioning forgeries."

"Is it true?" Nadine asked Landry, ignoring his rhetoric. "Is there some kind of financing behind your edition that allows you to sell it for less than it costs you to print?"

"You certainly don't expect me to talk about my business affairs," Landry snapped. "And to think that he's been waging this campaign of slander against me all because of some petty, unfounded suspicions."

"No, but there's something else," Andrei said. "A friend of mine in Salzburg—an Englishman with a Ph.D. in musicology—told me you authenticated the diary Braun was talking about, with all the clichés from *Amadeus*. In other words, you authenticated a fake."

"I've heard enough!" Landry shouted. "I have better things to do than sit here and listen to unfounded accusations. I'm leaving." Rising to his feet, he started to walk directly toward the door. When no one intervened to discourage him from leaving, he turned and said to the viscount, "I've had to listen to all of this. Enough is enough."

The viscount responded dryly, "No one is forcing you to stay against your will. But if you leave, it's an admission of guilt."

Landry contemplated what his departure would mean. Almost as quickly, he returned to his seat. "Then let's get it over with," he barked. "It's probably better that I stay. Otherwise these lies and innuendos would be made behind my back."

Immediately, I returned where the questioning had left off. "Dr. Landry, we need to know who your business associates are."

Landry insisted, "That's out of the question."

Nadine intervened delicately. "But we do know who paid Arneis—a check from Girard Resource Development was deposited in his account. And we've just confirmed that one of their clients is Syndicat International, one of the most flagrant crime organizations in the world. Have you had any dealings with GRD?"

Landry looked horrified. Just as he was about to speak, a different voice rang out, Maximilian De Angelis saying, "That's enough."

Taking his cue from Max, Landry shook his head. "I'm sorry," he replied. "I won't talk about my business associates."

Wolff continued to press him. "But what does this all mean? That you and Max are business partners?"

Nicoletta, who had been keenly following the discussion, looked at Max, who spoke to her calmly, as if to a child. "It's bad business practice to reveal the names of clients who have specifically asked to remain anonymous."

Nadine pressed on. "Who is going to tell us? Is it going to be you, Dr. Landry, or you, Max?"

Neither spoke and the viscount intervened. "Max, I heard a client of yours offered Matthew Pierce seven hundred fifty thousand dollars for his diary. Is that true?"

Looking uncomfortable, Max replied with exaggerated politeness, "*Monseigneur,* I'm not at liberty to reveal anything about my clients."

"Then tell us what you *are* at liberty to reveal!" the viscount said, raising his voice. "What is your role in the Mozart diaries?"

With every eye on him, Max looked at Nicoletta and said, "For me, the diaries are a business investment. That's all."

Immediately, I said, "That's not enough."

"Max," the viscount continued, with slow, simmering anger, "if you don't tell us what your role has been, I'm going to be forced to assume the worst—that you are responsible for what's happened."

Apparently unwilling to take responsibility in front of Nicoletta and the viscount, Max hesitated. Then slowly, he began to speak. "The diaries are, and have always been, my own personal project. Long before anyone else ever knew about them. I'm the person who decided to buy them."

There was a piercing silence in the room. Max continued, "Long before anyone else had heard about Mozart diaries, I had an offer to buy the first one that turned up. I've always had an interest in art, rare books, and antiques. My investment company specializes in locating investment opportunities for corporations and private clients, so it was a perfect merger of art and commercial interests."

"So you bought the diaries for clients as a business investment?" Nadine asked. "I find that difficult to believe . . . their prices are so inflated, they're only valuable on paper."

Without flinching, Max said, "Well, that's part of what my company does. We look for legitimate means to offset windfall profits that would put clients in higher tax brackets."

"In other words," I interrupted, "you devise money-laundering schemes."

Trying to keep his composure, Max snapped, "You can call it what you want, Pierce. I don't ask my clients where their profits come from; it's none of my business."

Wolff broke in. "And Landry's edition—is that a legitimate way to offset windfall profits?"

"I don't care to discuss that," Max replied. "Client confidentiality."

The viscount intervened. "So your clients bought the diaries at high prices regardless of whether they were forgeries?"

With reluctance, Max replied, "Yes. But this information can never leave this room. I was instructed to spend as much as necessary in order to guarantee the highest bid. That's all . . . they were an investment."

Andrei asked, "I'm confused. The diaries are forgeries?"

Max did not respond, so the viscount turned to Braun. "You said you saw many of them. What do you think? Are they forgeries?"

Braun spoke slowly, gauging every word. "Some are clearly fakes, as we've all heard. Like the *Amadeus* diary, which is a far-fetched forgery based on a tiny, authentic fragment. But Schott's Geneva diary was authentic; I don't have the slightest doubt about it."

"Dr. Landry," the viscount continued, "what do you think?"

In a decidedly pompous tone, Landry said, "The Naples

diary is clearly colored by the illness of the woman who wrote it, Bianca di San Felice," he replied. "The duchess was afflicted with sexual delusions before she died. But it has the ring of eyewitness testimony."

When he finished speaking, the viscount looked to me. "Matthew?"

"In my opinion," I said, "the main body of text of the Prague diary was by Mozart. But parts of it were forged, probably by a monk who disapproved of Mozart's candid admiration for Casanova."

The viscount continued questioning me. "And the diary you found in Milan?"

With all eyes on me, I replied, "During my convalescence, I contacted a number of Italian historians, who all say it contains rare, unusual information known only to specialists. Also, I compared watermarks and Mozart's handwriting at the time, and everything points to it being authentic."

"Unfortunately, Pierce," Landry countered, "you have a vested interest. The diary will have to be examined by others, many others, before any decision can be made."

Looking at Dr. Braun, I asked, "You examined it. What do you think?"

Pausing to gather his thoughts, Braun replied, "At first, there were things about it that bothered me: like the idea of Mozart saying he had been robbed of his childhood. Because in the eighteenth century, childhood was generally not romanticized like that."

Something critical occurred to Nadine and she said, "I sent a page to a man in Chicago who runs an optical laboratory. He uses polarized light and scanning electron microscopes to examine the ink and compared it with other pages from the eighteenth century. And he concluded, without a doubt, that the Mozart Milan diary is authentic. Arneis could fake handwriting using eighteenth-century paper, but no one can duplicate the molecular composition of ink that's over two hundred years old."

Looking at Braun, the viscount asked, "So what do you think now?"

Braun remained deep in thought until he broke his silence. "Then I'm inclined to believe it's by Mozart."

I felt an enormous wave of satisfaction sweeping over me; the foremost authority on Mozart documents had finally given me the answer I had been waiting over a year to hear.

Staring at Braun, the elderly Baroness Paumgarten interrupted, "And to think you called this young man a tenth-rate musicologist in front of everyone."

Immediately, another thought occurred to me. "There's something I've always wanted to ask you. The day I asked for the diary back, you seemed to know what I was going to say. The exact words, in fact. How do you explain that?"

Braun remained silent and Landry barked impatiently, "Why don't you just come out and say it. You've admitted just about everything else under the sun."

"All right," Braun shouted. "It's about time to get these things out in the open. Like your disgusting scheme to wrest my edition from me and ruin my reputation."

Without flinching, Landry replied sarcastically, "And how do you know about it?"

Braun shot back, "What difference does it make? The point is that you plotted to destroy me, and now you're exposed for what you are—a ruthless, twisted schemer."

"After what we've heard," Landry retorted, "you're hardly in a position to call anyone names." Deliberately prodding him, Landry continued, "So, you've been spying on us."

"No," Braun answered bitterly. "It wasn't spying. Peter Arneis, the forger, called it corporate espionage; big organizations with huge financial resources do it all the time to get their information. He offered to arrange it for me, and for once in my life, I knew what was going on."

Landry was livid. "So you paid someone to eavesdrop on me, isn't that it? Who, my chauffeur?"

"And keys?" Philippe asked immediately. "Like the master key that was missing from my desk for two days?"

When Braun didn't reply, Philippe shook his head in disgust. The viscount looked stunned.

After a long, painful pause, I said, "There's still something I don't understand—how a fake like the *Amadeus* diary could sell for eight hundred thousand dollars."

Braun shouted, "Landry claimed it was an authentic Mozart diary. He fell for an obvious forgery."

His comment hit a nerve, and Landry was clearly defensive. As Landry tried to explain, Braun plunged ahead. "With all your pretensions, all your corporate money, you put your name on a fake that was practically scripted from that stupid film."

Landry lashed back, "It's not that I didn't spot it—"

In a surprising burst of anger, Maximilian stood up and shouted at Landry, "That's enough."

An uncomfortable hush swept the room. The viscount, who had been following the events attentively, fixed his gaze on Max, then Landry. The viscount asked Landry, "What were you going to say?"

With all eyes on him, Landry sighed, then slowly began to speak. Maximilian, who had been glaring at him, again interrupted. "Not one more word . . ."

The viscount glared at Landry, waiting for him to continue. As Landry opened his mouth to speak, Max suddenly stood up and thrust his hand into the breast pocket of his dinner jacket forcefully. Landry's face blanched completely, and he froze in midword, his mouth open. In disbelief, he whispered, "My God, he's going to kill me."

In the silence, the entire room sat motionless. Staring at Max, Landry stammered, "I wasn't going to say anything."

With every eye in the room fixed on him, Max slowly drew out a silver cigarette box and sat down. He held it up and said with a debonair tone, "I hope no one's going to tell me I can't smoke in here!"

No one was amused, particularly the viscount. "So you're trying to intimidate my guests?" he asked, raising his voice. "To defeat the purpose of everything we're doing here? You think this is all a joke?"

Max looked directly at the viscount. "He already said everything he was going to say."

I could no longer hold back. "Dr. Landry, you started to say something about the *Amadeus* diary. Why you fell for a fake."

Landry, still white, replied softly, "I just wanted to make it clear to everyone that I immediately recognized that the diary was a fake."

Max's demeanor again changed. "*Shut up,* I said."

The painful silence that followed was interrupted by Nadine. "Maximilian, you're determined to keep Dr. Landry from talking. Then *you* tell us: if he knew the diary was a fake, why did he authenticate it?"

De Angelis took a few seconds to think, then crossed his arms and said, "It's a private matter. *Basta.*" He sat back in his chair, making no attempt to disguise his disgust.

"Then," I countered, "if you won't tell us, at least let Dr. Landry finish what he was going to say."

Nadine continued, "Dr. Landry, you'll have to tell us why you authenticated a forgery."

Although he was clearly shaken, he refused to speak. Cautiously, I intervened. "If you don't explain what's going on, then there's only one conclusion." The room was completely still. "You and your edition are linked to organized crime."

"No!" Landry protested. He was clearly in conflict: to explain his role was the only way to exonerate his reputation and that of his edition. Very tentatively, he said, "It was just a business deal, a private matter. I was assured it would disappear from circulation, that no one would ever know about it. A deal to help finance my edition of the Mozart letters. That's all there is to it."

Again I intervened. "That's not enough. The man who forged that diary was murdered. Who told you to say the diary was authentic?"

Landry looked at Max, who remained silent. Nadine spoke up. "I know more now about what happened to that diary. The auction in Zurich was only the first time it was sold. It was then purchased by Capital Investment Corporation in the Bahamas for 1.8 million dollars and a month later by the Finance Bank of Luxembourg for 4.1 million. The list is pretty long and we have a few gaps, but the last purchase we've been able to trace is to the

Credit Corporation of the Ivory Coast for eighty-six million dollars."

A gasp was heard around the room. Landry looked like he would choke, and couldn't resist staring at Max, who sat simmering with rage. Nadine continued, "Over eighty-six million dollars for a fake. It's probably now in a bank vault somewhere, with the investment strictly on paper."

But Landry was not about to utter another word. Nadine continued, "The men who tried to get Arneis to talk learned their techniques from the Mafia. Don't you find that odd? They tied his ankles, then his wrists behind his back, then his neck, and they explained how he was going to die: every time he moved, the rope would tighten, choking him slowly. Then they said that if he didn't tell them everything, it would break his neck. I'm sure he tried to stay still, but in that cramped, uncomfortable position, every tiny movement of his body, every breath he took, made the ropes dig in deeper. The kind of thugs they hire for that work enjoy it, and I'm sure it went on for hours. And when they heard the police coming, they took off. After torturing Arneis for hours, they didn't even bother to cut him loose. So he ended up exactly like they told him he would—with his neck broken."

As Landry's discomfort grew, Max's stare bored into him. Again I prodded him. "It's pretty clear now that you and your edition are linked to organized crime."

Landry began to mumble, "It was all the fault of that stupid English musicologist. Why did he have to show up out of nowhere?"

Seeing Landry beginning to lose control, Max interrupted, "What are you trying to do, Nadine? Intimidate sniveling cowards?"

The color in Landry's face had drained. After an excruciating pause, he said, "I didn't know anything about them at first. I only figured it out when they told me I had to authenticate that damn diary."

"*Basta,*" Max said forcefully. "Enough!"

My response was swift. "Let him talk," I shouted.

Landry was rapidly coming unraveled. "I always said it was a fake, but they had already paid so much for it. That's when it was decided—they needed them all, and would continue to buy them up even if they were fakes. They made me understand that I had to say it was genuine. But it was the way they did it . . . they showed me photos of what happened to their client, Arnold Schott, mutilated beyond recognition, his parts cut off and sewn into his mouth." He continued, "They weighed him down and dumped him in Lake Geneva. Because he double-crossed them, they said."

"Double-crossed them?" Nadine repeated.

"*Basta,*" Max insisted.

By now Landry was almost hysterical. "He sold them the diary that had to disappear, and then he had Peter Arneis make a copy of it. Schott was the one who thought of having Arneis make copies of the diaries. And after all the money they paid him."

With each word, Maximilian De Angelis was becoming more and more agitated. When Landry stopped for a second, I asked, "*They?* Who are *they?*"

With the entire room hanging on Landry's every word, he stopped. Then he looked at Max, who was seething with anger. After a moment of hesitation, a decisive expression crossed Landry's face—he had finally decided to reveal what he knew.

# CHAPTER 35

*The curious crime, the fine
felicity and flower of wickedness.*

—ROBERT BROWNING

Landry protested. "It wasn't my fault; I would never have gotten involved with them if I had known. At the beginning, I thought I was dealing only with Max and his company, the Swiss Investment Consortium. Everything went through them. They were all professional . . . leather briefcases and business suits. Until I wouldn't authenticate that fake diary. Then new people came in, from GRD. And I understood immediately—it was a front. I should have realized that it was all too good to be true—" When he realized what he had said, Landry stopped abruptly.

"And now," he continued, "they're going to get rid of me, just like they did Peter Arneis and Arnold Schott and that rare books dealer in Salzburg."

Braun interrupted. "No one got rid of the rare books dealer in Salzburg, thanks to me. I kept sending him anonymous notes and clippings, and he decided to stage his own death. He's gone into hiding . . . I saved his life."

Maximilian De Angelis, now more livid than I had ever seen him, lashed out violently. "I've never heard such a crock in my life." Turning to Braun, he shouted, "No one was going to kill him. You did him more harm than good. The notes you've been sending have just made people crazy. Just look how you upset my fiancée, and what you did to Alison Teal! You're even responsible for von Horvach's death!"

Nicoletta, who had been watching Maximilian, spoke with characteristic calm, unaffected by all the emotions surging around her. "Max," she asked quietly, "do you know who's behind the killings?"

With a surprisingly docile tone, Max answered, "No, Nikki. As you know, I have been managing the Swiss Investment Consortium for eight years. We make all kinds of investments . . . sometimes they're not very attractive to some people, but they're always legal. In the world of business, it's a simple fact that certain kinds of deals have to be made. And just because the United States has an embargo against this country or that . . . those countries still need the same things that every other country needs. So the problem is how to get it to them without breaking the law."

Nadine spoke up immediately. "And what kinds of things do they need, Max? Chemical and biological weapons, nuclear technology that gives them the capacity to build missiles that have only one purpose?"

Enraged by Nadine's provocation, Maximilian barked, "Don't preach to me, Nadine. The only issue that concerns me is whether or not it breaks the law."

"And if it breaks the law," Nadine replied angrily, "what do you do? Find a loophole, or transfer the deal to the Bahamas, or to Monte Carlo, or to Liberia?"

"You are so incredibly naïve," Max shouted. "This is a world of business. Business is what runs this world, it's what keeps it going. From the first moment there were two people on this planet, there was business. And as the world gets more and more complex, business gets more complex. But it's always been the primary force running everything. And after all the centuries, all the millenniums of war, business is still here. And so are we, aren't we?"

No one spoke. When Nadine finally went on, it was with calm logic. "It's still corruption. Plain, simple corruption."

"Don't use that tone of voice on me," Maximilian barked. "Corruption . . . what is it, anyway? What's corrupt to one person is legal to another. Look at the Catholic Church throughout the centuries. How they burned all those who didn't agree with them. Through all their wars, all the wealth they accumulated . . . if they were going to do something corrupt, they had an entire army of theologians say it was God's will. Corruption is nothing more than a word—it's just a fucking point of view."

The room was silent, until a voice emerged, that of the viscount. "Who is responsible for destroying the statues of my house? And killing the deer in my park? You say you don't know who's responsible for the murders, but you must have some idea who would commit such an act."

Max hesitated. Gauging every word, he said, "I have to be very careful about what I say."

The viscount was more resolute than I had ever seen him. "Is it the organization you work for? If so, why don't you just get out of it?"

"There are some business relationships, *Monseigneur*," Max said slowly, "where you can't just leave whenever you feel like it. When you become privy to certain information, you become indispensable, so to speak."

"Whoever they are," the viscount continued, "what are they trying to say by killing my deer and decapitating my priceless statues?"

"Some people," Max said quietly, "are not happy this meeting is taking place. But I can't say anything more. I admit I'm in over my head."

As Max sat motionless, Nadine went on. "You would have us believe you're a pawn in the hands of a ruthless organization. But I, for one, don't buy it. I've followed your business career, and seen how you spent the last twenty years buying and selling to anyone who would pay the price. And it seems to me you never did anything illegal . . . nothing that you could go to jail for, at least. Until a year and a half ago, when you crossed the line."

Max suddenly sat up. "That's preposterous," he replied.

"And I know," Nadine continued, "thanks to the confession Bruno Abruzzese made before he died. He named the people he was working for—and one of the names he cited was Maximilian De Angelis."

"You're bluffing," he said.

"And you sent the killer to the monastery," I interjected.

"That's a lie," he replied. Looking at Nicoletta, Max continued, "This is all a lie. They're lying."

Nicoletta looked momentarily disoriented and Nadine took advantage of the silence. Speaking directly to Max, she continued, "You were once the director of a legitimate investment corporation with a few clients from the world of international crime. But a year and a half ago, you decided to make the change. You were among several people invited aboard a yacht docked off the coast of the Bahamas. And I received a report from a reliable source that you were escorted to a private island where a meeting of the board of directors of Syndicat International took place."

Jumping up from his chair, Max shouted, "This is all a lie. I'm leaving." Looking at Nicoletta, he said, "We're leaving."

Quietly, Nadine turned to Nicoletta. "My uncle and I have known you since you were a child, your family is one of the greatest in Europe. But if you go through with this marriage, you'll drag your family name down beyond repair."

Enraged, Max continued, "This whole thing has been made up to destroy our marriage." Regaining his composure, he stopped and said quietly, "Nicoletta, listen to me. I love you— more than anyone or anything I have ever loved in my life. And I swear to you, they're lying. If you believe this nonsense, then stay here with all these fools. But if you love me, and believe in me, come with me now."

Holding out his hand to her, Max repeated, "Nicoletta . . . come with me . . . now."

Every eye in the room was on her. Max insisted again, "Nicoletta, I love you. Come with me, now."

As he waited for Nicoletta's reaction, a painful silence descended upon the room.

## CHAPTER 36

*Thou blind fool, Love, what dost thou to mine eyes*
*That they behold, and see not what they see?*

—SHAKESPEARE, *Sonnet* 135

Inexplicably, Nicoletta rose from her seat. And without looking at anyone, she reached silently for Maximilian's hand. In disbelief, I watched as they walked out together slowly, leaving the doors wide open behind them.

After they had disappeared from sight, Roberto stood up and screamed, "Goddamn it, why doesn't she see him for what he is?" Abruptly, he burst out crying, saying, "We were in love." People sat motionless as Roberto, head down, sobbed uncontrollably, pouring out his grief.

The guests of the foundation had been sitting for hours. By now, everyone was emotionally exhausted. Nadine sensed the mood and said, "With Max gone, I can't see any benefit in prolonging our meeting. If no one can think of a reason why we shouldn't adjourn . . . "

Eagerly, the guests began to get up. Philippe stood up quickly to say, "There will be a midnight buffet in the dining room." As everyone began to move in that direction, I chose to remain in the library to exchange a few words with Nadine. From the dining room, the familiar sounds of conversation began to mount steadily, and gradually they became a soft, tired roar in the distance.

With Ilsa at his side, Roberto sat slumped in his chair, drained of tears, as Nadine, the viscount, Štěpán, and I took seats near him. From the large doors, Andreas Wolff reemerged holding a plate of finger food, which he offered to each of us. He was followed by Jano, carrying tall glasses and a bucket with a bottle of champagne. Roberto, visibly depleted from his ordeal, refused Jano's offer, but within minutes, Elisabetta von Stahl arrived like a Minervan goddess, holding a chilled glass of draft beer. "Philippe told me what you like to drink," she said to Roberto. Smiling at her, he took a sip, but the disoriented expression again swept across his face.

As we sat together, Wolff turned to Nadine and the viscount. "So, what happens now?" he asked ironically. "More Syndicat International? More murders?"

Nadine spoke openly. "Syndicat International . . . we're learning more about it every day. But by the time we get the concrete documentation we need, it's reorganized as something else, in a new country, and the next day it's business as usual. And who knows what their next scheme will be? Maximilian initiated the whole project with the Mozart diaries because he sees himself as a great connoisseur of art and culture. But it ended up as just another money-laundering scheme—one of thousands. Unfortunately, it started him in directions where there's no turning back."

Andreas Wolff interrupted. "I didn't exactly follow how they did it . . . to get the value of a fake diary up to eighty-six million, for example."

Nadine replied, "It's an ingenious scheme and not at all a bad investment for those corporations affiliated with SIN. They were each guaranteed that a diary would be bought and sold for a return of over one hundred percent on their money. Those toward the end of the chain could easily stand to make twenty to forty million dollars for the transaction—not bad for a day's work. For the corporation left holding the diary at the end, it was only value on paper, but an opportunity to disguise massive illegal profits. So I suspect the final sale of each diary has been to a high-ranking member in the SIN family, who will keep it forever deposited in a bank vault somewhere."

"In private hands," I said, repeating the phrase so familiar in catalogues of Mozart's autograph scores and letters. Thinking aloud, I continued, "But they needed all of them. A kind of monopoly."

Nadine added, "So they can justify the extraordinary expenditures to their respective governments, who won't be able to challenge them."

Looking lost in thought, Ilsa said, "The part that makes me the saddest is what happened to poor Denise: to have left Rudi von Horvach's apartment after all she went through, with all those welts and bruises. And then to have to explain them to an insanely jealous boyfriend, who killed people for a living."

Elisabetta added, "Literally walking from one abusive man to another. Talk about fate being cruel."

Wolff looked over at the viscount, who looked tired, and asked, "How are you doing?"

Viscount de Laguerelle replied, "You might say, I'm beginning to feel all ninety-four of my years."

I ventured to speak. "I never expected Max to get up and leave like that. I was planning to confront him in front of Nicoletta. He tried everything in his power to get me to sell him the diary, and when he discovered the microphone Enrique planted, he decided to have my hot water heater sabotaged. Then he sent the killer to Prague. There's no question—Enrique's blood is on his hands."

Nadine answered, "I have to admit, I also never expected Max to just get up and walk out . . . and with Nicoletta. But it's all over now. We can't change the past."

"Andreas," I said, "you once told me you knew something about Max, that if Nicoletta knew, there would be no marriage."

He hesitated, then replied, "Max is a sexual tank, fucking everything in his path."

Skeptically, I asked, "And you think Nicoletta would leave him if she knew?"

Ilsa interrupted quietly. "I don't think it would make any difference now. She's already made up her mind to stay with him. I'm afraid what they say is true . . . love is blind."

Elisabetta, sitting comfortably at Roberto's side, answered, "But believe me, marriage restores its sight. Give them time."

Ilsa replied quietly, "No, they're in it for the long run. That's how it all begins, like with wives of Mafia members. They try to bury their heads in the sand because they love their husbands, but ultimately they end up living in a state of perpetual denial."

"What I'll never understand," I said, "is how Max found me at the monastery."

Wolff replied, "What did Braun call it? Corporate espionage. Apparently, there's been a lot of it going on."

Weakly, the viscount said, "That's something I can make sure never happens again at La Favorite."

Wolff asked Nadine, "So what happens now?"

Nadine replied, "We almost never get the kingpins, only the small fish."

With characteristic irony, Elisabetta replied, "And in case you didn't notice, this time you didn't even get the small fish."

Our intimate party was getting restless, and Wolff, Ilsa, and Elisabetta were soon standing up to join the other guests at the buffet dinner. The viscount appeared hesitant to leave and remained seated with Nadine, Štěpán, and me, along with Roberto, who looked comatose, unable to speak or react. "But at least we know now," I said. "Alison Teal killed Rudi von Horvach because she thought he was stalking her. Braun paid Arneis to forge copies of the diaries. And Max masterminded the whole money-laundering scheme." As an afterthought, I added, "And Max's business associates hired Abruzzese to get inside La Favorite."

Instead of the acknowledgment I expected from Nadine and the viscount, there was complete silence. "That's it, isn't it?" I repeated.

Nadine finally replied, "Yes, that's it."

The viscount, visibly irritated, suddenly spoke up. "Let's drop this ruse, Nadine. We've done something reprehensible, and it's time to admit it."

Nadine gestured to him to stop, but he continued, "All this talk about allowing people to tell what they know. And all the time, we've been hiding the truth from everyone."

"Please, Uncle René," Nadine said. "Don't do this."

"I don't care," he replied. "I'll never have peace of mind

until I say it. We're responsible for the murder of Denise." For a minute, I couldn't believe my ears. Looking directly at Nadine, the viscount continued, "You and your bodyguard convinced me to do it."

Nadine's face blanched completely. "It was a legitimate mistake," she insisted. "There was no way we could have known."

The revelation was too much for me. "What exactly did you do?"

"We were the ones who hired Abruzzese," the viscount shouted. Exasperated, he continued, "We brought in that lowlife and gave him complete access to La Favorite at night."

Stunned, I asked, "But why?"

Furious, the viscount replied, "To wire La Favorite for electronic surveillance. I knew it was a complete violation of privacy, but I agreed to it anyway. I had to know what was going on. And in taking that step, we created a living nightmare."

Nadine was visibly nervous. "Uncle René, you're not being fair to yourself or to me. Abruzzese wasn't the man we hired."

"You were supposed to be here when we hired him," the viscount screamed. Seeing the viscount in a hysterical state was unnerving.

"I had a crisis in my department," Nadine replied defensively. "There was no way of knowing someone else had been sent in his place."

"Who sent him in?" I asked, trying to intervene.

"Max and his associates, of course," Nadine blurted out. "They outwitted us."

"But we're just as bad as Max," the viscount continued. "He took a step in directions where there's no turning back, and so did we."

Nadine interrupted. "Please don't say that, Uncle René. We're not as bad as Max."

"This is making my head spin," I said. "So, the whole time we were here, you were eavesdropping on us. And the information was also going to Max?"

Nadine spoke quietly. "Between that and Braun bribing the chauffeurs, we found ourselves in the middle of a war."

"And the bankcard you gave me?" I asked the viscount.

Nadine spoke up. "Nothing elaborate . . . a computer chip. With your position monitored by satellite. That was for your own safety."

"Keeping tabs on me," I said, getting more enraged by the minute. "Except that all your surveillance ended up in the hands of Max and whoever else he's working for—Syndicat International?"

Neither Nadine nor the viscount spoke, and their silence indicated that what I had said was true.

The viscount spoke slowly. "I take full responsibility for what happened. I invited all these artists and friends, and at a certain point, I sat back and watched. And La Favorite turned into a place like the church in your Milan diary where they allowed vipers and poisonous snakes to run loose."

Stunned, I asked, "How do you know about the church in Milan? I never discussed it with anyone."

Taken aback, the viscount hesitated. Then he blurted out, "Do you really believe for one second that I didn't look at your diary in my safe? After all I've been through to find out what's going on?"

Dumbfounded, I replied, "This is too much for me to handle."

Softly, Nadine said, "You really must hate us."

Unable to reply, I looked away. Finally, I said to the viscount, bitterly, "All your talk about idealism and changing the world with a single act. And you and Nadine were the only people I believed in."

The viscount looked as if he had just been slapped. In a surprisingly humble tone, he replied, "At ninety-four I don't have much time left."

I was speechless as he continued. "Finding out what's been taking place with these diaries has become an obsession for me. But I never once expected that things would turn out this way . . . that my own guests would die, that you would be . . ."

The viscount did not continue; his own words seemed to choke him.

Overwhelmed and betrayed, I sat silently. It felt like an eternity before Nadine suggested that the viscount retire, but he gestured, *No*, with his hand. Softly, she asked me to accompany her to where the other guests were gathered, and she, Štěpán, and I left the viscount in the library, sitting next to Roberto, who remained speechless and motionless. Together, the three of us proceeded slowly toward the dining room. Scrutinizing Nadine, I tried to talk, but I couldn't. Deflated and angry, I felt my trust in her had been demolished. "You both betrayed me," I finally said, trying to control my simmering rage.

Seeing her devastated and helpless, I was stunned. Overcome with a painful emotion—pity—I couldn't continue blaming her. Finally I said, "Tell me what you're thinking."

For once, Nadine completely let down her facade of total competence and unbridled confidence. "To tell you the truth," she replied with a blank expression, "I'm beginning to ask myself, What's the use? Three people dead and Max walks away a free man."

We stood around the buffet table without speaking and I sensed how totally defeated she felt. And I felt exactly the same way: *What was the point of it all?* The sound of the doorbell in the distance startled me. "Jesus, who's that at this late hour?" I asked.

"Must be the driver picking up Max and Nicoletta," she replied. "They're obviously not wasting any time in leaving."

"Now that we know Max's role," I said angrily, "I'm having a hard time dealing with the fact that he walks off scot-free. Is it certain the police can't do anything?"

"What we found out," she replied, "would never stand up in court."

Bitterly, I replied, "I can't accept that."

With uncharacteristic coolness, Nadine answered, "Welcome to the real world."

"No," I said, refusing to accept her conclusion. "Nadine, there's something I have to say to Nicoletta before she leaves."

Before I could head for the front door, I felt a sudden, firm lock on my wrist. Looking down, I realized Nadine's hand was gripping me like a vise.

When I stared at her, I was speechless—her eyes were glazed, her face frozen. It was almost impossible to disengage her grip but, exasperated, I finally pulled away from her with all my strength. Followed closely by Štěpán, we headed in the direction of the front door.

At the main entrance, we watched as Max walked out, confident and debonair as usual, as if nothing had taken place. With him was Nicoletta, more cool and sophisticated, more beautiful than I had ever seen her. A surge of rage filled me as I saw her with the man who tried to have me killed.

"I have something to tell you before you leave, Nicoletta."

"Shut up, Pierce," Max responded, mildly irritated, as their luggage was loaded into the sedan. "Your brains are scrambled from all the drugs they gave you in the hospital."

"Nicoletta," I repeated, "before he was murdered, Enrique told me who sent the killer to the monastery. He said it was Max . . . he encrypted Max's cell phone."

"You imagined all that," Max retorted. "You don't even know the difference between your own hallucinations and reality." Taking Nicoletta's arm firmly and leading her to the car, he made small circles around his ear with his index finger to indicate I was insane. "Don't listen to him," he whispered.

"Nicoletta," I continued. "You're making a terrible mistake. There's more . . . "

Surprising me with the rapidity and force with which he moved, Roberto emerged from the foyer of La Favorite. Looking like he had just come out of a trance and carrying an elaborate carving knife from the buffet table, he leaped from the doorstep and lunged at Max, plunging the blade violently between his shoulder blades. Max's expression was one of complete astonishment, and he uttered an outraged exclamation of surprise. We stood frozen in shock—until Nicoletta's ear-shattering scream pierced the night, an unnerving combination of indignation and horror. Within a few seconds, I could make out the moonlit figure of Roberto, heading rapidly into the dark recesses of the viscount's park.

Stretched out on the steps below us was the massive figure of Maximilian. Kneeling next to him, Nicoletta placed his head on her lap, sobbing, her long brunette locks almost completely draping his head in a pose that reminded me of a gruesome Pietà. Within seconds I noticed a widening expanse of mahogany-black liquid, descending slowly and encompassing one step after another.

Too much was happening all at once for me to comprehend. A reverberation from deep within the park, more animal than human, punctuated the tomblike silence: the voice of Roberto, reminiscent of the mourning wail of a wolf. Under the strangely beautiful luminescence of the moon, it sent a fierce shudder running through me.

*"Que se passe-t-il?"* The sound of Philippe's enraged voice as he burst through the door ended abruptly when he realized what had happened. As guests began to crowd around the entrance, he slowly spread his arms to hold them back, including the viscount, whom he led away. By now, I was aware of a soft sound in the background: the muffled sobs of Nicoletta, her voice gradually becoming louder, until it yielded to convulsive gasps and moans. As I stood there with Nadine listening to the emotional torrent, I was overcome by violently conflicting feelings: vindication and pity . . . and somehow, inexplicably, of loss.

# EPILOGUE

*Every parting gives a foretaste of death . . .*

—ARTHUR SCHOPENHAUER

Despite the shocking revelations, saying goodbye to Nadine was difficult for me. In the time I had known her, I had almost begun to feel as if she were part of my family, and the feelings ran deep—far deeper than I had imagined. I sensed, somehow, that she felt the same way.

As Philippe stood at attention, Štěpán and Jano carried my luggage out of La Favorite and placed it carefully in the sedan. Suddenly, I felt the urge to demand an explanation from Nadine about what came over her that fateful night, when she grabbed my wrist and held me. But as she embraced me, an inner voice held me back. Instead, I asked, "What's going to happen to Roberto?"

Nadine sighed. "It was a wild, irrational act. A crime of passion. I imagine they'll plead temporary insanity." She placed a delicate kiss on each of my cheeks, careful not to disturb my balance. "But the viscount's told me he's going to cover the full legal costs; Roberto will have absolutely the best lawyers in the world. Unfortunately, he'll have to do some time, probably a brief residency in a mental institution."

She noticed I was supporting myself on an antique walking stick with a splendid silver handle depicting a deer's head. "It's a gift from your uncle," I said. "He sent it this morning with a note that he wanted me to have something to remind me of La Favorite until the time when I can return."

"He probably feels it's the least he could do," Nadine replied.

"Thank him for arranging to have my diary put on sale at Christie's next week," I said.

"How do the offers look?" Nadine asked.

"There have been advance bids ranging from forty to seventy thousand dollars."

"That's a far cry from what the diaries were getting when the prices were artificially inflated by bidders from GRD and SIN," Nadine replied, and I smiled ironically. "Are you sorry you didn't sell it to Max?" she asked. "When he offered you seven-fifty?"

Trying to repress an involuntary sigh, I said, "Of course I am, a little. But I probably never would have felt right profiting from a money-laundering scheme funded by organized crime. Anyway, if the bidding goes well, I could easily end up with sixty thousand after Christie's deducts their twenty percent commission. And I can sure use it now."

"Have you decided who's going to publish it?" she asked.

"Both Braun and Landry want it for the launching of their editions in 2006, the two hundred fiftieth anniversary of Mozart's birth. So I'm letting them both have it—Braun's will come out in German, Landry's in English. And I was surprised, they're both interested in publishing my transcription of the Prague diary, along with my conclusions about what parts are authentic . . . in a special section on disputed documents attributed to Mozart."

"So, what are your plans now?" Nadine asked.

"I'm heading to Geneva," I said, thinking of Suzanne. Nadine looked at me cryptically. "Some unfinished business," I added. "Plus, there was a fringe benefit from auctioning the diary. A university search committee member in Boston read about it and called me. They're offering me a tenure-track position. So I'm heading back to academia in September, in my hometown."

"These days," Nadine replied, with her smile that always appeared to be hiding secrets and great truths, "academia is no place for a scholar." Just before I climbed into the sedan, she added, "But you probably won't be doing it for long."

"What's that supposed to mean?" I asked.

"Oh, I don't know," she continued, smiling enigmatically. "It's just a feeling I have."

As the car pulled slowly away from La Favorite, I turned to look back and saw the estate, sprawled out and shrouded in an early morning mist that heightened the impression of aristocratic calm and detachment. With the solitary figure of Nadine disappearing slowly into the distance, I began to experience an overwhelming emotion of a different kind. It was as if I were somehow leaving behind part of myself.

With La Favorite disappearing from sight, my thoughts began to move in other directions. Recalling the gruesome scene the night Max was stabbed on the front steps of La Favorite, I remembered something: Nadine's glazed expression, just before Max was killed. And I felt her viselike grip on my wrist. In a rapid stream of consciousness, something else flashed before my eyes: the viscount sitting with Roberto in the library after everyone had left. Faintly, I remembered Nadine's comment the very first night I met her: "There's very little that happens at La Favorite that the viscount hasn't personally planned." And I realized that Max's death was no wild, irrational act.

# ACKNOWLEDGMENTS

Over the past seven years, many people helped and participated in the process of writing *Night Music*. Foremost, I would like to thank my friend and mentor, Paul René Doguereau (1908–2000), who heard and commented on each new chapter, sometimes until as late as four o'clock in the morning. His enthusiasm and critical insights were a constant source of inspiration.

The historical documents presented in Lucas Staehelin's *Die Reise der Familie Mozart durch die Schweiz* (1968) and Francis Carr's *Mozart and Constanze* (1983) were invaluable.

Early in the process, Arks Smith and Suzanne Leon helped considerably as editorial consultants. A remarkable team then shaped and colored the work: Jane Isay, editor-in-chief at Harcourt; Judith Riven, my literary agent; Lori Stoopak, copy editor; and Joseph Pittman, a consultant who took time from writing his own novels.

Several Mozart scholars read the manuscript and made invaluable comments. Daniel Freeman, who knows Czech language and culture intimately, contributed insights from his extensive background in eighteenth-century studies. Faye Ferguson's contributions were invaluable, as were those of Peter Branscombe, Michael F. Robinson, John A. Rice, and Marita P. McClymonds.

Specialists aided the technical writing: David Johnson, a psychopharmacologist; Debby Buchanan, a nurse; John L. Evans, an international consultant in justice and social policy; Rona Klein, a lawyer; Peter M. Schaeffer, a Latin scholar; and David Wilcox, a former Trappist monk. Anna Maria Busse Berger, Josette Melman, Jacqueline Mercorelli, and Alfredo Mandolini helped me with German, French, and Italian. And the monks of the abbey of Solesmes welcomed me into their world.

From the beginning, readers were a great source of useful comments. Anthony Ciuffo provided remarkable suggestions, as did Ennio Dell'Ovo, Ingrid Hesse-Peitchev, Jeffrey Lindabury, Sally Lavallée, and Edward LeMay. A book club offered a unique opportunity for an exchange of ideas: my thanks to Roberta and Edward Sapp, Samantha Seddon, Arleen Shabel, Hilda Stoolman, and Carol Leehive.

# *Night Music*

## Harrison Gradwell Slater

# A CONVERSATION WITH HARRISON GRADWELL SLATER

❧

*Q. What was your inspiration to write a novel based on Mozart? Where did the title come from?*

A. The idea for *Night Music* came to me during a high-speed train ride from Rome to Milan in 1991, just after I finished my nonfiction book, *In Mozart's Footsteps*. I mapped out the novel on a piece of paper ripped from a brochure on the train. At that point, I was writing my dissertation on Mozart and had no time to write the book. After receiving my Ph.D. in 1995, I immersed myself in *Night Music,* never suspecting that it would take seven years to complete the novel. I chose the title *Night Music* because it is the English equivalent of the German word *Nachtmusik* and comes from the congenial work "A Little Night Music" (said to have been written by Mozart in the course of a single day).

*Q. Why Mozart? What draws you to his music? Why do you think it has been so enduring?*

A. Like *Night Music*'s protagonist, Matthew Pierce, I first heard Mozart's great G Minor Symphony as a child, and something in my brain changed. Music became the major passion in my life, and that has continued to the present day. Mozart's music continues to delight and fascinate us today because of the spontaneity, perfection, and underlying element of passion that permeate everything he wrote.

*Q. To what extent then is the novel autobiographical?*

A. *Night Music* is largely based on reality—on my own life, on real issues of music research, and on real events. Still, I was convinced some people would conclude that the events and circumstances in *Night Music* could never happen. And I discovered in the process that truth is literally stranger than fiction. A simple case in point: The "narcoleptic baroness" is based on an important personality who was a friend of my adoptive father (who appears in the novel as the shadowy viscount). William Randolph Hearst did indeed bring in professional costume designers for his costume balls, and an old safe in the hands of Jules Verne's grandson was opened decades later to reveal the author's last (and previously unknown) novel. Mozart's beautiful pupil, Magdalena Hofdemel, pregnant at the time, was slashed with a razor by her husband, Franz, who then killed himself on the day after Mozart's death, and her life was saved by pumping air into her lungs with a pair of bellows from the fireplace. And, yes, academics do sometimes plan the destruction of rival scholars, students, and professors.

*Q. Many reviewers have noted that your fictional Mozart diary seems so authentic. How did you go about researching Mozart's life? How were you able to re-create his voice?*

A. Since 1988, I have been researching and writing about Mozart's life and music—a kind of "total immersion" in the life of the composer. Mozart's voice—and his personality and character—come through clearly in his letters. And much of the colorful material of the period—such as executions in front of the Milan cathedral, the "orphan machine," and silver votive ornaments in the form of "shapely breasts and asses" hanging in church—are cited in travel guides from the eighteenth century, one of which Mozart's father carried with him during their travels. Again, truth is stranger than fiction, especially in the eighteenth century, and I think these historical elements add a dimension of authenticity to the diaries in the novel.

During the years I researched my Ph.D. dissertation, I came across a number of previously unpublished Mozart and Mozart-related documents. I incorporated such material into *Night Music* to create a heightened participation: Readers become like the characters in the novel, using whatever resources they have to determine if the diaries are forgeries, authentic, or pastiche (counterfeit diaries built upon one or several authentic fragments). Because I had spent so much time in the area of scholarly writing, *Night Music* was a totally new experience for me, especially in terms of writing narrative. It was a challenge to incorporate the diary entries, as well as descriptions of Mozart's music and European cities, into the traditional framework of a novel.

*Q. Speaking of travel, Matthew Pierce ends up visiting many of the great cities of Europe. In what way, if any, does his journey parallel your own travels?*

A. Over the past twenty years, I've had the privilege of traveling to hundreds of cities around the world, particularly in Europe. When I was researching *In Mozart's Footsteps*, I traveled to fifty-five cities in nine countries, and during the seven months of research for that book, I was able to visit many extraordinary places. Many readers have told me that the descriptions of Nancy, Venice, Vienna, Salzburg, and other cities make them feel as if they were there. All the descriptions are derived from my own personal experience, with most of them literally written for *Night Music* as I walked through those cities.

The beautiful interiors of *Night Music* are largely based on the historical apartment in Boston's Back Bay that was created by my adoptive father, who passed away several years ago. His opulent style of entertaining, which we shared for more than twenty years, provided the basis for the musical evenings in *Night Music*. Plus I've had the privilege of living and entertaining in four countries, with many evenings filled with great musical artists, fine cuisine, and articulate guests.

*Q. In addition to being a writer, you are an acclaimed concert pianist. How does performing in front of a live audience compare to writing a book? Can you tell us about your own music?*

A. It's a totally different experience. Writing requires research and an astonishing amount of rewriting. Performing live requires enormous preparation, but at the moment of the concert, the artist must say everything in an instant. What is strikingly similar to writing is recording—it allows time for reflection and "rewriting" (additional takes, if needed) so that what is projected is refined and brought in line with the performer's conception. This is also similar to what painters and sculptors do as they perfect their works.

At the present time, my CD of the piano music of Mozart (which I play solo and with orchestra) is available, and readers have an opportunity to hear the *Sicilienne* from Mozart's A Major Piano Concerto, K. 488, which is described in the novel.

*Q. What are you working on next?*

A. My next novel will be a sequel to *Night Music*, with many of the same characters, but moving into the area of the occult and reflecting on the issue of people who have consciously embraced evil. The life, music, and letters of Chopin will be center stage, and I will be researching much of it in Poland and France.

But first I will be revising and updating *In Mozart's Footsteps*, published twelve years ago, which will come out in paperback for the first time (that will make it easier for people to carry it with them on their travels). I'll be traveling throughout Europe for a television series based on *In Mozart's Footsteps*, which will be filmed for the two-hundred-fiftieth anniversary of Mozart's birth in 2006.

# QUESTIONS FOR DISCUSSION

1. In many instances, Matthew Pierce comes across as a naive academic. Do you think he is responsible in part (or completely) for the traumatic events that happen to him? In hindsight, was there anything Matthew could have done differently? How does he change throughout the course of the novel?

2. Denise, Alison Teal, and Nicoletta Chigi are all involved in relationships with men who have disturbing qualities. In fact, abuse figures in *Night Music* both in the plot and in the diaries. Do you know anyone who has been in a similar relationship? What would you do in such a situation?

3. Consider the title of the novel. Why do you think so many important events in the story take place at night, including seduction and murder? Does the night have its own particular music? How does the time of day affect the mood of your favorite scenes?

4. *Publishers Weekly* described Slater's writing as "poetic, even musical." What do musical compositions and novels have in common (for example, structure)? How does reading a novel

compare to listening to music? If you are a fan of Mozart's music, has reading *Night Music* changed the way you listen to or appreciate his work?

5. Recently several high-profile scandals have involved journalists who have admitted to inventing sources and facts, and *Night Music* deals with issues of literary fraud throughout history. Why do you think respectable journalists and writers try to deceive and mislead their readers? In terms of the novel, does it ultimately matter if the diary Matthew found is authentic or not?

6. Mozart was clearly a celebrity of the eighteenth century. How does his celebrity compare to celebrity today? If Mozart had been poisoned by an obsessively jealous husband (regardless of whether he had been intimate with his piano student Magdalena Hofdemel), do you feel it would diminish the prestige of the composer or your appreciation of his music? Can you think of any popular musicians who have been murdered? How have their violent deaths shaped public opinion about their music?

7. How does the depiction of Mozart in *Night Music* compare and contrast to his depiction in the Academy Award–winning film *Amadeus*? What new facets of Mozart's personality emerge in the novel? If a film were to be made of *Night Music*, who do you see portraying the leading characters?

# MOZART AND HIS FAMILY AT A GLANCE

**Wolfgang Amadé Mozart**, who has been called the most universal composer in the history of Western music, was born in Salzburg, Austria, on January 27, 1756. During his lifetime, Mozart composed more than six hundred works, which have never ceased to delight and amaze his listeners.

Mozart's first compositions were written when he was five. In 1763, his father took Mozart, his sister, and his mother on a 3.5-year trip to perform for the most important courts in Europe. When Mozart was fourteen, he traveled with his father to Italy for the first time and was commissioned in Milan to write an opera. This was followed by commissions for two more operatic works, and by the possibility of being engaged as a composer by Ferdinand, the son of Empress Maria Theresa of Austria. Unfortunately, a perfunctory postscript on a letter to Ferdinand by the empress destroyed the possibility of Mozart's employment.

Mozart had been employed by the Archbishop of Salzburg, Count Colloredo. Unhappy with his servile treatment, Mozart asked to be released from his duties, and was granted his wish. He arrived in Vienna in 1781 and continued his life as a freelance artist, successfully composing works on commission. During the next ten years of his life, Mozart wrote his most renowned masterpieces, which include the last three symphonies, the Clarinet Concerto, "A Little Night Music," the Clarinet Quintet, and the operatic masterworks *The Abduction from the Seraglio, The Marriage of Figaro, Don Giovanni,* and *The Magic Flute.*

Mozart married Constanze Weber in 1782 and continued to concertize, compose, and diligently run a family. Although he lived an affluent life with Constanze, his debts became increasingly difficult to manage. When he received a commission to compose a Requiem under suspicious circumstances, he believed he was writing his own funeral Mass. Mozart's failing health plagued the composition of the Requiem, and he died on December 5, 1791, at the age of thirty-five. The location of his grave in St. Marx Cemetery in Vienna is unknown.

After Mozart's death, his music continued to be performed around the world, and his reputation grew from century to century. 2006 is the two-hundred-fiftieth anniversary of Mozart's birth, a year of celebration of the composer and his music.

Mozart's father, **Leopold** (1719–87), was a native of Augsburg who went to Salzburg to study at the Benedictine University. There he found a position as a violinist for the Archbishop of Salzburg, and met his wife, Maria Anna Pertl. In 1747, they married, and in 1756 (the year Mozart was born), his book on playing the violin was published. When Leopold understood the gifts of his two children (particularly those of his son), he dedicated his life to their education. He was a superb educator with a keen eye for business, and he traveled around Europe with his children, presenting them to the most prestigious courts and sovereigns, including Maria Theresa of Austria, King George III of England, and Louis XV of France.

Mozart's mother, **Maria Anna** (1720–78), was born in St. Gilgen. After her marriage to Leopold, the attractive couple began a family, with a total of seven children, of which only Mozart and his sister, Nannerl (a nickname for Maria Anna), lived. Although she was not particularly fond of traveling, Maria Anna accompanied Mozart to Paris in 1778 when Leopold was not granted leave by his employer. During an uncomfortable sojourn there, she died on July 3, 1778.

Mozart's sister, **Nannerl** (1751–1829), was a prodigy on the keyboard. Soon, however, her talents were overshadowed by those of her brother. Nannerl was attractive, fashionable, and refined. Along with Leopold, she disapproved of Mozart's decision to marry Constanze Weber. Nannerl married a magistrate, Baron Johann von Berchtold zu Sonnenburg, and moved to the same house in St. Gilgen where her mother was born. In 1801, after her husband died, she moved back to Salzburg and gave lessons on the clavier. She was almost blind and living in poverty on her death in 1829.

**Constanze Weber** (1762–1842) married Mozart in 1782, several years after her sister, Aloisia, rejected Mozart's suit. Although they had a successful and loving marriage, Constanze was criticized for not helping Mozart manage his finances. Of her six children with Mozart, only two, Carl Thomas and Franz Xaver, survived. After Mozart died, Constanze married Georg Nissen, who later wrote an important biography of the composer.